THE

FLOOD

Kassandra Montag is a poet and novelist. Her work has appeared in *Mystery Weekly* Magazine, *Midwestern Gothic*, and *Prairie Schooner*, among other literary journals. She has won the Plainsongs Award, New Year's Poet Award, and 1877 Award. She lives in Omaha, NE with her husband and two sons.

Praise for *After the Flood*:

'[A] moving account of a mother's love . . . By turns bleak and uplifting, this is a refreshingly original take on the dystopian post-apocalyptic subgenre'

Guardian

'Gripping'

Grazia

'A searing, deeply moving story'

Daily Mail

'A soaring, brilliantly imagined novel about love and desperation, set in an astonishing new world that still feels utterly gripping and contemporary. Kassandra Montag is a visionary new talent!'

Karin Slaughter, internationally bestselling author of *The Last Widow*

AFTER

THE

FLOOD

KASSANDRA
MONTAG

THE BOROUGH PRESS

The Borough Press
An imprint of HarperCollins*Publishers* Ltd
1 London Bridge Street
London SE1 9GF

www.harpercollins.co.uk

This paperback edition 2020
1

First published by HarperCollins*Publishers* 2019

A catalogue record for this book is available from the British Library

ISBN: 978-0-00-831959-5

Designed by Bonni Leon-Berman

Printed and bound in the UK by CPI Group (UK) Ltd, Croydon CR0 4YY

MIX
Paper from
responsible sources
FSC™ C007454

For Andrew

Only what is entirely lost demands to be endlessly named: there is a mania to call the lost thing until it returns.

—Günter Grass

The Valley

Apple Falls

Harjo

Broken Tree

Ruenlock

Wharton

AFTER THE FLOOD

PROLOGUE

CHILDREN THINK WE make them, but we don't. They exist somewhere else, before us, before time. They come into the world and make us. They make us by breaking us first.

This was what I learned the day everything changed. I stood upstairs folding laundry, my back aching from Pearl's weight. I held Pearl inside my body, the way a great whale swallows a man into the safety of his belly, waiting to spit him out. She rolled over in ways a fish never would; breathed through my blood, burrowed against bone.

The floodwater around our house stood five feet high, covering roads and lawns, fences and mailboxes. Nebraska had flooded only days before, water coming across the prairie in a single wave, returning the state to the inland sea it once was, the world now an archipelago of mountains and an expanse of water. Moments earlier, when I'd leaned out the open window, my reflection in the floodwater had returned dirty and marred, like I'd been stretched and then ripped into indiscriminate shreds.

I folded a shirt and screams startled me wide eyed. The voice was a blade, slipping metal between my joints. Row, my five-year-old daughter, must have known what was going on because she screamed, "No, no, no! Not without Mommy!"

I dropped the laundry and ran to the window. A small motorboat idled in the water outside our house. My husband, Jacob, swam to the boat, one arm paddling, the other clamping Row against his side as she struggled against him. He tried to hoist her onto the boat, but she elbowed him in the face. A man stood in the boat, leaning over the gunwale to pick her up. Row wore a too-small plaid jacket and jeans. Her pendant necklace swung like a pendulum across her chest as she struggled against Jacob. She thrashed and twisted like a caught fish, sending a spray of water into his face.

I opened the window and yelled, "Jacob, what are you doing?!"

He wouldn't look at me or respond. Row saw me in the window and screamed for me, her feet kicking at the man who held her under the armpits, lifting her over the side of the boat.

I pounded the wall next to the window and yelled out to them again. Jacob pulled himself over the side of the boat as the man held Row. The panic in my fingertips turned to a buzzing fire. My body shook as I folded myself through the window and leapt into the water below.

My feet hit the ground beneath the water and I rolled to the side, trying to lighten my impact. When I surfaced, I saw Jacob had winced; the pained, tightened expression still on his face. He was now holding Row, who kicked and screamed, "Mommy! Mommy!"

I swam toward the boat, pushing aside debris that littered the water's surface. A tin can, an old newspaper, a dead cat. The engine roared to life and the boat spun around, spraying me in the face with a wave of water. Jacob held Row back as she reached for me, her tiny arm taut, her fingers scratching the air.

I kept paddling as Row receded into the distance. I could hear her screams even after I could no longer see her small face, her mouth a dark circle, her hair standing on end, blowing in the wind that came off the water.

CHAPTER 1

SEAGULLS CIRCLED OVER our boat, which made me think of Row. The way she squawked and waved her arms when she was first trying to walk; the way she stood completely still for almost an hour, watching the sandhill cranes, when I took her to the Platte to see their migration. She always seemed birdlike herself, with her thin bones and nervous, observant eyes, always scanning the horizon, ready to burst into flight.

Our boat was anchored off a rocky coast of what used to be British Columbia, just outside a small cove up ahead, where water filled a small basin between two mountaintops. We still called oceans by their former names, but it was really one giant ocean now, littered with pieces of land like crumbs fallen from the sky.

Dawn had just lightened the horizon and Pearl folded the bedding under the deck cover. She had been born there seven years earlier, during a storm with flashes of lightning white as pain.

I dropped bait in the crab pots and Pearl came out from under the deck cover, a headless snake in one hand, her knife in the other. Several snakes were woven around her wrists like bracelets.

"We'll need to eat that tonight," I said.

She sent me a sharp glance. Pearl looked nothing like her

sister had, not thin boned or dark haired. Row had taken after me with her dark hair and gray eyes, but Pearl resembled her father with her curly auburn hair and the freckles across her nose. Sometimes I thought she even stood the way he did, solidly and sturdily, both feet planted on the ground, chin up slightly, hair always messed, arms a little back, chest up, as though exposing herself to the world with no fear or apprehension.

I had searched for Row and Jacob for six years. After they were gone, Grandfather and I took to the water on *Bird*, the boat he'd built, and Pearl was born soon after. Without Grandfather with me that first year, Pearl and I never would have made it. He fished while I fed Pearl, gathered information from everyone we passed, and taught me to sail.

His mother had built kayaks like her ancestors, and he remembered watching her shape the wood like a rib cage, holding people the way a mother held a child within her, sheltering them to shore. His father was a fisher, so Grandfather had spent his childhood on the Alaskan coastal seas. During the Hundred Year Flood, Grandfather had migrated inland with thousands of others, finally settling in Nebraska, where he worked as a carpenter for years. But he always missed the sea.

Grandfather searched for Jacob and Row when I didn't have the heart to. Some days, I followed languidly behind him, tending to Pearl. At each village, he'd check the boats in the harbor for any sign of them. He'd show photographs of them at every saloon and trading post. On the open sea he'd ask every fisher we passed if they'd seen Row and Jacob.

But Grandfather had died when Pearl was still a baby, and suddenly the enormous task swelled up before me. Desperation clung to me like a second skin. In those early days, I would strap Pearl to my chest with an old scarf, wrapping her snugly against me. And I'd follow the same route he had taken: scouting the harbor, asking the locals, showing photographs to people. For a while it gave me vigor; something to do beyond survival, something that meant more to me than reeling in another fish to our small boat. Something that gave me hope and promised wholeness.

A year ago, Pearl and I had landed in a small village tucked in the northern Rockies. The storefronts were broken down, the roads dusty and littered with trash. It was one of the more crowded villages I'd been to. People hurried up and down the main road, which was filled with stalls and merchants. We passed one stall heavy-laden with scavenged goods that had been carried up the mountain before the flood. Milk cartons filled with gasoline and kerosene, jewelry to be melted and made into something else, a wheelbarrow, canned food, fishing poles, and bins of clothing.

The stall next to it sold items that had been made or found after the flood: plants and seeds, clay pots, candles, a wood bucket, bottles of alcohol from the local distillery, knives made by a blacksmith. They also sold packets of herbs with sprawling advertisements: WHITE WILLOW BARK FOR FEVER! ALOE VERA FOR BURNS!

Some goods had the corroded appearance of having been underwater. Merchants paid people to dive into old houses for items that hadn't yet been scavenged before the floods and hadn't rotted since. A screwdriver with a glaze of rust, a pillow stained yellow and heavy with mold.

The stall across from these held only small bottles of expired medications and boxes of ammunition. A woman with a machine gun guarded each side of the stall.

I had packed all the fish I'd caught in a satchel slung over my shoulder, and I hung on to the strap as we walked up the main road toward the trading post. I held Pearl's hand with my other hand. Her red hair was so dry it was beginning to break off at the scalp. And her skin was scaly and light brown, not from sun, but from the early stages of scurvy. I needed to trade for fruit for her and better fishing supplies for me.

At the trading post I emptied my fish on the counter and the shopkeeper and I bartered. The shopkeeper was a stout woman with black hair and no bottom teeth. We went back and forth, settling on my seven fish for an orange, thread, fishing wire, and flatbread. After I packed my goods in my bag I laid out the photos of Row before the shopkeeper, asking if she'd seen her.

The woman paused, staring at the photo. Then she slowly shook her head.

"Are you sure?" I asked, convinced her pause meant she'd seen Row.

"No girl looks like this here," the woman announced in a thick accent, and turned back to packaging my fish.

Pearl and I made our way down the main road toward the harbor. I'd check the ships, I told myself. This village was so crowded, Row could be here and the shopkeeper could have never seen her. Pearl and I walked hand in hand, pulling away from the merchants as they reached out to us from their stalls, their voices trailing behind us, "Fresh lemons! Chicken eggs! Plywood half off!"

Up ahead of me, I saw a girl with long dark hair, wearing a blue dress.

I stopped in my tracks and stared. The blue dress was Row's: it had the same paisley pattern, a ruffle at the hem, and bell sleeves. The world flattened, the air gone suddenly thin. A man at my elbow was nagging me to buy his bread, but his voice came as though from a distance. A giddy lightness filled me as I watched the girl.

I rushed toward her, running down the path, knocking over a cart of fruit, pulling Pearl behind me. The ocean at the bottom of the harbor looked crystal blue, suddenly clean-looking and fresh.

I grabbed the girl's shoulder and spun her around. "Row!" I said, ready to see her face again and pull her into my arms.

A different face glared at me.

"Don't touch me," the girl muttered, jerking her shoulder from my grasp.

"I'm so sorry," I said, stepping back.

The girl scurried away from me, glancing over her shoulder at me anxiously.

I stood in the bustling road, dust swirling around me. Pearl turned her head toward my hip and coughed.

It's someone else, I told myself, trying to adjust to this new reality. Disappointment crowded me but I pushed it back. You'll still find her. It's okay, you'll find her, I chanted to myself.

Someone shoved me hard, ripping my satchel from my shoulder. Pearl fell to the ground and I stumbled to the side, catching myself against a stall with scavenged tires.

"Hey!" I yelled at the woman, now darting down the main

road and behind a booth with bolts of fabric. I ran after her, leaping over a small cart filled with baby chicks, dodging an elderly man with a cane.

I ran and spun in circles, looking for the woman. People moved past me as though nothing had happened, the swirl of bodies and voices making me nauseous. I kept looking for what felt like ages, the sunlight dimming around me, casting long shadows on the ground. I ran and spun until I nearly collapsed, stopping close to where it had happened. I looked up the road at Pearl, who stood where she'd fallen, next to the stall with tires.

She didn't see me between the people and stalls, and her eyes moved anxiously over the crowd, her chin quivering, holding her arm like it'd been hurt in the fall. This whole time she'd been waiting, looking abandoned, hoping I'd return. The fruit in my satchel that I'd gotten for her had been the one thing I was proud of that day. The one thing I could cling to as evidence that I was doing okay by her.

Watching her, I felt gutted and finished. If I'd been more alert, not so distracted, the thief never would have ripped it from my shoulder so easily. I used to be so guarded and aware. Now I was worn down with grief, my hope for finding Row more madness than optimism.

Slowly it dawned on me: the reason the blue dress was so familiar, the reason it had grabbed my gut like a hook. Yes, Row had that same dress, but it wasn't one Jacob had packed and taken with them when he took her from me. Because I found that dress in her bedroom dresser after she was gone and I slept with it for days afterward, burying my face in her smell, worrying the fabric between my fingers. It had stayed in my memory because it had been left behind, not because she could be some-where out there wearing it. Besides, I realized, she would be much older now, too large for that dress. She had grown. I knew this, but she remained frozen in my mind as a five-year-old with large eyes and a high-pitched giggle. Even if I ran across her, would I recognize her immediately as my own?

It was too much, I decided. The constant drain of disap-pointment every time I reached a trading post and found no answers, no signs of her. If Pearl and I were going to make it in this world, I needed to focus on only us. To shut everything and everyone else out.

So we'd stopped looking for Row and Jacob. Pearl sometimes asked me why we'd stopped and I told her the truth: I couldn't anymore. I felt they were somehow still alive, yet I couldn't un-derstand why I hadn't been able to hear about them in the small communities that were left, tucked high in the mountainsides, surrounded by water.

Now we were drifting, spending our days with no destina-tion. Each day was the same, spooling into the next like a river running into the ocean. Every night I lay awake, listening to Pearl breathe, the steady rhythm of her body. I knew she was my anchor. Every day I feared a raider ship would target us, or fish wouldn't fill our nets and we'd starve. Nightmares engulfed me and my hand would shoot out for Pearl in the night, rat-tling both of us awake. All these fears lined up with a little hope wedged in the cracks in between.

I closed the crab pots and dropped them over the side, let-ting them sink sixty feet. As I surveyed the coast, an odd, fear-ful feeling, a tiny bubble of alarm, rose in me. The shore was marshland, filled with dark grass and shrubs, and trees grew a little farther back from the shore, crowding up the mountainside. Trees now grew above the old tree line, mostly saplings of poplar, willow, and maple. A small bay lay around the shore's bend, where traders sometimes anchored or raiders lay in wait. I should have taken the time to scope out the bay and make sure the island was deserted. There was never any quick escape on land the way there was on water. I steeled myself to it; we needed to look for water on land. We wouldn't last another day otherwise.

Pearl followed my eyes as I gazed at the coast.

"This looks like the same coast with those people," Pearl said, needling me.

She'd been going on for days about raiders we saw robbing a boat in the distance. We'd sailed away, and I was weary, heart heavy, as the wind pulled us out of sight. Pearl was upset we hadn't tried to help them, and I tried to remind her it was important we keep to ourselves. But under my rationalizations, I feared that my heart had shrunk as the water rose around me— panic filling me as water covered the earth—panic pushing out anything else, whittling my heart to a hard, small shape I couldn't recognize.

"How were we going to attack an entire raider ship?" I asked. "No one survives that."

"You didn't even try. You don't even care!"

I shook my head at her. "I care more than you know. There isn't always room to care more." I've been all used up, I wanted to say. Maybe it was good I hadn't found Row. Maybe I didn't want to know what I'd do to be with her again.

Pearl didn't respond, so I said, "Everyone is on their own now."

"I don't like you," she said, sitting down with her back to me.

"You don't have to," I snapped. I squeezed my eyes shut and pinched the bone between my eyebrows.

I sat down next to her, but she kept her face turned from me.

"Did you have your dreams again last night?" I tried to keep my voice kind and soft, but an edge still crept in.

She nodded, squeezing the blood from the snake's tail down to the hole where its head had been.

"I'm not going to let that happen to us. We're staying together. Always," I said. I stroked her hair back from her face and a shadow of a smile crossed her lips.

I stood up and checked the cistern. Almost empty. Water all around but none to drink. My head ached from dehydration and the edges of my vision were beginning to blur. Most days, it was humid; it rained almost every other day, but we were in a dry spell. We'd need to find mountain streams and boil water. I filled Pearl's water skin with the last of the fresh water and handed it to her.

She stopped playing with her headless snake and weighed the water in her hand. "You gave me all the water," she said.

"I already drank some," I lied.

Pearl stared at me, seeing right through me. There was never any hiding from her, not like I could hide from myself.

I fastened my knife in my belt and Pearl and I swam to shore with our buckets for clam digging. I was worried it would be too wet for clams, and we both stumbled along the marsh until we found a drier spot to the south, where the sun fell warm and steady. Little holes peppered the mud plain. We began digging with driftwood, but after a few minutes Pearl tossed her driftwood to the side.

"We won't find anything," she complained.

"Fine," I snapped. My limbs were heavy with fatigue. "Then go up the mountainside and see if you can find a stream. Look for willows."

"I know what to look for." She spun on her heel and awkwardly tried to run up the mountainside. The poor thing was still trying to account for the motion of the sea, and she set her feet down too firmly, swaying from side to side.

I kept digging, pulling the mud in piles around me. I hit a shell and tossed the clam in my bucket. Above the wind and waves, I thought I heard voices coming from around the bend in the mountain. I sat back on my heels, alert, listening. A tension settled along my spine and I strained to hear, but there was nothing. I always thought I sensed things on land that weren't there—hearing a song where there was no music, seeing Grandfather when he was already dead. As though being on land returned me to the past and all the things the past had carried.

I leaned forward and dug my hands into the mud. Tossed another shell into my bucket with a clink. I'd just found another clam when a small, sharp scream pierced the air. I froze, looking up, scanning the landscape for Pearl.

CHAPTER 2

SEVERAL YARDS UP the mountainside, in front of shrubs and a steep rock face, a wiry man held Pearl, her back against his front, a knife at her throat. Pearl was still, her eyes quiet and dark, her arms at her sides, not able to reach the knife at her ankle.

The man had a desperate, off-kilter look on his face. I stood up slowly, my heart pounding in my ears.

"Come with me," he called out. He had a strange accent I couldn't place, clipped and heavy on the consonants.

"Okay," I said, my hands up to show I wasn't going to try anything, walking toward them.

When I reached them he said, "You move and she goes."

I nodded.

"I've got a ship," he said. "You'll work it. Drop your knife on the ground."

Panic rose up in me as I unfastened my knife and tossed it toward him. He sheathed it at his waist and grinned at me. Holes showed where teeth should be. His skin was tanned to a red brown and his hair grew in sandy patches. A tattoo of a tiger spread across his shoulder. Raiders tattooed their members, often with an animal, though I couldn't remember which crew used the tiger.

"Don'tcha worry. I'll care for ya. It's up thataway."

I followed the man and Pearl along the side of the mountain, winding our way toward the cove. Rough grass scratched my ankles and I stumbled over a few rocks. The man lowered the knife from Pearl's neck but kept his hand on her shoulder. I wanted to reach forward and snatch her out of his grasp, but his knife would be at her throat again before I pulled her away. Quick flashes of how things could go ran through my mind— him deciding he only wanted one of us or there being too many people to fight once we reached his ship.

The man started chatting about his people's colony up north. I wanted him to shut up so I could think straight. A canteen hung from the man's shoulder and swung back and forth at his hip. I could hear liquid sloshing inside and my thirst rose above even my fear as my parched mouth ached for water, my fingers itching to reach it and unscrew the cap.

"It's important we have new nations now. Important for . . ." The man cast his hand out in front of him, as if he could pluck a word from the air. "Organizing." The man nodded, clearly pleased. "That's how it was always done, back in the beginning, when we were still in caves. People aren't organized, we'd all be snuffed out."

There were other tribes who were trying to make new nations by sailing from land to land, setting up military bases on islands and ports, attacking others and making colonies. Most of them began as a ship that took over other ships, and eventually they began trying to take over communities on land.

The man looked over his shoulder at me and I nodded dumbly, wide eyed, deferential. We were half a mile from our boat. As we approached the bend along the mountainside, the ground dropped away at our side and we walked along a steep rock face. I thought about grabbing Pearl and leaping from the cliff to the water and swimming to our boat, but it was too far in this choppy water. And I couldn't know if we'd have a clean fall into the water or if there were rocks below.

The man had shifted to talking about his people's breeding ships. Women were expected to produce a child every year or so, to grow the raider crews. They waited until a girl bled before they moved her to a breeding ship. Until then, she was held captive in a colony.

I'd passed breeding ships when I was fishing, recognized them by their flag of a red circle on white. A flag that warned boats not to approach. Since illness spread so quickly on land, the raiders reasoned the babies would be safer on ships, which they often were. Except when a contagion broke out on a ship and almost everyone died, leaving a ghost ship, unmoored until it crashed against a mountain and drifted to the bottom of the sea.

"I know what you're thinking," the man continued. "But the Lost Abbots—we, we do things the right way. Can't build a nation without people, without taxes, without having people to enforce those taxes. That's what gives us the chance to organize.

"This yer girl?" the man asked me.

I startled and shook my head. "Found her on a coast a few years back." He wouldn't be so keen on separating us if he didn't think we were family.

The man nodded. "Sure. Sure. They come in handy."

The wind changed as we began to make our way around the mountain, and voices from the cove now reached us, a clamoring of people working on a ship.

"You look like a girl I know, back at one of our colonies," the man said to me.

I was barely listening. If I lunged forward, I could reach his right arm, pull it behind his back, and reach for my knife in his sheath.

He reached out and touched Pearl's hair. My stomach clenched. A gold chain with a pendant hung from his wrist. The pendant was dark snakewood, with the engraving of a crane on it. Row's necklace. The necklace Grandfather had carved for her the summer we'd gone to see the cranes. It was colorless except the drop of red paint he'd placed between the crane's eyes and beak.

I stopped walking. "Where'd you get that?" I asked. Blood surged in my ears and my body thrummed like a hummingbird's wings.

He looked down at his wrist. "That girl. One I was telling you about. Such a sweet girl. I'm surprised she's made it this long. Doesn't seem to have it in her . . ." He gestured with his knife toward the cove. "Don't have all day."

I lunged at him and swiped his right leg with my foot. He tripped and I smashed my elbow down on his chest, knocking the air from him. I stomped on the hand holding the knife, grabbed it, and held it to his chest.

"Where is she?" I asked, my voice all breath, barely above a whisper.

"Mom—" Pearl said.

"Turn away," I said. "Where is she?" I pushed the knife farther between his ribs, the tip digging into skin and membrane. He gritted his teeth, sweat gathering at his temples.

"Valley," he panted. "The Valley." His eyes darted toward the cove.

"And her father?"

Confusion furrowed the man's brow. "She had no father with her. Must be dead."

"When was this? When did you see her?"

The man squeezed his eyes shut. "I dunno. A month ago? We came here straight after."

"Is she still there?"

"Still there when I left. Not old enough yet—" He winced and tried to catch his breath.

He almost said not old enough for the breeding ship yet.

"Did you hurt her?"

Even now, a pleased look crossed his face, a sheen over his eyes. "She didn't complain much," he said.

I drove the knife straight in, the hilt to his skin, and pulled it up to gut him like a fish.

CHAPTER 3

PEARL AND I stole the man's canteen and shoved his body over
the side of the cliff. As we ran back to the boat I kept thinking
of his crew in the cove, wondering how soon they would start
searching for him. There was enough wind, I thought, to push
us south quickly. Once *Bird* got behind another mountain it'd
be hard to track us.

When we got back to the boat I raised the anchor, Pearl adjusted the sails, and we surged forward, the coast behind us
growing smaller, but I still couldn't breathe steadily. I hid from
Pearl under the deck shelter, my whole body shaking, not unlike how the man's body shook when he died. I'd been in fights
before, tense moments with weapons out, but I hadn't killed.
Killing that man was like stepping through a door to another
world. It felt like a place I'd already been to but had forgotten,
hadn't wanted to remember. It didn't make me feel powerful; it
made me feel more alone.

We sailed south for three days until we reached Apple Falls, a
small trading port nestled on a mountain that had been in British Columbia. The water in the canteen lasted us only a day,
but late on the second day it rained a small bit, just enough that
we weren't ill with thirst by the time we reached Apple Falls. I
dropped the anchor over the side and glanced at Pearl. She stood
at the bow, staring at Apple Falls.

"I didn't want you to see that," I said to Pearl, watching her closely. Pearl hadn't spoken to me much since.

Pearl shrugged.

"He was going to hurt us. You don't think I should have done it? You think he was a good person?" I asked.

"I just didn't like it. I didn't like any of it," she said, her voice small. She paused, as if thinking, then said, "Desperate people." She looked at me a little too intently. I always said to her, when she asked me why people were cruel, that desperate people did desperate things.

"Yes," I said.

"Will we try to find her now?"

"Yes," I said, the word out of my mouth before I knew I'd already decided it. A response beyond reason. Just the image in my mind of Row in danger and me moving toward her, with no choice, only one direction to move, the way rain falls from the sky and does not return to the heavens.

Though I was surprised to realize this, Pearl showed no shock. She merely looked at me and said, "Will Row like me?"

I walked to her, squatted, and wrapped my arms around her. Her hair smelled like brine and ginger and I buried my face in it, her body as tender and vulnerable as the night I birthed her.

"I'm sure of it," I said.

"Are we going to be okay?" Pearl asked.

"We're going to be fine."

"You said everyone is alone. I don't want to be alone," Pearl said.

My chest tightened and I pulled her close to me again. "You

won't ever be alone," I promised. I kissed the top of her head. "We better count these," I said, gesturing to the buckets of fish laid out on the deck.

Row is alone out there, I kept thinking, weighing each dead fish in my palm, one part of me asking how much it was worth, the other part imagining her alone on some coast. Did Jacob die? Did he abandon her? My hands shook with cold rage at this thought. He abandons people; that's what he does.

But he wouldn't do that to her, I argued with myself, feeling myself being pulled back into the hatred that had kept me awake at night for years after he left. I'd been blinded by love and now, I knew, I was blinded by hate. I had to focus. To remember Row and forget him.

The last three days we'd sailed, a part of me thought of Row incessantly. I had the sense that my entire body was plotting how to reach her, while my consciousness focused on tightening the rope at the block or reeling in fishing line, the small daily tasks that grounded me. There was both a low thrum of panic and shock at discovering she was alive, and a strange animal tranquility as I moved about the boat as if it were simply another day. It was what I'd dreamed of and hoped for and also what I'd feared. Because her being alive meant I had to go after her, had to risk everything. What kind of mother abandons her child in her hour of need? And yet, wouldn't taking Pearl on this journey be a kind of abandonment of her? An abandonment of the peaceful life we'd fought to build together?

Pearl and I loaded the salmon and halibut into four baskets. We had gutted and smoked the salmon already on our boat, but the halibut was fresh from this morning, which could give us bargaining power.

Apple Falls was aptly named—apple trees had been planted in a clearing between the peaks of two mountains. Thieves were shot by the guards of the orchard, who had watchtowers on each mountain. I was hoping we'd be able to trade for at least half a basket of apples, plus some grain and seed. At our last trading post we had only three baskets of fish and could barely trade for the rope, oil, and flour we needed. We needed to trade for some vegetable seeds so I could grow a few more vegetables on board. Right now we only had a half-dead tomato plant. Beatrice, my old friend at Apple Falls, would give me a better deal for my fish than at any other port.

Water rippled against the mountainside and the bank rose in a steep incline up the mountain, with a small peat ledge for a dock. A wooden boardwalk, half submerged, had been cobbled together over the years.

We docked our boat and paid the harbor fees with a crate of metal scraps I had found while hunting the shallows. *Bird* was one of the smallest boats in the harbor, but it was sturdily built. Grandfather had designed the boat to be simple and easy to maneuver. One square mast, a rudder, a punting pole, and oars on each side. A deck cover made from old rugs and plastic tarp where we slept at night. He'd made it from the trees in our yard back in Nebraska at the beginning of the Six Year Flood, when we knew that fleeing was our only chance to survive.

Water had already covered the coasts around the world by the time I was born. Many countries had been cut to half their size.

Migrants fled inland, and suddenly Nebraska became a bustling, crowded place. But no one knew the worst was yet to come— the great flood that lasted six years, water rising higher than anyone could imagine, whole countries becoming seafloors, each city a new Atlantis.

Before the Six Year Flood, earthquakes erupted and tsunamis struck constantly. The ground itself seemed heavy with energy. I'd hold out my hand and feel the heat in the air like the pulse of an invisible animal. On the radio we heard rumors that the sea- floor had split, water from within the earth seeping into the ocean. But we never knew for certain what happened, only that the water rose around us as if to swallow us up in a watery grave.

People called the years the coasts disappeared the Hundred Year Flood. The Hundred Year Flood didn't last exactly a hun- dred years, because no one knew for sure exactly when it began. Unlike a war it had no call to arms, no date by which we could remember its beginning. But it lasted close to a hundred years, a little longer than a person's lifetime, because my grandfather always said that when his mother was born New Orleans existed and when she died it did not.

What followed the Hundred Year Flood was a series of mi- grations and riots over resources. My mother would tell me stories of how the great cities fell, when electricity and the In- ternet faltered on and off. People would show up on doorsteps at homes in Indiana, Iowa, Colorado, clinging to their belongings, wide eyed and weary, asking to be let in.

Near the end of the Hundred Year Flood, the government moved inland, but its reach was limited. I was seventeen when I heard over the radio that the president had been assassinated.

But then a month later, a migrant passing through said he'd fled to the Rockies. And then later, we heard a military coup had taken over a session of Congress and members of the government had fled after that. Communication was breaking down by that point, the whole world reduced to a rumor, and I stopped listening.

I was nineteen when the Six Year Flood began and had just met Jacob. I remember standing next to him watching footage of the White House flood, only the flag on the roof visible above the water, each wave soaking the flag until it lay sagging against the pole. I imagined the interior of the White House, so many faces staring out of its paintings, water trickling down hallways into all its chambers, sometimes loud and sometimes quiet.

The last time my mother and I watched television together it was the second year of the Six Year Flood and I was pregnant with Row. We saw footage of a man lying on an inflatable raft, balancing a whiskey bottle on his tummy, grinning up at the sky, as he floated past a skyscraper, trash swirling around him. There were as many ways to react as people, she always said.

This included my father, who was the one to teach me what the floods meant. The blinking on and off of communication was familiar to me, the crowds of people at soup kitchens normal. But when I was six I came home early from school with a headache. The garden shed door was open and through the opening I saw only his torso and legs. I stepped closer, looked up, and saw his face. He'd hung himself from a rafter with a rope.

I remember screaming and backing away. Every cell in me was a small shard of glass; even breathing hurt. I ran inside and looked for my mother, but she wasn't home from work. Cell towers were down that month, so I sat on the front stoop and waited for my mother to come home. I tried to think of how to tell her but words kept wincing away from me, my mind recoiling from reality. Many days, I still feel like that child on the stoop, waiting and waiting, my mind empty as a bowl scooped clean.

After my mother had gotten home, we found a mostly empty bag of groceries on the table with a note from my father: "The shelves were bare. Sorry."

I thought when I had my own children I'd understand him more, understand the despair he felt. But I didn't. I hated him even more.

PEARL TUGGED ON my hand, pointing to a cart of apples sitting just past the dock.

I nodded. "We should be able to get a couple," I said.

The village was a clamoring, crowded throng of people and Pearl stuck close to me. We slung the baskets of fish on two long poles so we could carry them on our shoulders and we started up the long winding path between the two mountains.

I felt relief at being on land again. But as the crowd closed around me, I felt a new kind of panic, different from anything I felt when I was alone on the waves. An out-of-control sensation. Being the foreigner, the one who had to relearn the ever-changing rules of each trading post.

Pearl wasn't ambivalent like I was, hovering between relief and panic. She hated being on land, the only benefit being that she could hunt snakes. Even as a baby she hated being on land, refusing to fall asleep when we camped on the shores at night. Sometimes she got nauseous on land and went out for a swim to calm her nerves while we were at a port.

The land was filled with stumps of cut trees and a thick ground cover of grasses and shrubs. People seemed to be crawling over one another on the path, an old man bumping into two young men carrying a canoe, a woman pushing her children in front of her. Everyone's clothes were dirty and torn and the smell of so many people living close together made me dizzy. Most people I saw in ports were older than Pearl, and Apple Falls was no different. Infant mortality was high again. People would talk on the streets about our possible extinction, about the measures needed to rebuild.

Someone knocked one of Pearl's baskets to the ground and I cursed them and quickly scooped up the fish. We passed the main trading post and saloon and cut across the outdoor market, smells of cabbage and fresh-cut fruit lingering in the air. Shacks littered the outskirts of town as we traveled farther up the path, toward Beatrice's tent. The shacks were cobbled together with wood planks or metal scraps or stones stacked together like bricks. In the dirt yard of one shack, a small boy sat cleaning fish, a collar around his neck, attached to a leash that was tied around a metal pole.

The boy looked back at me. Small bruises bloomed like dark flowers on his back. A woman came and stood in the doorway of the shack, arms crossed over her chest, staring back at me. I looked away and hurried on.

Beatrice's tent stood on the southern edge of the mountain, hidden by a few redwoods. Beatrice had told me she guarded her trees against thieves with her shotgun, sometimes awakening at night to the sound of an ax on wood. But she only had four shotgun shells left, she had confided in me.

Pearl and I squatted and slid the poles from our shoulders. "Beatrice?" I called out.

It was silent for a moment and I worried it was no longer her tent, that she was gone.

"Beatrice?"

She poked her head through the tent opening and smiled. She still wore her long gray hair in a braid down her back and her face had deeper creases, a sun-etched rough texture.

She sprang forward and grabbed Pearl in a hug. "I was wondering when I'd see you again," she said. Her eyes darted between Pearl and me, taking us in. I knew she feared there'd come a day when we didn't return to trade, just as I feared there'd come a day when I'd come to trade and her tent would be taken over by someone else, her name a mere memory.

She hugged me and then pulled me back by my shoulders and eyed me. "What?" she asked. "Something's different."

"I know where she is, Beatrice. And I need your help."

CHAPTER 4

BEATRICE'S TENT WAS the most comfortable place I'd been in the past seven years, since Grandfather and I took to the water. An oriental rug lay over the grass floor, a coffee table sat in the middle of the tent, and off to the side several quilts were piled on top of a cot. Baskets and buckets of odds and ends—twine, coils of rope, apples, empty plastic bottles—were scattered around the periphery of the tent.

Beatrice scurried around her tent like a beetle, wiry and nimble. She wore a long gray tunic, loose pants, and sandals. "Trade first, talk later." She set a tin cup of water in my hands.

"So what do you have?" she asked. She peered into our baskets. "Just fish? Myra."

"Not just salmon," I said. "There are some halibut. Nice big ones. You'll get a big fillet off this one." I pointed to the largest halibut that I had positioned on top of a basket.

"No driftwood, no metal, no fur—"

"Where am I supposed to get fur?"

"You said your boat was fifteen feet long. You could keep a goat or two. It'd be good for milk, and later fur."

"Livestock at sea is a nightmare. They never live long. Not long enough to breed, so it's hardly worth it," I said. But I let her scold me because I knew she needed to. A maternal itch, the pleasure of scolding and soothing.

Beatrice bent down and sorted through the fish. "You could tan leather on a ship easily. All that sun."

We finally agreed to trade all my fish for a second tomato plant, a few meters of cotton, a new knife, and two small bags of wheat germ. It was a better trade than I expected and only possible because Beatrice was overly generous with Pearl and me. She and my grandfather had become friends years before, and after he passed away, Beatrice became more and more generous with her trades. It made me feel both guilty and grateful. Though I was known in many of the trading posts as a reliable fisher, Pearl and I still barely scraped by with our trades.

Beatrice gestured to the coffee table and Pearl and I sat on the ground while Beatrice stepped outside to light a fire and get started on supper. We ate salmon I had brought, with boiled potatoes and cabbage and apples. As soon as Pearl was finished eating she curled up in a corner of the tent and fell asleep, leaving Beatrice and me to talk quietly as the night grew darker.

Beatrice poured me a cup of tea, something minty and herbal, with leaves floating on the surface. I got the impression she was gathering her strength.

"So where is she?" Beatrice asked finally.

"A place called the Valley. Have you heard of it?"

Beatrice nodded. "I've only traded with people from there once. It's a small settlement—maybe a few hundred people. People who make it there don't normally make it back. Too isolated. Rough seas." She gave me a long look.

"Where is it?"

"How'd you get this information? Can you trust it?" she asked.

"I found out from a raider with the Lost Abbots. I don't think he was lying. He'd already told me most of the information before . . ."

I paused, suddenly uncomfortable. A flicker of understanding crossed over Beatrice's face.

"Was he your first?"

I nodded. "He captured Pearl and me."

"Those fighting lessons have paid off," she said, though she sounded more sad than satisfied. Grandfather taught me to sail and fish, but Beatrice had taught me to fight. After Grandfather passed away, Beatrice and I would practice under the trees around her tent, a few paces apart, me mimicking the motions of her hands and feet. Her father had taught her to fight with knives back during the early migrations and she wasn't gentle with me during our lessons, tripping me up with a heel, yanking my arm behind my back until it nearly snapped.

The tea steamed before me and I warmed my hand around the cup. I felt my body try to steady me with stillness, but a cascade still fell within me, as if inwardly I were scattering to pieces.

"Can you help me?" I asked. "Do you have maps?" I knew she had maps—she could charge wood and land for the maps she had, which was also why she had to sleep with a shotgun at night. I'd never heard of the Valley, but I hadn't heard of many places.

When Beatrice didn't say anything, I said, "You don't want me to go."

"Have you learned to navigate?" she asked.

Since I couldn't navigate, I only sailed between trading posts along the Pacific coast, which I knew well from sailing with Grandfather.

"Beatrice, she's in danger," I said. "If the Lost Abbots are there, the Valley is a colony now. Do you know how old she is? Almost thirteen. They'll be transitioning her to a breeding ship any day now."

"Surely Jacob is protecting her. He may pay extra taxes to keep her off the ship."

"The raider said she had no father with her," I said.

Beatrice looked at Pearl, curled into a ball, sleeping on her side, her face serene. One of her snakes lifted its head from the pocket of her trousers and slid over her leg.

"And Pearl? What of her?" Beatrice asked. "What if you go on this journey only to lose her, too?"

I stood up and stepped out of the tent. The night had grown cold. I sank my face in my hands and wanted to wail, but I bit my lips together and squeezed my eyes so hard they hurt.

Beatrice came out and set her hand on my shoulder.

"If I don't try—" I started. The sound of bats' wings beat the air above us as they cut across the moon in fluttering black shapes. "She's alone, Beatrice. This is my one chance to save her. Once they get her on a breeding ship, I won't find her again."

What I didn't tell her was that I couldn't be my father. Couldn't leave her on a stoop somewhere when she needed me.

"I know," she said. "I know. Come back inside."

I hadn't come to Beatrice only because she would help me, but because she was the only person who could understand. Who knew my whole story, going all the way back to the beginning. No other living person besides Beatrice knew how I met Jacob

when I was nineteen and didn't even know the Six Year Flood
had begun. He was a migrant from Connecticut, and on the
day I met him I was drying apple slices in the sunlight on our
front porch. It was over a hundred degrees every day that summer, so we dried fruit on the porch and canned the rest that we
harvested. I'd cut twenty apples into thin slices, lining them
on every floorboard along the porch, before stepping inside to
check the preserves over the fire. In the mornings I worked for a
farmer to the east, but in the afternoons I was home, helping my
mother around the house. She worked as a nurse only occasionally by that point, doing home visits or treating people in makeshift clinics, trading her care and knowledge for food.

When I came back out a row of the apple slices was gone and
a man stood frozen, bent over the porch, one hand on a slice, the
other hand holding open a bag that hung from his shoulder.

He turned and ran and I dashed across the porch after him.
Sweat trickled down my back and my lungs burned, but I
caught up to him and tackled him, both of us sprawling across
the neighbor's lawn. I wrestled the bag from him and he almost
didn't resist, his arms up to protect his face.

"I thought you'd be fast, but you're even faster," he said,
panting.

"Get away from me," I muttered, standing up.

"Can't I have my bag back?"

"No," I said, turning on my heel.

Jacob sighed and looked to the side with a mildly dejected
look. I had the feeling he was accustomed to defeat and stom-
ached it quite well. Later that night I wondered why I'd chased
a stranger and not been more afraid, when usually I took pains

to avoid strangers and feared an attack. Somehow, I realized, I'd known he wouldn't hurt me.

He slept in a neighbor's abandoned shed that night and waved to me in the morning. While I was weeding the front garden he watched me. I liked him watching me, liked the slow burn it gave me.

A few days later, he brought a beaver he'd trapped at the nearby river and laid it at my feet.

"Fair?" he asked.

I nodded. After that he'd sit and talk to me while I worked and I grew to like the rhythm of his stories, the curious way they always ended, with a note of exasperation mixed with delight.

Catastrophe drove us together. I don't know that we would have fallen in love without that perfect mix of boredom and terror, terror that bordered on excitement and quickly became erotic. His mouth on my neck, my skin already moist with sweat, the ground wet beneath us, the heat in the air making rain every few hours, the sun drying it away. My heart already beating faster than it should, nerves calmed only by enflaming them more.

The only photo we got at our wedding came from an instant-print camera my mother borrowed from a former patient. We were standing in the sunlight on our front porch, my belly already round with Row, squinting so much you couldn't see our eyes. And that's how I remember those days: the heat and light. The heat never left, but the sunlight dimmed so quickly during each storm that you felt you stood in a room where some god kept turning a light on and off.

Beatrice ushered me back into the tent. She walked over

to her desk, wedged between the cot and a shelf of pots. She rummaged through some papers and took out a rolled map that she spread out across the table in front of me. I knew the map wouldn't be completely accurate; no accurate maps existed yet, but some sailors had attempted to chart the major landmasses that now existed above water.

Beatrice pointed to a landmass in the upper middle of the map. "This was Greenland. The Valley is in this southeast corner." Beatrice pointed to a small hollow surrounded by cliffs and sea on both sides. "Icebergs" was written across the seas surrounding the small land mass. No wonder I hadn't been able to find Row after years of looking; I hadn't wanted to consider she could be so far away.

"It's protected by the elements and raiders because of these cliffs, so I'm surprised the Lost Abbots made it a colony. Traders from the Valley said it was safer than other land because it's so isolated. But it's hard to get to. This"—she pointed to the Labrador Sea—"is Raider's Aisle."

I'd heard of Raider's Aisle. A stormy section of dark seas where raiders lurked, often taking advantage of damaged ships or lost sailors to plunder their goods. When I passed through ports I'd barely listened to the tales, always assuming I'd never have to go near it.

"The Lily Black keep several of their ships in Raider's Aisle," Beatrice said. "News is they're moving a few more ships up north."

The Lily Black was the largest raider crew, with a fleet of at least twelve ships, maybe more. Ships made from old tankers fitted with new sails or small boats rowed by slaves. A rabbit tattoo marked their necks, and trading posts buzzed with rumors of other communities they'd attacked and the taxes they'd extracted from their colonies, working the civilians almost to death.

"And," Beatrice went on, "you'll have to deal with the Lost Abbots."

"But if the Valley is already a colony, the Lost Abbots will only have left a few men behind to guard it. I can get Row out and we can leave—sail somewhere else before they return."

Beatrice raised her eyebrows. "You think you can take them alone?"

I rubbed my temple. "Maybe I can sneak in and out."

"How do you plan to get there?" she asked.

I dropped my forehead into my palm, my elbow resting on the table, the steam from the tea warming my face. "I'll pay you for the map," I said, so tired my body ached for the ground.

She rolled her eyes and pushed it toward me. "You don't have the boat for this journey. You don't have the resources. And what if she's not still there?" Beatrice asked.

"I have some credit in Harjo I can use for wood to build a new boat. I'll try to learn navigation—I'll trade for the tools."

"A new boat will cost a fortune. You'll go into debt. And a crew?"

I shook my head. "We'll sail it ourselves."

Beatrice sighed and shook her head. "Myra."

Pearl stirred in her sleep. Beatrice and I glanced at her and each other. Beatrice's eyes were tender and sad, and when she reached out and grasped my hand, the veins in her hands were as bright blue as the sea.

CHAPTER 5

THE NEXT MORNING Beatrice and I sat in the grass outside her tent, making lures with thread she'd scavenged in an abandoned shack up the mountainside. I knotted the bright red thread around a hook, listening to Beatrice tell me about how things were before the old coasts disappeared. Born in San Francisco, she was a child when it flooded and her family fled inland. Sometimes when she talked, I could tell she was trying hard to remember how things were when she was young, before all the migrations started, but that she couldn't really. Her stories felt like stories about a place that never really existed.

The neighbors to her right, who lived in a one-room sod house dug out from the side of the mountain, were bickering, their voices rising and railing against one another. Beatrice told me about the Lost Abbots and how they began. They were a Latin American tribe, mostly people from the Caribbean and Central and South America. They began as many raider tribes began: as a private military group employed by governments during the Six Year Flood, when civil wars continued to destroy countries. After all known countries fell, they developed into a kind of sailing settlement, a tribe trying to build a new nation.

"Just last week, Pearl and I saw a small boat taken over by raiders north of here," I said. "It was a fishing family. I heard their screams and—" I squinted hard at my lure and bit the thread to cut it. "We sailed away." I had felt a heaviness in my gut when I placed my hand on the tiller, turning us south, away from their screams. I felt hemmed in and trapped on the open sea, left with few choices.

"I didn't feel bad," I confessed to Beatrice. "I mean, I did. But not as much as I used to." I wanted to go on and say: It's like I've gone dull inside. Every surface of me is hardened and rubbed raw. Nothing left to feel.

At first Beatrice didn't respond. Then she said, "Some say raiders will control the seas in coming years."

I had heard this before, but I didn't like hearing it from Beatrice, who was never one to deal in conspiracies and doomsday speculation. She went on to tell me news from a trading post to the south, how governments were trying to form to protect and distribute resources. How civil wars were breaking out over laws and resources.

Beatrice told me about how some new governments accepted help from raiders and willingly became colonies, controlled by raider captains. The raiders offered protection and gave extra resources to the burgeoning community—food, supplies the raiders had stolen or scavenged, animals they'd hunted or trapped. But the community was bound to pay back any help offered with interest. Extra grain from the new mill. The best vegetables from the gardens. Sometimes the community had to send a few of its own people to work as guards on breeding ships and colonies. The raiders' ships circled between their colonies, picking up what they needed; their guards enforced rules while they were gone.

My conversations with Beatrice followed the same rhythm

each time. She urged me to move onto land and I urged her to move onto water. But not this time.

Beatrice began telling me a story about something that had happened to her neighbors the previous week. She told me how in the middle of the day shouts and yelling had erupted, coming from the sod dugout. Two men stood outside the dugout, shouting and pointing at a girl who stood between her mother and father. The girl looked about nine or ten years old. One of the men stepped forward and grabbed the girl, holding her arms behind her back as she tried to run toward her mother.

The father charged forward toward his daughter, but the other man punched him in the stomach. The father doubled and the man kicked him to the ground.

"Please," the father pleaded. "Please—I'll pay up. I'll pay."

The man stomped on the father's chest with the heel of his boot and the father curled in pain and rolled to his side, his hand shaking and stirring up small clouds of dust.

The girl screamed for her father and mother, her arms held taut and long behind her as she tried to run toward them. The man who'd stomped on her father smacked her hard across the face, wound rope around her wrists, and knotted them. The other man lifted her body over his shoulder and turned around.

She didn't scream again, but Beatrice could hear her soft cries as the men carried her away.

An hour later the village had begun to swarm with people again, footsteps echoing on the dirt paths, bright children's voices calling to one another. Beatrice's neighbor across the road leaned out the open window of her shack to hang a dish towel on a peg. Everything had moved on as though a child hadn't just been taken from her parents.

Beatrice shook her head. "It was probably a private affair. Maybe a private debt being collected and no one wanted to interfere. They don't have control here—but still."

Both of our hands had gone still, the hooks glinting in the sunlight in our laps. Beatrice cast about for words.

"Still, I worry," she said. "A resistance is being organized here. You could join us. Help us."

"I don't join groups and I don't care about resistance. I'm not staying on land, waiting for someone to take her," I said, nodding at Pearl, who had caught a snake and was dropping it into one of our baskets. Pearl came and sat next to us, eyes on the grass, another snake still in her hands.

"They built a library, you know," Beatrice said softly, with pain in her voice.

"Who?" I asked.

"Lost Abbots. At one of their bases in the Andes—Argali. They even put windows in. And shelves. Books salvaged from before and new ones being transcribed. People travel for miles to see it. Some friends told me they built it to show their commitment to the future. To culture."

Beatrice's mouth tightened. Before the floods, she'd been a teacher. I knew how important learning and books were to her. How much it had pained her when her school closed and her students scattered across the country. I knew also of her lover who had been killed on his fishing boat three years before by a raiding tribe. She had been scared of the water even before that, and she cloaked this fear as a love for land.

"Little bit of good in everything," Beatrice said.

I thought of the raider on the coast talking about new nations and the need to organize people. I'd heard that argument before in saloons and trading posts. That the raiders' wealth could re-build society faster. Forcing people to go without would get us back to where we were sooner.

I described what a library looked like to Pearl. "Do you want to go to a place like that?" I asked her.

"Why would I?" she asked, trying to wrap the snake around her wrist as he resisted her.

"You could learn," I said.

She frowned, trying to imagine a library. "In there?"

I came up against this again and again with Pearl. She didn't even want what I so sorely missed, had no conception of it to desire it.

It wasn't just the loss of a thing that was a burden but the loss even of desiring it. We should at least get to keep our desire, I thought. Or maybe it's how she was born. Maybe she couldn't want something like that after being born in a world like this.

Beatrice didn't say anything more, and after we finished mak-ing lures I went into her tent to pack. I packed our grain in a linen sack, tucking it in the bottom of a bucket. I set the tomato plant in a basket and tucked a blanket around it, a gift from Be-atrice. I thought of Row, imagined her wrists cinched together with rope, her cries silenced or ignored. I shuddered.

Beatrice handed me the rolled-up map. "I don't even have a compass to give you."

"You've given me more than I hoped for," I said.

"One more thing." Beatrice pulled a photo from her pocket

and placed it in my hand. It was a photo of Jacob and Row, taken a year before she'd screamed my name in that boat as it sped away. Grandfather and I gave it to Beatrice so she could ask traders in Apple Falls if they'd been seen. In the photo Jacob's auburn hair had a gold sheen from the sunlight. His cleft chin and crooked nose, caused by a childhood schoolyard fight, made his face look angular. Row looked delicate with her small sloping shoulders and shining gray-blue eyes. They were my eyes, almond shaped, hooded. Eyes that looked like the color of the sea. She had a scar, shaped like the blade of a scythe, curving over an eyebrow and across a temple. When she was two she had fallen and cut her face on a metal toolbox.

I rubbed Row's face with my thumb. I wondered if Jacob had built them a house at the Valley. That's what he always said he wanted to do for me, years ago. Jacob worked as a carpenter like Grandfather. They began building our boat together, but after a while it was only Grandfather working on the boat. I had listened to their yelling and arguing for weeks and then suddenly it was quiet. That was two months before Jacob left with Row.

Beatrice reached out and tucked a strand of hair behind my ear and wrapped her arms around me. "Come back," she whispered in my ear, the phrase she whispered in my ear each time I visited. I could feel in how her embrace lingered that she didn't think I would.

CHAPTER 6

PEARL AND I set sail to the south, following the broken coast. It was rumored there was more wood for building boats down south in Harjo, a trading post in the Sierra Nevada Mountains. I'd use my credit at Harjo for wood and trade my fishing skills for help in building a bigger boat. My little boat would never handle the tumultuous seas in the north. But even if I could build a bigger boat, would I be able to navigate and sail it? Desperate people could always be found to join a ship's crew, but I couldn't stand the thought of traveling with other people, people I might not be able to trust.

I strung a line through a hook and knotted it and did it again for another pole. Pearl and I would fish over the side of the boat later in the evening, maybe even try some slow trolling for salmon. Pearl sat next to me, organizing the tackle and bait, dividing the hooks by size and dropping them in separate compartments.

"Who's in this photo?" Pearl asked, pointing to the photo of Row and Jacob sitting on top of a basket filled with rope.

"A family friend," I said. Years ago, when she'd asked about her father, I told her he had died before she was born.

"Why'd you ask that man about my father?"

"What man?" I asked.

"The one you killed."

My hands froze over the bucket of bait. "I was testing him," I said. "Seeing if he was lying."

The sky to the east darkened and clouds tumbled toward us. Miles away a haze of rain clouded the horizon. The wind picked up, filling our sail and tilting the boat. I jumped up to adjust the sail. It was midafternoon and the day had begun clear, with an easy, straight wind, and I thought we'd be able to sail south for miles without making adjustments.

At the mast I started reefing the sails so we'd bleed wind. Around the coast to the west, waves rose several feet, the crashing white water swirling under the dark sky. We'd faced squalls before, been tossed in the wind, almost capsized. But this one was driving straight west, pushing us away from the coast. A rag on deck whipped up into the air, almost smacking me as it flew past and disappeared.

The storm approached like the roar of a train, slowly getting louder and louder until I knew we'd be shaking inside of it. Pearl climbed over the deck cover and stood by me. I could tell she was resisting the urge to throw her arms around me. "It's getting bad," she said, a tremor in her voice. Nothing else scared Pearl like storms; she was a sailor afraid of the sea. Afraid, she'd told me before, of shipwreck. Of having no harbor.

"Take the gear under the deck cover," I told her, the wind catching my words and flattening them. "And bolt it down."

I tried to ease the tension of the sail's rigging, loosening the sheet, but the block was rusty and kept catching. When I finally got it loose, the wind picked up, knocking me backward against the mast, the rope flying through the block, sending the halyard soaring in the wind. I held on to the mast as *Bird* leaned left, waves rising and water spraying across the deck.

"Stay under!" I shouted to Pearl, but my words were lost

in the wind. I climbed across the side of the deck cover, running toward the stern, but I slipped and slid into the gunwale. I scrambled to my feet and began tightening the rope holding the rudder, winding it around the spool, turning the rudder so we'd sail into the wind.

Thunder roared, so loud I felt it in my spine, my brain vibrating in my skull. Lightning flashed and a wave crashed over *Bird*, and I grabbed the tiller to steady myself. I dropped to my hands and knees, scrambled toward the deck cover, and ducked inside as another wave hit us, foaming overboard.

I wrapped myself around Pearl, tucking her under me, clutching her with one arm and holding on to a metal bar drilled into the deck with my other hand. *Bird* rocked violently, water pouring under the deck cover, our bodies jostling like shaken beads in a jar. I prayed the hull wouldn't break.

Pearl curled in a tight ball and I could feel her heart beating like a hummingbird's wings against my arm. The wind was blowing straight west, pushing us out of coastal waters and deeper into the Pacific. If we were pushed any farther offshore, I didn't know how we'd make it back to a trading post.

Some dark feeling washed over me that felt like rage or fear or grief, something all sharp corners in my gut, like I'd swallowed glass. Row and Pearl rippled through my mind like shadows. The same question kept rising in me: To save one child, would I have to sacrifice another?

THE DAY MY mother died I had been at the upstairs window, four months pregnant with Pearl, hand on my belly, thinking of preeclampsia, placenta abruption, a breech baby, all the things I'd thought about when I was pregnant with Row. But now, with no hospitals, not even makeshift ones run out of abandoned buildings, they seemed like certain death. I knew my mother would help me deliver Pearl like she'd helped with Row, but I was still more nervous about this birth.

We had lost Internet and electricity for good the month before and we watched the horizon daily, fearing the water would arrive before Grandfather finished the boat.

In the block behind our house, a neighbor's front yard held an apple tree. Mother had to stretch to pick them, a basket hooked over her arm, her hair shining in the sunlight. The yellow and orange leaves and red apples looked so bright, almost foreign, as though I already was thinking of them as lost things, things I'd rarely see again.

Behind her I saw a gray wall building, rising upward toward the sky. I was perplexed at first, my mind too shocked to comply, even though this was what we'd been waiting for. The water wasn't supposed to be here yet. We were supposed to have another month or two. That's what everyone on the streets had been saying. All the neighbors, all the people pushing grocery carts full of belongings as they migrated west toward the Rockies.

I didn't understand how it was so quiet, but then I realized we were in the middle of a roar, a deafening crashing, the collision of uprooted trees, upended sheds, lifted cars. It was as if I couldn't hear or feel anything, all I could do was watch that wave, the water mesmerizing me, obliterating my other senses.

I think I screamed. Hands pressed on glass. Grandfather,

Jacob, and Row ran upstairs to see where the commotion came from. We stood together at the window, frozen in shock, waiting for it to come. The water rose as if the earth wanted vengeance, the water creeping across the plains like a single warrior. Row climbed into my arms and I held her as I had when she was a toddler, her head on my shoulder, her legs wrapped around my waist.

Mother looked up at the water and dropped the basket of apples. She ran toward our house, crossing the street, passing a house and almost reaching our backyard when the wave crashed around her. The wave dipped over her, its white spray falling around her.

I couldn't see her anymore and the water thundered around our house. We held our breath as the water rose around the house, climbing up the siding, breaking the windows and flowing inside. It filled up the house like a silo full of corn. The house shuddered and shook and I was certain it'd splinter into pieces, that our hands would be ripped from one another. The water rose, climbing each stair toward the attic.

I looked back out the window, praying I'd see my mother reappear, surface for a breath of air. After the water settled, the surface was still and my mother did not come up to break it.

The water settled a few feet below our upstairs window. We waded and swam through the water for weeks afterward but could never find her body. We later found out the dam had broken half a mile from our house. Everyone had said it would hold.

After Mother was gone I kept wanting to tell her about how things were changing, in me and around me, Pearl's first kicks, the water covering all the prairie as far as the eye could see. I'd turn to speak to her and be reminded she was gone. This is how people go crazy, I thought.

It was only a month later that Jacob would take Row. Only Grandfather and I were left in that house, sitting in the attic, that empty room the length of our house, as the boat slowly filled it.

A month after Jacob left we took the attic wall out with a sledgehammer and pushed the boat out of the house and onto the water. The boat was fifteen feet long, five feet wide, and looked like a large canoe with a small deck cover at the back and a single sail in the middle. We loaded the boat with supplies we'd been hoarding for the past year—bottles of water, cans of food, medical supplies, bags of extra clothing and shoes.

We sailed west, toward the Rocky Mountains. At first, the air was thin and felt hard to breathe, as if my lungs kept clutching for something more. Three months later I awoke with birthing pains. The wind was so strong it rocked the boat like a cradle and I rolled back and forth under the deck cover, gritting my teeth, clutching the blankets around my body, crying in the lulls between contractions.

When Pearl came she was glistening and pale and silent. Her skin looked like water. As if she'd risen out of the depths to meet me. I held her to my chest and rubbed her cheek with my thumb and she broke into a wail.

A few hours later, when the sun rose and she was suckling at my breast, I heard gulls above us. Holding Pearl at my breast was both like and unlike when I held Row at my breast. I tried to hold the feeling of both of them in myself but couldn't; one kept sliding away and replacing the other. Deep down, I had known that one couldn't replace the other, though I now discovered I had been hoping Pearl could replace Row. I placed my nose on Pearl's forehead, smelling her newness, her freshness. I mourned the loss of it, the loss I felt before it happened.

In Grandfather's last days he began speaking nonsense more and more. Sometimes talking to the air, addressing people he'd known in the past. Sometimes speaking in a dream language that I would have found beautiful if I wasn't so tired.

"Now, you tell my girl that a feather can hold a house," Grandfather said. I wasn't sure if by "my girl" he meant my mother, myself, Row, or Pearl. He'd call all of us "his girls."

"Who do you want me to tell?"

"Rowena."

"She isn't here."

"Yes, she is, yes she is."

This irritated me. Most of the people he spoke to were dead. "Row isn't dead," I said.

Grandfather turned to me, shock on his face, his eyes wide and innocent. "Of course not," he said. "She's around the corner."

A week later Grandfather died sometime in the night. I had just finished nursing Pearl and had laid her in a small wooden box Grandfather had made for her. I crawled over to where Grandfather slept, my fingers outstretched to shake him awake. When I touched him, he was cold. His skin not yet ashen, only slightly pale, the blood having settled. He otherwise looked the same as he always did when he slept: eyes closed, mouth slightly agape.

I leaned back on my heels, staring at him. That he could pass with so little ceremony stunned me. I had never expected sleep to take him, of all things. Pearl whimpered and I crawled back to her.

We were alone, I kept thinking. I had no one left I could trust, except this baby that depended on me for everything. Panic pressed around me. I looked at the anchor lying a few feet away. I'd heard of people leaping from their boats tied to their anchors. But this wasn't a possibility for me. It was as impossible as the water receding from the land and people standing up again where they'd fallen. Instead I took Pearl in my arms and climbed out from under the tarp into the morning sun.

I would carry him with me; he would still guide me. Grandfather was the person who taught me how to live; I wouldn't fail him now. I wouldn't fail Pearl, I told myself.

When I think of those days, of losing the people I've loved, I think of how my loneliness deepened, like being lowered into a well, water rising around me as I clawed at the stone walls, reaching for sunlight. How you get used to being at the bottom of a well. How you wouldn't recognize a rope if it was thrown down to you.

CHAPTER 7

AFTER THE STORM, we came out from under the deck cover and surveyed the wreckage. We'd lost all the rainwater from the cistern. I dropped to my knees in front of it and swore. The waves crashing overboard had filled the cistern with salt water. We'd have to empty it all and get back to land as quickly as possible before we got dehydrated. We had a small emergency supply of water I kept in plastic bottles, tied down under the deck cover, but it would only last a few days.

Pearl kept close to me as we sloshed through the water, across the deck toward the bow. She held her arm against her side, a bruise blooming where she must have fallen when trying to scramble under the deck cover with the tackle and bait. I squatted in front of her, kissed my finger, and touched it to her arm. A shadow of a smile flickered across her face. I brushed her hair from her face with my palm, took her head in my hands, and kissed her forehead.

"We'll be okay," I said.

She nodded.

"How 'bout you get the bucket and towel. Start wringing the water off the deck. I'll check the rudder."

At the stern, I inspected the rudder and tiller. A crack split the base of the rudder support and it was leaning to the side. Above me, our single sail fluttered in the breeze, a tear down the middle. The bottom yard swiveled in the wind. The storm had taken our punting pole and the tomato plant Beatrice had given us, but the rest of our supplies were stored in the hull or tied down under the deck cover.

I cursed and rubbed my face with my palm. We were losing time, I thought. How would we get another boat built when I didn't even know where we were?

"Oars are still here," Pearl called to me, her hands on the gunwale, looking down to where the oars were tied tightly to the sides of the boat.

I shielded my eyes from the sun and squinted against the glint of water, peering east. Or what I thought was east. I glanced at the sun and back at the water. How long had the storm gone on? It felt like forever, but it could have been only a half hour. I couldn't tell how far west we'd been pushed off our usual course, which was always two miles from the coast, straight north or south, tracking the bits of land that hovered above water.

Wreckage from another boat floated about a mile east of us, drifting our way. I squinted and grabbed the binoculars from under the deck cover.

It had been a salvage boat, made from various scavenged materials. A few tires were tied around a base of doors nailed together. A few dozen feet away, the cabin of a truck lay floating on its side, and a bright yellow inflatable raft floated nearby. Plastic bags and bottles were strewn across the surface of the water like trash.

"Grab the net," I told Pearl. I hoped there was food or water stored in those bags and bottles.

"There's a man," Pearl said, pointing to the wreckage.

I peered through the binoculars again, scanning the wreckage. A man clutched the raft of tires and doors, treading water and squeezing his eyes shut against each wave that rolled into his face.

Pearl looked up at me expectantly.

"We don't know anything about him," I said, reading her thoughts.

Pearl scoffed. "That doesn't look like a raider ship."

"It's not just raiders we should fear. It's anyone."

A nervous buzz spread through my veins. I hadn't brought anyone else on *Bird* and I didn't want to now. Someone sleeping right next to us under the deck cover. Sharing our food, drinking our water.

I glanced at the man and back down at Pearl. She wore the steady expression of already having made a decision.

"We don't have enough food or water," I told her.

Pearl knelt under the deck cover and pulled out her snake pot, a clay jar with a bright blue glaze. She lifted the lid and caught a small, thin snake just behind its head, its fangs out, its tongue a flickering red ribbon. She held him up to me and grinned. The snake opened and closed its mouth, biting the air. She squatted on the deck, cut its head off, held it by the tail over the water, and pinched it from tail to neck with her thumb and forefinger, draining its blood into the water.

"We can eat him," she said.

She never offered her snakes for meals. I turned back toward the wreckage, the man now only half a mile from our boat. I felt in my bones that he would bring us trouble in some way. Every sinew and tendon in me turned and tightened like rope on a pulley.

But I couldn't tell if the panic was from being lost or taking a stranger onto our boat. The fears mixed like blood in water and I couldn't separate them. I thought I could get us back to a trading post, but if I miscalculated and it took longer than expected and it didn't rain— I couldn't stomach the thought of us drying up like prunes under the sun.

The man was beginning to float away, pulled by a current. Watching him in the water reminded me of how Grandfather would sing "I will make you fishers of men" while he fished the rivers in Nebraska. He'd lean back in the boat, an umbrella propped in the corner to shade him, a pipe stuck in the corner of his mouth, and he'd chuckle to himself as he sang. He always found things both silly and serious. The chorus began repeating in my mind as the man floated farther away, and I felt it as an admonishment. I clenched my jaw in irritation. I had wanted Grandfather to guide me, not haunt me.

"Grab the rope," I told Pearl.

The man was barely conscious, so I jumped in the water and swam to him. I tied the rope around his torso and swam back to our boat. I climbed back onto *Bird* and Pearl and I hauled him up, bracing against the gunwale with each pull.

The man carried nothing but a backpack, and when we got him on the deck he sputtered and coughed up water, lying on his side, almost curled in the fetal position. Pearl crouched next to him, peering into his face. His dark hair fell loose and disheveled almost to his shoulders. He had a broad chest, long strong limbs, and skin darkened by the sun. He wore the rough-hewn look of someone accustomed to sailing alone. Despite this, he was handsome, in a still and solemn way, like a photograph of someone from another era. When he opened his eyes and looked at me I was startled by their light gray color.

"Sweetie, grab a water bottle," I said.

Pearl leapt up and got the water. I leaned forward to dribble a few drops onto his lips, but he jerked away from me.

"It's water," I said gently, holding the bottle in front of him to show him. He reached for it and I pulled it away.

"I'm going to give you just a little. We don't want you throwing up."

I knelt forward and dribbled a few drops on his lips. He licked the water quickly and looked at me, a pleading expression on his face. I poured more water in his mouth, half the bottle, my stomach clenching as I did so, and I thought about the heat, the water bottles we had left, and the miles to shore.

The man lay back, closing his eyes, leaning against the gunwale. Pearl and I let him doze. Pearl and I caught what we could from his wreckage in our net and sorted it on the deck. Not much of use. A few bottles of water, two spoiled fish, and a bag of dry clothing. We fished spare wood from the water to use for rebuilding the rudder. We tied his raft to the stern of *Bird* so we could tug it along behind us like a caboose in case we ever needed it.

I brought down the sail and examined the tear. When I finished mending it two hours later, it was uneven and puckered along the tear, but it would last until we got to shore and I could trade for more thread and material.

I walked over and kicked the man's shoe. He startled awake, his hands out in front of him.

"Almost dusk," I said. "Can you skin two snakes?"

He nodded.

Pearl brought the bucket of coals over to where the man lay, near the mast step, and poured them in a flat pan, the kind we once used to make birthday cakes. We were lucky it wasn't windy tonight. When it was windy we'd have to eat raw or dig into our stores of dried meat or flatbread. I sat in front of the pan with a box of kindling, arranging the twigs and leaves on top of the coals. Pearl lit it with her flint stone and knife.

"You didn't have to. I'm grateful," the man said. He had a soft, clear voice, like distant bells.

I was trying to decide if we should tie him up while we were sleeping. The uneasy feeling in my gut wouldn't loosen.

"Can you help me hoist the sail?" I asked.

"Gladly," he said.

He finished pulling the skins from the snakes and Pearl tossed them on the hot coals. The sun was low on the horizon, casting a gold glow across the water. The sun seemed to go down so much faster since the floods, now that the horizon had risen to meet the sun.

"I'm Daniel, by the way."

"Myra. Pearl. What's in your bag?"

"Some of my maps and instruments."

"Instruments?"

"For navigating and charting. I'm a cartographer."

He knows how to navigate, I thought.

Pearl scooped a snake off the coals with a long stick and

coiled it on the deck in front of her to let it cool. It was blackened and my stomach turned just looking at it. It smelled acrid. Snake meat was as tough as sinew, and I was weary of eating it.

"You remind me of someone I used to know," Daniel said.

"Oh, yeah?" I poked the snake still on the coals with a stick. What I really wanted to know was what schools of fish swam this far off the coast and whether they could be tracked.

"A woman I lived with for a year in the Sierra Madre. She didn't trust people, either."

"What makes you think I don't trust you?"

He rubbed his beard with his palm. "If you got any tenser, your muscles would break your own bones."

"Should she have trusted people?"

He shrugged. "Maybe some."

"And now?"

"She passed at the end of that year."

"I'm sorry."

Pearl tried a bite of the snake, chewing fiercely, the stench of the meat drifting toward me on the breeze. She laid it straight on the deck and cut it into three even pieces and tossed our two pieces to us.

"Who'd you make maps for?" I asked

"Anyone who wanted them. Fishermen. New government officials."

"Raiders?"

He sent me a hard look. "No. At least not that I know of."

"I'd think you'd have a better boat with that kind of work. Maps are more expensive than wood."

"Let's just say I've had bad luck."

I narrowed my eyes at him. He was holding something back.

Pearl whimpered and I saw why she'd been so silent during our conversation. She held up her handkerchief and ran her finger along a tear at the edge.

"It ripped," she said softly. "During the storm."

"Bring it here," I said, holding out my hand to her. She crawled to her feet and brought it to me. I examined the tear. "Well, this will be easy to fix since it's so near the edge. We can fold it like this and take the thread around in a thumb knot and it won't even fray, it'll just be stronger."

Pearl nodded and touched the handkerchief gingerly. "I'm still sleeping with it tonight." The red handkerchief had been Grandfather's. When he died we laid it over his face and it almost fluttered away on the breeze as we dropped his body into the sea, but I snatched it from the air. Pearl tugged it from my hand and after that she wouldn't let go of it, even in her sleep.

"You pay attention to the little things," Daniel said, watching us. He said it wistfully, like he was remembering something. He looked out at sea and his face was cast in shadow.

The sudden tenderness on his face turned something over in me, like lifting a rock and seeing the life beneath it. My chest went soft with a sudden movement. There was something about him that was beginning to put me at ease. Maybe it was the easy way he looked me in the eye, his frank way of speaking, his lack of charm. Jacob had been charming; he pretended to be simple and transparent while hiding what he actually thought. Daniel seemed like a man who carried guilt willingly and didn't skitter away from it, who labored under decisions.

I decided he could sleep free tonight, though I'd still sleep with one eye open.

"I have to," I said.

"No one has to do anything," he said, looking back out at the sea.

CHAPTER 8

DANIEL CALCULATED OUR position and estimated that if we sailed southeast for four days we'd be close to Harjo. Daniel repaired the rudder while Pearl and I fished. After watching the birds and the water for hours, Pearl and I finally attached our net to the downrigger and began trawling for mackerel. We fished for two days before catching anything, our stomachs rumbling through the day and night, and when the rope finally went taut at the downrigger I swallowed sharply to stifle the gasp of relief that rose in my throat.

We spilled a full net of mackerel on the deck, the dark stripes on their backs glinting and shining in the sun. Each was at least eight pounds, and I savored the weight of meat in my hands. I gutted them, one after another, while Pearl set up the smoking tripod.

I still kept an eye on Daniel and tried to keep my defenses up. But I was growing more comfortable with him, as it felt as if he'd already been with us for a long while. We were quiet most of the time, just listening to the wind pull against the sail, or the distant splash of a fish or bird. Just sky and sea for miles and miles, the three of us, alone.

The closer we got to Harjo, the more we sailed over the old world, transitioning from the Pacific into water that now rippled over cities in California. I often sailed this way because I had to stick close to the new coasts, but it always haunted me to sail over cities, over the mass graves they've become. So many people died not just during the floods but during the migrations, from exposure and dehydration and starvation. Feet bloodied from trying to climb mountains and outrun the water. Possessions abandoned up the mountainside the way they were along the Oregon Trail.

Some of the cities were so deep below, no one would see them again. Others, which had been built at higher elevations, could be explored with goggles and a strong stomach. Their skyscrapers rose out of the water like metal islands.

I used to dive and spearfish in those underwater cities, but more recently I'd done it only when I was desperate. I didn't like being in the water for long periods of time; didn't really like being reminded of how it once was. Once, I was diving and swimming through an old city that'd been nestled on a mountainside in the Rockies. Fish made homes in the wreckage, hiding amid the sea grass and anemone. I dove down into an office building that was missing a roof. A few desks and filing cabinets floated in the room, items around them nearly unrecognizable. Barnacle shells grew on a mug with a photo of a child's face, some birthday gift you once could get sent to you in the mail.

I swam deeper. A school of angelfish scattered and I speared one. As I turned to go up for air, the coiled rope I wore around my shoulder caught on the broken bottom handle of the file cabinet. I yanked at it, jimmying the cabinet loose from where it stood close to a wall. Out of the shadows, a skull tumbled along the floor toward me, settling a foot away. A flicker of movement from within the mouth. Something living inside it.

I yanked on my rope again to get free and the cabinet fell

toward me. I shoved the cabinet to the side so it wouldn't fall on me and my rope slid from the broken handle. In the space behind where the cabinet had stood, two skeletons lay on their sides, facing each other, as though in an embrace. Like falling asleep with a lover. One skeleton didn't have a skull, but by the way it was positioned, turned toward the other body, I imagined its head had rested on the other's chest. Positioned like they were waiting for their fate and chose to hold each other when the end came. Disintegrated clothing fluttered around them. Rocks lay on the floor all around their bodies. My oxygen-deprived brain recoiled before I realized they must have filled their pockets and stuffed their clothes with rocks so they could succumb to the water as it slowly inched upward around them, covering their arms that touched the floor first, a final whisper between them before it covered the arms that held each other. Otherwise the water would have separated them when it came, pulling them apart, floating their bodies before it sank them, miles apart.

I dropped the spear and swam for the surface. I traded for nets at the next post and from then on only dove when the nets came up empty.

I didn't know how to talk to Pearl about what lay beneath us. Farms that fed the nation. Small houses built on quiet residential streets for the post–World War II baby boom. Moments of history between walls. The whole story of how we moved through time, marking the earth with our needs.

It felt like cruelty to bury the earth, to take it all away. I'd look at Pearl and think of all she wouldn't know. Museums, fireworks on a summer night, bubble baths. These things were already almost gone by the time Row was born. I hadn't realized how much I lived to give my child the things I valued. How my own enjoyment of them had grown dull with age.

But other times, when everything was so dark out on the sea that I felt already erased, it seemed like a kindness that life before the floods had gone on for as long as it did. Like a miracle without a name.

BY THE THIRD day Pearl pulled Daniel into her games: hopscotch on deck with a piece of charcoal, naming games for each cloud or strange wave. The next day it rained for most of the afternoon and we sat under the deck cover, telling each other stories. Pearl got Daniel to tell her stories about places he'd been that we'd never heard of. I didn't know whether any of his stories were true, they seemed so tall, and Pearl never asked if they were true or not.

One morning while I was caulking a crack in the gunnel with hemp, Daniel and Pearl played shuffleboard with caps from plastic bottles. They'd drawn squares on the deck with charcoal and took turns knocking their caps into the squares with sticks.

"Why do you like snakes so much?" he asked Pearl.

"They can eat things bigger than them," Pearl said.

Daniel's cap skidded outside the square and Pearl cackled with laughter.

"I'd like to see you do better," Daniel said.

"You will," Pearl said, biting her lower lip as she concentrated.

Pearl knocked her cap into the square and cheered, hands raised in the air, jumping in a little circle.

Watching them gave me an unexpected good feeling, a warmth spreading slowly through me. It was like I was seeing a puzzle put back together after it had broken apart.

"Where will you go once we're in Harjo?" I asked Daniel.

He shrugged. "Maybe stay in Harjo, work for a bit."

We needed a navigator, I kept thinking. Ever since I'd found out he could navigate I considered asking him to stay with us, to help us get to the Valley. I felt like I could trust him—or was it just that I wanted to trust him because I needed him? Daniel was clearly hiding something. I could tell by the way his expression changed when I asked him questions, like a curtain falling over his face, shutting me out.

Pearl and I had never sailed with anyone else, and I liked being alone. Alone was simple and familiar. I felt sore from this division, one part of me wanting him to stay with us and the other part wanting to part ways with him.

The next morning, Harjo loomed in the distance, the sharp mountain peaks piercing the clouds. Sapling pines and shrubs grew near the water and tents and shacks climbed up the mountainside.

Daniel packed up his navigating instruments, hunched under the deck cover, his compass, plotter, divider, and charts spread out in front of him. I turned from Harjo and as I watched him put each instrument carefully in his bag, my chest grew constricted. Do you actually want to reach Row in time? I asked myself. Even if he taught me to navigate, I couldn't afford to buy the instruments I needed.

Only a few hours later we reached the coast. Seagulls fed on half-rotted fish on the shore. Pearl ran out among the seagulls, squawking and flapping her arms like wings. They rose up around her like a white cloud and she spun, her feet kicking up sand, the red handkerchief waving out of her pocket. I thought of Row watching the cranes, thought of my father's feet hanging suspended. I couldn't just do what I wanted anymore. I turned to Daniel, my chest tight.

"Will you stay with us?" I asked Daniel.

Daniel paused from stacking the tripod wood against the gunwale and looked at me.

"We're going to a place called the Valley," I rushed on. "It's supposed to be a safe place, a new community." Inwardly, I winced at the lie. I hoped he didn't already know the Valley was a Lost Abbot colony.

His face softened. "I can't," he said gently. "I'm sorry. I don't travel with other people anymore."

I tried to hide my disappointment. "Why is that?"

Daniel shook his head and thumbed a piece of charred wood in front of him, the ash snowing on the deck. "It's complicated."

"Could you just think about it?"

He shook his head again. "Look, I'm grateful for what you did, but . . . trust me. You don't want me with you much longer."

I turned from him and began loading the smoked mackerel into a bucket.

"I'm going to trade this at the post. We can meet after if you want your share," I said, my last attempt to be appealing, hoping he'd reconsider.

"That mackerel is all yours. I owe you much more than that," he said.

Damn right, I thought.

"I'll carry it to the post for you and be on my way," he said.

I called to Pearl to follow us into town. We climbed rock steps leading up the mountain slope to where the town lay, wedged between a cluster of mountains.

Harjo hummed with motion and voices. A small river cut down a mountain and fell in a waterfall into the sea. Twice as many buildings had been built in the year since I'd been this far south, with a flour mill half constructed up one side of a mountain and a new log cabin next to it with the word HOTEL in bold letters across the façade. Last year, the town was just beginning to farm basic crops like corn, potatoes, and wheat, and I hoped there'd be grain for a decent price at the trading post.

The trading post was a stone building with two floors. We stood outside of it and Daniel handed me the bucket of mackerel.

"Where will you go?" I asked.

"First? The saloon. Have a drink. Ask the locals about work." He paused and rubbed his jaw. "I know I owe you my life. I'm sorry I can't go with you."

"You could," I said. "You won't."

Daniel gave me a look I couldn't read—one that seemed both regretful and admonishing. He bent down in front of Pearl and tugged on the handkerchief hanging out of the pocket of her pants.

"Don't you lose that lucky handkerchief," he said.

She slapped his hand. "Don't you steal it!" she said playfully.

His face flinched almost imperceptibly, a slight tightening of the muscles.

"You take care," he said softly.

Several people exited the post and I stepped out of their way.

"We have to go," I said.

Daniel nodded and turned away.

He was a stranger. I didn't know why I felt a twinge of grief while I watched him walk away.

THE CREDIT I had in Harjo would buy me less than I thought. I stood at the counter, biting back irritation, shifting my weight from one leg to another.

A middle-aged woman with deep wrinkles and a pair of eyeglasses with only one lens hobbled around the counter to look into my bucket.

"Last time I was here I was told my credit was equal to about two trees," I told her.

"Costs have changed, my dear. Fish has gone down, wood has gone up."

She pointed to a chart on a wall which detailed equations: twenty yards of linen equaled two pounds of grain. It ran down to things as small as buttons and big as ships. She clucked her tongue when she saw the mackerel. "Oh, lovely. You must be an excellent fisher. Not easy to catch this much mackerel 'round these parts. And you were the one last year with the sailfish, right?"

"I want to talk to you about wood—"

"You don't want to buy or build here, dear. We're growing by leaps and bounds. The mayor just put a limit on cutting lumber. We hardly have any saplings and there haven't been any shipments in three weeks. I'd go farther south if I were you."

My stomach dropped. How much time was it going to take

to find wood, much less build a boat? Would Row still be in the Valley by then?

"Do you have a salvage yard?"

"Small one, up past Clarence's Rookery. Where you sailing, if you don't mind me asking?" The woman began weighing the mackerel and tossing it in a bin beside the scale, the meat landing with a thud.

"Up north. What was Greenland." I glanced around the shop and saw Pearl looking at an advertisement pinned to the wall by the front door.

The woman clicked her tongue again. "You won't get up there in a salvage boat. Sea's too rough. If you ask me, stick around here. Richards told me they found a half-sunk oil tanker off the coast down south a few miles. Going to try and excavate it and renovate it. You know that's what I'd love—a nice spacious tanker to spend my last days on."

I used my credit on linen for a new sail. The woman and I negotiated back and forth over the mackerel, finally settling on trading it for an eight-foot rope, a chicken, two bags of flour, and three jars of sauerkraut and a few Harjo coins. Pearl and I had tried to avoid scurvy by trading fish for fresh fruit in the south, but sometimes a whole bucket of fish would only get us three oranges. Sauerkraut lasted longer and was much cheaper, but you had to find a place where cabbage grew to get it.

I handed Pearl the box of sauerkraut to carry and she said, "You got it."

"My one bright spot," I muttered. The little bell attached to the door rang as another customer stepped inside. I smelled stone fruit and my mouth began to water and I turned around to see a man carrying a box of peaches to the counter. The scent clouded my mind with longing.

"We need to tell Daniel about the advertiser."

I glanced down at her in surprise. I'd been trying to teach her to read in the evenings with the two books we owned—an instruction manual for hair dryers and Edith Wharton's *House of Mirth*—but didn't know if my lessons had really stuck.

The advertisement asked for a surveyor, displaying pictures of a compass, divider, and plotter, with the words EARN MONEY, QUICK!

"You read that?" I asked.

She glared at me. "Of course. Where's the saloon?"

"It's pretty far. Besides, I'm sure he'll run across the advertisement on his own."

"You're only pretending like you don't want to see him again, too!" Pearl said. She jiggled the box, the jars clinking against one another.

I smiled despite my disappointment. She always could disarm me. I never could read her half as well as she read me.

CHAPTER 9

THE SALOON WAS a run-down shack with metal siding and a grass roof. Light filtered through dirty windows made of plastic tarp. In the dark, voices were disembodied, lifting and mixing in the shadows and the rank smell of dirt and sweat.

Upturned buckets and stools and wood crates served as chairs around makeshift tables. A cat lay on the bar, licking its black tail while the bartender dried canning jars with an old pillowcase.

Daniel sat at a table with a younger man who had the look of a runaway teen; disheveled, jaunty, like he could make use of anything and leave anywhere at a minute's notice. Daniel leaned forward to hear what the younger man was saying, his brow deeply furrowed and his fists clenched on the table. His face was turned toward the door, as if trying to block the commotion of the bar from his view.

Pearl and I were in his eyesight, but he didn't notice us. Pearl tried to step toward him but I caught her shoulder.

"Wait," I said. I ordered moonshine at the bar and the bartender placed a teacup of amber liquid in front of me. I pushed a Harjo coin, a penny with an H melted into the copper, across the bar.

When the younger man stopped talking, Daniel leaned back in his chair, arms crossed over his chest, his eyebrows low and heavy over his eyes, his mouth a tight line. The younger man got up to leave and I thought about slipping out after him. I had wanted to see Daniel, to convince him to help us, but we didn't need to get involved in whatever he was part of.

Pearl leapt toward Daniel before I could catch her. He jumped when he saw her and he forced a smile and tried to level his face into a friendly expression.

"The advertisement even had a picture of your tools," Pearl was saying, moving her hands in excited circles as she told him.

Daniel smiled at her, that same sad smile he often wore around Pearl.

"I appreciate you coming to tell me," he said.

Daniel wouldn't look me in the eye, and I felt tension coming off his body like steady heat.

"Maybe we should go, Pearl," I said, setting my hands on her shoulders.

An old man from the table next to Daniel's tottered toward us and laid a gnarled hand on my arm. He smiled widely, showing a mouth with few teeth. He pointed in my face.

"I see things for you," he said, his voice coming out wheezy, stinking of alcohol and decay.

"Town prophet," Daniel said, nodding to the old man. "He already told me my future."

"What was it?" I asked.

"That I'd cheat death twice and then drown."

"Not bad," I said.

"You," the old man pointed in my face again. "A seabird will land on your boat and lay an egg that will hatch a snake."

I glanced at the old man. "What does that mean?"

"It means," the old man said, leaning forward, "what it means."

I felt a blankness in my head, like my thoughts had nothing to connect to. A white fear rippled through me. Why did the prophet talk about snakes and birds? I shook myself inwardly. Snakes and birds were some of the only animals not extinct. He probably brought them up in everyone's fortunes. But Row and Pearl's faces rose up in my mind, their lives like tenuous things that could drift away.

"Myra," Daniel said. He touched my arm and I startled, stepping away from him. "It doesn't mean anything."

"I know." I glanced around the dark saloon, the silhouette of heads bent over drinks, bodies slumped toward tables in fatigue. "We should go."

"Wait—can—can I stay one last night on your boat?" Daniel asked.

I glared at him. "So you don't have to pay for the hotel?"

He tilted his head. "I'll help you fish in the morning."

"I can fish on my own."

"Mom, stop. You can stay, Daniel," Pearl said. I glanced at Pearl and she raised her eyebrows at me.

"Who were you talking to?" I asked.

"Just an old friend," Daniel said. "I'm only asking for one more night. I like being around you two."

He ruffled Pearl's hair and she giggled. I regarded him coolly, arms crossed over my chest, wishing I could read his face the way I could read the water.

"But you're still not coming with us?" I asked.

A pained expression crossed his face. "I shouldn't."

He looked down at his hands on the table and I could feel him resisting us. As though there were two magnets in him—one pulling him away and another pulling him closer.

BEFORE SETTLING ON our boat for the night we searched the coast for firewood. The rule in most villages was anything small or damaged, like driftwood, could be claimed by anyone. Anything larger was considered property of the village and needed to be bought. If you were caught taking good wood that could be used for building you could be thrown in prison or even hanged.

The three of us drifted apart across the beach, scanning the sand for driftwood or kindling. I picked up a piece of dirty cloth and pulled up a clump of dried grass and stuffed them in my pockets. Daniel walked toward me, carrying a few sticks and an old paper bag.

"I was thinking, you might want to reconsider your trip," he said.

"Why's that?" I asked.

"Atlantic crossings are rough. Your boat is suited to the Pacific coast. It'll be expensive to build another one." Daniel kicked sand off a rock. "News in the saloon earlier was about how the *Lily Black* has a new captain, who is using biological warfare now. Rabid dogs, smallpox blankets. They start an epidemic, cut a population in half, and then take it over and make it a colony. They're looking at northern villages."

"Yeah, I've heard that," I muttered and bent to pick up a discarded shoe. I took the shoelace out, stuffed it in my pocket, and tossed the shoe aside.

"I know this Valley place sounds nice, but . . . is it worth the risk?" Daniel asked.

I looked at him. When he met my eyes I saw he knew I had another reason for going. His question set me on edge. I realized I couldn't see Pearl anywhere on the beach. "Where's Pearl?"

Daniel turned and looked over his shoulder. "I thought she was just over thataways."

I scanned the beach. No sign of anyone, except a couple of people farther down the beach, behind a cluster of rocks. Pins and needles spread down my spine. I had heard of children just disappearing. Parents turning around and them being gone. Kidnapping was a new form of pickpocketing, and seemingly, for those good at it, just as easy.

"Pearl!" I called, trying to stay calm.

"Maybe she went back to the boat?" Daniel asked, in a carefree tone that enraged me.

"Of course she didn't," I said, glaring at him. "Pearl!" I screamed.

"Calm down—"

"Don't tell me to calm down!" I shouted at Daniel. "What do you know about losing a child?"

I took off running, calling Pearl's name, sand flying off my heels. To my left the mountain rose in a steep rock face and to my right the ocean stretched past the horizon. I leapt over a pile of seaweed and kept running and calling for her. It was eerily quiet on the beach, everything gone still. Even a small boat a mile from the coast seemed anchored, stuck in place as though painted into the landscape.

I stopped running and quickly turned in a circle. There was

nowhere she could have gone; it felt like she'd been lifted up into the sky. Panic rose up in my chest. I could hear Daniel's footsteps behind me, and farther behind him the cries of seagulls.

Pearl crawled out from a crevice in the mountain, a crack at the base only three feet wide, and she held a bundle of driftwood.

"All the wood is in the cave," she called out to us.

I inhaled sharply. Her small body silhouetted by the darkness behind her, both familiar and strange, someone made from me and separate from me.

I ran to her and pulled her into a hug before pulling her back from me and tilting her chin up to face me.

"You need to stay in sight," I said.

"I found the wood."

"Pearl, I'm serious."

Daniel caught up to us.

"She always overreacts," Pearl told Daniel as I stepped into the crevice to pick up an armful of wood.

He reached forward and tousled her hair. "No," he said. "She doesn't."

CHAPTER 10

WE LIT A small fire on deck inside the metal lid of a trash can. We grilled half the chicken from our earlier trade and I started making a small loaf of bread. Pearl got two small pans from beneath the deck cover, along with a cup of water from the cistern.

The sun set as the chicken grilled, and I swore I could smell lilacs drifting toward us from land. Daniel and Pearl laughed at me when I told them this. They teased me about wishful thinking. But it was just land—being close to land stirring my memories. Smelling fresh-cut grass or in-season flowers. Expecting the mail at noon. All these memories like a phantom limb. Maybe that was the real reason Pearl and I stayed on the water.

Pearl danced a little jig for Daniel and showed him her two favorite snakes, their thin heads sliding above the rim of her clay jar when she lifted the lid. She pleaded with him to tell her a story. He told her about how he grew up in the Upper Peninsula of Michigan and spent hours hiking through the woods as a child and once stumbled upon a moose.

"What is a moose?" Pearl interrupted him.

Daniel looked at me. "Well, they are big . . ." he started.

"Like a whale?" Pearl asked.

"Uh, maybe a small whale. But they have fur and antlers."

Pearl frowned in confusion and I could tell she was trying to imagine it but had no reference.

"Think of a really big goat, with really big horns," I told her before Daniel started his story again.

"Then the moose pulled its ears back and dipped its head low and charged at me," Daniel made a quick gesture with his hands and Pearl jumped. "It was only twenty feet away and I knew I couldn't outrun it. So I raised my arms and yelled at it."

Pearl giggled. "What did you yell?"

"Get away from me, you beast! Be off! Go away!" Daniel mimed waving his arms and yelling. "It was pretty ridiculous, but it worked. I pretended to be bigger."

The firelight flickered across their faces, sending a warm glow over every surface. I kneaded the flour and water on the back of the pan, listening to them. It was good for Pearl, being around another person, I thought.

"Are there any moose now?" Pearl asked.

I shook my head. "They're all gone."

"Maybe there are a few somewhere," Pearl said.

"Maybe," Daniel said.

We ate the chicken and I baked the bread in two pans, one pan on top of the other to make a small oven. After it got dark, Pearl curled under the deck cover and Daniel and I sat in the moonlight, the fire dying to embers, our voices flickering on the wind.

"The reason you won't travel with anyone anymore," I said. "Is it that woman you told me about?"

"A little. And because it gets too complicated when other people get involved."

I tilted my head and he sighed.

"My mom and I lived alone during the Six Year Flood. She

was diabetic. When the water started coming I loaded up on insulin, traveling to the local hospitals that weren't already ransacked or flooded. Got quite a bit. But most of it got stolen before we took to the water. We headed west and did okay for a while, but she died two years later of DKA."

I remembered what I'd yelled at him on the beach and I looked down at the deck and scratched the wood with a fingernail, a cloud of shame building up in my chest.

"It was difficult . . ." Daniel paused and glanced out at sea. The moonlight caught the top of the water's ripples, carving silver scythes into the black surface. "Knowing the end was coming for her . . . knowing I couldn't do anything, no insulin left to be found. We tried adjusting her diet." He let out a hoarse sound as though he were clearing his throat. "That was impossible with so little food left. Everyone grabbing at what was left."

I remembered those days, the rush of excitement when you found a box of cereal in an empty cabinet in a neighbor's house. And the way your heart dropped when you grabbed it, only to find it weightless, the contents already taken by someone else.

People raided gas stations and shops. And they filled other buildings to the brim. Schools, libraries, abandoned factories. So many people sleeping in rows, on their way somewhere else they hadn't decided yet. Most of them kind and frightened. But some not, so you stayed at home most of the time.

"I'm sorry," I murmured, and when I looked up at him the pain on his face hollowed my stomach.

Daniel raised his shoulders up to his ears. "It's happened to everyone, hasn't it?"

I nodded and felt an odd stirring in my bones. I held his gaze and felt like I was losing control, like I was floating in a sea so salty it held me up.

I remembered that we hadn't just scavenged for food; we also taught ourselves to grow it. Row and I started a vegetable patch in the front yard where the sun was strongest. She once stood in that garden, holding a radish she'd pulled, a pleased grin on her face, sunlight bright on her face. Even in the upheaval there were incandescent moments like that—moments I'd spend the rest of my life reaching for.

"I'm not going to the Valley just because it sounds nice," I said, surprising myself. "That's where my daughter is. My other daughter."

If Daniel was surprised, he didn't show it. His stoic expression stayed unchanged as I told him about Jacob taking Row from me, about how I hadn't heard of them for years until just a few weeks ago, and now Row was held in a colony in the Valley and I had to try to save her. To get her out before they moved her to a breeding ship and my chance was closed forever.

"I know the risk," I said, my voice faltering. I glanced at Pearl under the deck cover. "I know. I just . . . I just have to try." I shrugged and looked away, then looked back at him, his eyes locked on me, his face shadowed. "The thought of not trying feels like suddenly not having bones in my body. My body goes loose and empty." I shook my head and brushed a palm over my face.

"I'll come with," he said, his voice barely audible above the lapping waves against the boat.

"What?"

"I'll help you get there."

"That isn't why I told you," I said. But I wasn't so sure. A part of me had known it was my last card to play. Or maybe I wanted some human connection in a vast dark sea. I couldn't sort it out. "Why are you changing your mind?"

Daniel looked away and reached forward for a stick and stirred the coals.

"I think we can help each other," he said. "I—I've been lonely. Besides, it would be good to go northeast. I haven't been that way before."

The uneasy feeling I had in the saloon returned to me; it drowned out the relief I'd felt when he'd changed his mind. I shifted my weight, leaning to the side, one arm under me. Why was he changing his mind? I couldn't believe it was just because he wanted to help me find Row. I tried to push the uneasiness away. You've always had trouble trusting people, I reminded myself.

When I glanced back at Daniel his eyes were closed, his head leaned back against the gunwale. He looked innocent, and I didn't believe that, either.

CHAPTER 11

AFTER I LOST Row, before I gave birth to Pearl, I wished I wasn't having another child. Part of me wanted Pearl more than anything and the other part felt I couldn't meet her, couldn't look into her face. It all felt too fragile.

I couldn't regret my children, but I also couldn't be free from them, from the way they had opened me up, left me exposed. I had never felt as vulnerable as I had after birth, nor as strong. It was a greater vulnerability than I ever felt facing death, which only felt like a blank expanse, not like free-falling, which was how I felt every day trying to care for Pearl in this world.

What was most different about mothering Pearl compared to Row wasn't that I was on water with Pearl and on land with Row. It was that I was all alone with Pearl after Grandfather passed. With Row, I worried about her falling down the stairs as we played in the attic. With Pearl, I worried about her falling from the side of the boat while I hooked bait. But it was only with Pearl that no one else was there to help keep an eye on her. Paying such close attention turned my mind inside out, flayed my nerves.

When Pearl was a baby I carried her in a sling almost every moment, even when we slept. But when she was a toddler I had a harder time keeping a handle on her. During storms, I'd tie her to me with a rope to make sure she didn't get swept away. I trained her to stay near me at ports and taught her to swim.

Pearl had to do everything early: swimming, drinking goat's milk, potty training, helping me work the fishing lines. She learned to swim at eighteen months but didn't learn to walk properly until she was three. Instead of walking, she scuttled about *Bird* like a crab. Her childhood was the kind I'd read about in frontier stories, the children who knew how to milk a cow at six or how to shoot a rifle at nine.

At first this made me pity her in a different way than I'd pitied Row. But then I realized that being born later, after we were already on water, could be a gift. As a young child she could swim better than I ever would, with an instinctive knowledge of the waves.

So having Daniel on board made me feel like I could breathe again. I noticed he kept an eye on her the way I would, keeping her in his peripheral vision, one ear attuned to her movements. Daniel, Pearl, and I kept sailing south. At night, we'd all sleep under the deck cover, the wind whistling above us, the waves rocking the boat like a cradle. I slept on my side with Pearl tucked against my chest, and Daniel lay on the other side of me. One night, he rested his hand tentatively on my waist, and when I didn't move he reached his arm around the two of us, his arm heavy and comforting, grounding us.

Sometimes, on nights that peaceful, I'd imagine us three going on like that, forgetting about the Valley, making a quiet, simple life on the sea. I began to look forward to the moments when Daniel was close to me, both of us standing near the tiller or huddling under the deck cover during a rainstorm. We could be silently working on mending a rope, our heads bent above the fraying fibers, our hands swiftly weaving, and I'd feel a serenity at his body being near mine.

But I'd remember Row, tugging her blankie behind her on our wood floor, her head cocked to one side, her expression a mix of curiosity and mischief. Or how she'd push the coffee table against the window and sit on it with her perfectly straight posture, watching the birds. Naming them by their colors: red birdie, black birdie. I'd feel her as though she were beside me. A warm tide rose and flooded my veins, pulling me toward the Valley as if I had no choice at all.

I PICKED SARDINES and squid from one of the nets I'd fished with that morning and dumped them in our live bait jar, a large ceramic canister that once was used to hold flour in a kitchen. We kept the jar tied down next to the cistern and only filled it with live bait when we could spare the meat.

I kept scanning the horizon as we approached the mountaintops of Central America. When we were about fifteen miles from the closest coast we signaled to a merchant ship by waving our flag, a blue square of fabric with a fish in the middle. The ship's own flag billowed in the wind, purple with a brown spiral that looked like a snail shell.

People had communicated by flags before Grandfather and I took to the water. Sailors said that the Lily Black had been the first to raise a flag, using it to identify the different ships within their tribe, and later, to invite another ship to surrender before an attack.

So Grandfather and I made a fisherman's flag by cutting a fish out of a white T-shirt and sewing it onto a blue pillowcase. As soon as Pearl was a toddler I taught her the three different kinds of flags, because I needed her to be my second set of eyes on the sea, to alert me to who could be approaching us if I was busy fishing. So she learned how some flags were a plain color: white to communicate distress, black to indicate disease, orange to refuse a request. Others told what kind of ship you were: a merchant ship, fishing boat, or breeding ship. And the last kind were the tribal flags, flags with symbols on them to show the identity of a new community, like a family crest.

Though the Lily Black were the first to set up this communication, they were also the first to subvert it. Now it was rumored that the Lily Black liked to sail under false flags to get closer to an enemy and to raise their own flag right before an attack.

So as we approached the merchant ship, I kept my eyes on their flag, my hands on the gunwale, fearing they'd take it down and replace it with a raider tribal flag.

"I think you can relax," Daniel said. "You can't stay in a permanent state of hypervigilance."

"I've always avoided this part of the Pacific because I've heard raiders have a stronghold here."

"I thought you avoided this area because you can't navigate?" Daniel grinned at me and brushed my arm with the back of his hand.

I suppressed a grin and glanced at him, the wind tossing my hair in my face. "After the trade, we should troll and head a bit farther east for sailfish."

Daniel looked out at sea. "How can you tell?"

I pointed to frigate birds flying low and diving into the water a few miles east. Grandfather had taught me to watch the birds. "I also saw schools of tuna and mackerel. The water is warm here. Sailfish can get you eighty pounds of meat. It's worth going off course."

"Okay. We've just got to be careful, sailing so close to the coast without aiming to dock."

I knew he was concerned about the mountains just under the surface of the water and the boat running aground, shredding the hull. Sometimes you could see shadows darkening the water where the mountains rose up to meet the sky, and when you sailed over them, you could look down and see the rocky peaks like ancient faces floating in the deep, looking back up at you. The ocean churned above them, its currents eddying among the rocks, coral springing up anew, new sea creatures adapting and forming in the dark.

I wouldn't be here for whatever new things would grow out of this new world; I'd be ash before they sprouted fully formed. But I wondered about them, wondering what Pearl would live to see and hoping they'd be good things.

We pulled alongside the merchant ship and traded our fish for a few yards of cotton, thread, charcoal, and goat's milk. When I asked them about wood, they told us we needed to go even farther south to get good prices. A knot twisted in my stomach. We couldn't lose even more time by sailing farther off course.

When we parted ways with the merchant ship, it sailed northeast toward a small port on the coast and Daniel adjusted our tiller so we'd turn southeast, toward where I thought there might be sailfish. Pearl played with a snake on deck as I repaired crab pots, weaving wire between the broken slats of metal. There was always something to be fixed. The rudder, the sail, the hull, the deck, the tackle and bait. Everything always breaking and me barely able to keep up, time slipping through my fingers all the while.

We sailed toward the diving birds. Pearl and I trolled with brightly colored lures made of ribbons and hooks. The water ran clear and the wind breathed easy, one of those lovely sailing days that made me feel like I was flying. I caught sight of a sailfish near the surface, its sail cutting the water like a shark's fin, and I dropped a line with live squid on the hook.

I let the line drift, occasionally moving it, watching the water and waiting, careful to bait the sailfish and not follow it. It took two hours before the sailfish bit and jerked me against the gunwale. My knuckles whitened as it almost tugged me into the sea.

Daniel leapt forward to steady me. "You okay?" he asked as he helped me screw the pole into the rod holder on the gunwale.

I nodded. "We can't lose this one."

It swam with astonishing speed, its sail cutting the surface of the water, and our boat lurched toward it when it reached the end of the line. It gave a powerful run, swimming in a semicircle at the end of the line, then fighting the line, diving into the air, sending a spray of water around it.

No coast lay in sight; the world was so flat and blue, your eyes could get tired of it. It was disorienting—this much space. Like a person needed something to dwarf them. Even the clouds were as thin as gauze.

A shark circled our boat, swimming closer and then farther away. At first I thought the shark was tracking the movements of a school of mackerel under us, but then I realized it was hunting our sailfish.

"We should try to reel it in quick," I told Daniel.

"I thought you said it's better to let them wear out before you reel them in? How are we going to handle this thing?"

I put on my leather gloves. "You and Pearl reel him in. I'll catch him by the sword. Once I've got him, you help me lift him out of the water by grabbing his sail and under his torso."

The pole that held the sailfish had been a titanium fence post before Grandfather fashioned it into a fishing pole. It didn't bend or break against the sailfish's weight, but the rod holder on the gunwale creaked and screeched, threatening to rip lose.

Daniel cranked the reel, straining with each pull, sweat gathering at his temples. The sailfish kept fighting, lunging into the air and whipping its body around. Water sprayed our faces. Its body slammed against the boat as it fought. I blinked away the salt caught in my eyes and lost sight of the shark.

When the sailfish was close enough to grab, I leaned over the gunwale and reached for it. It jerked on the line, its head pulled from the water, the hook glistening in its mouth.

I grabbed its sword and it almost slipped out of my hands, slick as an icicle. The sulfuric scent of coral and seaweed drifted around us. We must be close to mountaintops, I thought fleetingly.

Daniel locked the reel in place and leaned over the gunwale to grab the sail. Out of the corner of my eye, I saw the shark reappear. It bumped the hull and we rocked slightly.

Dread gathered like bile at the base of my throat. The shark dove deeper into the water, its shape cloudy and then invisible in the depths. The sailfish's eyes darted to and fro. Its gills fluttered and its scales tremored, spinning sunlight in a kaleidoscope. Even it seemed to have a fresh wave of fear roll over it.

It opened its eyes wide and ripped its sword from my hands in a violent lurch and dropped back into the water with a splash.

"Dammit," Daniel muttered, reaching into the water to grab the sail.

"Daniel, don't!" I said.

The shark pierced the water, mouth open, catching Daniel's forearm in its teeth and shaking its head in a violent toss before dropping back into the water. Daniel screamed, falling forward toward the water.

CHAPTER 12

I CAUGHT THE back of Daniel's shirt, braced against the gunwale, and yanked him hard. We both stumbled backward and fell to the deck. Blood streamed from his arm, running along the cracks between the wood.

"Pearl! Grab the fabric!" I shouted.

I couldn't see the wound past the blood. Skin and tendons hung from his arm. Had he severed an artery? Was the bone crushed?

Pearl ran to the deck cover and returned with the fabric I'd gotten in Harjo. I pressed it against his arm.

"It's going to be okay," I told him, my own blood pulsing in my ears. "We just need to stop the bleeding."

He squeezed his eyes shut. His face was pale and his breath came in quick shallow bursts.

"Pearl, hold this here and apply pressure," I said. She held the fabric against the wound as I took off my belt and hooked it around his upper arm, above his elbow. I cut a new hole in the leather with my knife, tightened the belt, and fastened it in place.

I leaned back on my heels to get a better look at him and laid my hand on his shoulder. "Breathe," I said. "Try to stay calm."

The sound of wood on rock filled the air, a rumble growing into a dull roar. The boat rocked abruptly, knocking me to my side.

Daniel's eyes flew open. "Mountain. Mountain!" he said frantically.

I leapt up, ran to the stern, and looked over the gunwale. The tops of mountains glimmered just below the surface, pocked with crevices and peaks, small blooms of coral sprouting in the shadows. We were running aground on mountaintops.

I turned the tiller, yanking the rudder as far to the right as it would go, and felt the boat start to shift. A strong wind caught the sail and we surged forward. Beyond the bow, several peaks protruded a few feet above the water. We needed to turn farther to the right, and faster.

"The sail!" I called to Pearl, but she was already at the block, working the rope through. I joined her, pulling the rope, fumbling to release a knot.

Pearl's hands shook and tears streamed down her face. "We're going to be in the water," she cried.

"We're going to be okay," I told her.

I dropped the knot, pulled my knife from its sheath, and cut the rope, releasing the sail so it let out, bearing us away from the wind.

But it was too late. The rocky tip of a mountain stood a foot above the water's surface and was only twenty feet in front of us. I grabbed Pearl and pulled her close.

Bird tilted to the left as we ran over the mountain, water sloshing over the deck and Daniel rolling toward the gunwale. Pearl and I tumbled against the mast and clung to it. The boat slid over the mountain, the sound of cracking wood thundering around us.

The hull hit the water again with a thud and *Bird* almost

leveled. I ran to Daniel, pulling him up beneath his armpits and propping him against the gunwale. He clutched his arm against his chest and gritted his teeth. *Bird* started to lean to the right. We were taking on water. I stood up and scanned the horizon, hoping to see land, but found none.

"Pearl, grab the bucket and a torch," I said.

I opened the latch door in the deck and peered into the cavity between the hull and deck. Interlaced boards blocked my view, but I could hear the rush of water. Pearl handed me the torch, a branch with a piece of fabric wrapped around one end and a plastic bag over it to keep it dry. I ripped the plastic bag off the end and Pearl struck her flint stone against it.

I jumped through the hole, my feet hitting water when I landed. The flame only illuminated a foot around me, casting deep shadows between the interlaced boards. To the right I saw the hole, near the bottom right of the hull. The water inside was already two feet high. We could sink in an hour or less.

I pulled myself out of the hole and grabbed a bucket from Pearl. She'd already tied a string to the handle, and I dropped it into the hole and pulled it up, water dripping and sloshing over the rim.

"Pearl, while I haul water, you pack food and Daniel's instruments into our bags. And bottle some of the water from the cistern."

"It won't all fit."

"Don't take the flour then."

"Okay," Pearl said. She turned and disappeared beneath the deck cover, dragging out bags and tossing them on the deck in front of her.

I dropped the bucket again and again, my arms and back beginning to ache.

"Shit," I muttered. I wasn't buying us any time. I tossed the water over the side of the boat, and it caught the light in a bright curve, sparkling like crystal. I squeezed my eyes shut and reopened them. *Bird*, I thought, thinking of Grandfather's hands as he made her, his callused palms running over the wood.

I WATCHED *BIRD* sink as I clung to Daniel's raft. Daniel and Pearl sat on top of the raft, clutching the sides so they wouldn't be knocked off with each wave. There was only room for two without it sinking; I put Pearl on so she'd be safe and Daniel on so he'd stop pissing me off by bleeding into the water. We each wore a backpack stuffed with supplies.

Bird pitched to the side and seemed to hold steady as the water filled her. I felt that the water was filling me, its weight inescapable. But then a gurgling sound came from *Bird*, water pulling her down, and she disappeared from sight like a coin dropped in a wishing well. I sucked in air. *Bird* was the last thing tying me to my mother and grandfather, and without her I felt suspended, cut loose from them. I stifled a sob and clutched the raft more tightly.

I held my knife in my other hand, scanning the water for the shark.

"It will wait till we tire," Daniel said, watching me, concern softening his voice.

I glared at him. You'll tire first, I thought, half tempted to pull him into the water if I saw the shark again. "I told you not to reach for the sailfish," I snapped.

"I told you we should've stayed on course and gone straight to port," he snapped back. "Navigating this close to the coastline is impossible."

A small strangled sound came from Pearl, a sob caught in her throat. She hadn't stopped shaking since the first collision.

I reached my hand up to grasp her white knuckles. "Pearl, sweetie. We're going to be okay."

"I don't want you in the water. The shark," she cried.

"I've got my knife," I said, holding the blade up so it glinted in the sun. I forced a smile and squeezed her hand. "We'll be fine."

Pearl's tears fell on my hand over hers. A wave splashed in my face and I swallowed salt water and felt rage unfurl inside me. I cursed myself. I never should have let him on board.

All my tackle and bait, most of the food stores, the fresh water in the cistern. All sunk, drifting to the seafloor. Even if we made it to land, I'd have nothing to trade for food or new fishing supplies.

"Myra, I see something," Daniel said.

"Shut up."

"Myra—"

"I said shut up," I said, clutching my knife tighter.

"It's a ship," he said, reaching into a bag for the binoculars.

"Give them to me."

I peered through the binoculars, scanning the horizon until I landed on a ship. It was larger than a fishing boat, about the size of a merchant vessel. I squinted through the binoculars, searching for a flag.

"I don't know who they are," I said. Strangely, they seemed to be sailing straight toward us, though I was doubtful they could see us yet. They seemed almost three miles from us, and we were such a small speck in the vast sea. I doubted they could see us unless they were searching for us.

I gnawed on my lip, already dry from salt and sun. I gazed toward the ship, only able to see a small shadow on the horizon without the binoculars. The ship could save us or condemn us to a worse fate than taking our chances on the open sea.

"You should wave them down," Daniel said, reaching into the backpack for our white flag.

"We don't know who they are," I repeated. "I'd rather face my chances on the open sea than chained in the hull of a raider ship."

"It's worth the risk," Daniel said.

I glared at him. Worth the risk for him, I thought. He wouldn't survive on the open sea long, but Pearl and I might. At least for a few days, and if the currents were right, maybe we'd make it to the coast.

He seemed to read my thoughts. "You two won't make it long. We're still several miles from the coast. This isn't well-traveled territory; someone else won't come along."

I glanced back at the ship. I remembered talking with my mother up in the attic, sitting on the top step, as Grandfather had fitted *Bird*'s joints. We talked about the latest reports we'd heard, how far the water had come, what buildings in town to avoid. Jacob was gone, meeting up with some of his new friends I didn't know. Row carried a pail of water past us and set it next to the others, clustered around the perimeter of the attic. The city water had been shut off the week before and we were collecting rainwater in all our buckets and bowls. Row knelt in front of the bucket and leaned forward, grinning into her reflection.

"Hi," she said to herself and giggled.

Grandfather had smiled at her and patted the side of *Bird*. "She'll be a good boat to start out in," he'd said.

I was surprised when he said this—I never imagined we'd leave *Bird*, not after it'd taken so much work to build. I was so young, I wasn't accustomed to loss and impermanence the way Grandfather was. I hadn't known how to expect it or accept it.

My heartbeat quickened and I tried to breathe deeply. No choice but to move forward, I told myself.

"Hand me the fishing wire," I said. I pulled my torso up on the raft and treaded water. I pierced the fishing wire through the fabric, tying it around the oar to make a flag.

When Daniel lifted it into the air with his uninjured arm I felt a cold weight in my stomach, like I was waiting to receive a sentence. I kept my eye on the ship as it grew larger and felt an unfurling sensation in my limbs, a movement of growing anticipation, a sense that this ship would change everything.

CHAPTER 13

WHEN THE SHIP approached, I feared it would collide with us. Before we were in the shadow of its hull, I caught a glimpse of several sailors moving on board. The ship itself had two sails and looked about sixty feet long. The name SEDNA was painted in black block letters on the hull. It reminded me of a merchant sailing vessel I'd seen in history books as a child. There was a small poop cabin, a goat in a pen on the deck, and a small canoe hanging from the wall of the cabin.

Daniel had grown paler as we waited, and now his eyelids hung heavy over his eyes.

"Stay awake," I said sharply to him.

Pearl still clutched the side of the raft with white knuckles, her eyes wide, watching the ship draw near. Dehydration stung my throat and I swallowed and blinked my eyes to try to clear my head. Even my blood felt fuzzy with fatigue.

A ladder dropped from the ship's gunwale down to the sea while the ship was still ten feet away.

"We'll have to swim," I told them.

Pearl's eyes grew wide with terror and Daniel nodded in a drunken way.

I cursed under my breath. "I'll swim with each of you. Pearl, come on," I said.

Pearl wrapped her thin arms around me and we swam to the ladder. After I got her started up it, I went back for Daniel.

He was so heavy and his limbs moved so sluggishly, I felt a surge of panic that we'd both sink, his weight pulling me down. I thrashed furiously through the water, yanking him along. Once we reached the ladder, he grabbed it with his good hand.

"You go first," I said. If he fell, I wasn't sure I'd be able to save him, but I'd try, I realized with surprise.

Daniel scaled the ladder easier than I thought he would, going slowly but steadily. I had a feeling he'd collapse soon as he got on deck, so I pulled myself up the ladder quickly, my mind buzzing, thinking of Pearl alone up there.

A man grabbed my arm as I came up over the gunwale and I startled, put my hands on his chest to push him away, and was met with kind dark eyes.

"Woah, easy there, just helping you over. This gunwale is tall," the man said, lifting me from the gunwale to the ground.

He was attractive, his face angular but friendly. He had black hair and light brown skin; wore a bandanna around his neck and leather lace-up boots.

"I'm Abran," he said, shaking my hand. "Welcome to *Sedna*. Glad we made it to you in time." His hands moved as he talked in quick bursts.

"Myra," I said, glancing around at the crew, trying to decide what I thought of them. "This is Pearl and Daniel."

"We normally take weapons," Abran said as my hand flew to the knife sheathed at my waist. "But we want to welcome you onto our ship in good faith," he said watching me carefully. "We actually know a bit about you. We have a friend in common—Beatrice in Apple Falls."

My eyes widened in surprise. "Beatrice," I said softly.

"She said you always have a good catch. We didn't expect to catch you." Abran and a few others chuckled and I glared at them.

"Then, at Myer's Port"—Abran pointed behind him toward the trading post—"some merchants said they got a good trade with you, so we wanted to catch up with you. I was worried we wouldn't find you. Wayne had you in view and then it seemed you disappeared. You're lucky we were already coming after you."

The world was so small now, and since I visited the same trading villages every year, often during the same season, I was a regular. Names of trustworthy fishers and traders were swapped over whiskey or amid the smoke of a tobacco pipe at trading posts.

"What kind of ship is this?" I asked. The ship was much too big for the average fishing boat and it didn't have the usual display of wealth you found on a merchant vessel.

"We're a community," Abran said, and I looked him over skeptically.

"But we should"—Abran gestured to Daniel—"we should get him treated. Jessa and Wayne—" A young woman and middle-aged man stood a few feet away, watching us. Jessa was petite, with a heart-shaped faced and fair complexion. Wayne had blond hair so bleached by the sun it looked white, and a splash of tattoos across his arms. "They're going to salvage whatever is left of your raft."

I nodded. Abran led the way across the deck to the poop cabin, near the stern. The poop cabin was a square, one-room building with a curtain separating the room in half. On this half of the room, the door into the cabin faced a long table and on the wall opposite the door there was a small window. Along the length of the table, shelves and baskets lined the wall, brimming with maps, books, rope, tackle, and cords.

Sunlight poured through the window and landed in a square on the table. It felt odd to be blocked from the wind on a ship, to move with the waves but not feel the wind on my body.

"If you use an ax instead of a sword, you have more force behind it. Really, it is better," said a voice from behind the curtain.

"Mmm-hmm," murmured another voice, the voice of a mother only paying half attention.

Abran stepped forward and pulled the curtain back to expose a tiny kitchen. A teenage boy of about seventeen was stirring a bowl of something that smelled like tomatoes in vinegar, the sweet, pungent smell making my stomach clench in hunger. Next to him, a middle-aged woman was standing on a stool, searching for something in a cabinet above a counter.

"Marjan," Abran said, gesturing to the woman. "She's our quartermaster and cook. And Behir," he said, gesturing to the young man. "This is Myra, Daniel, and Pearl."

Marjan turned on the stool and smiled at us. "Hello. We finally found you." She had a square face, brown skin, glittering black eyes, and a black braid down her back. Something about her expression and the way she stood, grounded and calm, reminded me of Beatrice and I felt a surge of sadness.

Behir walked toward us, holding out his hand for us to shake, a wide smile on his face. Warmth radiated from him. He looked like a taller and thinner version of his mother, with the same bright eyes and kind demeanor.

Marjan got down from the stool and set a bag of grain on the counter. She stepped forward and stumbled over the stool and almost fell, but Behir caught her elbow and held her upright. "You okay?"

He asked the question with such tenderness, I felt that buzz in my veins, the electric shot when Pearl did something thoughtful for me. I had met so few other mothers with children still living. It seemed I only now met one without the other—childless mothers or orphans. I stared at them, drinking them in briefly before Abran said my name.

"What?" I asked.

"Can you get Daniel on the table while I get my supplies?" Abran asked. Abran walked to the shelving along the wall and pulled down a tackle box.

I dropped my backpack to the floor and helped Daniel lie down on the table. I pointed to a stool in the corner for Pearl and she settled into it, tucking her knees up under her chin. She was surprisingly quiet, her eyes moving about the room, watching Abran.

Abran peeled the bandage off Daniel's arm, slowly and gently, careful to not pull Daniel's flesh away with it. Daniel gritted his teeth, his eyes squeezed shut.

"Marjan, can we have the whiskey?" Abran called. Abran looked at me. "We have some painkillers, but they're only for the crew," he said apologetically.

I nodded, surprised he'd even mention painkillers. Only the wealthy had hoarded drugs, and it was even rarer to mention it to strangers for fear of inciting theft.

Marjan brought a clay bottle to the table and held Daniel's head up so he could drink it.

Abran loosened the tourniquet and pinched Daniel's fingers, the blood slowly coloring them.

"It got the ulnar artery, which is why you lost so much blood. It looks like it is already beginning to seal up again, though. The wound isn't as deep as you'd think. Mostly got your skin and some muscle tore up. I'm always glad when things aren't as bad as they seem. We'll sew you up, get some alcohol on it," Abran said.

His chattiness put me on edge. "Are you a doctor?" I asked.

"Was."

And he grew quiet. Asking about a person's past always made them open or close, and I always wanted to know which it'd do.

Abran dipped his needle in the bottle and strung it with a very fine thread. He handed me a rag and I mopped up the blood around Daniel's arm.

Abran bent forward, his face only a few inches from Daniel's arm. He worked slowly, smoothing the torn skin down and stitching along the jagged edges. Daniel's arm would be a jigsaw of scars by the time it healed.

"Where were you headed?" Abran asked.

"Andes. To trade," I said.

"Same with us. That's where we're planning to find a place to settle. You have plans to stay on the water?"

His questions made me feel peevish, and I hoped Pearl wouldn't pipe up and give anything away. The less they knew, the better. At least until I knew more about them.

"Like I said before, we've heard about you. That you're a good fisher. Dependable. You go up and down the coastal villages with plenty to trade. Small, independent operation. That's rare now. And it's getting harder to do with everyone else teaming up." He glanced up from Daniel's arm to look at me, his eyes inquiring.

"How did you get such a big ship? I guess these are becoming more common, too," I said.

Abran's eyes flickered over me before returning to Daniel's arm. He understood my other question.

"I ran into some bad luck, then some good luck, and had expensive resources to trade. It got me extra wood and some good builders. Then I got a good crew that keeps us going." Abran straightened and wiped his needle with the rag. "We don't deal in the raider's market."

From the kitchen, the sound of clanging pots, pouring water, and stoking of coals filled the cabin. The smell of cooking meat wafted past the curtain. Abran looked over at Pearl, quiet in the corner. "And what do you think of our ship?" he asked Pearl with the easy friendliness of someone accustomed to strangers.

"It's nice," she said softly.

Something in Pearl's bag moved.

"What's in the bag?" Abran asked, sharpness edging his voice.

"Snakes," she said.

Abran looked at me.

"Pearl!" I gasped. "You packed your snakes? We could have packed the flour!" I looked at Abran. "I'm sorry. She beheads the poisonous ones, so those aren't venomous. We can give them to you to eat."

"No!" Pearl said.

"Pearl!"

Abran gave me an uncertain grin. "We'll speak about the rules of the ship later. We do have a rule about sharing everything."

An uneasy feeling came over me. I had heard of people being held on ships as slaves to repay debts. These people had rescued us, sheltered and fed us, and we'd be in their debt. "We'd like to be on our way as soon as possible," I said. "How can we repay you?"

"We can discuss that later," Abran said, dabbing extra blood from Daniel's arm with a wet rag. "For now, he needs rest. Swelling is normal, oozing isn't. Come to me if you see any signs of infection."

Abran saw the concern on my face and reached out and gave my arm a squeeze. "It will be fine." He clapped his hands together and pushed a lock of hair from his face. "Now, how about I give you a tour of the ship. That way you know your way around." He smiled at me warmly and spread his hands wide in a welcoming gesture.

He had an animated energy about him, a charisma that made me feel uneasy, and then I realized why. He reminded me of Jacob.

CHAPTER 14

PEARL WANTED TO stay with Daniel, so I left them in the poop cabin while Abran gave me a tour of the ship. Before we left the cabin, we peeked in on Marjan cooking chicken stew over hot coals, the smoke filling the cabin and billowing up through a giant hole in the ceiling.

He showed me around the deck and we passed the goat's pen and three large cisterns, their metal gleaming in the sunlight. I hoped Pearl could have some of the goat's milk before we left the ship, but I didn't ask. I didn't want our debt to grow even larger.

We climbed down the deck hatch to get into the hull, where we walked through the quarters, small rooms sectioned off with thin walls. The bathroom had a chamber pot and pitcher and basin. Across from the bathroom was a room with fishing supplies, and next to it was Abran's room, the captain's chambers. It was the size of a large closet, with a small cot along one wall and a small dresser. The largest room was the crew's quarters, crammed with bunk beds and shelving for clothing and personal items. A man lay in a bottom bunk, groaning, the skin on his leg inflamed with a red rash.

"John is ill," Abran said quietly, and we exited the room.

Crates were stacked in the back corner of the hull, with odds and ends spilling out: spare pieces of rope, wood, broken blocks and tackle. We walked into a storage room next to this and a man rooting through a box of small metal pieces jumped.

"Thomas," Abran said, "this is Myra. Thomas is our boatswain."

Thomas limped a few steps forward, favoring his right leg. He followed my eyes and said, "Broken ankle never healed right." His skin was a deep brown and his black hair was shorn close to his head. He shook my hand and smiled.

"I can't find a metal eye for the flagpole," Thomas told Abran.

"I think there is an extra one in that crate," Abran said, pointing.

Thomas rummaged through the crate, pulled a metal eye from it, and left the storage room.

I couldn't keep my eyes off the crates of canned cabbage, bags of flour, sugar, salt, beans, and corn, and boxes of salted pork and tea piled on shelves. Buckets of water anchored the bottoms of the shelves. I tried to imagine what it would be like to live on a ship with so much food in reserve, so much variety. Not just fish with some flatbread, every day and night until you reached a trading post. It felt so safe, so calm, to stand in a room like this on a ship, with food carefully packaged and labeled.

"A lot of food," I said softly, fingering a can of cabbage.

"We ration carefully and trade with reputable traders who give us a fair trade. Everyone here has a job and they do it well," Abran said.

Abran gestured that we move on and led me to the armory. Guns, knives, bombs, bows, arrows, and a few clubs filled the shelves. I turned and looked at Abran, waiting for him to say something.

He shrugged. "Every ship needs to protect itself" was all he said.

"Yes, but where'd you get all this? This many weapons, these days . . ." I trailed off into silence. These weapons were worth more than *Bird*. I stared at them, metal glinting in the dull light from the kerosene lamp Abran was holding.

"I stole them," Abran said.

I looked up at him, waiting for him to go on.

"Found a stash of weapons buried by a raider ship. A reserve stash. It was marked with a raider flag on the boxes, so I took it."

I paused, still watching him, considering his story. It was common for raiders to stash resources, especially expensive re-sources like weapons or medicine, in hidden locations so they could return to them if their ship was robbed. But what was uncommon was to find these hidden locations.

"How'd you find it?" I asked.

The ship creaked as it turned to the right, the floor tilting, the weapons clattering against one another on the shelves.

"Luck," Abran said. "Saw some raiders up the mountainside close to where I was living. They were rummaging around for a bit. I knew there was nothing up there to get their attention for so long—no water, no good hunting. So after they left I checked it out."

Abran smiled and tilted his head, a lock of black hair falling in his eyes. "I've gotten lucky a few times. Hopefully that luck will last me a bit longer." He looked at me closely with a slight smile playing on his lips.

"Where all have you sailed?" I asked.

"Up past what was Alaska, and throughout the Caribbean and around the Andes. Now we're searching for a place to settle."

"To settle? Why? When you have this kind of ship?"

"Being on the water, it's not permanent." Abran hung the kerosene lamp from a hook in the ceiling. "We want a community. I want to build a community of people where certain values are upheld. Where everyone works, and everyone has a chance at a better life."

"And what place will that be?" I asked, trying to straighten a smirk from the corners of my mouth. I took a step back to lean against a shelf, the handle of a rifle digging into my shoulder blade.

"I know I sound idealistic," Abran said. "But you have to risk idealism to have hope." He took a step closer to me and I felt a magnetic pull coming from him. He spread his hands in an open gesture, like he was trying to welcome me into some shared idea. "Besides, we aren't meant to live on water."

"I don't know if what we're meant for really plays a role anymore."

Abran stopped and lifted the kerosene lamp from the hook. "We should go back to the deck. Check on Daniel."

"I'm sorry. I didn't mean to mock. I'm just cynical, I suppose."

"You may think you have no beliefs or hopes, but you do. It's better you be aware of them since you already have them," Abran said, turning and leading the way out of the armory. We climbed up the ladder and onto the deck.

"I understand your concerns," Abran said. He walked to the gunwale and leaned against it, scanning the sea.

"What concerns?"

"Your . . . your hesitancy. Your reluctance to trust us. We aren't looking to take anything from you. In fact, we are looking for a few more people to join our crew."

I was silent for a moment and then asked, "Why would you want us to join?"

"Remember how I said everyone here has a job? Well, we have a need for someone who can fish. We had a fisher, but he, well, isn't here anymore." Abran seemed nervous and rushed on. "Like I said earlier, we've heard stories about you—about a mother and a daughter who always have good catches, even when other fishers come up dry. You have a reputation for being able to read the water."

That's what Grandfather had called it. Reading the water. He told me that the water would tell me what it held, I only had to listen and respond. We'd look for a deep basin when ice-fishing for walleye in winter or drop lines near frogs when fishing for bass in summer. And when it was quiet, he'd tell me how to read the water on the ocean, too, remembering his days of fishing off the banks of Alaska. Nebraska, he'd always say, had been an ocean, and it was easy to believe with only wind and sky and waves of grass in all directions. But that didn't mean he wasn't still homesick for the sea. When the water came to Nebraska, he'd stare out the window and murmur, "The seas fall away and they rise again."

I felt Abran's eyes on me and lifted mine to meet his. A jolt of longing caught me by surprise. I wanted life on a ship like this. I wanted the bunks, the crates of food in the hull. But I thought of Row, alone in the Valley, and felt a second gravity on my bones, a resolute weight spreading through me.

"So, you'll think about it?" Abran asked, brushing his finger against my forearm to get my attention.

Inwardly, I bristled. We knew nothing about who these people were. I knew Abran hadn't told me the full truth of how he got all those weapons in the armory. But a part of me wondered if the risk of trusting them was worth it. I wondered if I could convince them to change course to the Valley. This kind of ship could handle northern seas. Already I was weeks behind schedule.

"Yes," I told him. "I'll think on it."

CHAPTER 15

PEARL SHOVELED THE chicken stew into her mouth at supper. She raised her bowl, pouring the last bits into her mouth like water from a pitcher into a basin. The chicken stew had carrots and celery in it, and I hadn't tasted either in at least two years. I tried to hide how famished I was by eating slowly, but I fooled no one. As soon as Pearl's and my bowls were empty, Marjan held up the ladle and asked if we wanted more.

"Yes," Pearl said greedily, stew dripping off her chin.

Marjan laughed and ladled more stew into her bowl. I wondered if they had food this good every night or only when they had guests to impress.

We were sitting around the table in the poop cabin and I noticed a wood sign hanging above the door: A MAN'S CHARACTER IS HIS FATE. I stifled a laugh.

"Something funny?" Wayne asked.

"You don't think circumstance has anything to do with it?" I asked, pointing up at the sign.

"Maybe we don't always make our fate, but we decide how to meet our fate," Abran said.

"Or the gods decide our fate," Marjan said, a small smile playing on her lips.

Thomas and Wayne chuckled. It seemed to be an inside joke.

"I'd love to know what they were thinking," Thomas said shaking his head.

"When the floods came?" I asked.

"When they made us," Thomas said.

The room grew quiet, only the sounds of wooden spoons in clay bowls. After a few minutes Jessa started talking about repairing a crack in the mainmast, and then the conversation moved to what they needed at the next trading post. The conversation moved lightly, and I relaxed, watching their familiarity and ease. I felt a sense of warmth at that table, surrounded by the crew. I tilted my head, watching their hands move, their shoulders relax, their quick laughs and the occasional eye roll.

They're like a family, I thought. It wasn't something I saw much anymore, this communal comfort. I'd been alone so long, it made me uncomfortable, and it also filled me with longing. I remembered evenings gathered around the candlelit table back home, dusk still sending a haze of light across us. How my mother would bring us bowls of oatmeal or baked potatoes. Jacob, Row, Grandfather, Mother, and I would joke about the weather, reminisce about years before, talk about tomorrow. And the light around us would die down and space would shrink to just the five of us, our voices flickering like the flame, going on into the night.

I wondered how each of them had gotten here and what they had done before. What their secrets were and how well they kept them. What would happen if we did join them? I noticed Daniel was watching me as I watched the crew, his face troubled as though he could read my thoughts.

"I know you're considering joining them," he said, his voice low so no one else could hear.

"And?"

"Bad idea."

"Why?"

Daniel just shook his head and leaned back in his chair, his injured arm crossed over his chest.

The crew's conversation moved to Thomas talking about an old friend who now lived in Harjo.

"He admitted to trading with raiders. Says he can't make it otherwise." Thomas's voice was soft and regretful. Thomas kept a sensitivity that reminded me of the previous world, a gentleness in his body that looked like trust.

Wayne slammed his hand on the table, rocking our bowls and silencing everyone.

"That's bullshit. Total bullshit! Can't make it otherwise? Might as well be slitting throats himself. Might as well be raping children—" Wayne pointed at Pearl and she stared at him wide eyed.

"That's enough," Abran said, standing up, his hands on the table, glaring at Wayne.

"No, it's not," Wayne said, shoving his chair backward so forcefully it toppled over. "Not even close."

Wayne strode out of the room, his shoulders so broad he could barely fit through the doorway without turning sideways, his hair grazing the doorframe.

"Wayne lost his wife," Abran said quietly, sitting back down.

"Not just lost," Jessa said. "Killed in front of him."

I didn't ask by who. But I knew that Abran wasn't lying when he said they didn't trade on the raider's market. Or if they did, most of the crew didn't know about it.

· · ·

WHILE WE WERE cleaning up supper, Marjan left with a plate of food. When she came back into the cabin a few minutes later, she said something quietly to Abran.

Abran closed his eyes and nodded.

"John," Thomas said, leaning forward and gripping the back of a chair. The crew went still and quiet, like the air had gone out of the room.

Abran nodded again. "John passed this evening. We'll do the sea burial tonight."

Abran walked over to me and tilted his head so I could hear him speak softly. "We were expecting this, but it's still a blow." Abran looked around at the crew. They seemed to move languidly, against a new gravity. "He was with us almost a year. He was a good seaman."

"I'm so sorry. What—"

"Sepsis. Started as a localized infection on his foot. Cut it stepping on something." Abran shook his head. "He was always about deck without shoes."

We all moved out onto the deck. The sun hung low and the sky grew overcast. *Sedna*'s flag now flapped in the wind, square gray fabric with a red sun in the middle. Seagulls' calls fell and rose around us as Marjan wrapped John's body in sailcloth. His mouth was twisted in a grimace, and I wondered how long he'd been in pain, if his face had forgotten other expressions. I could imagine him shaking with fever, heat coming off his body, his breath short and labored.

Wayne tugged at his thick blond mustache and bristled. "An entire sailcloth?"

"We can spare it," Marjan said.

"He was one of us," Abran said.

Wayne folded his arms over his chest, nodded, and looked down.

I was surprised. It almost felt too extravagant, this show of loyalty. An entire sailcloth could go for two whole baskets of fish.

When they finished wrapping him in the sailcloth, each crew member murmured a good-bye to John. Abran went last, and after saying his good-bye he said to the crew, "John believed what we believed in: in a haven, a place for us to settle. Where we can build what we know will sustain us and continue on after us. We can honor his memory by moving forward."

Thomas and Wayne then lifted John's body over the gunwale and let him drop to the water. The dark water rose in a splash around him. I would never get over how quickly the water could swallow a person; it would always frighten me.

Afterward some of the crew stayed on deck, murmuring to each other or standing apart in silence. Marjan fingered a necklace at her throat as if it were a string of prayer beads. After some time passed, Marjan returned to the kitchen to clean up and I volunteered to help her.

When I came back out under the black sky I saw Pearl and Daniel at the bow, talking and laughing. Pearl stepped back from Daniel and did a little spin, the starlight carving her silhouette out of the darkness. She wrinkled her nose like she did when she found something really funny. I wondered if Row laughed and moved like that, with abandon.

Across the deck Abran tightened rope at a block. He nodded at me and smiled. He'd want an answer from me soon. I squeezed my eyes shut, wishing Pearl and I were still on *Bird*, not shoved into a different life with people I knew nothing about. I had always expected danger from others, even when I was younger.

Back when I was seventeen, I had walked down a street several blocks from my home, scavenging for food and warm clothes in abandoned houses. I'd jimmy open broken windows or check back doors. Many of the homes on the street were empty, people having already moved on to higher altitudes. In the years before, Nebraska had been crowded with migrants, but then the entire state felt like a ghost town.

I passed crocuses in a front yard and bent down to pick a few. Behind me I saw a man walking toward me. He wore disheveled clothing, his face slightly pink from drink or illness. He was someone I had passed earlier that day, at the park. We had locked eyes before quickly moving on in opposite directions.

Was he following me now? I dropped the flowers and hurried on down the street. I turned the corner, heading home.

He followed me, picked up the pace. My thoughts lurched and scattered. Should I run? But then he'd chase, and I likely couldn't outrun him. Better to stand my ground.

He was only a few paces behind me when I whipped out my knife and whirled around.

He stopped and held up his hands. "I don't mean to bother you," the man said. He reached into his coat pocket and took out a plum and set it on the concrete between us.

"I just wanted to say you have beautiful eyes." He paused as if struggling with something. He bit his lip, and his face was so haunted I felt hollowed. "They remind me of my daughter's eyes." He backed away from me quickly, leaving the plum behind, a small gift.

I tucked the knife back into my belt and took a bite of the plum. It was sweeter than anything I'd tasted in months.

Pearl's laugh pulled me back to the deck. She was flapping her arms like a bird and cackling madly. I thought of this crew and how I always acted like it was me against the world. Always ready to pull my knife. Grandfather used to tell me this attitude would sometimes give me what I needed, but not always.

This could be good, I decided. You could fish for them. You could convince them to sail north.

I watched Pearl for a few more minutes. Now she was lifting Daniel's good arm and trying to get him to twirl. She laughed when he pretended to lose his balance and fall into the gunwale. I liked seeing Pearl from a distance like that, to stand back and observe her without me. It felt like a window into her future; it was how she'd be once I was gone.

CHAPTER 16

AFTER I TUCKED Pearl into bed I met Daniel upstairs near the bow of the ship. Stars blinked overhead, clear and bright as diamonds strewn across black velvet. They were so bright, with no other lights to dim them. The night sounds of the sea swarmed around us; waves lapping the side of the boat, rope groaning against metal blocks, the wooden twist of the halyard straining against a light wind.

"We should change your bandages," I said.

"Just because I think they may be good people doesn't mean I think we should stay with them," Daniel said, his voice low.

"Why are you so set against it?"

"What about the Valley?" Daniel asked, turning from the water to face me.

"I'm still going," I said quietly. A mile away some large creature surfaced and disappeared again.

"You're going to try to convince them to go there, aren't you?"

"What if I do?"

"Don't."

"Why?"

"When you try to convince them, are you going to tell them it's a Lost Abbot colony?"

I frowned at him, searching his face in the moonlight. "I didn't tell you it was the Lost Abbots. I only told you it was a colony."

"I talked to some people in Harjo," he said, turning from me, leaning his elbows on the gunwale.

"I know. I saw. What else did you talk about in Harjo?"

"These people are looking for a safe place to settle. That's not why you're going."

"It could be a good place to settle. It has natural protection against invasions since it's between two mountains. It's also hard to get to, so they won't suffer as many attacks."

Daniel looked at me hard.

"I can't tell them why I'm going, Daniel. They won't go then. They'll only go if they think it's a safe place to settle."

I couldn't tell them the truth: that I was going to rescue my daughter and that it was an unsafe place to settle, because if it was safe, what was I saving her from? I could tell Abran was cautious, prizing stability among his community above all things. I couldn't be the unstable link and think I could convince them to change course. I needed to insinuate myself, become the person they couldn't lose.

"Do you think I have the time and resources to build a boat like this?" I asked.

"Wasn't that your original plan?"

"Did you agree to come with me because you knew I wouldn't actually get there? You knew a plan like that wouldn't work. How far did you think I'd get? Where are you wanting to end up?" I said, my voice rising. I clenched my fists at my sides. Thomas and Jessa, talking near the stern, glanced over at us.

Daniel shook his head and let out a low, angry laugh. "You might not know this, but things get complicated fast when you travel in a big group. Maybe I shouldn't have agreed to this."

Sedna tilted on a wave and we surged forward at an angle. We hurtled through the night like a lone fish in a pond with no banks. I bit my lip and reached out for Daniel's hand on the gunwale. "Please," I said.

He pulled his hand away and looked at me intently. "I don't want another thing to regret."

He turned as if he was going to walk away from me, then turned back. "What happens in a big group like this is people start wanting different things."

I waited for him to go on, the ship creaking in the water, the low moan of its parts straining against each other.

"That woman I told you about earlier who reminds me of you? Well, she and I joined a big ship, of about ten people, in the Caribbean three years back. We were mostly scavengers, for metal, meat, wood, fur. Some of us could trap along the banks. One fished some, but it was never too profitable for us. Well, half the people wanted to start a breeding ship and partner with some raiders."

I stiffened, and he swallowed and paused before going on.

"We were starving, the ship was deteriorating, we couldn't fix it, we couldn't settle on land without enough resources to trade for a place to settle. We may as well have been in the middle of space, floating among the stars, for all our options. Well, Marianne . . . Marianne wouldn't stay quiet. Railed against it. She and I planned to get off the ship at the next trading post and live like beggars, doing whatever we could just to get off the ship. But the night before we docked, some of the crew beat me and locked me in the hull of the ship. Then they raped Marianne. I heard it through the floorboards. I stayed up all night, bloodying my wrists against the rope, listening to her screams. In the morning it was silent. When they got me out, she was gone. She had jumped off the ship with the anchor tied to her ankle."

I couldn't speak for a moment. He ran his palm back and forth across the gunwale like he was trying to wipe it clean. I took his hand and covered it with mine.

"I'm so sorry," I said.

"I killed them," Daniel said, his eyes stricken and haunted. "The next morning, when they let me out, I . . . I went mad. I killed each and every one."

A chill ran through my body but I kept hold of his hand.

After a few seconds, Daniel said, "I don't think anything like that will happen here. These people are too good for that. But . . . something will go wrong."

I couldn't disagree. I felt my eyes brimming with tears, and I blinked them away and tried to steady my strained voice. "She's alone, Daniel. I have to help her."

Daniel nodded and laid his other hand on top of mine.

"Will you still come with us?"

Daniel didn't say anything for a minute. Clouds shifted and moonlight brightened the sea. "I gave you my word."

"Things changed. You can leave us if you want," I said, hoping he wouldn't.

Daniel shook his head. "I won't."

CHAPTER 17

THE NEXT MORNING the sky held a soft gray cast and an orange glow spread above the water where the sun would soon rise. I stood on deck, awakened early by hunger pangs. Though I had eaten well last night, I knew it'd be days before my stomach settled after having been empty so long.

"You're up early."

I turned and saw Abran walking toward me, his hair ruffled and unkempt, his skin still soft and full from sleep, not yet wind beaten and raw from sea air.

We both stood in silence for a few moments, watching the sun rise. It cast a pink light across the water, and I imagined I could feel its warmth even before it fully rose.

"I hope this isn't too intrusive, but—are you and Daniel a couple?"

I raised my eyebrows to ask if it was a serious question.

Abran blushed and went on, "We've never had a couple on board. Our sleeping arrangements are communal and I'm not sure we have space to accommodate—"

"We aren't a couple," I said.

"Oh. Okay. Good."

"And we've decided to stay," I said.

I could feel Abran smiling at me, but I didn't turn to face him. I was trying to think of a way to bring up the Valley to him, to see if he'd even consider changing his route.

"That's wonderful news," he said warmly.

"Daniel knows how to navigate," I said.

"I know. Marjan talked to him about it. A fisher and a navigator. What luck. Thomas and I have been navigating, but we aren't too skilled at it. It will be good to have an expert on board."

"With a navigator like Daniel you aren't confined to the Pacific and Caribbean."

"Meaning?"

"Meaning you could consider other places beyond South America for a place to settle. There's a place in southeast Greenland called the Valley. I've heard that it's a peaceful community, a good place to settle—"

Abran shook his head. "You'd have to cross Raider's Aisle to get there. It's considered worse than the Caribbean."

"You don't think some of that is tall tales?"

"It's not worth the risk." His voice was sharp and final.

Irritation twisted inside me and I took a breath, nodding and offering a stiff smile, but Abran saw through it.

"Sorry," he said, "but I have a responsibility to these people. Can't take on unnecessary dangers."

"I understand," I said. I had a sinking feeling, a strange helpless flutter. I'd have to try to persuade him in other ways. Maybe if we ran into trouble farther south, I could convince him the north was no worse. But that'd waste so much time. I felt there was a ticking clock inside me, urging my blood into faster rhythms, making my mind buzz like something pinned to a wall.

"Look—I actually should have explained to you earlier, but we have some rules," Abran said.

I nodded and bit my lip. Of course. I should have asked about the rules. Every ship had rules new members had to agree to.

"We have them written down in the cabin, and I'll have each of you sign your name to the list. Even Pearl. No lights after nine o'clock. Meals are in the cabin at eight, noon, and six. On odd days of the week we do sponge baths with water from the cistern if there's enough in storage for drinking. No stealing or skimming from your own work. Things like keeping a few fish to trade on your own at posts. Everyone has equal vote on major decisions. Desertion in battle or any attempt at mutiny is punished with marooning. Lost a few people with that. That's it, mostly."

"By suggesting another course—"

Abran laughed. "That's not mutiny. Least I hope I don't have to worry about that from you," he said, nudging me with his elbow.

"You've had to maroon people before?"

"Two guys started trying to decide everything. Starting with small things: who we traded with, where we fished, where we docked. But then it went further. They got into deciding rations on food and oil and changing course, all without wanting to cast a vote. In the end, they wanted to get rid of me. Thomas found out and came to me. We left them on a small island in the northwest part of the Rocky Mountains. We left them with a few supplies."

When I didn't say anything, Abran grinned and said, "Doesn't work out with everyone. But I'm pretty sure it's going to work out with you."

I hoped he was right, but the knot in my throat wouldn't loosen.

• • •

DANIEL SET UP his navigating instruments in the cabin that morning and calculated our location, two thousand miles from Alahana, a village in the Andes. The plan was to stop and trade there before heading farther south.

A stingray leapt from the water a mile away. Sometimes trevally, known to like clearer, coastal water, were found swimming with stingrays for hunting cover. I sat on the deck with a bucket of anchovies, pinning them on hooks. I'd try to catch the trevally with small fish and bright lures, and then I'd try bottom-water trawling for shrimp and cod before we got too close to the coast. Their downrigger, anchored near the rudder of the ship, was much larger and stronger than mine had been, and I was anxious to try it. Maybe after I had a good catch I could bring up the Valley to Abran again.

Abran walked past, waving at me as he entered the cabin. His charming, confident wave reminded me of Jacob once again. I thought Abran's similarity to Jacob would make me dislike him, but it didn't; it made me feel strangely close to him. Familiar. Like we'd known each other longer. Abran would tease me about the hours I spent on deck, taking few breaks, and I'd tease him about always looking busy but not getting much done. He'd chuckle and shake his head, reach out and give me a gentle shove. Whenever I spoke to him I could feel myself easing back into some pattern.

Pearl watched Jessa and Wayne as they wove a rope through a new block and tackle near the mainmast.

"That's not how it's supposed to be done," Pearl announced. "They don't know what they're doing."

Jessa and Wayne glared at us.

"Can I go tell them how to do it right?" Pearl asked.

"No," I said.

Jessa walked over to us and pointed to the snakes woven around Pearl's wrists.

"Does she need to wear those?" Jessa asked.

"I don't see why it's a problem," I said.

Pearl glared at Jessa and started stroking one of the snakes with her finger.

"It's not sanitary. They're dead," Jessa said.

"Charlie isn't," Pearl said. Charlie was the snake Pearl kept alive in her jar down in the quarters.

"Snake meat doesn't spoil as quickly as fish; you can keep it in the skin for a few hours," I said.

Marjan came out of the cabin and walked toward us.

"The meat will go bad. We need it. It's breaking the rules," Jessa said.

"Is the meat bad?" Marjan asked.

"No, I won't let it go bad. She just likes to play with them after she catches them. I'll smoke them soon as I'm done with these lures."

"It's not efficient," Jessa said.

Marjan held up a hand. "It doesn't need to be. The girl likes them and the meat isn't bad. It's fine."

Jessa looked like she was going to argue further, but she rolled her eyes and turned on her heel. Marjan offered a small smile and shrugged.

"Can I help?" Marjan asked. "I just finished weaving."

I nodded. "Hook them near the tail, so when we pull them through the water it'll look like they're swimming."

"It's lovely to have a child on board. She reminds me of my girl," Marjan said, glancing at Pearl. She sat cross-legged next to me. She wore flat leather sandals and a loose cotton tunic and pants. "So spirited."

"And belligerent," I said.

Marjan fingered the necklace, rubbing her finger over a small wooden bead. I'd seen other people wear necklaces like this. A new bead was added to the necklace when the wearer lost someone close to them. Marjan's necklace had three beads.

Marjan noticed me watching her. "She was seven when the water reached Arkansas," she said. I quickly looked away. I didn't really want to hear her story; I didn't know how close I wanted to get to these people. I was scared of them, scared mostly of their kindness. It brought something out in me I didn't recognize—something that felt both tough and tender, like some living thing underground that I'd forgotten about. Something that had shriveled without oxygen, without attention, but still survived.

"That's when we traveled west, to the Rockies. She . . . she died on our journey there. Maybe in Kansas, Oklahoma. I don't know. The water pulled her out of my hands. Then Behir and I got separated from his father and brother during a flash flood." Marjan's voice went quiet. I had the feeling she had told this story over and over in her own head, trying to make sense of what had happened and never finding any.

"They never surfaced. I . . . I don't think they made it. If I had been with them when the flood came . . ." She shook her head. Her face was tight, but her eyes didn't fill with tears. "Might not have made a difference."

"I'm so sorry," I said.

Marjan nodded thoughtfully, offering me a small smile as though to comfort me.

"You watch your girl," she said.

"I will," I said, my chest tight.

We fell into quiet, our heads dipped over the hooks, the small fish squirming in our fingers. Abran exited the cabin and we both looked up at him. He smiled our way before climbing up the mast to adjust the sail. He still wore the bandanna around his neck.

"He likes you," Marjan said.

"He seems like the type of person who likes everybody," I said.

"Mmm. Not really. He's a good captain, though. He takes things very seriously. This new community. He's been planning it and working toward it for four years now. Very slowly building up resources and a good crew. He does sometimes . . . let the pressure get to him. It can all be lost very easily."

Marjan looked at me out of the corner of her eye, studying my face. She seemed to be measuring me, trying to figure out if I'd be the weak link.

We finished hooking the anchovies and strung lines through the pole eyes and cast them over the side of the boat.

"He knows the other way it can be," Marjan said. "The other way you can live. That drives him."

I know about that, too, I wanted to say. How to live one way; how to live without.

CHAPTER 18

ABRAN BURST INTO the cabin during breakfast.

"Okay, they're about a half mile away. Do we have the baskets ready?" he asked.

Marjan pointed to the baskets of fish lined against the wall near the kitchen curtain. Abran clapped his hands together. "Okay, first trade in a while. These people are great, we should get some good stuff. Let's get in position."

At daybreak Abran had spotted a friend's ship and flagged it over for a trade. Before breakfast I had rushed about the deck, checking the fish I had caught and smoked and loading it in baskets. These were friends he had traded with many times before in the Caribbean, and he was hoping to not only get a good trade for the fish, but hear news of the south.

"I'm thrilled to see them again," Abran had told me. "I'd heard rumors that they'd been attacked by a raiding tribe."

Once they were close enough, we threw a rope over to them so our ships would anchor each other. Their ship was close to the size of *Sedna*, but more weathered and neglected. There were holes in the sails, missing rope and block from some of the rigging, and cracked, dry wood along the hull.

Abran, Wayne, and I boarded their ship for the trade by dropping our canoe into the water, paddling closer to them, and climbing a ladder they'd dropped. I stayed in the canoe with the baskets of fish and Wayne dropped a rope over the side so he could pulley them up. Once all the fish were lifted onto their ship, I climbed the ladder myself.

When I climbed over the gunwale I was hit by a stench: a smell of rotten fish, feces, and decay. I glanced at Abran and saw shock on his face. A short, portly, elderly man with white hair and pale, sunburned skin hobbled toward us, wearing a threadbare tunic. The ship felt like a ghost ship, and I wondered if anyone else was on board.

"Robert," Abran said, shaking the man's hand. "It's been too long."

"Too long indeed," Robert said in a high-pitched voice that sounded like a horse's whinny.

"We brought fish to trade," Abran said, proudly gesturing to the baskets of fish.

"Lovely," Robert said, eyeing the fish. "Haven't eaten in days."

My shoulders tensed. He was clearly lying. Even Abran's exuberance was beginning to fade, a line forming between his eyebrows as he studied his old friend.

"And you?" Abran asked, looking around their ship for what they had to offer.

"Nothing to trade, I'm afraid," Robert said.

"But you responded with the trade flag," Abran said. Once we had raised the trading flag—a blue flag with two yellow hands—they had raised their trading flag in return.

"You shouldn't have waved us over if you didn't have anything to trade," Wayne said.

Robert grinned and was quiet. The entire ship was too quiet. I wanted to scramble back over the ladder into the canoe.

"Mary!" Robert called toward the cabin on the poop deck.

A woman came out of the cabin and I stifled a gasp. Her eyes had been plucked out, scar tissue thick and white in place of where her eyes had been. Blood vessels threaded through the scar tissue like thin red rivers. She stood in the doorway of the cabin, facing us as if on display. The woman was heavyset, much better fed than anyone I'd seen in a long while.

Abran took a step backward, almost stumbling, shock tightening his face. "Mary . . ." he whispered. Abran looked at Robert. "Who did this to you?"

"We've not been well, my friend," Robert said. He clasped his hands in front of him and seemed oddly satisfied. "Now we rely on the goodness of others." Robert spread his arms wide.

Abran squinted at Robert. "What happened to you? This isn't you." Abran's muscles had gone tense, his body poised to lunge at his friend. My heart hammered in my chest.

Robert shrugged. "We weren't making it on our own. There isn't enough fish."

The blind woman walked toward us, and a man came out of the cabin behind her, holding a sawed-off shotgun. Abran took another step back, holding his arms out and pushing Wayne and me behind him.

"Robert, don't do this. The rest of my crew is at the ready," Abran said.

Wayne pushed Abran's arm out of the way and pulled his pistol from the holster.

"Wayne, calm down," Abran said.

"I think we all know how this will go," Robert said. "You've already boarded. How will your crew get you back, full of bullets?"

Wayne cocked his pistol and raised it and Abran swore at him and pressed his arm back down.

"We don't want to hurt you. We just want something to eat," Robert said, patting his stomach and grinning.

Abran scanned the ship quickly, searching for an out. My hands had gone cold and clammy. Abran's face had sharpened into wrath, his brows pulled together, his jaw set tight. He'll do what he wants, I thought. Abran talks about stability because he doesn't have it within him; he needs to surround himself with it. I felt like the world was slipping away from me and I needed to reach out and grasp it.

"I'll get more," I muttered to Abran. "I'll get us more."

He kept staring at Robert and didn't seem to register my voice. In a short glimmering moment, the sun hot on our backs, the water buzzing with light, I thought Abran would charge Robert, his body poised to pounce, but the moment snapped shut and Abran raised his hands.

"Fine. Fine," Abran said, spitting the words out.

"Abran—" Wayne said.

"To the ladder. Now!" Abran bellowed. He turned toward the rope ladder.

Wayne narrowed his eyes and, without holstering his pistol, climbed over the gunwale onto the ladder.

Robert smiled again and bent to pick up a fish from the basket, weighing it in his palm. I felt a flutter of fury but stepped back, trying to usher Abran onto the ladder.

"You still going south?" Robert asked as Abran swung his leg over the gunwale.

Abran glared at him.

"There's no good land left in the Andes," Robert said. "That's my gift to you, old friend. A bit of knowledge. Don't go south. I can't tell you of all the people going there looking for a place to settle. Dying along the way, only to arrive with half their crew to a packed village or a rocky coastline where they can't even dock. You'll have to go elsewhere." Robert grinned, his smile mostly a grimace. "Not sure where."

CHAPTER 19

AFTER WE GOT back on *Sedna* Wayne raged about revenge, about bombing them and sinking them. Abran disappeared to his quarters and Marjan was left to calm Wayne down.

"Couple baskets of fish," she said. "It's best we move on. We run across them again, you can be sure they'll get something else from us."

In spite of this, I could tell she was furious, rubbing her beads between her fingers, her eyes narrowed and her voice sharp.

Over the next two weeks we all stayed busy with work around the ship, repairing a crack in the mast, fishing, mending nets, and sailing south. When I'd asked Abran if we should consider Richard's comment about the south, Abran had shaken his head and turned away from me.

Pearl and I visited with the other crew members as we worked, but Daniel kept to himself. He only talked with Pearl about his maps and charts, teaching her how to use a sextant and compass. When I came into the cabin to get some extra twine and stood at the shelves, rummaging through the boxes, he came up behind me and laid his hands on my shoulders and asked me how I was. When I turned and looked at him, I felt strangely unmoored and I stepped away.

"Fine," I said. "I can't believe we're going south after what—"

"He still thinks it's the best option. He's captain."

I nodded and returned to the deck to check our lines. A

few hours later Pearl and I caught two trevally, and when we dropped the net to bottom-trawl, we caught twenty pounds of shrimp and a few cod and rockfish. We loaded our catch into buckets and baskets while Thomas and Marjan helped set up the smoke tripod.

"I knew we'd be glad to have you," Abran said, surveying the fish. He reached out and touched my arm and smiled.

I smiled back. I hadn't expected to fulfill my promise so quickly after we'd been robbed, but I was grateful for it. I could use this good standing.

I often caught Abran watching Pearl and me while we fished, his gaze like the sun on my back. When I'd turn to look at him he'd look away. While reeling in lines or scaling fish, I'd think of the tenor of his voice in the morning, the slight huskiness sleep left behind. At the breakfast table I'd catch myself looking at his hands. I'd pull my attention back to what Pearl was telling me about an old map she'd found of the world before.

At night, when I couldn't sleep, I'd wonder what he'd do if I knocked on his door. I could hear Daniel snoring above us, his breath heavy. He barely moved when he slept, as if his mind had evaporated from his body, leaving him hollow and thick with stillness. Unlike me, who tossed and turned, my dreams bubbling up out of unconsciousness, thrashing my limbs and grinding my teeth, awakening to the sounds of other people sleeping.

That night the whole crew was in high spirits over our good catch and Wayne pulled out his handmade guitar after supper. It was a wooden box with wires strung tight over a hole in the middle, and Wayne played a few old Irish ballads on it. Abran brought moonshine up from the storage room and we passed the bottle around. Marjan, who could almost never be found doing anything but working, even set down the straw hat she was weaving to listen to Wayne play and laugh at Jessa's attempts to dance a jig. The ship creaked and moaned, the wind pushing us to the right, the floor tilting slightly. The kerosene lamp rocked on its hook. Thomas and Daniel were deep in conversation and Pearl stood in front of Wayne, clapping as he finished a song.

"Do ya wanna know why she's named *Sedna*?" Behir asked Pearl.

She nodded.

"She doesn't need to hear this story. She's just a child," Abran said, taking another swig of whiskey. He had a slight slur and he slouched back in his chair, more relaxed than I'd ever seen him before.

Wayne set the guitar down on the table and chuckled. "There are no children anymore. Besides, this story is about a child."

He said it almost with menace. I'd felt this menace in taverns and shops at ports before. The sidelong glances and tightening around the lips when people saw Pearl. Children were both a reminder of loss and a kind of rebuttal of it.

With their vulnerable faces and skin not yet tough from the sun, they were a reminder of life before, when we all could be a bit more tender. Children had been the future, but did we even want the future anymore? The question itself was an uncomfortable betrayal of our bodies and of history, our inevitable march forward through time. Who were we without people who would come after us?

I turned from Wayne and asked Abran, "Who named her *Sedna*?"

"Thomas picked the name. He's been with me the longest, helped me get all this started," Abran said.

Thomas smiled at me. "We need the Mother of the Sea on our side, considering the circumstances," he said with amusement.

Pearl climbed into the chair next to Behir. "There once was a girl," Behir began, "who was a giant and the daughter of a god. But because she was a giant she was very hungry, so hungry that she attacked her parents so she could eat them. To protect themselves, the mother and father had to take the daughter away. The father took his daughter on his kayak, telling her he would take her to an island far away. But when they were out in the ocean, he threw her over the side so she would drown. She clung to the side of the kayak, begging for her life, but her father cut her fingers off. She drifted to the bottom of the seafloor, where she rules over the monsters of the deep. Her fingers became seals, walruses, and whales. Sedna is a vengeful sea goddess, and if you do not please her you will see her anger in the swells of the sea and she will not release fish for you to catch."

Behir lifted his hands and wiggled his fingers, and Pearl giggled.

"What does she look like?" Pearl asked.

"She has snakes for hair and blue skin," Behir said.

"I want to look like that. What happened to her parents?"

"Not sure. Story doesn't say."

"I think they ended up in the sea, too," Pearl said.

Marjan began collecting the plates, the aroma of vegetables and fish still heavy in the air. Pearl had begun to put on weight since we joined *Sedna,* but that wasn't the only way she'd changed. She was more open with other people, less sullen and more lighthearted.

As the sun set, Thomas, Jessa, Behir, and Wayne left the cabin for their evening duties and Daniel offered to take Pearl down to the quarters and tuck her in. Abran wrapped up the leftover fish and Marjan and I wiped down the dishes. We were quiet, letting the revelry of the evening fade into silence.

When we were finished with the dishes, Marjan and I turned to leave.

"Myra," Abran said. "Will you stay a minute?"

I sat down next to Abran.

"I wanted to check in and see how things have been going." Abran set his mug of moonshine down on the table, the hammered tin a dull bronze. His face was flushed.

I told him things were going well and waited for him to speak. He seemed like he had other things on his mind.

"Can I ask . . . Daniel—how'd you meet him?" Abran asked.

"I rescued him after a storm."

"And you trust him?"

"Why shouldn't I?" I asked.

Abran shrugged. "I get a weird feeling from him. He spends a lot of time poring over maps and notes."

"He's diligent," I said defensively.

Abran nodded and paused. "I hope you aren't too disappointed that we aren't going to that place," he said.

"It's fine," I said quickly. "Just heard good things about it. Do you think Robert was telling the truth? About the south?"

"Wouldn't surprise me," Abran said, rubbing his palm over

his face. He looked like a wounded boy, lost and alone, his eyes glazed over with astonishment at where he'd ended up.

"Did he do that to her? The woman with no eyes?" I asked.

"No. Mary is his niece. The rumors I'd heard were true. They must have been attacked by raiders and spared if they became a beggar ship. The raiders torture crew members until captains agree to their terms. Robert wouldn't have submitted otherwise." Abran shook his head. "Not the Robert I knew."

"I've only heard of breeding ships," I said.

"The Lily Black just began making beggar ships, and a few other raiding tribes have followed. Beggar ships acts like merchants, pretending they want a trade. Once they steal your goods they deliver them to whichever tribe owns them and get to keep a good cut of it themselves."

I could tell the change in Robert had hit Abran hard, harder than he wanted to let on. Losing people through betrayal was the hardest. I reached out and squeezed Abran's hand.

Abran looked up at me. "This is why I have to do this. I made a promise. That I'd do something right."

"Who'd you promise?" I asked.

"My brother," he said, taking another swig of moonshine. "That's not what I want to talk about. I want to tell you about the community we're building."

He went on to describe a democratic community where everyone had a vote and everyone had a job. Where children were safe and the elderly were cared for. Where trading was only done with reputable traders and boundaries were enforced by a small military. I didn't understand what was new about his idea, how it was realistic. Even if you could create this sort of haven, you'd forever be defending it from someone trying to take it. Hadn't people always tried to create a safe haven, only to have it slip from their fingers, more elusive than the fish of the deep?

"We all need one another," he said. "Now more than ever."

"Why are you telling me this?"

He started and looked at me as if just now noticing I was there.

"You . . ." he murmured. "I think you get it. Get how fragile this is. When I saw how frightened you were when you waved us down. Some people . . ." Abran looked into his drink and shook it to break the reflection. "Some people have forgotten how to be afraid. Lost too much. I don't ever want to stop being afraid."

We looked at each other. I knew exactly what he meant.

"I'm grateful you were there," I said.

"Me, too," he said, reaching across the table to lay his hand over mine. I broke his gaze and he withdrew his hand. He finished his moonshine and pushed the tin mug away. He stood, took the kerosene lamp from its hook, and turned toward the door. At the threshold he turned and looked at me, the kerosene lamp sending flickers of light and shadow across his face.

"What happened to Pearl's father?" he asked.

"Dead."

"I'm sorry. That had to be difficult."

I smiled tightly and nodded. Not so much, I thought.

"Come to me. Anytime. With anything," he said, stepping away, leaving me in darkness.

I stayed in the dark, rocking with each wave, listening to the creaking of the ship in the night. The wounded look on Abran's face came to me once more. Was I any better than his false friend? Wasn't I pretending to be a friend and actually deceiving him by aiming to convince him to sail to the Valley without telling the full truth?

I squeezed my eyes shut and opened them again, the darkness flooding over me. I thought of Marjan, losing her husband and two of her children. I knew I was greedy. I still had one child, healthy and vibrant as the day she was born. Wasn't she enough?

But it wasn't about Pearl being enough—it was about me being enough. This journey was changing her life, but it had less to do with her than it had to do with me. With proving that whatever Jacob thought about me when he left was wrong. Maybe he thought I couldn't make it in this world. Maybe he thought I couldn't help them. That they didn't need me.

Out of the darkness, memories of Row rose up. The roundness of her cheeks. The way she had smelled like cinnamon in the morning after eating her oatmeal. I imagined all the memories of her I didn't have but wanted. Her reading a book in the summer, with light from a window falling bright on the pages. Moments that would be snuffed like the flame on a wick if I didn't help her. I kept the other image of her at bay, lingering at the edges of my mind's eye: the image of her boarding the breeding ship, her small form shadowed by the men around her.

CHAPTER 20

I WENT TO his room that night for two reasons. I wanted to be touched. And I wanted to start trying to change his mind.

I stood before his door, snores and rustling coming from the crew's quarters. I was hesitant to knock and alert anyone of where I was, but I couldn't enter without knocking. So I laid my fingers on the door and tapped lightly.

I gasped when he opened the door, surprised that he heard me. He wore only his trousers and his hair was disheveled. The candle he held cast a warm glow around us.

"Can I come in?" I whispered.

"Of course," he said, opening the door wider and peering behind me to see if I was alone.

Once I was in his room I realized I didn't know what to say or do. I felt unsure of myself, confused about how to move forward. I stood there, dumbfounded, looking around in the dim light of several candles. I could smell the faint scent of tobacco, unwashed linen, and wet wood. A wooden box was turned upside down for a table and books were piled several feet high along the walls. A quilt lay on the bed, and several books were strewn across it.

"Were you reading?" I asked.

He smiled guiltily and shrugged. "Breaking the rules . . ." he said, gesturing to the candles.

"I won't tell." I grinned at him. "How'd you get all the books?"

"Been collecting them for years now. They're harder to come by now than they were in the beginning. So many of them tossed in fires for warmth back then. But I hear there's a library now in the Andes, so people must be saving them again. It feels like good fortune to have them around."

"It does," I said, surveying the books and wondering if it was the same library Beatrice had told me about, started by the Lost Abbots.

There was nowhere to sit but on the bed. Abran gestured for me to sit down and I did. My face felt warm and I didn't know where to put my hands.

"So," Abran said, sitting next to me. "Why did you stop by?" He leaned toward me, his arm between us, fist wedged in the mattress. His weight was tilting me toward him. I leaned away to steady myself from falling into him.

I cast about for something to say and surprised myself with honesty. "I was lonely. I wanted to be in here. See you."

Abran set the candle on the table and tucked a strand of hair behind my ear. "I'm glad. Nice to have you here."

I was wearing Row's crane necklace, and he reached out and touched the pendant lying between my breasts.

"A crane," he said softly. "I hear they're gone now. The wind is not right for them."

I had a feeling they were still somewhere, somewhere we did not know about. At least, I wanted to believe they were. I raised my eyes to his and he looked at me with such intensity that I felt myself unraveling, blood rushing from my head, making me feel dizzy.

I stood up and crouched before a pile of his books, running

my finger across the spines. I hadn't liked school, but I had loved to read. The local school closed for good when I was fifteen, and before that I had only attended sporadically. I was thirteen when the library shut down. It was left unlocked and migrants slept inside. I'd go and walk through the rows of books and take home whatever I liked, piles and piles of books that later would swell up when the house filled with water. When I was alone on *Bird* at night, with nothing but the dark sky and dark waves to speak to me, I'd ache to flip through the pages of books, to feel the connection of another mind.

Abran and I were both quiet, and then he asked, "What are you thinking about?" He laid a hand on my shoulder and I felt him beckoning me back to the bed.

"I want Pearl to be able to read more books. To be able to be somewhere safe. Like the Valley."

I felt him stiffen and he removed his hand from my shoulder.

"I don't want this to be a problem," he said.

I turned to face him, keeping my body open, my shoulders relaxed, dropping my knees to the floor, my hands on either side of me, my eyes beseeching. Childlike, innocent, harmless.

"It won't be," I said softly.

His face softened and he said, "Okay. Tell me about it."

"It's hard to get there, so there aren't as many threats. It's isolated. There are resources. More land, less people. Vegetation does well there now with the increased humidity. Since it's a valley, you're naturally protected from storms and attacks."

"But I doubt there are many trees. In the north the soil hasn't adapted yet. How would we build?"

"We can scavenge with materials already there."

"Wouldn't we need more resources to make that kind of journey? More food, more weapons?"

"I can get us more fish; we can trade more. You already have so much."

"It could also risk everything I've built."

"If you really want to build this community, you need the right land. Otherwise you'll be back on the water in less than a year."

"I can't take that kind of risk," he said. I felt him slipping away from me, like he was an oyster shell closing before my eyes. He looked away from me and he suddenly looked very tired, fatigue etched in the lines and hollows of his face.

I stood up and sat on the bed next to him and touched his shoulder.

"You're right," I murmured. "It's too much of a risk."

"The thing is—we aren't just looking for land, we're looking for the right land. I had hoped the Andes would be our best bet. There are lots of villages and ports there. We need to settle somewhere close to a village so we can trade, but we also need to have enough space and resources on the land to farm, raise livestock, cut trees for building. We can't just settle anywhere and expect to survive."

I knew he was right. Villages and ports were often overcrowded and the lands around them were often mined for every resource, leaving them barren and uninhabitable. The rivers were drained to irrigate farmland in the villages and trees cut to trade at the ports. Or the land itself seemed unwilling to support life; rocky soil with no chance of growth or marshes holding only rotten water and strange animals.

"We'll find what we need," I assured him, wondering how I could convince him about the Valley.

He looked back at me, his brow furrowed in concern, his eyes heavy with worry. "What if I can't do this?"

I cupped his face with my palms. "You can."

He leaned in and kissed me, pulling me toward him. I softened against him. I began to untie the bandanna around his neck, but he stopped me.

"Don't," he whispered.

"It's okay," I said.

His hands softened and I untied the bandanna, feeling scar tissue on his neck beneath the fabric. It was raised, pink, and rippled as though from a bad burn, and I turned my face into his neck to kiss it.

He pulled me down to lie on the bed, my hands on his chest, feeling his heart hammer against my palms. We both tried to move quietly, our bodies straining against making noise. As his tongue slid in and out of my mouth I became wetter and wetter, heat and liquid spreading, making me ache. I turned my head to the side, watched the candle's shadow flicker on the wall. We peeled our clothes off, the room around me a blur of stillness against our motion. I arched my neck, my hands moving up to his hair, thick and warm between my fingers.

He slid into me and something in me contracted and expanded, a fluid motion, a rising and rising. We moved together, our breath hot, our nerves spinning, and I felt myself splitting, teetering on an edge. He pushed into me again and again, like some other animal's faster pulse, and I rose out of the dark depths as though bursting through the water's surface into sunlight, unfurling in a bright white spot, a sudden high spark that left me heavy-lidded and drowsy.

He pulled out before he finished, my hands on his hips, directing him out to spill on the quilt. We lay in the quiet, my body tucked into his, his arm around my waist. My mind fluttered clumsily, like a butterfly with a hole in its wing, over people and places. Row when she ate a crayon, blue streaming down the side of her chin. The meadows my grandfather and I would walk through to get to his favorite fishing lake. And how Daniel almost smelled like that, like floral woods and grass that's never been cut. I hadn't noticed how much Daniel smelled like home until I was lying next to someone else. I wanted sometimes to tuck my face into his neck and breathe him in.

Abran shifted his weight, turning over. The last time I'd slept with someone, Jacob and I had conceived Pearl. I remembered how his hair had fallen into his face when he moved over me. I'd liked how his shoulders looked from that angle; I'd liked the warmth coming off his chest.

We'd just had an argument about Row playing outside alone, and the argument had brought a sudden closeness.

We were already talking less in those days. He was looking at me differently by then, too. He'd always been so captivated with me, but then, after Row, after the flood got worse, after we stopped talking, there was this distance in his gaze. Like we were strangers. But not even that, not even that much mystery. Like we were people who'd half known each other in a lifetime before.

When we conceived Row it had been our decision. Our

way of thumbing our noses at the world. And it wasn't just us. During the Hundred Year Flood birth rates didn't drop like you'd expect, but remained steady. Some people who had wanted children decided they couldn't care for them with water approaching their doorstep. And others, who had never felt particular on the subject, suddenly started having a child a year, birthing them like flowers in spring, to remind themselves of how fertility felt. But so many of these children died in their first couple of years, along the migration routes, typhoid and cholera wiping out refugee settlements.

If my being pregnant worried my mother, she never let on. The local hospital where she'd worked as a nurse was closed at that point, but she still held free clinics in an abandoned warehouse a few blocks from our house, and she began stocking up on supplies for a home birth—sterile gloves, scissors, painkillers.

Unlike Row, Pearl was a surprise. We had been using old condoms scavenged from the local drugstore, and one day in April I realized I hadn't bled in over a month. I panicked and went to Jacob, and when I told him he just stared at me and then looked away, his jaw set, desperation in his eyes.

Abran's breath grew heavier and slower, and I whispered, "I should go," lifting his arm off my waist.

"You should stay," he said, lifting his head groggily.

"The others shouldn't know," I said, sitting up, reaching for my shirt. "Let's just keep this between us."

Abran looked at me cautiously as if trying to discern my reasoning. "Okay," he said.

I tiptoed down the dark hallway, feeling along the walls to find my way back to the crew quarters and my bunk. When I got into bed I heard Daniel shift above in his bunk. I hoped he had been asleep. We had been quiet. He couldn't have heard, I told myself.

CHAPTER 21

WHEN I WOKE the next morning I heard Pearl murmuring a prayer of St. Bridget, pulling the edge of her handkerchief inch by inch through her pinched fingers. She moved the handkerchief the way I'd seen my grandmother move the beads on her rosary. Grandfather had taught Pearl the prayer during long evenings we spent on the boat, after the fishing lines had been rolled up and moonlight lay heavy on the water. The words comforted Pearl, and I caught her doing it when she was alone, trying to be brave.

We were late waking; everyone else had already gone upstairs for breakfast.

I reached out, rubbed Pearl's shoulder, and pulled her close, tucking her head under my chin.

"What is it, sweetie?" I asked.

"We'll sink," she said before resuming the prayer. ". . . perforating Thy delicate feet, and not finding Thee in a pitiable enough state to satisfy their rage . . ."

"What makes you say that? Pearl?" I gave her shoulder a little shake.

My grandfather was not especially religious, but the prayers had been passed down to him through the generations. He often recited them while he was working, with a jovial voice, the harsh words and dark sentiments odd on his tongue, which was neither austere nor reverent.

I hadn't liked it when he taught the prayers to Pearl, feeling that they were too violent and disturbing for a young child to memorize.

The ancient prayers were stories of suffering, he would say. Stories we would do well to remember.

I wasn't sure what the remembering would offer her, but I wanted her to keep a part of him, so I let him teach her the prayers.

"... pulled Thee from all sides, thus dislocated Thy limbs ..."

"Pearl," I said firmly, pulling the handkerchief from her hands.

"No!" she said, grabbing the handkerchief back from me. "They'll cast us overboard and we'll sink. Like Jonah. But we won't be swallowed by a whale. We'll be swallowed by another ship."

She was always having nightmares about shipwrecks, about going down into the sea, trapped in the ship, her grave the dark cold water.

"No, no, Pearl. Did you have another bad dream? That won't happen."

Pearl's face pinched and reddened. "We've been cursed and they will see it. The sea will take us. The sea will not rest," she wailed, covering her face with her handkerchief.

I pulled Pearl into my chest and rubbed her back. "No, honey. No. Those are stories you've heard."

Pearl's small body shook and I squeezed my eyes shut. What struck me, hardening like a stone in my chest, was that she was right. The sea would eventually take us in some form, and we would disappear beneath its surface. I couldn't stop its rising; I couldn't keep us afloat forever. I'd brought her into this world, and some days all I hoped was that I wouldn't be around when she left it.

She turned her face up from my chest, her voice small and singular like a bird's. "I don't want to be alone. You'll go with me?"

"I'll go with you," I said.

Her cheeks were rosy. I tucked a strand of hair behind her ear. "I'm here. Always," I whispered in her ear. I felt her relax against me, her fingers going limp around the handkerchief.

DANIEL AND I butchered fish on deck, slitting open the stomachs of wahoo, pulling out their guts, and tossing them in a bucket. The noonday sun burned against our backs and sweat kept falling in my eyes. All I could smell was fish guts and salt. Salt in my body and salt from the sea; I felt I couldn't escape it.

I chopped off a dorsal fin and head, pushed the fish aside, and reached for another.

Pearl was helping Marjan peel potatoes in the cabin. I could see her head, bent over her task, through the open doorway. It was the last of the potatoes. We needed to port soon and trade for vegetables.

"I heard you go to his room last night," Daniel said, his voice quiet. Sound of blade against wood, the dull scrape of shoving the head away from the body.

"And?" I was surprised to see sadness, a sort of melancholy regret in his gray eyes. The way he looked at me made me feel exposed.

"Did you tell him everything? About Row?" Daniel asked.

"You know I didn't."

"But you were trying to convince him to go to the Valley, weren't you?"

"I also like him," I said, hoping it'd shut him up.

A wounded look crossed his face and he slit a fish's stomach and yanked the guts out. He tossed them in a bucket. Behir and Abran's voices, chatting and laughing about something, drifted our way.

"You know what you haven't mentioned this whole time?" Daniel asked.

"What?"

"Jacob. You've talked about Row, but you won't talk about Jacob."

He waited to see me react to the name. I shrugged, but I felt a burning in my spine, a dull buzz between my ears. I assumed Jacob was dead from what the raider on the coast had said, but he still felt strangely alive to me, some otherworldly presence that penetrated me wherever I was, like some ghost beyond my reach. Back before I assumed he was dead, I had at times longed for his death, but sometimes, I had also longed to have him with me again. To not be alone. To be with someone familiar.

"Do you ever wonder why he did it? Did you ever think he'd do such a thing?" Daniel asked.

"No," I lied, my voice cold as steel. I gripped the knife tighter.

"I didn't mean—"

"Yes, you did," I said, my throat tight. "You meant to imply he left because I was somehow terrible. You meant to imply I should have known. You meant to imply it's my fault she's gone—" My voice cracked and I shut my mouth, pressing my tongue against the roof of my mouth, blinking furiously to clear my eyes of tears.

Daniel reached out to touch me and I hit his hand away.

"Don't touch me!" I hissed.

"I asked because . . ." Daniel shook his head and looked down. "It must have been terrible."

His voice faded and I watched him warily.

"No," I said. "I never imagined he could do such a thing. And yes, I've wondered why. I suppose he thought I'd be a liability. I was pregnant. It made him nervous."

"I didn't mean—" Daniel started.

"Yes, you did. Don't make me speak of him. Don't pry. I thought better of you."

Shame colored Daniel's face and he looked down at the fish before him, the single eye staring back, the scales glittering in sunlight. He wiped his bloody hands on a rag.

"You're right. I'm sorry. I know how it feels . . . to want to change what has already happened."

I felt skepticism like an itch in my spine, but when he looked up and his eyes met mine I saw he was telling the truth. His eyes were tender and calm, like an open palm stretched out for me to take. I also saw regret in him, but a kind of half regret. The kind of regret you have when you feel bad about something, but not bad enough to stop doing it.

I gave a short nod and returned to the fish before me. I felt uncomfortably warm and exposed, like I'd walked naked a long while and needed shelter. We resumed our work in silence.

Part of me felt like I knew Daniel. And yet he was absent

somehow, removed. He was holding himself back from me for some reason. As though each time I was with him I was only seeing a small part of him. This dance of taking a step closer and then a step back.

Those questions Daniel asked me I had already asked myself. During those early years on the water I would constantly ruminate on why Jacob left without me and took Row from me. For years and years I blamed myself. I must have somehow pushed him away, I thought.

But over the years a different picture emerged: one filled with other, small disappearances he'd enacted during those years we were together. How when Row was a newborn, crying for hours from colic, he'd leave the house for days, staying with friends and leaving me alone to tend to her. There was never any mention of taking turns, only his turn. He was charming and fun, but when things became difficult, he seemed to disappear on me. He'd had a habit of disappearing, and the floods simply brought his final disappearance.

He could be the most generous person I'd ever met. And he could be ruthless in his weakness, always looking for an out. Someone who could talk big but never follow through. I held on to this side of him and started to blame only him.

What I hadn't told Daniel was that Jacob had actually asked me to leave with him once. He had been skittish about reports that water was coming our way. He didn't think the boat Grandfather was building would be big enough for all of us or done in time.

I was out in the front lawn, weeding our vegetable patch. I pulled a dandelion and tossed it in the bucket.

Jacob grimaced, looking at the house across the street from us. All the windows were boarded up from the inside, and if you walked past it you could smell decay. The neighbor hadn't come outside for months and we weren't sure if he was alive in there.

"I think we should leave early," Jacob said.

I stood up and brushed dirt off my pants.

"What do you mean, early?" I asked.

"Davis told me the dam could break. Besides, it's not going to work—all of us on that boat."

I glared at him. Jacob had never gotten along with my grandfather.

"Davis has a motorboat. I'm trying to talk him into letting us take off with him and his family."

"All of us?"

"Your mom and grandpa can take the boat they're building. They'll be right behind us. It's more suited for two anyway."

I stifled the urge to tell Jacob to fuck off. I was already worn to the bone, trying to prepare for our departure, and here he was losing his nerve. "I'm not leaving without everyone," I said. "We stick together. We're a family. All of us."

Jacob sighed and glanced up at the attic, where we could see Grandfather through the window, bending over the boat. On the sidewalk near my feet, puddles of water had slowly grown from cracks in the cement. As if the earth were so waterlogged it was now bubbling up from below, too.

"Myra, you're not listening to me."

"Yeah, you're right. I'm not. Why don't you help us out, instead of making other plans? We're still stockpiling food. You haven't been hunting in days."

Jacob had backed away from me, shaking his head. I could never understand why he couldn't just help us. He always hovered at the edges of my family as if he weren't actually a part of it. But I still never imagined he'd just leave. He needed me, didn't he?

I kept my rage at Jacob tucked so deep inside me, I could sometimes feel it roiling out, barely contained. I felt when he left that I had been gripping the edge of a boat like Sedna had and he had cut each of my fingers off, watching me drift to a watery grave. And a part of me wanted to rise up from the depths and pull him down with me.

More than I wanted to admit, I was disappointed when I heard he was dead. I had wanted to see him again; it had been a burning desire that I hadn't even fully acknowledged.

But why see him again? To demand answers? To enact revenge?

After I killed that raider on the coast I would sometimes imagine it was Jacob's body crumpled at my feet and I would wait to see how it would feel, holding that image in my mind. But no feeling came. Only emptiness.

My rage still beat on like a second heart. I wondered, if I saw Jacob in the flesh, could I kill him so coldly? Did I actually want to?

Maybe there was something else, beneath the anger, beneath the pain. Some third option, between revenge and absolution, that hovered just beyond my consciousness, waiting to be named.

I knew I hated him too much to not still love him.

CHAPTER 22

I CREPT THROUGH the dark hallway to Abran's room several nights a week for three weeks. I knew our nights together would have to come to an end soon. He was becoming too serious about us, starting to say "we" too often. I wanted to convince him to go to the Valley before I ran out of time, but I knew I couldn't push it. Abran was the type of person who had to feel it was his idea.

On these nights Abran loved to share stories from his past with me. I'd lie half awake, half asleep, Abran's lips brushing my hair, and he'd tell me about where he'd been and who he'd known. He didn't often ask questions about me, and I didn't offer many stories of my own. After a while I got the sense that he wasn't sharing stories with me so much as confessing. He needed to tell it all, all the little details, to get to the darker parts.

One night, we lay naked on our sides, the quilt pulled halfway up our bodies, the candlelight jumping and falling like a wave. Abran talked about the community he wanted to start, his plans for distribution of labor.

"Why did you promise your brother about starting the community?" I asked.

Abran was silent and I turned over to look him in the face. Abran looked at me warily and kissed my forehead. I pushed his dark hair from his face.

"My brother, Jonas . . . he felt guilty," Abran said. "We had done some bad things. He wanted to build a safe place. A place we'd want to live."

I thought of the man I'd killed on the coast, the terrifying way his body jerked as I waited for him to bleed out. I sometimes lay awake at night thinking of the man. I thought of who he was before the floods. How he could have been a neighbor, a man I walked past while carrying groceries up the front stoop, someone who said hello and continued on his way, under the dappled sunshine, among the fallen leaves on the sidewalk.

"What did you do?" I asked.

Abran spread my hair tips like a fan across the pillow's edge. My hair, once silky, had grown coarse from the constant salt, wind, and sun.

"Got in with some people. Got out eventually . . ."

It was rare for Abran to be reluctant to speak.

"I think we should tell the crew about us," he said.

I stiffened. "Not yet."

I was already worried the crew knew about our nighttime visits. I felt like Wayne and Jessa watched us with strange, bemused looks on their faces, and Marjan had given Abran an extra pillow for his bed last week.

"Don't make me wait forever," he said, grinning and nudging my shoulder.

I smiled and felt a chill in my veins. I did feel something for Abran, but whatever I felt, I knew it couldn't last. I'd been here before, wanting and needing, ready to be disappointed.

We lay in silence for a few minutes, and I reached up and touched the scars on Abran's neck. "A man I killed close to Apple

Falls had a tattoo on his shoulder," I said. I thought of Abran's charisma, the way he naturally gathered everyone around him. So often the raiders I'd encountered were charming, could charm you before you knew who you were dealing with, and then it was too late.

Sedna creaked and rumbled, the rubbing of the sea against the ship making a low growl. Abran and I held each other's eyes for a moment before he spoke, saying, "Lily Black."

I raised my eyebrows and felt a drop in my stomach. I had suspected he'd been part of some raider ship, but it had felt abstract and distant. That he had been part of the Lily Black made them feel more present, as if it somehow brought them closer to us. I'd heard of them tracking people who'd left their crews and joined other ships. Should we be keeping a lookout for ships following us?

It wasn't easy to find people anymore, I reminded myself. Tracking someone on the open sea was nearly impossible. Besides, raiders got into so many battles, it was likely that half the crew Abran had been with was already dead.

"I heard that in the early days the Lily Black had started as a few families protecting their land. By the time I joined them they were a military tribe," Abran said, sitting up. He rested his arms on his knees, his back a long curve. I sat up and placed my hand on his spine.

"They came to us, to our home. My parents were both surgeons. During the Hundred Year Flood they moved up to a gated community high up in the mountains with other friends. They'd kept their old medical textbooks and used them to teach my brother and me the family business. My parents pinched drugs from the hospitals where they worked before they closed. People would travel to us to receive medical care and we treated them out of our living room. They paid us in food and scavenged items. For a while, we could live like the world wasn't completely collapsing . . . until the Mediterranean War."

Abran made a choking sound and swallowed. I rubbed his back.

"But some of my parents' friends had ties with the Lily Black and they needed a military base during the war, so they moved in. An outbreak of dysentery spread through our community and surrounding areas. My parents died when I was twenty-six. Jonas and I talked about fleeing south, but we didn't have enough food to make the journey. Then Jonas got sick. We met a man who offered to treat Jonas and let us join his ship. We started as cabin boys, mopping up the deck, running ammunition belowdecks. We didn't know what all they did when we first joined, and once we joined . . . it was too late to leave. No one was calling them raiders back then. We thought they were protecting themselves . . . not attacking others."

Abran shook his head and looked around the room as if searching for a window to look out of. He looked so pained, so lost, that I rubbed his back and whispered, "You're not the same as them."

"Everything was so confusing in those days," he said. "So many people and yet so few. The world felt like it kept expanding and contracting. We transported goods, we traded, we fought other ships, but everyone did. We tried not to think about it."

Abran laid his hand over the scars on his neck as if hiding them. "Then they put the rabbit on our necks. They started to get more serious about colonizing villages on land. Jonas and I were already talking about trying to start our own community. It was Jonas's idea. He felt even guiltier than I did. His health was failing; he wasn't sleeping at night. We made a pact that if either of us didn't survive leaving the ship, the other would go on and still start a community where certain things . . . certain things wouldn't happen. So when we left the Lily Black I stole from our crew to start *Sedna*. I still know about where they have some resources hidden. They have medicine—mostly antibiotics—hidden northeast of here."

"Antibiotics?" I asked.

Abran shook his head. "It's too dangerous to go after any of it. Better to stay as far away as possible from those places. Sometimes they leave men behind to guard them."

My heart sank, but I tried not to show my disappointment. "Have you told the others? About the Lily Black?"

"No. I don't want them to know."

"They won't hear about it from me," I said. And I meant it. His secrets were his.

"Your brother . . . ?" I said.

Abran shook his head and lay back down, his hand over his eyes. I lay next to him. *Sedna* rocked abruptly and a few books fell from the table. Abran lifted his head from his pillow and propped his face on his knuckles. "Do you really think we could make it through the northern Atlantic?"

"Yes," I said. "With this ship we have a better chance than many."

"If we made it out there, we would have it mostly to ourselves. Not many people can journey that far north."

He was repeating my own words back to me. I stayed silent, letting him ponder it.

"I've been thinking more about what Robert said. I don't think he was lying," Abran said. He traced the vein from my hand up my arm with his fingertip. I felt a thrill, a thrumming in my bones. It felt like I was close; after weeks of carefully planting seeds, I was now finally seeing some green poking through the dirt.

"Are you sure you trust him?" I asked, playing the devil's advocate, giving him the resistance he needed.

"Not at all," Abran said. "But I've heard the same thing elsewhere about the south. At each trading post. I was just fixed on going south because . . . that's where Jonas and I had talked about going."

Abran rubbed the tender skin on the inside of my wrist with his thumb. "That day, I think Robert felt powerful and wanted to give me something . . . something I didn't want."

I realized Abran could read people better than I'd expected. How well could he read me?

"I've been thinking about it more and more, and everything you say is right. The isolation, the resources. I've been scared of the risk, but I'll regret it if I don't try," Abran said.

Elation poured through me, as if a dam had broken. I couldn't believe I'd finally done it. All the gentle coaxing and the casual reminders had paid off. Already I could see the shores of Greenland, the rocky coast and crisp, cold air. I tried to ignore a darker undercurrent tugging at me—images of guards patrolling the streets of the Valley, the meager rations in dining halls. Public beatings and spontaneous house searches. At least you're moving closer to her, I told myself. I took Abran's hand in mine, felt the calluses on his palms.

"But it isn't up to me," he said. "We have to put it to a vote with the rest of the crew."

CHAPTER 23

ABRAN TOLD ME we'd hold the vote for changing our destination to the Valley the next evening. He wanted to ask Daniel to chart out the route we'd take before we voted, so he could share with the crew the details of how long it would take. I didn't tell him that Daniel had already charted a course.

That morning after breakfast Abran pulled me aside and told me we needed more provisions for the journey. I needed to catch more fish than I had if I was going to prove to the crew we could make it across the Atlantic. I couldn't stop thinking about the vote as I went about my morning chores, considering each crew member and which side they'd fall on.

Sedna approached a small mountain range a few miles away. Thomas stood at the bow with the binoculars, keeping an eye out for mountains just below the water. I felt like we were losing time by traveling farther south, but Abran insisted we wait until evening for the vote. The water was warmer and we were getting closer to channels and estuaries between the broken coastline, so Pearl and I began trolling for bluefish with live bait.

When I wasn't watching the water and our lines, I kept glancing up at the mountains. A half mile from the mountain range a tiny island stood about fifty feet above the water. Daniel was navigating us to sail through this half mile between the coastline and island so we wouldn't have to maneuver around the land mass entirely. As we drew closer to the island we would begin skirting around it, turning farther south. It was tiny, only a half mile across, and a cluster of short trees grew on top, looking like a shelter where people would camp out. I had the distinct feeling that we were approaching enemy territory, as though we were traveling in a desolate land and saw the campfire of our enemy up ahead and didn't know where they had gone.

Pearl and I dropped a net to trawl for live bait and Abran stopped next to me as I worked the downrigger.

"Is trawling really a good idea here?" Abran asked. "Since we're so close to the coast, couldn't the net catch on something?"

"We need more live bait," I said. He was right—it was a terrible place to trawl. I probably wasn't even getting the right depth, but I wanted a full net to show off before the vote.

"Okay. It's just putting such a drag on our speed. The sails aren't large enough."

"It'll be quick—"

"Abran!" Thomas called from the bow.

Abran ran up to the bow and Thomas handed him the binoculars. We were pivoting around the small mountain island, skirting close to the coast, passing through a small channel of water between the island and the coast. It seemed risky to sail so close to the coast, and I wondered why Daniel had charted this route instead of one farther out to sea.

I squinted to see what Thomas was pointing at. I thought I could see the bow of another ship behind the island. Maybe it was just a fishing vessel. People tended to fish close to the coast, as they could get to a port to trade more easily.

The island was less than a thousand feet away and Jessa had adjusted the sail at the halyard so we'd catch the north wind and turn farther south. Wayne stood at the tiller, turning the ship so we'd pivot around the island, and I reeled in the net on the downrigger as quickly as I could.

Behir, Jessa, and Marjan scrambled to the bow and I followed them. Pearl tried to follow me, but I turned and pointed to the cabin.

"Go to Daniel," I told her.

"What is it?" Pearl asked.

"Go!" I commanded.

Pearl glared at me but obeyed, retreating to the cabin, where Daniel was working on calculations. We rounded the island and almost sailed into two ships that seemed to be anchored side by side. The northern wind pushed us even closer to them, our ship now only a hundred feet away.

Abran lowered the binoculars and yelled to Wayne at the tiller, "Turn toward the coast! Keep along the coast!" Panic edged his voice and he gripped the gunwale. I squinted over his shoulder and saw raiders from the larger ship boarding the other, a fishing vessel, clubs and knives in their hands, a black flag flapping in the wind from the bow of the larger ship.

Sedna shifted toward the coast, but we were trapped between the island and the coast, not able to turn away from the ships. A man on the fishing boat took a hatchet in the chest and fell to his knees. Screams reverberated around us, so heartrending that it felt like they came from our own ship. Two raiders got a rope around one man's neck, the other end of the rope fastened to the stern of their ship, the rope's slack trailing in the water between the two ships.

They're going to keelhaul him, I thought distantly, bile

building in the back of my throat. I swallowed it and wanted
to run.

A raider wrestled a baby from her mother's arms, the baby
and mother screaming the same scream, the mother clawing at
the man. Another raider grabbed her arm and ripped her back.
The man with the noose around his neck screamed and charged
the raider and someone grabbed his rope and he was yanked
back, tumbling backward, red in the face and gasping.

"We need to stop," Jessa whispered, her eyes wide.

I was thinking the same thing, but I didn't say anything. I
stood rooted on deck, my hands itching for the weight of knives
in my palms but my feet unmoving, some part of me aware that
if I didn't do anything we'd sail right past, isolated, with no
losses to count as our own.

Behir touched Jessa's arm. "Come on," he told her, trying to
pull her back to the cabin.

"We need to stop!" Jessa screamed, running toward Abran.
She grabbed him by the shoulders and shook him.

"Behir—please," Abran said, his hands on Jessa's waist, trying to move her toward Behir. His face was pained, with some
new stillness behind his eyes. Like he was shut down, a part of
him silenced and tucked away.

Behir stepped forward and took Jessa's arm, but she turned
from him, reaching her hand out to the fishing ship, her hand
opening and closing in a grasp.

The raider who held the baby climbed back on his ship. A
woman on the raider ship walked toward him and took the baby,
disappearing down into the hull with him. My stomach clenched
and I knew what would come next. They would keep the mother

separate from the child, transfer her to another ship or base. They'd raise the child to be part of their crew, to raid ships at sea or to guard colonies on land.

The screams continued, but they were muted, like I was hearing them through a closed door. Breath left my lungs and I felt weightless. I was a feather in the wind, swaying on my heels, my knees almost buckling beneath me.

Behir held Jessa as she screamed and dropped to her knees. I backed away from them, the need to flee like a fire in my chest.

The raiders boarded their own ship again, taking their plunder with them. The raiders opened the door to a small birdcage and a bird flew from it, darting straight up and to the west, as if pulled by some invisible string in a predetermined direction. We passed them, the distance between us widening.

I was grateful for the distance. I didn't want to see the rest; I knew all they would do. They'd take the mother with them and whatever water was left in the fishing boat's cistern. They'd leave the captain on the fishing boat, and once the raiders' sails gathered wind the rope would rip him from his feet, his body slamming against the gunwale and tumbling into the sea below. He'd follow them like bait on a hook for a day or two, smashed to bits against the barnacles on their boat, shredded by coral on the mountains just under the surface, swallowed by the sea. And then he'd hang from their bow, wet and purple, the sun drying his hair until it went soft, fine as the downy hair a baby loses before he's born.

CHAPTER 24

JESSA WOULDN'T COME up from the crew's quarters for three days. Wayne paced the deck of the ship, ranting and raving about turning our ship around and attacking the raiders. Everyone let him rave, with an unspoken understanding that he'd quiet down in time and everything would return to normal.

When Jessa did come up from the quarters, she first stormed into the cabin where Abran was talking with Daniel, demanding to know why we hadn't helped the people on the fishing boat.

I stood in the kitchen with Marjan, the curtain pulled aside, watching as Abran tried to reach out and comfort Jessa. She knocked his hands away.

"We aren't prepared to attack a raider ship," Abran began.

"Bullshit!" Jessa cried. "We have a whole armory!"

Abran shook his head. "Jessa—we can't save each ship that is threatened. Our loyalty is to each other—we can't save everyone else."

Tears streamed down Jessa's face. She wanted to go back in time, I realized. She wanted to save herself by saving them. I knew that feeling and that need. How much in my life could I rewrite by saving Row?

I was struck again with the feeling of running, of backing away from her. Seeing her was a little too much like looking in the mirror.

After Behir helped Jessa down to the quarters and Marjan

and I returned to descaling fish, Marjan leaned closer to me and whispered, "It happened to her."

The hairs rose on my arms as if they could keep the truth out, make all my surfaces impenetrable. "What?"

"She had a baby."

I jiggled the knife between muscle and scales. I don't want to know, I thought. I couldn't touch that kind of grief, I couldn't be near it. It felt like a contagion, like someplace I'd been, where if I returned, I might not survive again.

Besides, I didn't need Marjan to tell me. I already knew Jessa had suffered the same thing as that mother. Her scream had that tenor—that tenor of reliving something that shouldn't have been endured in the first place. I knew it, but I couldn't bear to have it named to me, where I'd have to acknowledge it.

But why not? Why did I keep wanting to hold them all at arm's length?

Maybe, I thought, if everyone has lost what you've lost, you can't use them to get her back. You can't stomach deceiving people who have suffered as you have. It's easier to not know too much.

"Wayne and Jessa were both in the military," Marjan said. "Wayne was in a combat unit, Jessa did work in intel. When part of Wayne's unit joined the Lily Black and he refused to join they were taken captive on a ship. Wayne, his wife Rose, and Jessa."

Marjan continued on, telling me how Jessa was pregnant with her dead boyfriend's child when they were taken captive. They were slaves on the ship for half a year before Rose was murdered when she was found stealing supplies so they could escape. Throat slit as she stood before Wayne and Jessa. A month later Jessa gave birth and her daughter was taken from her, to be raised on a base with children from breeding ships.

After that, Wayne hid Jessa in an empty barrel that he wheeled on shore during a stop at a trading post. He left her behind and boarded the ship, since he was always followed by guards during stops on land. Back on the ship, he lit the sails on fire and leapt into the sea during the chaos, swimming back to the port. He and Jessa found each other and swam two miles to another mountaintop, hiding in the woods until the Lily Black gave up on finding them and sailed from the area. They were starving on that same mountaintop a month later when Abran and Thomas came across them. Over the next few days I watched how the crew cared for Jessa, taking meals down to the quarters and speaking to her about small tasks to be done around the ship, gently pulling her out of herself. I remembered how alone I'd been once Grandfather passed away, just Pearl and me, her tiny body nestled against mine, her cries in the night so desolate it felt as if we could be the only two people left in the world.

It made me want to join them, to be invited into their secret language of gestures and expressions. To have a place. Even though I was part of them, I still felt like I was on the outside looking in. These two impulses—to be close to them and to hold them at arm's length—kept rubbing against each other, putting me on edge.

I thought of the small fishing vessel Pearl and I had seen plundered before we'd found out Row was held captive in the Valley. How it had been easier to believe it was only Pearl and me in this world; everyone else felt vaguely abstract. And now it all felt too close. Like I suddenly had more responsibilities than I could carry and I couldn't choose between them all.

Four nights after the attack we gathered in the cabin for the vote. Abran described the Valley, sharing the details I'd told him—some true and some not. I tried not to squirm when Abran talked about how safe it was. It would be safe, once the Lost Abbots were gone, I reasoned with myself.

Abran talked about how there were only a few hundred people settled in a peaceful village and there was plenty of land to spare.

"We can invite them to join our community, if their values are the same as ours," Abran said.

"What if they don't want to?" Wayne asked. "How will our community grow since it's so isolated up there?"

Abran paused, clearly uncertain. My heart sped up and I worried that he was reconsidering holding the vote.

"Expansion can be a problem anywhere. It's not the number of people, it's the right people," Abran said.

We were only a week's sailing from Alahana, the village in the Andes where we planned to trade. But if the crew voted for the Valley we'd turn north and slip up through the Panama Canal, now a gorge that spanned hundreds of miles, and enter the Caribbean Sea. We would stop and trade instead at Wharton, a small village in what had been southeastern Mexico.

While Abran talked about the Valley I watched the crew, trying to anticipate how they'd each vote. Marjan was placid and unexpressive, while Behir looked eager and intrigued. Jessa kept exchanging skeptical looks with Wayne, and Thomas sat in the corner frowning.

The wind howled outside and Pearl stood in the doorway, watching the seabirds flying above deck, scouting our ship for food. Daniel sat next to me, arms crossed over his chest, chin down so I couldn't see his face.

Abran talked with his hands, his expressions animated. But there was something desperate beneath his charisma, an anxiety. It was clear it was easy for him to be persuasive and to get people to follow him. Though I was uncertain about whether he could hold people together long-term. I thought of what Daniel had said about being in large groups, how the values of a group can change. How laws are only laws if everyone is following them.

"So we need to put it to a vote," Abran said, clapping his hands together.

"We should discuss it some first," Wayne said. "First, where did we get this information?" Wayne glanced at me before looking back at Abran.

My face flushed and I squeezed my hands together under the table, trying to loosen the clamminess. They knew. They probably all knew.

Abran paused and I could tell he was considering lying. "Myra, here. She told me about it. She got the information from trustworthy sources. People who have traveled and traded there."

"Sounds like a tall tale," Wayne said. "Too good to be true."

"I didn't know Greenland had high enough elevation for habitation," Behir said.

"That's Iceland you're thinking of. Completely covered," Marjan said.

"It will be almost impossible to get there. Storms. Raiders," Wayne said.

"But if we do make it, we'll be safer. We'll have a chance to build something with little outside interference," Abran said.

I wanted to argue that the size and durability of this ship made the journey safer, but I kept quiet. If anyone persuaded them, it needed to be Abran, someone they already trusted.

"Why do you want to go?" Wayne asked me. "You know someone there?"

"No," I said, lying instinctively. "I think it's our best chance. At really settling."

"We already know there isn't good land in the Andes," Abran said.

I was surprised by how certain he sounded. Perhaps the attack we had witnessed made him keener on the isolation of the north.

"We don't know anything until we're there," Wayne said.

"We do need to get off the water," Thomas said, his voice coming so quietly from the corner that everyone startled. "That attack . . ." Thomas shook his head.

"But we'll be on the water even longer if we go to the Valley. The journey will be twice as far as reaching the Andes," Jessa said.

"But once we're there we'll be more isolated," Behir said. "We won't have to deal with as many attacks."

Guilt curdled my stomach again. I imagined *Sedna* arriving at the Valley and everyone discovering it was already a colony. The shock on their faces, their rage as they turned to me. Would I lie even more and say I hadn't known about the colony? We would not only have to attack the guardians left behind, but we'd have to face the Lost Abbots once they returned, as they did every season, making their collection rounds.

"Okay, okay," Abran said, holding his hands out. "We don't have time to discuss every possible detail. Let's just vote."

Everyone seemed to go quiet and still, and I searched their faces, my heart speeding up, my fingers tingling.

"For everyone in favor of changing our destination to the Valley, please raise your hands," Abran said, raising his own hand.

My hand shot up and I surveyed the room. Daniel, Behir, and Thomas also raised their hands. Five. We were the majority. We were actually going.

Abran asked for the vote against the Valley, but I wasn't paying attention anymore. Relief seeped through me and my bones felt loose in their joints. Some part of me had never believed I could really get them to change course. I felt that my life was always taking me farther from Row and that I'd always be fighting tooth and nail to help her but never getting any closer. But that wasn't true; we were turning toward her. For the first time, I'd be going in the right direction.

Jessa and Wayne were talking angrily near the kitchen, throwing me dark looks, but I paid them no attention. Daniel stood up to leave, not facing me. I'd thought that maybe he wouldn't vote for the Valley, to spite me for not listening to him about joining *Sedna*. But that's not the sort of thing he would do, I thought, as I studied his back, his shirt plastered to his spine with sweat.

When I turned to leave the cabin, I felt Marjan's eyes on me and I looked up at her. Marjan's eyes held a reproach as I passed her, full of sadness and caution. Like she could see something I couldn't. Guilt pulled my elation back the way the sea recedes at low tide, crawling backward, leaving the sand wet and slightly sunken. I might be able to turn the current, but I wasn't like Daniel or Abran, thinking of others, keeping their promises.

I thought of how Row must be living. What room would they keep her in? A dug-out basement of a shack? A small room with cinder-block walls? Would she have even a window?

They'd try to keep her healthy. This comforted me only a little. Did she know what awaited her?

I'd do anything to save her, I reminded myself.

I pictured her braiding her long dark hair in a quiet room, light from a window falling in her lap. Wearing a linen tunic in a color lighter than her skin. Her face in shadow. I couldn't even imagine it, my mind denying me this. Telling me I must see it to know it.

CHAPTER 25

WE PASSED OVER Panama and into the Caribbean. One morning at breakfast, when we were a week away from Wharton, Abran assigned duties to everyone to prepare for our trade.

"We only have two major trades before we cross the Atlantic. Wharton and Broken Tree. It's vital that we have a huge inventory at both these posts. Without the necessary supplies we can't make the journey. This is our one chance," Abran said.

The spirit on the ship changed as we got closer to Wharton. Everyone talked about what they wanted from a trade. Marjan wanted yeast and Thomas wanted a hacksaw. Jessa wouldn't stop talking about lavender soap she'd gotten before from a soap maker in Wharton, the kind with scented oils in it to make your skin soft and fragrant.

"We'll have to trade for lye to make soap ourselves this time," Marjan told her gently. "We need to focus on food stores. Wharton has good beekeepers. The honey will be moisturizing and also help minor skin infections. And we already have coconut oil and aloe."

Marjan kept a close inventory on oils and aloe, giving a small jar to people when their skin started to crack. My skin had grown softer since being on *Sedna* because salt water didn't flood the deck as often as it had on *Bird*, each wave sending it splashing over me.

I remembered when Grandfather was still around and we could trade for carrot seed oil and raspberry oil to protect our skin from the sun. When I could no longer afford that, Pearl and I depended on long clothes and hats we made or got in trades to protect us.

Marjan began cleaning up the breakfast dishes. Pearl stood in the doorway again, watching the seabirds. She stood like a cat ready to pounce.

Abran talked about various duties, assigning Pearl, Behir, Jessa, and me to fishing. Daniel needed to redo calculations for navigation up through the Caribbean. Wayne would continue sealing the seams of planks with wooden plugs before he checked the ammunition stores. We'd be crossing raider territories in the Caribbean and needed to establish shifts for keeping watch at the bow.

Pearl leapt out of the doorway, pouncing on a seabird, and scrambled back to her feet with the bird squirming in her fist. I stepped out of the cabin onto the deck, the sunlight blinding me.

"Nice catch," I said, shielding my eyes.

"Her name is Holly," Pearl said.

Voices spilled out of the cabin. What did she catch? someone asked. A bird, someone answered.

"We could get a bit of meat off her," I said gently, squatting to look at the bird more closely. Its beak was short and curved and its feathers were a soft cream.

"But I wanted to keep her," Pearl said.

"Honey, you can't. She'll fly away."

I stepped back inside and Pearl followed, the bird still in her fist.

Marjan nudged my elbow. "Are you going to . . . ?" She nodded at the bird.

"It's hardly any meat," I said.

"The amount doesn't matter," Wayne said. "We all share everything."

I stiffened. "I don't think this needs to become a problem."

"The child wastes resources. We have rules. We all have to follow them," Jessa said.

"She's never wasted anything," I said, my voice so cold I felt Pearl shift closer to my side.

"It's not just about this. You always have to get what you want. You just joined. You don't have the same rights," Jessa said.

"That's enough," Abran said. "They absolutely have the same rights. Everyone does. It's one of our laws."

"Another rule is about sharing all resources," Wayne said, leaning against the wall, folding his massive arms over his chest.

Abran sighed and shook his head. "They're right," he said, addressing me in a quiet voice. "We can't make exceptions. Everything caught belongs to the whole crew. We can't keep pets."

I didn't even want Pearl to keep the bird as a pet. It was ridiculous. But somehow I felt primed for attack, to help Pearl keep her bird.

Marjan opened her palm in front of Pearl. "I'll do it so you don't have to."

Pearl stepped back from Marjan, then ran toward the door and tossed the bird into the air. The bird became a small white spot in the blue sky, smaller and smaller.

"Pearl," I said and closed my eyes in frustration. "You can't just do whatever you want."

"She'll have to be disciplined," Abran said quietly. "No supper tonight."

I stared at him. She was already thin, and I wasn't going to let her go without food while there was food on this ship. He waited for my response, so I nodded, planning to tuck some food away for her to snack on in bed that night. No food was allowed in the crew quarters for fear of rats. So we'd be breaking two rules in one day. How could I expect Pearl to live in this society, when I flaunted their laws? I had underestimated how difficult it would be for Pearl and me to adjust to living among a community. We couldn't go on living for just the two of us, I thought, never minding the wider world and the needs of others.

As everyone left the table Pearl tugged on my shirt so I'd squat next to her.

"Is Charlie a pet?" Pearl asked me, quietly so no one else could hear.

"Is Charlie still alive?"

"He's my favorite," Pearl said.

"He's not poisonous, is he?" I asked.

Pearl's eyes widened. "Of course not."

I couldn't tell if she was lying to me. "He better not be. No more live ones. We have to abide by their laws. And keep him hidden. And I'm almost out of bait, so he doesn't get any more ballyhoo."

She scowled at me. "Soon as we're in Wharton I'm catching frogs for him," she announced.

I began fishing, and by afternoon I had only caught two bluefish and had to pull up the lines to preserve the rest of the bait. The water seemed empty of anything living, as if we were sailing through a sea of poison. I adjusted the rope on the downrigger, shortening it with a series of knots, so we could do midwater trawling and maybe catch some of those schools of fish the blue-fish were feeding on. That was probably the problem—we were still close to the mountains and I probably didn't have the depth right.

Daniel walked up to me with a mug of steaming tea as I tossed the bluefish fillets in a bucket of salt. Clouds to the east were rolling west.

"We'll likely go through a small squall midafternoon. Better pull up the net after lunch," Daniel said.

"Okay." I knotted the rope, yanking it tight. Daniel's shirt was unbuttoned and I caught a glimpse of a long scar, the raised white line traveling from his clavicle and ending under his ribs.

It felt nice to stand next to him, the salt wind on our skin, the day cool and clear. I thought back to how we'd been on *Bird*, before we'd joined *Sedna*. The long quiet nights on the deck under moonlight, talking. It felt like ever since we'd joined *Sedna*, I'd barely seen him, but that wasn't true. I just had barely been alone with him.

"This is a mess," Daniel said. A mile away we could see a small island, not large enough to be inhabitable, but large enough to cut open the hull. "Navigating through this has been a nightmare. We should be farther east, but Abran wants to save time."

"He's worried about resources." And dissention from the crew if rations grew too tight. No need to make the crew doubt the change of destination.

"Saw something the other day," Daniel said. He looked at

me pointedly. "I think you've seen it, too. Abran used to have a tattoo on his neck. Now he has burn scars. The other day he changed that handkerchief he always wears. Thought I wasn't in there; I was in the kitchen, putting water on to boil for Marjan."

"So? Lots of people have tattoos," I said. It was true; they were an easier form of jewelry. Some people had names of lost loved ones tattooed on them. I took a sip of the tea. Leaves drifted to the bottom of my cup, fragrant in some sweet way I couldn't place, like mint but more bitter.

"It was a raider tattoo. Why else would he burn it off?"

I pretended to ignore this and tried to imagine what the rabbit had looked like on Abran's neck. There had been a faint outline under the scars. It had begun with blue ink, but whoever had done it must have run out, because midway down it was black.

"You know," Daniel said, as though he were reading my thoughts. He said it calmly, as though he pitied me. It made me want to smack him. "You know what crew he was with."

"So? So what are you saying?" I felt defensive, like Daniel was stirring up trouble. I'd finally gotten the vote to change our destination to the Valley. We weren't unstable. The path ahead was clear. We were going to make it there in time.

"Take the easy road once, he'll take it again," Daniel said.

I rolled my eyes. "Must be nice, living in your world of perfect choices."

"I'm just worried about you. I think you should be more careful."

"More careful who I sleep with?"

Daniel squinted at the horizon. "I think you know what I mean."

"I can take care of myself, thanks."

"I wasn't just talking about you," Daniel said, turning to leave.

"I'm just saying the tattoo doesn't change anything," I said. I meant about the journey, but I realized he took it to mean my feelings for Abran.

"That's the last of the tea," he said over his shoulder before disappearing into the cabin.

CHAPTER 26

WHARTON WAS MORE beautiful than I expected, with stone ruins and small thatched huts climbing up the mountainside, cypress trees bright green and heavy, and multicolored birds I'd never seen before flitting through the sky. The color was overwhelming after the salt-stripped colors at sea, the soft blues, greens, and grays, and the faded brown of driftwood.

Even the fish were brightly colored outside Wharton. I fished for snapper in the mangroves and grass beds as we neared the coast. Their yellow and orange fins flashed in the sunlight and Pearl kept saying, "Pretty, pretty," when she cut them up.

Daniel and I loaded the baskets, bins, and buckets of smoked and salted fish in silence. Each day that we drew closer to Wharton I felt him becoming tenser, his words terser, his movements abrupt and restless. On deck, he'd start to say something, only to walk away and shake his head.

One day he said to himself, "Well, I guess I'll find out."

"Find out what?" I asked.

He looked at me blankly, surprised to see me next to him, though we'd been knotting lures together for the last half hour.

The crew helped set the fish out on the dock for the port master, who jotted down the amount on a small piece of yellowed paper and handed it to us. The stench of smoked fish made me dizzy. I was sick of smelling it every day and couldn't wait to get on land and ask for a cup of tea. Something fragrant.

Already I could smell lavender and ginger, wafting down from a stand set up near the harbor.

"*No te llevas la plaga, verdad?*" the port master asked, surveying us all with a grimace and looking over our shoulders at *Sedna*.

"*No, por qué preguntas?*" Abran asked.

"*Tuve que desviar un barco esta semana. La mitad de la tripulación estaba negra y podrida,*" the port master said.

"What did he say?" I asked Abran.

"He asked if we were carrying the plague. Said they had to turn a ship away—half the crew was black and rotted."

We carried the fish up to the trading post, a large stone building near the harbor. The stones fit together oddly, some still lying in heaps outside the building, as if they'd collected more stones than they needed and then abandoned them at the building site. I had the chilling sense the building would collapse on us when we were inside.

Abran bartered at the counter with the shopkeeper, first trading a few fish for Wharton coins. I wished I knew Spanish so I could help with the trade—Marjan had told me that Abran never bartered hard enough. Most villages had their own currency, but coins couldn't be traded between villages since there was no agreement over value. We gave two coins to each crew member.

We asked for rope and fabric for sails, candles and wood, fabric for winter clothes. We weren't sure how cold it would be in the Valley. Temperatures seemed moderate in most places, a temperate maritime climate, but we wanted to be prepared. We'd heard of storms people called *chaacans* up north; storms that were like a blizzard at sea, a winter hurricane. A cyclone of water spun while the sky flung snow in straight winds, the water and snow turning to ice in the wind, shattering against ships and rocks.

We emptied our containers of fish at the post and refilled them with our trade. We carried everything back to the ship and then the crew disbanded to explore the village.

Daniel turned to me and dropped his coins in my palm. "For Pearl. Get something that will keep her warm. Something for her feet. She may not be able to run around barefoot there," he said.

I tried to give the coins back. "I was going to use my coins to get her something. Don't you want to go to the saloon?" I said, thinking of my longing for a fragrant cup of tea.

"Get her two things, then," he said curtly and walked away.

Pearl wanted to go with Marjan to check out a stand of woven baskets, so I made my way back to the trading post alone. I stepped over large puddles, the humidity in the air heavy like a wool coat. Children played in the muddy lanes, old men pushed carts of potatoes or carrots, and women fanned themselves next to their stalls.

The stalls were loaded with old-world and new-world objects sitting side by side. Rope, candles, and wood bowls made from materials found at the tops of mountains. Matches, knives, and plastic bottles saved from down below and brought up during the migration.

I glanced longingly at a pile of pillows. I remembered how it felt to wake up in a real bed, with soft pillows, the regularity of an alarm clock, the sudden cold water from a faucet to wash my face. Most of all I remembered the stillness and stability, how every surface wasn't always moving.

Smoke curled out of the holes in thatched roofs. A woman strung her washing on a line. Through the window of one stone cottage I could see a woman churning butter.

Close to the harbor, a collection of larger homes clustered around a communal courtyard, where pigs, goats, and chickens wandered in and out of small lean-tos.

I stopped and starred. These homes were built before the floods. Some were made of bricks, some with siding. The roofs had shingles. One was a colonial with pillars in the front.

I thought of Abran telling me about the gated community high up on a mountain that he'd grown up in. I wondered what it would be like to grow up that way during the Hundred Year Flood: no strangers on your doorstep, no guarding your house at night with a shotgun for fear someone would try to loot you. Did they have someone patrol that gated perimeter, keeping people at a distance, only letting people in to be treated? Guarding what they had so they could keep sharing their skills and hoarding medicine?

I wondered who lived in the houses—people who became wealthy before or after the floods? Sometimes those people were one and the same, the wealthy who grew wealthier in disaster, able to turn catastrophe to their advantage. I thought of Abran and the wealth on *Sedna*. All those shelves of stored goods in the hull. I imagined Abran and me in a house like the one before me, in the Valley, building a new community. How quickly would we build gates, face inward toward a courtyard to protect what we had?

An emaciated girl shoveled shit into a bucket in the court-yard, red welts visible on her upper back where her shirt didn't cover. I shuddered and hurried on. In most ports the line be-tween indentured servitude and slavery was unclear. People went to rich houses and agreed to work for food and shelter and were never able to leave, because where could they go?

In the trading post I wandered between the shelves, pausing. I fingered a clear jar labeled "toothpaste" and smiled. I hadn't thought of brushing my teeth in years.

A blanket, made with dyed wool, sat on one shelf and I rubbed the thick fibers between my fingers. Clothing was piled in barrels with a label on the front telling the customer what was inside: "Women, Sweaters" or "Men, Socks." I sorted through the barrels of clothing, searching for sweaters and trousers that would fit Pearl. She had grown out of most of the cloth-ing she wore now, her ankles visible beneath the hem of her pants. Some ports had weavers and seamstresses, making new clothes, but mostly we still wore clothes salvaged from before the floods.

The shopkeeper left the counter and walked up to me. "Going north?" she asked in a thick accent.

"Yes," I said.

"We've got more in the back, this way," she said, waddling between the overstuffed shelves to the back of the room, where blankets, boots, and coats were piled.

"Where up north?" the woman asked. The woman had black hair pulled into a tight bun at the base of her head. Though she walked slower than a turtle, she wore a no-nonsense expression in her pinched lips and slightly raised brows.

I paused. Normally I kept where I was going under wraps. I didn't like sharing my routes. But trading posts were the best places to pick up information.

"We're going to the Valley, up in—"

"Oh," the shopkeeper interrupted. "You know about the epidemic, don't you? Well, I guess it's not an epidemic anymore."

I dropped the blanket I'd been holding back on the shelf. "Epidemic?"

"Apparently there was some attack. Raiders. The village was so well defended—I guess the Valley makes an invasion tough. So they decided to subdue them a different way. Threw a body in their well. Somebody who'd died of the plague. It's back." The woman shut her eyes and shook her head. "Black death. Talk about evolution. We thought we'd overcome all that and here it is, wiping us out all over again."

I gripped the shelf. "When? When did that happen?"

"Hm. Maybe two or three months ago? It's been some time. After the raiders exposed the village and the epidemic killed half the population, they subdued the rest of the population and made it a colony."

"The Lost Abbots," I said softly.

"Oh, so you already know. Why are you going then?" She turned and straightened a couple of boots.

I didn't respond, my mind racing ahead. I had been so busy figuring out how to get to the Valley that I hadn't considered how it became a colony in the first place. I knew biological warfare was becoming more common, but I hadn't wanted to dwell on it. Why hadn't I stopped to think of what could actually be happening in the Valley?

Did Row even survive the epidemic? *Didn't think she'd make it.* Wasn't that what he said? He made it sound like she was being held until she was old enough for the breeding ship. So she must have survived the epidemic. Unless the epidemic wasn't over—would it still be there when we arrived?

I racked my brain, trying to remember what I'd heard about biological warfare and epidemics. Didn't rodents still carry the plague, even after it seemed to have disappeared? Wouldn't we, who hadn't yet been exposed, be more susceptible to it when we landed in the Valley?

I'd worried about starvation, storms, raiders, but I hadn't spent any time thinking about illnesses. How quickly they could wipe out a whole community. I hadn't thought about illnesses because I could do less about them than I could about anything else.

You could hold your child's hand as an illness broke them down, but that was all, I thought.

You can't protect them from everything.

You couldn't protect Row from her own father.

Maybe he was protecting her by taking her away from me.

"You okay?" the shopkeeper asked.

"Hm?" I asked.

"You look pale," the shopkeeper said.

"Is it still there?" I asked.

"Well, I'm sure they've boarded up the well by this point and burned the bodies. But you never know. Fleas could be carrying it. Some places eradicate it pretty well. It's easier on isolated islands, especially if there isn't too much travel. But we had to quarantine someone coming from Errons, up north, where there'd been an outbreak. Just to be on the safe side, keep him monitored awhile."

I fingered a pair of sheepskin boots on the shelf. They were Pearl's size. I would be exposing her to the plague by going. I would be resigning Row to a life on a breeding ship if I didn't.

I'd never imagined having to choose between them. Before them, I'd had few difficult choices to make. It was more like my life was an open expanse and I was waiting for something to appear on the horizon, waiting for my life to begin. With the world changing so quickly, it was hard to be ambitious or to make plans. When the floods kept getting worse, life both moved quickly and went stagnant. Schools closed, so I dropped out and never returned. People weren't pursuing careers like they used to, they weren't making life plans. They were trapping squirrels in their backyard and breaking into convenience stores. So I worked odd jobs—at factories, farms, ranches. I cleaned hotel rooms and picked corn. Anything that would let me work with my hands. I didn't move out of my parents' home and look for my own place because no one did. Several generations lived under the same roof, helping each other survive, as towns swelled with crowds and died down to ghost towns in a matter of months.

But then Row came and my life broke open. When I first held her, I felt a sudden shift in perspective. I could at once see my life from a great distance and settle more deeply into it, as if what came before had been merely preparation.

The main thing she taught me was that there was no going back to before. There was no later, no "let's wait and figure something out." There was only now, all the neediness of the present, hands against your skin, wails filling the room, a body to be rocked. There was always only moving forward.

The north would be cold, I thought. I bought the boots for Pearl.

CHAPTER 27

THE FIRST THING I needed to do was convince Abran to stop where his old crew had hidden the medicine. If the plague was still contagious in the Valley, we would need something to protect us. I wasn't going to sail into the Valley and watch Pearl succumb to a disease that rotted her from the inside out.

I found Abran in a saloon, but he was so drunk, he kept slurring his words and swaying on his feet. I left the saloon without telling him the news. I'd have to convince him later, when he was sober.

As I stood in the street outside the saloon I felt the overwhelming desire to confess and share the burden. Daniel, I thought. I could tell Daniel my plan to get the medicine and ask for his help.

I found Pearl first, in the mangroves, sitting against a cypress tree, feet tucked under her, whittling a piece of wood. Five dead snakes lay beside her, draped over a rock. Her snake pot was wedged between tall grass and a cedar tree. I walked over to Pearl, climbing around ferns and over fallen branches. She was whittling a bird out of a cypress branch. I squatted next to her and hugged her.

"Hey, careful!" she said. "Don't smoosh them." She gestured to her dead snakes on the rock.

I remembered when Pearl first caught a snake. She was five and we both were diving and I was spearing fish. When I came up, Pearl was treading water, holding on to a tiny snake, one hand pinching him behind the head, the other holding its body. It lay limp in her hands, only its eyelids moving.

"Pearl, that isn't a fish. We're only catching fish," I said nervously. "How did you know to catch him behind the head?"

She looked at me like I was stupid. "I saw he had teeth."

After that she caught a few more in the water and would stroke them, calling them her babies. When on land, she'd spot their burrows and stalk them or entice them out of hiding with frog legs. She caught mostly young, small snakes and I'd let her play with them for a short while before making a meal of them. We'd feed them scraps of fish, frogs, insects, or small mice.

When she caught them on land, I'd warn her that I didn't know if there were laws against hunting snakes.

"Laws, laws, laws," Pearl would sing, petting the snake.

Most villages had an overpopulation of them, but still wanted them around to control disease-ridden rodents. The rats seemed to know the floods were coming before we did, scurrying up the mountains, digging new homes. One woman in a saloon told me she saw a pack of rats climbing the mountainside one morning during the Six Year Flood, their brown coats glossy in the sunlight, darting over rocks and across fallen trees.

Some people kept snakes on boats to hunt mice, favoring the thin, long ones that weren't poisonous. Handmade guidebooks of poisonous snakes were distributed in ports, to alert people which ones to avoid.

"They're actually cleaner than cats," a man at a port told me.

"Cats?" Pearl asked.

"You saw one once, in Harjo," I explained.

Pearl had shrugged. "Must have looked boring; I don't remember."

I worried about Pearl getting bit all the time. But I also knew she had a skill, and it was a food source. And she needed both. So I made her pore over the guidebooks and avoid the poisonous ones, which she promised she did, but I knew how much she liked to push limits.

I reached out and smoothed her hair from her face, and she swatted my hand away.

"Where's Daniel?" I asked her.

She pointed east, where he stood ankle deep in water about twenty feet away, shrouded by cypress and cedar trees thick with lichen and mushrooms. A small bag was slung over his shoulder, bulging with mushrooms.

"It's for my sister," Pearl said, setting the bird in my palm. The wings looked like a fish's fins, short and lined.

"Your sister liked birds," I said.

An expression of recognition and pleasure crossed Pearl's face briefly and vanished. "I know."

I thought of Row in the Valley with the epidemic rotting those around her. I thought of her in a bed somewhere, boils on her wrists, fingers blackened, breath ragged in her throat. When she was sick as a child she liked me to pinch each of her fingers, one by one. I'd stroke her hair from her wet brow and then press her tiny finger between my thumb and finger and release it. We'd watch the blood come back to the tip, each of us marveling at her body. She said I was "pressing her" and it made me think of pressing her like a stamp, reminding both of us she wasn't going anywhere.

I lifted the lid of Pearl's snake pot. A mass of snakes slithered over one another, trying to lift their heads above the rim of the pot and into the sunlight. I slammed the lid back down.

"Pearl, how many do you have?"

Pearl shrugged. "Six? I have trouble counting." She grinned slyly at me.

"You're only supposed to keep one or two. We need them for tonight's supper."

"No, we'll eat fish."

"No, most of the fish has been traded for goods. We're at port, remember?"

"Why haven't you caught more?" Pearl asked, her eyes narrowed in accusation. "There's a poison one in there."

"Pearl, take it out and cut its head off."

Pearl shrugged. "You go ahead."

"Pearl!" I couldn't handle snakes like Pearl. I felt my face flush and wiped sweat from my brow with my arm.

She lifted the lid and her hand darted inside and shot back out, gripping a snake behind its head, fangs exposed, its tiny tongue flickering out of its mouth. She placed its head against the splayed base of the cypress tree and cut its head off. She held the head up to me and giggled.

"Yum, yum, yum," she said, the fangs bopping up and down as she jiggled the head.

"You should bury it so someone doesn't step on it," I said.

She began peeling the skin off it and I reached forward and caught her hand. She had a deep cut in the middle of her index finger, bright red and scabbed over.

"When did you get this?"

She ripped her hand out of my palm.

"It's fine," she said.

"You let me know if it hurts or gets any redder," I said, my nerves already sparking on like small lights. Even the smallest cuts could get infected, and once sepsis set in there was little you could do.

I kissed the top of Pearl's head and she shrugged away from me, but as soon as I turned to leave, she asked, "You're leaving?" with a hint of sadness.

I told her I'd be right back and climbed around a cypress tree, the bark smooth against my hands. Sunlight filtered through the trees, and it felt subdued and delicate compared to the brightness on the open sea. At my feet, a small turtle dove into the dark water.

"Thought you'd be drinking with the others," Daniel said when he saw me.

Thought you'd be talking to someone shady somewhere, I thought.

I waded into the water with him, my toes sinking into the mud. There was too much life around us; I felt like it would blot me out. Everything felt too close. Birds flitting between trees, snakes sliding into the swamp, water lilies floating with their faces to a sun that was shrouded by trees. The honeyed smell of flowers and grass mixed with all the decaying wood, giving the whole place an odor of something sweet and half rotted.

I stood facing him, feeling reluctant. Better to say it quick, I thought.

"There was an epidemic in the Valley," I told him, watching him pluck a mushroom from a tree.

I told him what I'd heard in the trading post. I tried to hold my face steady, but I felt the edges of my mouth tighten. Between his neck and shoulder there was a hollow filled with shadow. I wanted to place my face in it. To breathe him in and rest.

He waded around a small tree and several bushes to reach me and took my shoulders and pulled me into him. I sank my head against his chest. He already smelled like flowers and plants; I couldn't taste salt when my lips brushed his neck. It surprised me how much better I felt as soon as I was in his arms.

He reached up and brushed my hair with his palm. He swallowed, his throat moving against my forehead. I felt he wanted to say something more, but he stayed silent a moment and then we broke apart.

"Are you going to tell Abran?" Daniel asked. He tucked a strand of hair behind my ear.

I looked at him warily. I hadn't decided how much I wanted to tell Abran, but I had a sinking feeling that I'd have to tell him everything—not just about the epidemic, but the Valley being a colony—in order to convince him to stop for the medicine. But the rest of the crew couldn't know. I wanted to work it out alone with Abran.

"Abran's old crew has medicine hidden just north of here," I said. "It's on our way."

Daniel took a step away from me and shoved his hair out of his face. He cursed and looked up at the sky.

"You don't want to go anywhere near where raiders hide their stashes," he said.

"I know, but—"

"If this happened a few months ago—" Daniel stopped short and looked down at the dark water.

"Then she's already dead. Is that what you were going to say?"

"You're dealing with hypotheticals. It's dormant there by now."

"Maybe and maybe not. We haven't been exposed; we haven't built up an immunity. And how long until other raiders use biological warfare? The point is we have resources right in front of us," I said.

Daniel's jaw was set and he looked across the swamp at moss hanging from the branches. It swayed in the light breeze.

"Every time we take a turn, I keep thinking you're going to back out on me," I said. That's why I came to him, I realized. I wanted to stop feeling like if I turned around he would be gone.

Daniel watched a bird flying between the trees. He turned something over in his mind, his jaw twitching. I touched his arm.

"Are you with me on this?" I asked.

Daniel looked at me, his gray eyes tender and distant, like he was remembering something he'd forgotten. Then something shifted like a curtain being drawn back from him, and he stepped forward and took my hand. I felt like I could breathe for the first time in that thick air, inhaling a deep breath and letting it go.

"I'm going to help you get to your girl," he said. "I promised you that, and I'm not leaving now."

CHAPTER 28

IT WAS STARTING to get dark on my way back into the village. I needed a drink, so I headed for a saloon tucked into the mountainside, close to the harbor.

A large ship was anchored in the harbor and several men walked along the dock, herding several girls in front of them. One of the girls looked younger than fourteen, her belly rounded with child. Her hair was cut short around her face and her temple was branded with a T, the scar bubbled and pink, glistening in the twilight. She glanced up at me and quickly looked away.

"Move along," one of the men said, swatting their legs with a belt.

I hurried along the rock face, the path tilting toward the sea as I rounded the bend. Beyond the saloon, shacks and tents climbed up the mountainside, some glowing from within by lantern light. A low murmur of people ending their day drifted down to the sea.

I slipped into the saloon, went straight to the bar, and threw back a whiskey. The room was thick with smoke, light from the lanterns and candles heavy and foggy in the small space. There were chinks in the wood slats of the walls and the dull light of twilight shone between these holes.

Someone tapped my shoulder and I turned and saw Behir.

"You look pale," he said.

I shook my head and then told him what I'd seen in the harbor. While raiders could settle debts by taking people captive in various ports, normally slave trade itself was conducted in small bays and inlets just outside trading ports.

Behir nodded. "Wharton is a base now. Even the water just around the ports is taxed. That's all I've heard from the fishermen all night." Behir gestured to a group of dark-skinned men sitting behind us at the next table.

"Which tribe?" I asked.

Behir shrugged. "Lost Abbots. They have a stronghold here in the Caribbean—bases, colonies, you name it. All night it's been talk of taxes, public beatings, the slave trade." Behir shook his head, his young face etched with worry. "It's why I'm glad we're not just trying to settle in some port. That's what my mom wanted, but I kept telling her you never know if a port is already a haven for raiders. Already under their thumb. We didn't know Wharton turned until we got here."

Something turned over in my stomach and I felt the urge to tell him that the Valley was already a colony.

I ordered another whiskey instead. I downed it quickly, focusing on the heat in my throat. We were both quiet for a while and I watched the light dim between the cracks in the walls. Behir was listening intently to the men sitting behind us. I couldn't recognize the language they spoke.

"What are they—?"

"Hindi," Behir said. "My mom insisted I learn, said it would come in useful." He rolled his eyes. "She's always right."

He leaned closer to me and whispered in my ear. "You saw those big houses close to the harbor? I guess this man who lived in one—a broker back in the day or something—was a distant cousin of the family that started the Lost Abbots. So they came to an arrangement. The Lost Abbots could make this a base if they shared what they looted from other communities with Wharton. To help grow the society here. Wharton also gets free protection from the Lost Abbots from other raiding tribes."

Behir paused and listened more closely to the men. "Government officials here could keep their jobs; stay in leadership," he said. "Sounds like Wharton's a democracy of some kind, they hold votes every year. But there's a lot of bribery."

I shook my head and we fell silent again, twisting our drinks on the table. Next to us two women were arguing about the floods.

"She preserved us. We're still here," one said.

"She tried to wipe us out," the other said.

"She destroyed everything so we could rebuild."

"We're not rebuilding; we're going extinct."

"Well, God will save us."

"If there is a god, he has a different idea of goodness than we do."

I could tell Behir was listening to them as he turned his glass in circles on the bar in front of us. He seemed so young. I wanted to comfort him but didn't know how.

"You remember seeing that bird?" he asked, interrupting my thoughts.

"Bird?"

"Let out of the cage on that raider's ship?"

I nodded.

"I asked Abran about it later. He said raiders are using homing pigeons now. To communicate with other ships or ports after they've made a conquest."

This hit me like a wave and I rocked on my stool. Would the colony in the Valley be able to send out a message to the rest of the Lost Abbots before we killed the guards left behind? Would the Lost Abbots return before we could set up defenses?

Behir shook his head and went on. "Apparently they train them to fly between their ships. Abran said they shoot them dead above other ships because the bird won't land. Doesn't recognize a ship not part of their fleet and gets confused. They call it 'dropping a message.'" Behir paused and rubbed his thumb on his cup. "With them communicating, it will be so much harder to hide from them—" Behir's voice almost cracked and I took his hand.

"We don't need to hide from anyone," I said, stuffing down my own fears. I took a deep breath and assumed that calm and in-control expression I so often put on when Pearl was with me. I squeezed his hand once and drew my hand back. "We won't need to hide because we will fortify the Valley."

It surprised me that I believed what I said. I saw it now in my mind's eye—all of us working together to build something. Abran's vision was infectious. While I had thought I was above the idealism of it, here I was, secretly yearning for what he was trying to accomplish.

Behir nodded and grinned at me. "You're right," he said. He drank the dregs in his cup, the scent of elderberry and bark wafting toward me. "I think I'm going to head back to the ship. Almost everyone is back there."

I nodded. "I'll be there soon," I said, wanting suddenly to be alone, as if some barrier had been crossed and I now wanted to go back behind it.

"I almost forgot." Behir pulled something out of his pocket and set it on the bar in front of me. It was a pair of small snake-skin gloves. "I bought them for Pearl. For going north. She— she reminds me of my little sister. I guess I just wanted her to have something nice."

I touched them with the tips of my fingers, the skin surpris-ingly soft. "Thank you," I said.

These people deserve to know where they're going, I thought as Behir left the saloon. I pushed the gloves away from me and dropped my head in my hands.

CHAPTER 29

THAT NIGHT I walked along the dark hallway to Abran's room. Over the last few weeks I still visited Abran at night, though infrequently and without warning. Abran seemed so distracted with sailing the ship through these new waters that he no longer asked that we tell the crew about us. I was beginning to feel that if I stopped visiting him at night I wouldn't miss it. But it was the only private place I could try to convince him to stop for the hidden medicine.

As I stood at his door, my knuckles light on the wood, I thought of Daniel in the mangroves, the way his beard brushed my forehead when I lay my head on his chest.

Abran opened the door and I smelled whiskey on his breath. He closed the door behind me, careful that it didn't make a noise. He even moved cautiously back to his bed, looking over his shoulder at me like I was a stranger.

A half-drunk bottle of whiskey sat on his bedside box, tipping to the right on the uneven surface. It wasn't the same jug of whiskey we kept in the storage room and brought up to the cabin for celebrations. Perhaps he bought it with his two extra coins in Wharton. I didn't want to consider the possibility that he had been skimming our trades and had used the extra money to purchase alcohol for himself.

"You'll have to pace yourself if it'll last the Atlantic crossing," I said, trying to sound lighthearted and teasing, but an edge crept into my voice.

"Hopefully we'll all last the Atlantic crossing," he said. He collapsed on the bed, lying on his back, hand over his eyes.

"What is it?" I asked. He was making me nervous. I couldn't convince him to stop for the medicine if he was already feeling anxious and defeated. His small room reeked of sweat and liquor, of nights with no sleep, turning over and over in a small bed as the waves thrashed against the sides of the ship.

"Wharton was my brother's favorite post. Reminded him of home, I think." Abran sat up in bed, a line between his brows, his mouth pressed into a firm line. I could tell he was about to collapse and I gritted my teeth in impatience. The tension fell from his face as he began to sob, dropping his forehead to his palms.

I sat next to him and folded him into my arms, rubbing his shoulder and whispering into his hair, "It's okay, it's okay."

After a moment, he leaned back from me. "It was my fault."

I shook my head. "No, it wasn't."

"It was. It was our plan, but it . . ." Abran looked around the room, stunned and lost. "Our plan was to steal their supplies while the ship was docked and the crew was on shore, drinking and finding whores. It was only a few miles from here. We were going to hide the resources we stole up the mountainside. The plan was to set one of the ship's small boats free, to drift with the current, as a decoy, so the crew would follow it when they returned to the ship."

Abran grew quiet and neither of us spoke for some time. The sea seemed to build a wall of noise around us, thundering against

the wood, the ship creaking in the night. Then Abran continued, "Jonas went back on the ship to free a slave kept down in
the hull. We fought about it. I didn't want him to do it, the slave
wasn't . . . wasn't well anymore and it could put us in more danger. But Jonas went down below while I lowered the boat and
released it into the water. Then I went back up the mountainside to hide, waiting for Jonas to join me. But screams filled the
air. The slave was screaming and hollering and attacking Jonas.
Probably thought Jonas was going to execute him or something.
Couldn't understand he was being set free. Then it was silent. I
thought Jonas had knocked the slave out to quiet him. I was just
about to come out of hiding, go back to the ship, when I saw a
few of our crewmates coming down the dock, toward the ship."

Abran sank his head into his hands. "I watched, thinking to
Jonas, Get away, get away. I wasn't sure if he was still on the
ship or had slipped away. It was dark. I couldn't see. A couple of men finally dragged him up from the hull—I think he
was unconscious—the slave must have knocked him out. One
draped him over the gunwale and the other blew his head off.
They flipped his legs over and he fell into the sea."

An echo of grief shuddered through me. No wonder Abran
was as frightened as he was driven, I thought. I reached for
Abran's wrist, pulling his hand from his face, and put my palm
in his. "You couldn't have stopped it."

"I could have." Abran pulled his hand away and shook his
head. "No sense now. No sense in anything now."

I felt him slipping away from me, so I reached out and shook
him. "Abran, stop. The whole crew is depending on you. We
have things to worry about here and now." I told him what the

shopkeeper in Wharton had told me, not just about the epidemic, but about how the Lost Abbots used biological warfare to make the Valley a colony. My whole body went rigid; my tongue felt stuck in my mouth. I felt fear like a piece of metal I couldn't swallow. We had nowhere else to go. He couldn't change our route now, I told myself.

Abran listened glumly, without any apparent shock or concern. "I've heard of that. Biological warfare."

I had held my breath while he spoke and now let it out in a quick exhale. I leaned back from him, watching his face. Once again, he reminded me of Jacob, the way he sat hunched forward, defeated and disinterested. Whenever things got stressful Jacob would check out, slowly closing himself off. "You could lose everything you've worked for," I said carefully.

"There will always be something," Abran said, reaching for the bottle on the table. He took a swig and I resisted the urge to grab the bottle from him and fling it against the wall. Adrenaline buzzed in my veins. It was too abstract for him. Had he lost too much to care anymore? Was this an episode he'd pass through, or was this a different side of him I hadn't seen before?

"Did you know?" he asked. "About it being a colony?"

"Of course not," I lied. "But it isn't a base. Not like Wharton is now. It's only a colony. They'll only have left a few guards behind. What we really need is the antibiotics."

"Yeah, you said that." Abran stood up and paced the room.

"Do you still have the coordinates?"

Abran nodded. "A little island just south of Broken Tree, our last port before we cross the Atlantic. It's called Ruenlock."

"And they aren't using it as a base?"

"They never use hiding places as bases. But sometimes they return to hiding places, to restock or pick up resources to trade." Abran paused. "But even that is unlikely at this place. Our Lily Black ship broke apart a year after I left, killed half its members, got a new captain. I heard all about it from a friend in Apple Falls. After that breakup there's no telling if they still kept the coordinates of all their hiding places. They certainly aren't leaving people behind to guard in each hiding place. But also, no telling if it hasn't already been found and ransacked by someone else."

"We could put it up for a vote." I had the sneaking suspicion that Abran only put things up for a vote when he felt certain the crew would vote in favor of what he already wanted.

"Last time I messed with raiders' resources my brother got killed. Because I didn't know how to handle it. It doesn't go like you'd expect. You can't understand."

"Everyone could get sick. We need to still try—"

Abran shook his head. "The weather will be getting worse the closer we get to winter. We can't lose any time on extra stops. Those winter storms up north . . ." Abran shuddered. He was more scared of the crossing than I'd thought. He sat on the bed next to me and put his arm around me.

"Aren't you concerned? Aren't you worried about the crew being exposed? And the colony?" I asked. I had been prepared for him to threaten changing our destination; I hadn't been prepared for this apathy. I realized as I stared at him that I wasn't just worried about Pearl getting sick; I was worried about the whole crew. Worried that this crew needed someone who wasn't going to disappear on them when they needed a leader. If he isn't going to tell them, I need to, I thought. A wave of nausea rolled over me. What if they refused to sail to the Valley?

Abran turned his bloodshot eyes on me. "Hon, there's something around every corner. I'm done trying to be ready for it."

He slipped his hand under my shirt, fingers finding my breast. His grasp was drunken and rough, his mind elsewhere, my body between his hands like a toy. It was the first time I didn't want him touching me. He grabbed my chin and turned my face toward his and I pushed him back.

He reached for my wrist and I jumped up from the bed. I grabbed his whiskey bottle and flung it against the wall. The shards littered the floor in a melody like wind chimes on a front porch.

"You're not the only one on this ship," I said.

Abran fixed his eyes on me, black and glittering in the candlelight. "Neither are you, sweetheart."

CHAPTER 30

I AVOIDED ABRAN after that evening and we didn't speak again about the epidemic in the Valley. Two days later we celebrated *Sedna*'s fourth birthday. Marjan was preparing a menu of smoked cod, potatoes, collard greens, peaches, and beans. Everyone kept finding excuses to walk through the cabin to get a smell of the food cooking in the kitchen. We'd been on a strict diet of salted fish and sauerkraut and we all were ready to taste something different.

Marjan stepped out of the kitchen to look at the canned goods in the storage room in the hull, leaving Pearl and me with a bucket of potatoes to peel.

"What does Row look like?" Pearl asked, soon as Marjan left the kitchen. Normally she asked me questions about Row when we lingered in the quarters in the morning, after everyone had gotten started on the morning chores.

"A bit like me," I said. "Dark hair, eyes like the sea."

"And does she like snakes?" Pearl asked.

Marjan walked in and smiled at us in her absent, kind way. "Forgot the towels for laundry. Stinking up this whole kitchen with mold."

I didn't respond to Pearl's question so she nudged me with a potato and said, "Well, does she?"

"Honey, just one second," I told her, pretending to be carefully cutting rot out of a potato.

Marjan bustled out of the kitchen with a stack of wet, moldy towels.

"Pearl, we need to keep Row just to ourselves," I said. "She's our secret."

When Pearl looked at me I expected to find surprise or curiosity in her look, to ask why in a high voice, but instead I found a certain, sure expression that said, *I already know she's supposed to be a secret.* She wore a slight teasing grin, like she'd been needling me and enjoying my anxiety.

"Do you know why she's a secret, Pearl?"

"We're going to get her. And it's dangerous there, so no one can know."

I stared at her. She'd always known we were traveling to rescue Row, ever since that day on the cliff. But at what point did she realize we were deceiving the crew? Had my anxiety about the crossing let her know how dangerous it was? Had she heard me talking with Daniel in the mangroves after I'd found out about the epidemic?

She returned to peeling her potato with sure, swift strokes of her knife, a pleased look still curling her lips in a slight smile. Sometimes, when I saw the woman in her, I was frightened. She'd be stronger, more willful than I. I was teaching her to deceive, and she was learning my lessons well. I was teaching her how to make it in this world.

Marjan came back into the kitchen with a few cans in hand and shooed us out of the kitchen, telling us she wanted to finish up by herself.

The evening cooled, and by the time we reentered the cabin the kerosene lanterns had already been lit. The smell of fresh-baked bread felt warm and enveloping as we stepped out of the wind. A platter of cod with a tomato and peach salsa sat in the middle of the table, smelling bright and sweet.

Before we sat down to eat, Marjan pulled back the curtain to the kitchen and stepped forward carrying a small cake on a platter. She had a candle stuck in the middle, one of the old ones from before the floods, with a pink swirl wrapping around from base to tip.

She sat it on the table in front of me and said, "You said Pearl was born in the fall. I figured today is as good as any to celebrate. Children deserve to have their birthdays celebrated."

I was stunned and couldn't speak. I didn't remember when I'd mentioned Pearl's birthday being in the fall, but Marjan had remembered. Both my girls had been born in the fall, but I'd never known what day Pearl had been born on.

Pearl beamed up at her and thanked her and then looked at the cake, a wide smile fixed on her face, her hands clasped together. She'd never seen a cake before. Its glaze of frosting glistened under the kerosene lamp and I smelled the unmistakable scent of flour and sugar and egg and wondered how Marjan had pulled it off when we only had flour and no eggs or sugar.

"Happy Birthday!" the chorus came up around Pearl and she gripped her palms tighter together, her nose wrinkled in delight. She was buoyed by the attention, but I felt that my skin had been pulled back from the muscle. Sudden bright pain filled me at this display of affection by the people I was betraying. I couldn't do both, I realized. I couldn't be part of this crew and also betray them.

I remembered Row's last birthday I celebrated with her. She was turning five and my mother had also made a cake without enough ingredients. It was slightly sunken in the middle, but it still tasted sweet. The icing was pink and Row swiped some from the top and licked her finger.

The rain had stopped briefly, and we all gathered at the window, hungry to see sky without clouds. A rainbow stretched behind our neighbor's house and into the dark sky, and then it faded, just as quickly as it appeared. And I'd thought then how each moment snaps shut, faster than the shutter of a camera.

Everyone had returned to the table and gathered around Row and sung to her. She beamed and giggled and clapped her hands and I felt so proud of us. I had looked around at each of their faces—Grandfather, Mother, Jacob, and Row—and had thought how much we needed each other. How sticking together was our only hope.

Marjan placed a hand on my shoulder and I forced a smile back at her. I looked around the small circle formed around Pearl and me, searching each of their faces. They were clapping and smiling, Wayne stomping his foot in rhythm with the birthday song, Behir stepping forward to give Pearl a teasing pinch on the arm.

The song finished with a cheer and several hugs, each person stepping forward to wish Pearl a happy birthday and to say how happy they were that she was on *Sedna* with them. She kept nodding and giggling, drunk on their affection. Everyone began sitting down except me, chair legs scraping the wood floors and their chatter dying to a low murmur. In the quiet before Marjan began serving the food I felt that *Sedna* was tilting, but it was just me, clutching the chair in front of me, almost losing my balance.

These people have treated you like family, I thought numbly. How had I not realized it until now?

Because you didn't want to, I thought. Because of what you have to do if they aren't strangers, if you owe each other something.

I looked around at them, thinking of everyone they'd lost. Jessa's baby. Abran's brother. Wayne's wife. Marjan's husband and children.

I thought of losing Grandfather and how until I'd joined *Sedna* it'd been so long since I felt that I could sleep at night, that I wasn't the only one responsible for everything. I remembered the emptiness in the pit of my stomach when I knew I wouldn't listen to another human voice until Pearl learned to speak, those long days of her crying and babbling and silence, madness always lurking right at the edge of my mind.

I thought of Marjan's hands as they made Pearl's cake, those hands that did so much for the good of everyone, the invisible work we all enjoyed. I looked at Pearl, ready to take her first bite of the cake, made by people who cared for her as if she were their own child. Just as how when Grandfather was with me, Pearl wasn't just my child. She was his, too; I didn't have to shoulder the whole burden of raising her.

But that wasn't the worst of it. The worst of it was that Pearl knew we weren't just deceiving them; we were using them for our purposes. Undermining them and everything they'd fought and suffered for. As she smiled at everyone smiling back at her, she knew.

I was strung between my choices, stretched to the breaking point. I had to rescue Row. But I couldn't do it this way. Not anymore. My heart rose higher in my throat until I felt like I was choking.

"I lied to you all," I said, so softly I felt it could have been only a thought.

"What?" Wayne asked.

Daniel's face softened in a way that made me feel like he was taking my hand.

"I lied to you all," I said.

"What?" Wayne said again, this time in angry disbelief.

"Just let her finish," Daniel said sharply.

"I wanted to go to the Valley because my daughter is there—she's being held captive by the Lost Abbots. The Valley is a colony—" The crew exchanged shocked looks and Abran glared at me. He set one palm down on the table like he was going to spring up out of his chair. I felt like I was running out of breath, so I rushed on. "They made it a colony after they used biological warfare to attack and subdue everyone. There was an epidemic—the plague—this was months ago. I don't expect—" Wayne stood up so quickly his chair toppled over backward, and Abran held up a hand to tell him to wait. "I don't expect you to forgive me for deceiving you. I'm telling you because there are antibiotics hidden on an island that we'll pass soon. If we stop for them, we'll have protection in case the epidemic isn't gone yet. And also protection against future biological warfare. I think we should put it to a vote. Vote on whether to stop for the antibiotics."

Abran's face hardened as he watched me, hatred darkening his eyes.

"What makes you think we're still even going to the Valley?" Wayne asked. He looked like he wanted to reach out and snap my neck.

I took my eyes off Abran quickly, and my voice grew quiet once again. "You have nowhere else to go."

Marjan's face held so much sadness, I had to look away from her, and I didn't dare look at Behir or Pearl. The room was so silent, I heard the rhythmic clinking of a broken block out on deck, above the soft lapping of the waves against the boat. The sweet smell of the tomatoes and peaches had soured to an acidic scent and hardened in a glaze over the uneaten fish.

"I could throw you off this ship right now," Abran said, his voice cold and even. "But what would I do with Pearl?"

"You're not doing anything to Pearl," Marjan said sharply.

My heart thudded in my chest and my tongue was too dry in my mouth to speak. I tried to remember the ship rules and various punishments. But they wouldn't maroon Pearl, I kept reminding myself. This both comforted and terrified me. She would be safe and I would be separated from her.

Daniel stood up. "Whatever you do to her—"

"Daniel, stay out of this. It doesn't concern you," I said. If they did anything to me, I needed him to stay and take care of Pearl. I knew I could count on him for that.

"Did you know about this?" Wayne asked Daniel.

"No, he didn't. I kept it a secret," I said.

"Take her down to the hull," Abran said.

Wayne thundered around the table, throwing aside a spare chair, and grabbed me beneath my armpits and yanked me from the table like I was a rag doll.

"Stop!" Daniel roared, charging at Wayne. Abran leapt up and stepped in front of him, slamming his elbow into Daniel's chest and plowing him backward against the table. Pearl jumped up from her chair to dash after me, but Thomas caught her in one arm, her hand stretched out at me, calling my name.

The darkness outside hit me like I'd been dunked underwater, voices tumbling from the cabin like sounds from a sunken ship. As Wayne pulled me toward the hull, I heard Pearl's cries, her high shrieks begging them to stop.

CHAPTER 31

WAYNE TIED MY wrists with rope and shut me in the storage room, locking the door from the outside. I sat on the floor and leaned against bags of flour on the bottom shelf. A calendar had fallen off the wall and lay at my feet. Marjan kept a careful inventory on the calendar. Her neat script filled each day, listing what supplies had been lost and gained that day. Each day had a diagonal line through it until what must be today: October 5.

I reached out and touched the paper, pulling it closer to me. Row's birthday was October 2. Just a few days before. She had just turned thirteen. I'd first bled when I was thirteen, and undoubtedly she would soon, if she hadn't already. Her body was a clock I was racing against. And now who knew if I'd ever reach her in time.

The footsteps above me quieted and stilled. I tried not to think and dozed against the shelving, tossed to the ground when *Sedna* hit a wave. After some time, when I figured it was morning, the door opened and Abran stepped in.

I sat up straight. "Is Pearl okay?" I asked.

"She's fine. Marjan is with her."

He shut the door and leaned against it. I waited for him to speak.

"Did you lie about the resources?" Abran's voice was cold and even. "About the materials for houses, the wells, the safety of the layout, the good soil?"

"It is good land," I said. I sifted through my memories, trying to remember what was true and what had been lies.

"You've put everything I've built at risk. Everything. Were you even planning to help us build a community there? Or just get your daughter and run?" Abran asked.

I looked down. I had mostly only thought of how to rescue Row and keep Pearl safe. I hadn't thought much beyond that. "Whichever was best for Row and Pearl," I told him.

"Is someone else waiting for you there?"

"What do you mean?"

"Your husband. The father of your girls. Did you just tell us about your other daughter to win you some sympathy? A mother rescuing her daughter, not a wife wanting to be reunited with her husband? Seems like something you would do," Abran said, shaking his head at me as he spoke.

"No," I said. "My husband is dead."

Abran paced the small space of the storage room. "We discussed changing our destination, but you were right—we don't have any other good alternatives. Not a lot of land left." Abran flung out his arms and laughed. "They wanted to know how you knew about these antibiotics and I told them you had a friend who told you about it." Abran shot me a sharp look. "I still don't want them knowing about my time with the Lily Black."

"I'm not saying anything," I said.

Abran just glared at me and shook his head. "I've spent years building their trust. You undermined me. *I* decide what they need to know. I could maroon you for this."

I struggled to stand with my hands tied behind my back, but I made it to my feet. I lifted my chin and narrowed my eyes. "You need me."

Abran took a step toward me. "You're easy to replace."

We both knew that wasn't true. Abran reached out and turned a can so the label faced us. We were running low on inventory; half the shelves were bare.

"It was Marjan. Well, and Daniel, but we wouldn't listen to him. Marjan spoke on your behalf. Said she couldn't really blame you. And Behir agreed, and then, we couldn't really do anything without them on board." Abran shook his head. "So we aren't marooning you, but we also aren't letting you join us when we get there. You'll help us take care of the Lost Abbot guards, and then you'll be left alone. To die in the wild or try and sail somewhere else, I don't care. You'll be dead to me. We'll take Pearl and your other daughter—if she's still alive. But not you."

I nodded, but a cold terror gripped me and I tried to hold myself steady. He's angry, I reasoned with myself. This will all settle. At least the worst hasn't happened—at least you and Pearl won't be marooned. This will buy you time.

But the image of being separated from Pearl and Row, being left alone to die, chilled me. I'd have to find a way to become necessary. To prove myself so they wouldn't exile me. "And you'll be fishing for us day and night. I want you out there working the nets and lines until your fingers bleed," Abran said, pointing to the deck.

I nodded again. Abran stepped behind me and cut the ropes that bound my wrists. As the relief receded from my body it left a heaviness, a deep ache settling on my chest. I had thought my fishing would save me, since I could keep the crew from starving. But that wasn't it. It was Marjan and her mercy. Mercy she had because she knew loss as intimately as I did.

"And they voted to stop for the antibiotics. Just like you wanted." Abran's face twisted in a sneer.

I knew his anger was a thin veil over brokenness, disappointment. I took a step closer to him and was surprised when I didn't smell alcohol on his breath.

"I'm sorry. I really am," I told him.

Abran let out a low laugh. "You're not very good at apologizing. Do you even regret it?"

I paused and then shook my head no.

He tossed his hands up behind his neck, elbows pointing out, and turned from me.

"I trusted you more than I trusted most of my crew," he said. "What a fucking moron I was. I thought you could be a big part of this. You and I. Together. I thought we'd be side by side building this place . . ." He tossed out his hand as though to gesture to an imaginary place where we could be, building something different.

I wanted to defend myself, to ask him to imagine my position.

"I know. I'm sorry. I'm sorry about us," I said.

"Us?" Abran tossed his head back and laughed. "You think 'us' matters, compared to this?" The agony in his voice told me that it did. That the betrayal hurt more coming from me.

"You knew it was a colony the whole time and you were leading us blind!" Abran said, his voice barely above a whisper. He stepped closer to me and something in his eyes made me take a step back. He leaned in and roared in my face, "You knew!"

He lunged forward and grabbed me by the throat, but instead of squeezing, his hand went limp at the touch of my skin. His face collapsed to my chest and he began to sob.

I wrapped my arms around him and smoothed his hair.

"I'm losing it, Myra. Losing all of it," he murmured into my chest.

"No, you aren't. We're going to make it there and you're going to set up the community you promised. This doesn't change that. I'll do what I can to help and then I'll leave."

He stepped away from me and wiped his face with his arm. He opened the door and turned back to look at me.

"The hell of it is, I actually liked you," he said.

"I liked you, too," I said, softly, but he shook his head and walked away.

CHAPTER 32

When we neared Ruenlock, the sun was already high in the sky. I thought of a clock's hand ticking around the sky in a circle. The closer we got to the island, the tenser Daniel became, his eyes focusing into slits as he turned the tiller. He kept scanning the horizon as if scared he'd miss something.

The coast was a rock-strewn mountainside littered with pines and evergreen shrubbery. Wayne was stationed in the rigging with the binoculars to keep an eye out for any other ships or signs that raiders were on the island. So far no one had seen anything.

Pearl came and stood beside me.

"You're doing all this for my sister, aren't you?" Pearl asked.

"All what?" I asked.

"Meeting raiders. That's why everyone is so worried."

"We're not meeting with raiders. We're stopping here to pick up supplies."

"This isn't a trading post," Pearl said.

"Pearl. I'm doing it for us. All of us."

She gave me a measured look. She lifted her hand, the one with the cut finger. The skin around the cut was bright red, pus oozing from the wound.

"It hurts," she said.

"Pearl!" I took her finger in my palm and a clammy sweat

broke out on my back. I pushed my hair back from my face and swore.

"Is it bad?" Pearl asked. I could tell she was trying to steady her voice.

I pulled her close and kissed the top of her head. "It will be fine. I promise."

Abran walked up to us. "Let's dock there," he told Daniel, pointing ahead to a small rock outcropping less than half a mile from the coast. "Then Myra and I can paddle to the coast with a canoe."

"Can't dock there," Daniel said, not bothering to look at him.

Abran stiffened. "I said to dock at the outcropping. I don't want to bother with the anchor. We'll need to be able to get out fast if need be." Abran's hands were twitching and he jammed them in his pockets.

"I don't think you want a hole in the hull," Daniel said. "The rest of the mountain is too near the surface."

"I don't think you want to disobey my commands," Abran said.

Daniel smirked at Abran. I stepped between them.

"We can drop the canoe here without anchoring. We'll only be gone . . . maybe two hours?" I looked at Daniel, hoping he'd back me up.

"We'll drift some, but I can circle back," Daniel said.

"You need to be here when we're done," Abran said. Sweat shone on his brow and he gnawed on his lip.

"He'll be here," I said.

Wayne and Thomas helped us drop the canoe into the water and Abran and I climbed down the ladder into it. As we paddled to the shore I kept trying to look between the trees, to see signs of people or a camp. There were still no boats in sight, but that didn't mean they weren't anchored just beyond my view, around a bend or in a cove.

We pulled the canoe ashore and hid it among the pines. Abran read aloud from a small notebook.

"There's a hollow in the side of the mountain, up beyond a cluster of spruce. There's a small stream that flows on the right-hand side. Follow the stream up the mountain to the hollow."

The stream was easy to find, pouring into the ocean between several pines, making a tiny waterfall. We began our ascent and very quickly we were out of breath, pausing often to drink from our canisters.

Tiny purple flowers bloomed alongside the stream, reminding me of wildflowers alongside the road in Nebraska. How odd, to remember driving in a car, watching things fly past. Telephone poles, flowers in ditches, mailboxes. Half-invisible things until you missed them.

We had climbed about a half mile and still had not seen an outcropping of spruce.

"Are you sure about the spruce?" I asked. "Maybe some other tree?"

Abran shook his head. "I took careful notes on all the hiding spots."

"You go that way, I'll look this way. Only a few paces. We can't lose each other," I said.

We separated. There were only pines as far as I could see, no spruces in sight. I kept looking down at my feet, stepping carefully between rocks to avoid tripping and tumbling down the mountainside. I had a heaviness in the pit of my stomach, a premonition that we wouldn't find what we were looking for.

I stumbled over a rock and looked down. A handmade cigarette stub lay next to the rock. I picked it up. It smelled more like soot than tobacco. The dirt close to the rock held several perfect shoe prints, leading away from where I stood. The cigarette and the prints were too unspoiled to be old. Someone else was on this island.

I glanced over my shoulder, peering through the trees. I saw Abran walking toward me, his hand out, beckoning me to follow him.

"I found it," he said.

"Sshh, idiot," I whispered, quickly clambering over the rocks toward him.

"I should have written that it was a little to the left of the stream, not directly visible from the stream," he said. He led me past a cluster of spruce trees to the front of an opening in the mountain face. Moisture clung to its walls like beaded sweat and the depths of the cave stretched back into darkness.

"I found this," I said, holding the cigarette stub out in my palm. "And footprints."

"Shit." Abran dropped his head and swore again. "We shouldn't have come!"

"We don't know who it belongs to. Calm down. Let's just keep quiet, get what we need, and get out."

"I knew we shouldn't have come!"

"We're already here. I'm not leaving without checking. Do you have the torch?"

Abran looked around, his shoulders hunched to his ears.

"Abran!" I hissed.

"What? Yeah, yeah." Abran unzipped his bag and pulled out a stick with a gasoline-soaked rag at the end. We lit it and Abran glanced over his shoulder one last time before we entered the cave.

I followed him, stepping onto a ridge that lined the rock wall of the cave. A pool of water lay in the middle of the cave and I heard a trickle farther back, where the light from our torch could not reach.

Abran was several strides ahead of me. "We have to be quick," he said.

The ridge along the cave wall was slick and littered with small pebbles and I almost slipped, catching myself against the wall, my hands flying across its smooth surface, looking for something to grasp and steady myself. The light jumped in shadows around Abran and he stopped at the back edge of the pool. I could only make out his silhouette, and I crept closer toward him. Behind the pool, bats screeched and collided against one another in a flurry of wings. They dove from the rock ceiling the way birds dive to catch fish, only I couldn't see what they were catching in the low light.

Abran crouched at the water's edge, dipping his hands just below the surface. He knelt and wedged the torch between two rocks. Then he slid his feet in and slipped under the water.

The water was too dark to see him. I waited a moment. There was a rustle outside the hollow, but when I glanced out the opening I was blinded by the sun and couldn't see anything. The cave smelled like a mouthful of dirt, and I had the sudden urge to gag.

Abran surfaced and I jumped. The water made dark ripples around him.

"I think it's on a rock ledge, under some mud and plants. Can you hand me the rope?" he asked.

I took the rope from my shoulder, uncoiled it, and handed one end to him. He dove underwater again with it. When he came back up, he lifted himself from the pool and crouched dripping wet beside me.

We both pulled on the rope, straining against the weight, the rope burning my hands. Finally, the edge of a rust-covered metal box broke the surface of the water. Abran leaned forward, grabbed a metal handle, and pulled it toward us. It thudded against the rock ledge and Abran knelt before it, working on the rust-covered hinges.

"Is it the one you remember?" I asked. A bat screeched behind us and I ducked, hands over my head.

"I think so," he said. "I'm not sure. There's no lock. I thought we locked them."

One of the hinges was too rusty to open, so Abran hit it with a rock until it broke. The sound of the rock against the metal echoed in the cave, growing quieter and quieter like a ripple disappearing until out of sight.

Abran lifted the lid and we peered inside. The contents were submerged in water and Abran pulled out clear plastic bags holding bottles. He held them up to the dim light of the torch.

"Penicillin, tetracycline, amoxicillin," he read, setting the bags on the rocks. He reached in and pulled out more plastic bags, these holding rounds of ammunition.

"I thought you said this hiding spot was only for medicine," I said, frowning.

Abran paused. "It was." He was very still, like he was listening for something. The wind rustled the branches of trees just outside the cave.

"There aren't locks on the trunk because they've refilled it. Refilled it and haven't left the island," he said.

I took my knapsack from my shoulder and started shoveling the plastic bags into it.

"They could be waiting . . ." Abran said, his eyes dilated even though he was staring into the bright opening at the end of the cave. "Could be a trap."

"Fill your bag," I said, smacking his shoulder. I kept wiping my palms on my pant legs. Between the water on the cave walls, water in the trunk, and sweat now dripping from my brow, I couldn't get dry. I thought of the others on the boat. Had Daniel spotted anything while they waited? I almost hoped that if they did, they would sail away without us.

We filled our bags and extinguished our torch, darkness falling over us like a blanket. We crept along the rock ledge, our hands feeling along the wall for balance. Abran slipped on a wet rock and fell against the wall. I grabbed him by the arm and pulled him up.

"Thanks," he muttered, his face only inches from me. I smelled alcohol on his breath.

"Do you have whiskey in your canister?" I asked.

"A tiny bit. Helps me focus."

I gripped his arm so tightly that he whimpered and tried to pry my fingers loose.

"I swear to God, Abran, get your shit together," I whispered.

I let go of him and he stumbled forward. He grasped the edge of the rock wall and peered around the corner. "Looks clear," he whispered. "Let's try to make it to the stream."

I nodded and we bolted from the cave, trying not to stumble on the rocks, dodging trees and fallen branches. When we reached the stream, Abran held out his arm to halt me. We both crouched behind ferns and bushes growing along the stream. We crept down the mountainside, along the stream, glancing between the trees as we went, listening for anything unusual. Seabirds in the trees made a raucous noise, their thin voices like the edge of a blade. The sun was so bright I kept squinting, the muscles in my face sore and stiff.

Abran's hand shot out in front of me. He placed a finger to his lips and then pointed. Between two pines, a thin man in a long black coat smoked a cigarette. He had a tattoo of a rabbit on his neck. He was humming a tune we could barely hear over the birds' constant screeching.

CHAPTER 33

ABRAN AND I dropped to our stomachs, our arms tucked under our chests, our chins resting in the dirt, eyes locked on the man. Grass scratched my arms and rocks dug into my legs and chest. Abran breathed heavily next to me, his breath coming out loud and ragged. I elbowed him and put my finger to my lips. He dropped his head to the ground, his shoulders shaking and the dirt muffling his breath.

The man gazed at the trees in the direction of our ship. Blood pounded in my ears. Could he see our ship below, or were the trees obscuring it?

The man finished his cigarette, tossed it on the rocks, and meandered our way. The birds fell silent and we could hear the tune the man still hummed, some ballad that sounded Irish and ancient. All his hair was shaved off except for a long braid from just above the nape of his neck. The rabbit tattoo on his neck was in profile, and the single red eye of the rabbit seemed to stare straight at me.

The trees cast long shadows in the grass before us. I wondered how long we'd been gone and if Daniel had had any trouble holding the ship's position. The man approached the stream, squatted, and washed his hands, then stood and dried them on his long coat. We were tucked in the bushes on the opposite side of the stream. I could feel Abran go even tenser beside me, feel how he was ready to burst like a man held underwater.

The man turned from where we were lying and began strolling along the stream. Abran and I both let out the breath we'd been holding. The man walked a few paces away from the stream, his back now to us. Abran lifted his head, turned to me, and nodded.

We crept to our feet, crouching behind the bushes, keeping an eye on the man. A voice split the silence and Abran and I both jumped. I couldn't hear what the other person shouted, but I thought I heard the word *ship*.

"How far out?" the man called back.

"We got to go," Abran muttered, sweat glistening on his face, his hands shaking.

"Not now," I hissed, holding his forearm to keep him from bolting.

Abran ripped his arm from my grip and rushed headlong down the stream. I swore and darted after him, stumbling over rocks, arms up to block being whipped by low branches. I hit a loose patch of stones and skidded, catching myself against a tree trunk.

A bullet splintered the trunk next to my head. I didn't turn to look; I broke into a run. Voices thundered behind me, yelling and cursing. Another gunshot rang out. Abran ran several paces ahead of me, branches thrashing against him as he broke through the underbrush. I smelled blood but I didn't know where it came from. I went dizzy and the landscape before me seemed to blur.

Below us I could see the cluster of pines where we'd hidden the canoe. Abran tripped and fell on the escarpment above the pines. He tumbled down, thudding against the rock with each roll until he disappeared into the tops of the trees, the needles shaking from the collision.

I dropped to my side and slid down the escarpment, snapping branches from the pines as I fell, tumbling beside Abran next to the canoe. Abran tried to climb to his feet but was moving so slowly, I grabbed his arm and yanked him up. He moaned, and when I took my hand away it was covered in blood.

The footsteps of our pursuers grew louder, the breaking of branches and flying rocks creating a din above and behind us. We pulled the canoe toward the water and splashed in and threw ourselves inside as a rain of bullets peppered the water around us. Gunshots reverberated like an echo. They felt both far away and like they were coming from within me, as if I'd already been splintered and flung across the water.

I tossed an oar to Abran and we paddled in a frenzy, our bodies leaning forward, sweat in our eyes. A bullet rocked our boat, and I turned to see a hole and the water pouring through it. The moment widened and I felt that I was falling into it, my attention breaking and scattering.

Sedna was only twenty feet away and Daniel had already lowered the ladder. Wayne was on deck, firing a rifle. We ran the canoe straight into the side of the ship. It rocked and almost capsized, the salt water stinging my eyes. Abran leapt from the canoe and grabbed the ladder, swinging on it before his legs, flailing in the air, found a rung and began to climb.

The canoe was already drifting from the ship and I paddled

closer again, dropping the oar as I leapt from the canoe toward the ladder. My fingers grazed the rope, but it slipped from my hands and I fell into the water. I clawed the side of the ship, small waves rolling into me. A spray of bullets littered the hull and I ducked underwater.

When I resurfaced I swam for the ladder and reached it. The crew was yelling orders at each other and I felt the ship twitch as sails filled with wind. The ship heaved and turned as I climbed the ladder, and I slammed against the hull.

I clung to the ladder and the water beneath me receded. Someone was pulling the ladder up. When I collapsed over the side of the gunwale my hands were raw and one was bleeding. I stared at it in confusion.

Thomas was at the tiller, yanking it as far to the right as it would go. Behir dropped down from the rigging, a spare rope coiled around his shoulder. Daniel was at the mainmast, securing a block. Everyone was shouting to each other, but I couldn't make sense of it.

The hatch to the hull lifted and Pearl's face appeared. I sent her a look that said *stay down,* and she dropped the hatch and disappeared. I dropped my head back against the gunwale, the blood from my hand staining the wood, settling into the weathered grain.

We did it, I thought. We got it. I tried to steady my breathing but it still came out in spasms.

There was no more gunfire, and when I turned and lifted myself to my feet, I saw that the island was already small in the distance. Daniel had caught a western wind and it was driving us east quickly.

Marjan knelt beside Abran and helped him take his shirt off. He had a cut on the outside of his biceps, but no bullet wound. He must have been cut by a sharp branch. Marjan wrapped a cloth around his arm and picked up his backpack. I handed her mine.

The hatch lifted again and I nodded that Pearl could come out. She ran toward me and I squatted and enveloped her in a hug. She tucked her head into my neck as she had when she was much smaller.

"I got it, Pearl," I whispered into her hair. "Your finger will feel better soon."

I could feel her smiling against my skin and she nuzzled closer.

"Oh, no," Marjan murmured. She had emptied one of the bottles into her palm and was looking at it.

"What?" I stood up.

Marjan held her hand toward me.

The bottles didn't hold pills. They held seeds.

CHAPTER 34

I STARED AT the seeds dumbfounded.

Antibiotics. It had the names of antibiotics on the bottles, my mind kept repeating, as if repeating it would make it true.

Someone slammed into me and I sprawled, knocked out of breath, my head ringing from hitting the deck. Abran grabbed me by my shirt and dragged me a few steps. He knelt and grabbed me beneath my arms and rammed me against the cabin wall. Before I could catch my breath, he shoved his forearm into my neck.

I clawed at his arm, the space between my thoughts growing wider as I gasped for air.

"I told you I didn't want this. This is all on you," he said, his face inches from me, his voice hoarse and unrecognizable. His eyes were bloodshot and his face red. My toes brushed the deck in desperate swipes.

Daniel pulled Abran back and flung him to the deck. He pulled a pistol from his holster and cocked it at Abran.

Marjan stepped between them, her hands up.

"Put it away," she said quietly.

Pearl ran to my side and I massaged my throat, trying to bring back my voice.

"What the hell happened out there?" Wayne asked. "Why were there raiders?"

Daniel glanced at me, but I kept my eyes on Abran. I raised

my eyebrows at him and gave him a warning look that asked him, *Do you want me to tell?*

Abran gave an almost imperceptible shake of his head.

"Coincidence," I said. "They're everywhere."

Wayne glared at me. I saw now that my bag was in his hand, the zipper half open. He must have rummaged through to see what we got.

"I don't want to hear it from you," he said. He looked at Abran, who slowly climbed to his feet.

"Turns out raiders found the hiding spot before we did and removed the medicine and used it to hide other stuff," Abran said.

"Well, fuck," Wayne said. "I hope these couple rounds of ammo and little garden seeds are worth it. They'll be on our tail, now."

"Last I remember, this wasn't my choice. It was all of yours," Abran said.

"They will have trouble tracking us," Daniel said.

"You think they can't communicate with other ports?" Wayne asked. "We stole from them. It was the Lily Black, wasn't it?"

Daniel glanced at me and I could tell he was piecing together that Abran had been with the Lily Black. We all were quiet and then Abran nodded. Wayne kicked the side of the cabin and swore.

Wayne was right. Open sea, each port, each island, could be a place where more of their crew was hiding. And they'd be on the watch for us. Not so much to get back what we stole as to assert themselves, to remind us and everyone else that they

were people to be reckoned with. A new nation that could protect itself.

"When we stop at Broken Tree we'll slip in, trade, and slip
out," Abran said. "No telling anyone that we're going to the
Valley, so they can't track us. Once we're on the open sea we'll
be in the clear."

Wayne waved his hand in a dismissive gesture and dropped
the bag. "Don't think for a second it will be that easy," he said.

I knelt beside Pearl and took her finger in my palm. It was
bright red and still oozing pus. I felt her forehead. She was hot
with fever.

I leaned back on my heels and squeezed my eyes shut. The
Lily Black following us and attacking us felt inconsequential.
Like talking about a chess move. It seemed so silly, all this arguing, squaring our shoulders, stomping our feet like horses
before a race.

Fear held steady in Pearl's eyes like a lily floating on water.
We both knew the finger would have to go.

I'D RATHER HAVE cut off my own hand than take away any part
of her. But the fever continued to rage and I knew if we didn't
act quick, the infection would spread and she'd lose more than
a finger.

I sharpened my knife on the whetstone in the cabin. Dim
light filtered through the dirty window. Daniel lit the lantern
overhead so we could see better. Pearl sat in the corner of the
cabin, on a stool, her hair glowing red in the low light.

Abran only had limited surgical training from his parents, but he said he remembered enough to do it. To do it better than the rest of us, at least. As soon as we decided he'd do the amputation, I made him walk me through the procedure. A clean cut near the knuckle. Pressure and a bandage to stem blood loss. New tissue called proud flesh would form a scab over the wound naturally and offer a barrier against infection.

When Abran came into the cabin he wouldn't look at me, but busied himself with setting out clean cloths and the alcohol to sanitize the blade and the wound.

I stepped forward to hand him the blade and smelled alcohol on him. I looked down at the bottle of alcohol, unopened. Abran saw my face and stepped away from me, slightly swaying on his feet.

Drunk. Again. Drunk now, when I needed him to be sober. My mind unfurled in a white spiral of rage and I steadied myself against the table. One hand on wood, grounding myself. Abran dropped his eyes to the ground and muttered something I couldn't hear. My hand shot out and I jabbed him in the chest.

"Leave," I whispered.

"Myra, I said I'll do it," he said.

"Leave now. I don't want you to fuck it up," I said.

Abran's face reddened and he ducked out of the cabin. Daniel and I helped Pearl lay down on the table. She was so hot she felt like a glowing ember. I wiped sweat from her brow and pushed her wet hair back from her face. Daniel set a codeine pill on Pearl's tongue. We only had a few left, but Marjan insisted that Pearl should take them during and after the operation. Daniel put the bottle of alcohol to Pearl's lips and she took a few gulps, grimacing and sputtering, liquid dripping from her chin.

"How long will it hurt?" Pearl asked.

"For a while," I said, dabbing her face.

"Are you sure I can't keep it?" she asked.

"Honey, at this point, it's only getting worse. This will save you."

Her eyes darted around the room like she was searching for a way out of this and then she shut them, squeezing them tight. Daniel held her other hand and whispered something in her ear.

I unwound myself like the spool of a kite, the better part of me drifting away. I floated above, a drifting, incapable thing. Something untouchable, fluttering in the wind with nowhere to go, nothing to do.

Down below I cut clean and she cried out and Daniel pressed the bandage to the stump and she shot up into my arms and I held her as she sobbed, the both of us shaking, until the light died and we were only voices in the dark, warm skin, eyelash on cheek, lips in hair, a tangle of limbs, a single shadow in the gathering darkness.

CHAPTER 35

AFTER WE GOT Pearl bandaged and asleep in her bunk I went into the kitchen to help Marjan butcher the carp I'd caught earlier.

"You don't need to do this now," Marjan said softly.

"Can you hand me the bucket?" I asked. I couldn't stop and think right now. But the more I tried not to think of Pearl, the more she resurfaced in my mind. I'd failed her. I'd failed her. I bit my lip so hard I tasted blood.

Marjan handed me the bucket and I tossed a handful of guts in it. I slid the knife between the scales and the meat, jiggling the fillets loose. I set the fillets on the counter and noticed Marjan watching me.

"Did you know the raiders would be there?" she asked. "On the island?" When I didn't respond right away she went on. "The friend who told you about the antibiotics. Was it the same one who told you about the Valley?"

"Yes. She sailed there a while back. Left resources along the way."

Sound of blade on wood, a dull scrape to move the head aside.

I tossed the head in the pile and dipped my knife in the bucket of water, scraping it against the edge to clean it. "And no, of course, I didn't know the raiders would be there."

"I wasn't trying to suggest . . ."

"Look—I'm not going to apologize," I said. "If the antibiotics were there, it could have helped her. Could have helped us all in the Valley."

Marjan laid her knife down, wiped her hands on her apron. "I just wondered whether if you had known they were there, would you still have gone?"

She was asking how much I'd risk. I turned and looked at her, my eyes burning with unfallen tears.

"I'd have gone."

A WEEK PASSED and Pearl's incision healed as well as we could hope. Each morning and evening I cleaned the wound with honey soap Marjan had made and changed the bandages, wrapping the gauze carefully and knotting it, keeping my eyes on her face; trying to discern how she was adjusting.

One day after I'd bandaged Pearl's hand, I went to the cabin to gather hooks and bait for a day of fishing. I found Daniel hunched over his papers and navigational instruments, writing.

"Hey," I said.

Daniel jumped, flipped over the page he'd been writing on, and tucked it under a map.

"Hey," he said, not turning around, sitting there, looking at the map.

"Planning new routes?" I asked.

"No, just wanted to map out a few backup routes. Case of storms."

I stepped around the table so he had to face me. "Can I see?"

"I'm not finished."

Daniel tapped his foot on the floor and rapped his pencil

against the table. Normally, he was as composed as a deer: quiet, alert, poised. Ever since Pearl's amputation Daniel had grown quieter and more removed. Sometimes during evening meals he'd watch her with this intense yet gentle expression, a look that reminded me of how I felt about her.

"Is this about the Lily Black following us? Even if they try, you think it will be that easy?"

"The world's a small place now."

I sat down. Seeing Daniel so agitated made me feel uneasy.

"What is it?" I asked.

"Hm? Nothing. The raider you saw on the island—did he have any other tattoos? Anything other than the rabbit on his neck?"

I shook my head. "Not that I saw, but he had a long coat on, so more could have been covered."

Daniel didn't react, and the absence of a reaction seemed odd. He looked right through me like I wasn't there. After he was quiet a moment, he said, "You ever worried you love your older daughter more because she isn't here?"

My spine tensed. "I love her because she's my child. Love her more than what?"

"Sometimes I just wonder if it's really about you. What you can do. What if she's fine?"

"How could she be fine? The Valley is a colony. Jacob undoubtedly abandoned her, as he did me."

"I thought you said he was dead."

"Whatever. Point is, the raider said she didn't have a father. No one is helping her. She'll be boarding a breeding ship any day now."

"I can't help but wonder if your responsibility to Pearl is greater. Because she's here," Daniel said.

My bones felt loose in my joints. I opened my mouth to speak but had no words.

I stood up and slammed my chair against the table. "You know nothing about it."

He looked up at me. "That's how it is with me. I love the people who aren't here."

"Well, that's you. You know—you don't know the half of it."

I knew it was sometimes easier to love ghosts than the people who were around you. Ghosts could be perfect, frozen beyond time, beyond reality, the crystal form they'd never been before, the person you needed them to be. Sometimes I wanted only the good moments to surface in my memory. My father sitting next to me while I played cards and he did a crossword puzzle in an old newspaper. Running toward my father through the backyard, into his arms, to be tossed up into the sky. The smell of autumn when he brought in firewood, and how I'd kneel beside him to stack the wood in the fireplace and feel warmer even before the fire was lit.

In these memories I'd pushed away the girl on the stoop, the girl who knew some things are absolute and that she couldn't have been enough. I sometimes needed to pretend for a while that she was someone else and that my story had ended differently.

Daniel stood up and walked closer to me. "I worry about the weight of all this on you . . . if something more happened to Pearl—"

"Whether or not Row's fine in the colony isn't all that matters,"

I interrupted. "I don't trust that Jacob told her the truth. That he kidnapped her. What if she thinks I abandoned her? What if she doesn't remember how I tried to reach her? She won't be fine if she thinks I just let her go."

Daniel reached out to touch my arm but I hit his hand away. "I'm sure that's not what she thinks," he said softly.

"You know what happens to kids who are abandoned? Who don't believe they're worth anyone staying around? It changes how you see yourself. Everyone else is walking around fine and it's like you have a fucking hole in your chest and the whole world can reach in and touch anything in you. You have no armor. You never feel safe. I'm not just saving her from the Lost Abbots, I'm saving her from that. She . . . she has to *know* that I'm here for her."

My throat started to close up. I took a step away from Daniel and rubbed my hands over my face. I thought of my father hung like a fish from a line, his feet moving ever so slightly in the breeze that came in the shed. I thought of telling Daniel about what had happened and how it had opened up a need in me I'd never satisfy. I looked up at him and he looked back at me like he pitied me, like he guessed there was something wrong with me. I wanted to wipe that look off his face.

"Myra, I'm sorry, I didn't mean . . ."

I pointed in his face. "Don't *ever* assume you know me."

Daniel nodded. Seagulls' cries grew louder outside, the frenzied caws of diving for fish and fighting the wind. I was beginning to accept I'd always feel like this—caught between my daughters, caught between my past and future, wrestling toward an uncertain hope. Like being caught between the sea and sky, always hunting the horizon.

DANIEL RETURNED TO his maps and I rummaged through the shelves for new line. The cabin was so quiet, we both jumped when Pearl and Behir opened the cabin door and strolled inside. Behir disappeared into the kitchen and Pearl plopped down beside Daniel.

"I'm hungry," she said. She had her favorite snake wrapped around her wrist. His head hovered above her missing finger, his black tongue undulating in a wave.

I eyed him cautiously. Pearl had told me he wasn't venomous, but I still hated seeing him outside of his jar.

"Lunch isn't for another hour," I told her.

Behir pulled the kitchen curtain aside and set a loaf of bread in front of Pearl. We were beginning food rations and I knew Behir would have to answer to his mother later.

"Are you only giving this to me because I lost a finger?" she asked. Then she grinned and said, "It wasn't my favorite finger anyway."

I could tell Behir saw right through her bravado. That façade of disregard when you're crumbling inside. He knelt beside her and said, "Who's this guy?"

"Charlie stays with me now," Pearl said. She smirked. "He's my right hand." She erupted into a fit of giggles, her hand without Charlie covering her face, but when she removed it, her face was red and wet with tears.

"Let me show you something," Behir said, going to the shelves to pick up the binoculars.

He took her left hand and led her out onto the deck. Daniel and I followed.

"I saw them just before we came into the cabin," Behir said, leading her to the bow of the ship.

About a mile away the water broke and an orca dove up into the air and disappeared again. Then another. Their black backs gleaming in the sun. Ripples lost in the waves that tumbled over them. Their calls rising up in song, each voice folding over the other, a chant in a foreign tongue.

"Early this morning they were really close to us," Behir said. "And I got a close look. See that big one there? She's the leader."

Behir handed Pearl the binoculars and she peered through them.

"She has a deep scar up her belly. Something big must have got her. But all the rest follow her. She's the mother ship. She's the strongest now."

Pearl smiled at Behir.

Daniel stood so close his arm brushed mine. I watched Pearl watch the whales and felt an unfolding inside me. A stirring in my chest. Standing there, watching something greater than us, reminded me of taking Row to watch the cranes. How much we needed to see a beautiful creature that was not us, that had little to do with us.

Unbidden, a vision came to me of Pearl, Row, and me living in a small stone cottage on a cliff overlooking the sea. White curtains fluttering in the sea breeze. A small woodpile stacked against the house. A stone chimney releasing a curl of smoke.

Pearl's and Row's voices high-spirited and bright, a new sound as they spoke over one another and their voices mixed.

I hadn't allowed myself to have a dream in so long it felt foreign, uncomfortable, like a muscle gone weak. I pressed deeper into it, saw us on a bed reading a book, a quilt heavy and warm over our legs. The smell of bread cooling on a counter.

The whales came up out of the water and crashed back again, sending up a spray of white water. Rising again and again. Their bodies drawing a healing arc over and over, a movement they had to repeat to go on breathing.

CHAPTER 36

BEFORE WE DOCKED at Broken Tree, everyone discussed our last port stop during breakfast. What we needed to trade for, which merchants would give the best deals, and what we'd do if we ran into trouble.

"We can't mention to anyone that we're heading to the Valley. Much less chance of the Lily Black ever finding us once we're out in the Atlantic," I reminded everyone.

I had stayed up all night wondering if we could skip our last trade at Broken Tree. I had crept into the storage room and stared at our bare shelves and the crates of smoked and salted fish I'd caught. Our best bet was trading quickly and slipping out in case the Lily Black were there.

"And everyone stay close to the harbor, in the first few shops or saloons. We need to be able to collect everyone quick if we need to get out. We're not going to be able to stay the night," Abran said.

A murmur of groans went around the table.

"It will be our last day on land," Behir said. "Shouldn't we rest up before starting the Atlantic crossing? The Lily Black probably isn't even there."

"No," Abran said. "We'll set sail directly after our trade."

We docked our ship and carried the crates into the village. I hadn't caught half as much fish as I'd hoped. These past few weeks none of my previous techniques had worked. It was like

I'd lost the ability to read the water, to do the right thing in the right place.

Even Abran looked at the half-full crates disapprovingly when we loaded them onto the dock. I wished we could have filled less crates to hide how little I caught, but we always took the same crates into ports so we'd be able to haul our traded goods back to the ship.

Broken Tree was shabby compared to Wharton, so many buildings made of scrap metal and mismatched wood planks tied or nailed together. The streets stank of trash and manure. They were all dirt, no stone or laid planks, with potholes that deepened and connected into large fissures.

"Don't twist your ankle," I told Pearl, pointing out the crevasses.

She readjusted the bag slung over her shoulder gingerly, with her maimed hand. I had told her she couldn't bring Charlie into the village.

"Don't tell me how to walk," she snapped.

We were so low on food that last night we'd eaten two of her snakes. She'd refused to eat that night and had sat at the table, chin tucked into her neck, kicking the table with one foot. She had asked to be excused and I said no, she'd wait out the meal. That night she had lain curled in a ball at the foot of the bed, and I suspected it was about more than her snakes, about never having control, everything moving out from underneath you.

The eastern side of the village was covered in trees, but the western side was full of crop fields. Barley, wheat, potatoes, cabbage. Workers knelt between the rows, straw hats shading their faces, backs bent under the noonday sun. They looked like peasants from a seventeenth-century Dutch painting. It caught my breath and I briefly felt suspended in time, beyond the loop of years.

The salt breeze coming off the sea roughened every edge; the stone, metal, and wood of the buildings were cracked and patched with mud and clay. Near the shoreline, built into the crevasse in the mountain face, stood an old Catholic church with a sign that said STORE on the front. It was clear the church had been built before the water came. It wasn't made from scavenged materials; it wasn't a patchwork of broken and abandoned materials. It was made of cream bricks, all mortared with clean lines. It was eerie, the way the church stood, silhouetted against the bright sky, one of the only buildings from before the flood that I'd seen in years. It looked like it had been dropped down from the sky.

"It's like someone knew," Jessa said, her voice awestruck as she gazed at the church. The perfect corners, the thick walls. A small circular window right under where the roof came to a point in the middle. An actual door with hinges in the front. Like nothing that existed anymore.

"Knew we'd need a store, I guess," Marjan said.

Marjan still prayed with the sun every morning and evening. When I asked her about it she said it was a habit she was scared of breaking. "I have faith," she had said. "But only for every minute out of a hundred. So I act on that one moment even when I'm not in it."

We carried the fish to the trading post and traded for the last essentials we'd need for the Atlantic crossing. Rope, tackle and block, scrap metal and wood for repairs around the ship, potatoes and cabbage and flour, fabric and a couple of buckets of salt.

We didn't have enough fish to trade for the food we wanted: the sausage, eggs, fruit, or poultry. I'd need to catch more fish on the voyage than I had been if we were to make it without starving.

When we finished trading, most of the crew wandered along the stalls set up on the roads, browsing the goods with their two coins or venturing beyond the main road to one of the saloons that overlooked the ocean.

"Come with us to the church?" I asked Abran.

"No," Abran said, glancing away, rubbing his hands together in an anxious gesture. "I'll be around."

I watched him walk away, a dull anger thrumming in me. Had he hidden some of the fish to trade for alcohol? How much alcohol did he have stashed in his room?

I was tempted to follow him but walked with Daniel and Pearl to the church instead. A black stone on the front door held an engraved inscription. It told the story of a rich man who lived at the foot of this mountain. He'd had a dream that God wanted him to build a church at the top of the mountain for future peoples. So he'd had it done. The date read two decades before the floods.

I'd heard other strange reports of similar premonitions people had had before the water came. Premonitions or dreams or visions. But no one I knew of had acted on it.

Tables and stalls were set up inside the church, divided by the main aisle, which led straight to the altar and the crucifix.

The church was a long rectangle and sunlight poured through long thin windows on either side, giving the air a luminescent glow. Daniel took Pearl to look at a stall filled with wool gloves and hats.

I smelled charcoal and gasoline and turned around to see a booth with combustion equipment: lighters, ferrocerium rods, bow drill fire kits, and little bags of charcoal and bottles of gasoline. They were charging the equivalent of a week's worth of food for a small bottle of gasoline. I shook my head and stepped away, and a plaque with a carving of Christ's face caught my eye. It was a station of the cross, the style of the carving dramatic, overwrought, baroque. The agony was exquisite on Christ's face, the expression both transcendent and the pain of an animal.

"We only dropped one body." The woman's voice came from behind me, the accent thick, perhaps western European, but I couldn't quite place it.

The hair on the back of my neck stood up and I kept looking at Christ's face, straining to hear the other person this voice addressed.

"Well, it's easier up north than in the Caribbean. Bodies decompose too fast in that heat," a man said in a low growl. The voice was somehow familiar, but I didn't dare turn around to look.

"Yah. Ammo is so short, we're building bombs now. Much more effective. You set them out, kids walk on them, people start panicking, all over. You take 'em out, go in, and get what you need. We got salvaged materials for a new ship being collected by the dock."

"Keep your voice down."

"We need to take another colony and then focus on building a bigger fleet. Governor is already paying our tax. There are several wealthy colonies of other nations to the east. I have my scouts there now," the woman said.

"Good. I got a message from Ruenlock last week. A ship raided our supplies there. Name was *Sedna*. Need to pass on the info to other bases in case they stop at any ports," the man said.

"Which nation?"

"Didn't seem to be with a nation. Maybe an independent ship. Either way, need to shut them down fast. News can't spread we've been robbed without striking back. But that's not all. One of the men on Ruenlock said he spotted an old crew member who stole from one of our ships years ago. Goes by Abran, rumors are he might be the captain of *Sedna*. Even more reason to keep our eyes out."

I heard footsteps, soft on the stone floor, and the voices drifted away. Terror thrummed in my throat. I laid my palm against the cool stone and leaned my forehead against the back of my hand, trying to steady my breathing. We needed to get everyone out of Broken Tree. I looked around for Daniel and Pearl, praying they were near the door and we could slip out quietly. I turned in a circle and saw them several stalls down the main aisle, looking at small wooden figurines.

The man and woman who'd been talking had their backs turned to me and were walking away, toward a booth piled with oars made out of salvaged plastic. When the woman turned her head I saw she had a rabbit tattoo on her neck. I quickly crept toward Pearl and Daniel, slipping past a merchant and customer haggling over prices.

"Mom, look. This is so pretty—" Pearl started when she saw me.

"No, we're not buying it. Daniel," I said, tugging on his sleeve and pulling him a step away from Pearl.

I jerked my head in the direction of the couple, who were still turned away from us. "They're Lily Black."

He was silent, his jaw twitching like he was grinding his teeth.

"You *never* listen to me," Pearl said, stepping between Daniel and me.

"Pearl, not now. We need to alert the others as quietly as possible and get out," I whispered.

Daniel nodded and we walked down the main aisle, past the stalls, toward the front door. A toothless old woman pushing a cart filled with gauzy fabric blocked our way, murmuring apologies, and two children holding hands stepped gingerly in front of us, tiptoeing along, as if they weren't sure the floor would hold.

A pregnant woman with burnt skin and hair cut close to her scalp reached out and grasped my arm, asking me to buy her wares. I shook her off and lurched forward, stumbling into Daniel, who had abruptly stopped.

Daniel unsheathed a knife from his belt. He gripped it down by his thigh, keeping it hidden but ready.

I followed his gaze and jumped when I saw the couple now standing in the main aisle, walking slowly in our direction as they browsed the stalls and chatted in low voices. The woman was so thin the upper bones of her rib cage protruded from her chest, and she kept licking her huge front teeth like a rodent. I could only see the profile of the man's face—his high cheek-

bones, small nose, and sharp jaw. He had the same rabbit tattoo on his neck, the red eye seemingly omniscient, taking in
everything in all directions. One black earring glinted from his
ear. The way the man stood, shoulders back, spine straight, feet
placed wide, gave the impression of a man who wanted to take
up other people's space.

I held out my arm to keep Pearl behind me, but she clawed
at my hand and stepped beside me. When she saw them, she
scooted back behind me.

I stood frozen. They blocked our exit. Daniel's shoulders
were hunched toward his ears, his body angled sideways, poised
for attack. His knuckles whitened around the knife handle.

The man turned his face toward the altar and I saw him
clearly for the first time. He looked like Daniel would when he
was older.

CHAPTER 37

AMID THE ROPE and cloth and figurines and wool hats, the swirl
of voices continued, but it all slowed and narrowed. My blood
coursed more warmly in my veins; it sped its inward rush.

I placed my hand on Daniel's arm, tense as tightly coiled
rope under my palm. This jolted him and he glanced at me, then
Pearl. His eyes narrowed and dilated and I could almost see the
decision in his gaze, the momentary blankness in his face as he
held two possibilities in his mind.

"C'mon," he said, grabbing me by the arm and propelling me
backward, away from the main aisle, past booths, past people
hunched over tables. The commotion of people browsing and
pushing past each other swallowed us up. We lurched out of
the booths, facing a long wall. Daniel's head whipped back and
forth, searching for an exit. Up toward the darkened front of the
church, to the side of the altar, a thin strip of sunlight glowed.

I clutched Pearl's hand tightly and we made for that light,
scurrying as quietly as possible. We stumbled into the sunlight,
squinting and still trying to quiet our breathing.

Raiders had different punishments for stealing, and I tried to
remember what was most common. Taking a hand? Captivity
and slavery? Most of the time they tried to use a punishment
to strike a deal, always with the aim of growing their forces.
Pay taxes on everything you earn or they'd take two of your
best men.

They wouldn't be after us if we hadn't stopped in Ruen-lock, I thought. I did this; this is on me. Abran was right to be against it.

A toothless man grinned at us as he hobbled past. Wind gusted against the church, shuddering the trees and making the old man stumble.

"I'll get Pearl to the ship and set the sails. You gather the others," Daniel said. He kept his eyes on the door we exited, but it was too dark inside to see anything.

"Did they see us?" I asked. I pulled Pearl against me so the back of her head touched my stomach. My hands rested on her shoulders and she placed her hands on top of mine.

"I don't think so," Daniel said, glancing over his shoulder.

I kissed the top of Pearl's head and her hand lingered in mine as Daniel pulled her away. They made for the docks and I hurried through the village to the first saloon. I found Wayne, Jessa, and Thomas and told them the Lily Black were here and we needed to set sail. They leapt to their feet, knocking over stools, pulling on jackets. They told me Marjan was already on *Sedna* with Behir. We agreed I'd go find Abran and then meet them back at the ship.

I found Abran in the next saloon, throwing back a shot of whiskey, sitting in the back, chatting with a bald man who wore a leather jacket.

"The Valley is completely protected and has such fertile land," Abran was saying when I approached, his back to me. Abran spread his fingers wide on the table, tapping the tips of his fingers on the table as he spoke. He was leaning forward in his chair and I could imagine that half grin spread across his face, the look of confidence and ease. I wanted to smack his head so hard it hit the table in front of him.

The man he was talking to saw me and nodded at Abran, who turned to me.

"Myra! My favorite lady," he said. "Have a seat." He pulled the chair out next to him.

"Thanks, but we really need to go," I said, trying to catch Abran's eye to get him to see I was serious.

"Don't be rude!" Abran laughed and turned in his seat to motion to the bartender. "This is my old friend Matty. Matty and I go way back."

"Abran . . ." I said.

Abran held up his hands and laughed again, his face visibly flushed even in the half-light. "We can trust Matty. I know I said don't tell anyone, but I wasn't expecting to run into an old friend. Matty is the real deal."

The bartender dropped off three shots and Abran toasted Matty. I left my glass on the table.

"And we just got some good resources. Found some." Abran smiled as though he was proud. "So we're all set," he told Matty.

I laid my hand on Abran's shoulder and dropped my head next to his and spoke into his ear, "It's not just who we talk to, it's who can overhear us."

"You're paranoid." Abran tossed the shot back. "I'm sharing all this with Matty so he can join us. He's a fisher. And it's not like you've done a great job of late."

"Matty, please excuse us," I said, yanking on Abran's arm and pulling him up from his chair.

"What the hell?!" Abran said.

A narrow door around the corner of the bar held a sign labeled STORAGE, and I steered us through the door, into a tiny dark room filled with shelves of liquor. A stench of yeast and rotten fish hit me like a wall when we entered. A small window above our heads let in a slant of light.

"Myra, I'm just happy to see my friend. You're overreacting."

I pushed him against the shelves. "Snap out of it," I hissed. I placed my hand over his mouth and leaned into him. "You've been recognized. Ruenlock has contacted the Lily Black about us. And the Lily Black is here. We need to get back on the ship now and set sail."

Abran's eyes widened and he pulled my hand from his mouth. "Where are—"

The door opened and I expected the bartender to tell us to get out, but a man and woman slipped in and shut the door swiftly behind them. The woman was the one I'd seen in the church store, but the man I hadn't seen before. He had the same rabbit tattoo on his neck, didn't wear a shirt, and had his long, greasy hair tied in a ponytail. My mind scrambled around the thought: How many of them were in Broken Tree?

"Where is it?" the man asked.

"What?" Abran asked.

At first I thought he was buying time by playing stupid, and I watched him carefully for any sign he might be giving me. A sign to attack, to dart for the door. A flick of the wrist, eye contact, the angle of his feet on the floor. But he stood as he had before they entered, head slightly forward, shoulders relaxed, hands at his sides.

The man stepped forward and punched Abran, sending him

sprawling against the shelving behind him. The storage room went almost completely dark; a cloud passing across the sun. I could hear them breathing and Abran gasping, could just barely see him doubled over, hand over the left side of his face.

"We got a message that we've been robbed. You match the description of the people."

The man stepped forward, but the woman touched his arm with her knuckles and he stopped. She drew her knife from her sheath and rubbed the blade on the tail of her shirt as though she were cleaning it.

Abran grasped a shelf and pulled himself upright. He knocked a bottle over and it crashed, the collision like a thunderclap, the glass shards spraying out around our feet.

The man took a step toward Abran, his boot crunching the glass. He reached out and pulled the bandanna down from Abran's neck, revealing the scars.

"So it's true," the man muttered, looking back at the woman. "He must be the one they talked about. Stole from us years ago. Have a habit of it?" the man asked Abran. "You've been on our wanted list a long time."

"On our ship," Abran said. "It's all on our ship. We'll give it all back."

I glanced at Abran out of the corner of my eye. He had to know they wouldn't take back what we stole and then peacefully leave our ship. His eyes were downcast, his mouth a thin line; his face gave away nothing. Was he really going to lead them back to the ship? This gave me a hurtling sensation, of being pushed hard and fast. They weren't going anywhere near Pearl.

"Okay, take us there. You go first," the man said, stepping aside, leaving space for Abran to pass between him and the woman.

"Okay," Abran said. He didn't look at me, didn't gesture in any way. His hands were at his sides and he still looked hunched over, as though trying to make himself small and invisible. The acrid smell of vinegar permeated the room from the broken bottle and I blinked rapidly to clear my head.

Abran stepped between the man and woman and they both watched him pass, eyes on his hands. As soon as Abran stepped past them toward the door, the man unsheathed his knife. The man's weight was on his back leg so he could lunge at Abran and bury the knife in his back.

I unsheathed my own knife and darted toward the man in three quick paces. I leapt on his back and he spun around, trying to throw me off. I clung to him, yanked his head back with a fistful of hair, and ran my knife across his throat.

The woman caught my arm and pulled me from him and tossed me into the wall, my head slamming into the metal siding. I crumpled to the floor and the woman kicked my stomach, the hard tip of her boot like a stone being jammed between my ribs.

Abran collided with her and they both sprawled across the floor; he tumbled off her and groaned as he curled into a ball. I blinked to clear my vision, but everything still seemed sideways.

The woman crawled onto her knees and grasped a shard of glass. It twinkled in the slant of sunlight from the window, a radiant burst. She stood up and made for Abran, who was scrambling toward a spare board leaning against the side of the wall.

I tried to jump up to my feet, but my legs wobbled and crumpled beneath me. My lungs pumped for air, but I still felt breathless. I crawled forward, pulling my body over the shards of glass, pain bright and sharp in my torso. I couldn't make it in time.

As she stepped past me I raised my knife and drove it down through her foot into the floor, nailing her in place.

She shrieked and bent down to stab me with the glass, but I rolled aside. She yanked at the knife, but Abran raised the board and swung it down over her head with a thud.

Abran reached down and hauled me up under my armpit, his hand bleeding through my shirt and wetting my skin. He pushed me out the door in front of him and we stumbled over a fallen chair, people looking up at us as we passed through the saloon, hurrying for the door, the smell of blood and liquor and smoke heavy in the air. It caught inside me so thickly that I couldn't shake it loose even when we got outside.

We ran for the ship. Daniel was at the rudder, Jessa in the rigging, and Thomas at the mainmast, adjusting the sails. Abran and I raced down the dock, stopping at the dock post to untie the rope mooring us. Abran and I leapt onto the ship just as it was beginning to drift from the dock.

I stumbled and rolled across the deck, bursts of pain shooting across my chest. Pearl came out of the cabin toward me, but I waved for her to go back into the cabin.

"Behir!" Marjan shrieked. Jessa screamed from the rigging

and began climbing down. Wayne caught Marjan as she ran to the gunwale and she almost doubled over, her hands out-stretched toward the dock.

"Behir!" she shrieked again.

I stood up and looked toward the dock and then I saw. They had Behir.

CHAPTER 38

"Stop the ship," I yelled.

"Myra!" Abran yelled, stepping toward me. "They aren't going to just hand him back."

I knew he was right, but I didn't care. "Drop the anchor!" I shouted to Daniel.

"If we drop the anchor we aren't getting out of here before they surround us!" Abran shouted.

A man held Behir against him, a knife to his neck. Behir looked just as Pearl had the morning on the coast when we were collecting clams. Eyes wide with terror. Hands limp at each side. Like he was inside a well sucked clean of oxygen and a lid was slowly being rolled over the top.

The man with the black earring we'd seen in the church strolled up the dock with another woman at his side, a short blonde with only one ear. They stood next to the man holding Behir and crossed their arms, leaning back, relaxed, like they were waiting for something.

Daniel and the man with the black earring stared at each other. A powerful, pleased expression crossed Black Earring's face. Like he was challenging Daniel to something.

Daniel swallowed and clenched his fists, his face tightening in a pained way. I knew he was deciding something.

"Take me instead," Daniel called out. My heart raced. His voice sounded small and innocent; I barely recognized it. Everything sharpened, as if every surface rose higher, the mast straightening, the gunwale vibrating with new energy. Seconds lengthened and I tried to think but came up against a blankness in my mind.

Black Earring just shook his head at Daniel like he was a child who was mildly disappointing. Who couldn't measure up. Then he looked at the man holding Behir.

Daniel ran the length of the ship, toward the bow, where the anchor lay. Behir saw him and gave a slight shake of his head.

No, no, no resounded in me, echoing up from my feet.

I ran to the gunwale, waving my arms over my head. *Sedna* was already drifting from the dock; we needed to get the anchor dropped.

"We'll give you whatever you want!" I shouted to them. "Just let him go!"

The man who looked like Daniel gave a slight smile, a sad smile that looked like regret. He nodded at the man holding Behir and I squeezed my eyes shut. Marjan screamed and I heard her collapse on the deck. The sun shone against my eyelids and I saw only red, my body aflame as though I'd swallowed fire. The whole world became a howl.

When I opened my eyes again Behir lay in a crumpled heap at the man's feet and the man wiped the knife against the tail of his shirt. I grabbed the gunwale with both hands to keep from falling. Then I turned from the dock and saw Pearl standing in the doorway of the cabin, her face wet with tears.

WE HELD A funeral for Behir, but Marjan wouldn't speak at it. We gathered at the bow of the ship and she stayed behind us, like a shadow. When we had finished and turned around, she had already disappeared.

After the funeral, we all assembled in the cabin and Abran shared what had happened in the saloon at Broken Tree. That we'd killed one of theirs and they likely knew we were heading for the Valley. Abran didn't mention his past with the Lily Black or that he'd been recognized.

"You told us not to talk about the Valley," Wayne barked.

Abran closed his eyes and nodded. "I was just talking with a friend. But we may have been overheard. Behir . . ." Abran paused, his eyes flickering over Marjan. "Behir was killed because of Ruenlock. It's how they work; they punish any offense. Since they made their point, it's unlikely they'll follow us."

A murmur of concern rose from the crew. I squinted at Abran, wondering if he believed this. Between his past with the Lily Black and whatever connection Daniel had to that captain, I doubted they were through with us.

Daniel had to be a relative of that man—it wasn't just that they looked similar, it was the way they looked at each other across the length of the ship and the dock. With familiarity and recognition. I wondered if anyone else had noticed. The look they gave each other was almost a kind of bartering, like something would be exchanged. And Daniel had offered to give himself up.

I thought of how Daniel pored over maps and sometimes hid his notes when I entered the cabin. I remembered Harjo, how startled he had seemed to be found talking to a stranger. How he'd disappear into saloons alone, as if he were secretly gathering information. Abran had been right. Daniel was hiding something. For all his talk of how hard it was to track someone, had we been tracking the Lily Black all this time?

He had to know how dangerous that was. But maybe he didn't care. My blood quickened in rage at this thought. I needed to catch Daniel when he was alone and confront him about it.

Sedna was darker without Behir on it. We always relied on him for his wit and warmth, his refusal to be bleak even when the earth cast misfortune upon us. When a whirlpool ripped a net full of fish from the downrigger. When the sky flattened and pounded us with rain and wind.

Marjan stayed in Abran's room and he stayed in the quarters for a month. We delivered food to her and she sometimes requested visitors, but otherwise she made herself scarce about the ship, slipping away from us like a ghost.

Then one day she came up to the cabin for breakfast, her presence somehow brighter and refined, like she was a blade sharpened in the fire and pounded into a new shape. I found myself wanting to be close to her, to simply stand beside her and clean fish in the kitchen, or scan the water at the gunwale for mountaintops when we were close to coasts. Normally I couldn't get far enough away from people who had lost someone. It was like remembering a nightmare when you wanted to forget it. But somehow this was different. I wanted to reach out and touch her shoulder.

Maybe it was because I loved her enough to sit with her, her grief like a third person in the room, palpable, with a shape of its own. A shape that I knew would change over time, evolving as only grief could.

Or maybe I wanted to comfort her as penance to ease my guilt. We wouldn't have been in Broken Tree without all that came before, all the turns we had taken at my bidding.

The night after we lost Behir I dreamed that I was drowning. The water around me was dark and it kept rising and I kept swimming and it kept rising, the surface pulling away from me. My fingers kept reaching for the sunlight at the surface and I swam until my lungs almost burst, my legs knotted and weak. Pearl shook me awake right when I thought I'd stop trying and let myself drift to the black bottom.

That night Pearl didn't sleep at all but tucked herself into the corner of the bed and leaned against the wall. Her hair was wild and curly around her face and she looked like a doll on a forgotten shelf. I reached out to touch her cheek and she blinked but otherwise didn't move, her chest rising and falling faintly, like an animal in hibernation, not fully awake or asleep. I wrapped her in my arms and rocked her as I had when she was only a baby.

She shouldn't have seen it, she shouldn't have seen it, I kept thinking.

A FEW DAYS after Behir died I found Abran alone in the quarters. Everyone else had gone up to the cabin for breakfast and Abran sat on his temporary bunk, trying to tie a rag around his injured hand. A candle sent a dull glow across half his arm and then tempered out into darkness.

"What happened at Broken Tree?" I asked softly.

"What do you think happened?" Abran spat on the floor and leaned forward, trying to knot the bandage by pulling the fabric with his teeth and other hand. The rag slipped from his teeth and unraveled and he flung his good hand out across the small table, sending the candle flying.

The flame went out when it hit the floor. I didn't say anything. Wax dripped onto the floor. I picked up the candle and placed it back on the table.

"I hope no one else heard you talking about where we're going," I said.

"Why? You worried we won't go there anymore?"

I squatted in front of him and took his injured hand in both my hands.

"No," I said. It was too late to turn back, too late to try to find somewhere else. The whole crew was weary to settle. And Abran's confidence was slipping. He'd sail us straight into hell if it made him look stalwart. He watched me bandage his hand, his eyes lost and clouded, barely the man I'd visited at night. I remembered what Marjan had said about him months ago when I first joined *Sedna*. That sometimes the pressure could get to him. Was this what she meant? Had he done all this before? I thought of how scared he was of the Lily Black, how haunted by his brother's death. I pitied him, yet my pity was stretched thin. I needed him to be who I thought he was.

I pulled the bandage tight and he winced in pain.

"You pull yourself together," I said softly.

"Or what?" Abran asked. "You gonna lead a mutiny?"

I yanked the bandage so tight that blood stained through and Abran ripped his hand from mine.

"You're not acting like a captain. It's not a mutiny when there's no captain," I said.

CHAPTER 39

LATER THAT DAY I found Daniel in the cabin after hours, working on calculations. He had been avoiding everyone, even Pearl and me. A candle flickered on the table next to him. I wondered if he had asked Abran if we could work late and use light, or if he was ignoring the rule. I guessed the latter.

Daniel didn't look up when I came in, but I sensed he knew it was me.

"Thought you'd be in bed," he said.

The air had a sulfur smell, a pungent odor that seemed both green as life and black as decay. We had to be passing over mountaintops, thick with algae and plankton and new growth, plants that hadn't yet been named.

"Is he a relative? Father? Uncle?" I asked.

Daniel kept scribbling on his notepad, but I saw the muscles in his neck tense. He picked up the sextant, measured a space on the map, and set it back down.

"What I want to know," I continued, "is if we were following them." I tried to keep my voice steady, but I heard it quiver as though it came from someone else.

Daniel paused in his writing. He leaned back in his chair, dropped his pencil, and stretched his fingers out in front of him on the table.

I felt a wave of fury pass through me, shaking me in my bones. I couldn't trust him. He was like all the rest. I curled my hands into fists at my sides. My skin felt warm to my own touch. *Sedna* groaned against a wave and tilted to the side, then righted herself. "Now Behir is gone and they'll follow us to the Valley."

Daniel dropped his head in his hands and cursed. "It's too far. Not worth it to them." But I could tell he didn't believe this.

"Not worth it? All I've heard is how they execute anyone who betrays them." I stopped short, remembering my promise to Abran.

"They want more colonies," I said, switching tack. "They could decide to take the Valley from the Lost Abbots and take us down along the way. You acted like you wanted to keep us safe, not take risks—all the while you were leading us to danger, sailing straight into it." My voice rose and shook, and I restrained myself from leaping forward and hitting him.

"You and Pearl were never supposed to get involved," he said.

He stood up and turned to me and shook his head. His face was creased in anguish, his eyes bright and intent. I could feel he wanted to reach out and touch me. To comfort me. To be comforted. A cascade of fury built up in me, like a flame slowly crawling up my spine.

"I'm so sorry," he said.

"Sorry?" I lunged at him and pushed him. He stumbled backward. I pushed him again. "How could you?" I pushed him again and again until his back was up against the wall. "After I pulled you out of the water? And now—this whole time—" I punched his chest, pummeling him with both fists. He caught my wrists and held them.

I twisted free of his grip and stepped back from him. I almost felt calmer. Attacking him eased my anger, but it wasn't just that.

Beneath my rage was relief—relief that I could blame someone else, that Behir's death wasn't all my fault. I needed to escape the clutches of guilt the way a fish needs to escape the net.

"Were you leading us to them?" I asked again. "Were you repaying a debt?"

"No." Daniel shook his head and rubbed his face with the palm of his hand. "Yes. I mean, somewhat."

When I clenched my fists again he held up his hands.

"My older brother. I was tracking him . . . hunting him."

Daniel was silent; I waited for him to go on.

"He was in the navy years before. When the floods got worse and the world was breaking up, he always talked about how new nations would form. He wanted to be part of it, to protect people. He had all these principles about how people should be and what their place was." A grimace tightened Daniel's face. "Wanted to make sure I knew my place, which was beneath him. Jackson . . . he seemed almost excited about everything falling apart. Like he knew in this new world he'd have a bigger hand in it all. Hammering something of his own out of the chaos."

Daniel paused, and a roll of thunder split the silence. Lightning flashed and Daniel flared before me.

"Jackson fought in the Mediterranean War with this commander—Clarence Axon. Jackson was like a son to him. Axon had already started the Lily Black—they were a private military group the U.S. had hired to help in the war. Once the war was over Axon wanted to make Jackson captain of one of his ships. So Jackson came back home to get my mom and me, to take us with him."

Daniel paused again. I could tell he was deciding how much to tell me.

"Things got bad between him and my mom. We owned a boat we were going to use to escape, and Jackson stole it during the night, just disappeared. But he didn't take just the boat. He knew I'd stored all her insulin on the boat, so he took all that, too. He knew my mom would die without it, and he left me to nurse her to death. At first, I didn't try to find him, but then Marianne died and soon after I ran across him in a port. It was like an awakening. I . . . I tried to kill him then and there."

Lightning flared and *Sedna* shook in the clutch of a wave. Daniel ran a hand over his face and looked away. I thought of Daniel's impulsive wrath, the story he'd told me of killing his old crew after they raped Marianne.

"He promised if I tried that again, if I came after him, he'd end me. Before I met you, I heard he was making colonies in the northeast, so I wanted to head there."

"When I saved you, you mean," I snapped.

"I thought I'd be able to track him at a port and do it quietly. No one else was supposed to get involved."

"You're an idiot," I said. "And so am I for trusting you. How are you supposed to take out the captain of a Lily Black ship and no one else gets involved?"

"I don't know. I didn't . . . for all I knew, he'd take me out first. That part didn't matter as much. It's—it's about looking someone in the eye and saying, *you did this*."

I crossed my arms over my chest. I, too, had longed to face Jacob and hold him accountable. To speak what I knew was true and make him hear it. But I pushed this aside and held on to my anger.

"Here I thought you were helping me. That you wanted to protect Pearl—"

"I do want—"

"Shut up. Did you track him at each port we stopped at?"

"I asked around—people in taverns and shops. Some said they had been in Wharton but were moving farther north, around Broken Tree."

"So we stopped there instead of Brighton," I said. Brighton was a small trading post south of Broken Tree that we passed in favor of docking at Broken Tree. At the time Daniel had claimed he'd heard of typhoons hitting Brighton during that season. "How in the world did you think you wouldn't bring us into it?"

Guilt tightened the lines in Daniel's face. His body seemed to sag, his joints going limp, his shoulders folding forward. He ran his hand over his face. "I was hoping I could contain it. I hoped."

"You used me," I said. This knowledge felt like a burn I kept rediscovering on my body, surprised by the pain each time it brushed against something else. "You wanted the vote for the Valley as much as I did. Because you knew you could steer us closer to him."

When Daniel didn't say anything, I hurried on. "If the Lily Black hadn't been in the northeast, would you have agreed to come with me? To help me?"

Sedna rocked with another wave and the candle on the table began sliding near the edge. Daniel stepped forward and picked it up. The flame sent shadows dancing against the cabin walls.

"No," Daniel said softly, closing his eyes as he said the word. "Not then. I wouldn't have. But who I am now, yes, I would. I want to be with you and Pearl. But I also want that part of my life from before finished, tucked away. I can't . . . I can't reconcile it. It's like two halves of one life, and I don't know how to connect them."

I thought of all the times my life seemed to break away into a new direction. My father's suicide, my mother's death, Jacob taking Row, my grandfather's death, boarding *Sedna*. Myself fluid as water, changing shape with each event. But also not, some hard undefinable center in me, like a stone, that was neither altered nor touched by fate.

The wind howled and water pounded against *Sedna*. It felt like the whole world was trying to break into our small ship and tear us apart.

"I don't expect you to forgive me," Daniel said.

"Good, I'm not going to."

Daniel glared at me, set the candle back on the table, and crossed his arms.

"I'm surprised how judgmental you are, considering."

"Considering what?"

"Given the chance you'd take revenge. On Jacob."

"Of course I want a reckoning. But what does that matter? He's dead."

"You don't have to forgive me. But you understand. I know you do," Daniel said. "You understand the need to set things right and move forward."

"I understand that we are about to set off on the longest crossing of our lives and that we don't know if we'll be followed.

I understand that we just lost—" My voice caught and I swallowed. I tried to say his name, but my throat kept closing up.

Daniel stepped forward, his arms out toward me, but I jammed my hand into his chest, pushing him away.

"Pearl shouldn't have seen that," I said, my voice finally breaking, my shoulders heaving in a sob. "What if it broke something in her?"

I began shaking. *Sedna* lurched sideways and I almost fell to the floor, but Daniel caught me. He held me by my arms, keeping distance between us, settling me on my feet.

"Nothing is broken in her," he said. He placed his thumb at the bottom of my chin and tilted my face up to his. "And what happened. That's not on you. That's on me. That will always be on me. I will carry it."

He wiped a tear from my face with his thumb and I stepped away. The sobs kept coming and I felt like I couldn't breathe, so I made for the door, anxious for the wind to scour me clean. I paused in the doorway to look back at him.

He stood where I'd left him, in front of the candle, a soft glow fanned out behind him. I could only see his silhouette, his whole body made of shadow.

CHAPTER 40

IT HADN'T RAINED for days and our cistern held only a few inches of water, so we went on water rations. We all were dehydrated, wandering about the deck, licking cracked lips, blinking dry eyes. There were more squabbles and bickering, people stomping away from one another, shooting cold glances across the breakfast table. Losing Behir at the beginning of crossing the Atlantic didn't just break our hearts, it felt like some ill omen hovering over us, ready to drop from the sky and swallow us up.

The goat contracted some illness, sores peppering her throat, red and blistering under her fur. She began wasting away in wild-eyed pain, wailing at night, skittering away from our touch during the day. Thomas finally put her out of her misery and cleaned up her pen, returning it to just another part of the deck, but the outline remained, scratches from her hooves on the wood deck. We debated whether or not the meat would be safe to eat but we finally agreed not to risk it. We couldn't afford a sick crew on top of our troubles. But I did skin her and tan the hide before we dropped her body overboard. Nights were growing colder, and Pearl could use it as an extra blanket.

Thomas and Wayne built a second canoe to replace the one we'd lost at Ruenlock. This one was smaller but would still work as a tender to shore.

After trolling for fish and catching nothing, I hauled in the lines, checked the baits, and strung a few more lines. Weather had been calm the past week, but soon we would be entering what sailors called Tempest's Trail, a passage in the North Atlantic that was known for heavy winds and rain. More ships lay at the bottom of that part of the sea than I wanted to know. The rain would be good for the cistern, but we feared how well *Sedna* would handle the winds.

While I was fishing Abran crossed the deck from the hatch to the cabin, glancing at me, the expression on his face dark and preoccupied. When I went into the cabin to drop off some tackle I heard him speaking sharply to Marjan.

He saw me loading boxes on the shelves and said, "Do you mind?"

Marjan held a list and stirred a pot over the stove. The scent of fish curdled my stomach.

I left the cabin and returned to trolling. Daniel stood near the bow, binoculars up to his face, scanning the horizon. I knew he was searching for any signs of the Lily Black. I'd found him up in the rigging just yesterday with the binoculars. We hadn't seen anyone for the past week; we hadn't even passed another ship. But the isolation didn't erase the feeling that they could be following us.

My bare feet started to go numb on the chilled deck, so I went downstairs to get my boots. I was alone in the quarters, pulling on my boots, when Marjan walked in and set an empty liquor bottle on the table next to me. I tied the laces to my boots, leaned back, and sighed. It was a glass bottle, similar to the one I'd seen in Abran's room weeks earlier.

"He's going through more than before," Marjan said.

I nodded. "How bad is it?"

"He's been trading the ship's goods for alcohol. He stores smoked fish in a separate bucket and goes up and trades it after we've finished with the ship's trade at each port."

I stared at her. "You've known this whole time? How long has this been happening?" I tried to remember when I started to notice a difference in Abran. It was around when we stopped in Wharton—he had claimed he needed to unwind because Wharton was close to where his brother died.

"For years," Marjan said. She looked weary. Her worry lines had deepened and her gray hair had thinned around her temples. She wore her usual blue tunic and it brought out the blue in a vein that split her forehead like a small river.

"Years?" I asked.

"It's not always this bad. It ebbs and flows. Worse when he's stressed," Marjan explained.

"What about the rules? Why hasn't anyone said something to him?" I asked.

"The rules . . ." Marjan shrugged. "The rules are just some ideas Abran had. He's never enforced them. It's more of an honor code, but now . . ."

"But why hasn't someone stopped it?" I asked.

Marjan closed her eyes and gritted her teeth. I suddenly felt like a small child asking questions that didn't have anything to do with this world. When she opened her eyes again they seemed to glitter with vigor, a tireless momentum. I wondered how much work she did around *Sedna* that no one knew about. She was always slipping in and out of rooms, attending to business the rest of us only had a half knowledge of.

"Sorry," I said. "I know it isn't that easy. I'll try to talk to him."

"There won't be enough to make the crossing," Marjan said. "So he'll go through withdrawals. I'm starting a dosing schedule to wean him. I was hoping you'd help me."

"Of course. Anything."

Marjan nodded, picked up the bottle, and wrapped her shawl around it. Since Behir's death, I'd felt so much shame I thought it would burst straight out of me, splitting me in two. And beneath that shame I'd felt abundant fear, fear like another gravity, pressing me down, making me feel smaller and smaller. To stand up straight with all that weight on me took more strength than I thought I had. With each day that passed, the need to confess had grown and grown.

She turned to leave and I reached out and touched her arm.

"Wait," I said. My body tensed and my hands went clammy. "I'm sorry." When she faced me, I felt as if the ground had dropped out from beneath me. I thought of my mother, her dark eyes and quick laugh. The way she had tried to hide her fear so as not to burden me, breathing into the weight of it, tilting up her chin and forcing a smile. Each mother is different except in the ways she is broken, right to the marrow; even the softest parts can crumble.

I hurried on. "Earlier I wouldn't apologize, and I said I wasn't sorry about Ruenlock, but I am. I'm sorry I deceived you all, I'm sorry about—" My throat closed up and I blinked quickly to clear my eyes.

Marjan patted my arm as though she were a mother comforting a child. Her eyebrows knit together in concern and thoughtfulness. If she had moments when she blamed me, now wasn't one of them. I'd seen flashes of anger cross her face when she was working, hanging the laundry to be washed in an approaching rainstorm. Memories surfacing in the stillness. But if she blamed me, she never mentioned it.

Marjan's necklace now held four beads instead of three and it gave me an ache in my chest just looking at it. I wondered if she'd kept an extra bead hidden somewhere all this time, perhaps in her bunk, knowing she may one day need it.

The room seemed to hum with a deep quiet that enveloped us. I thought of how birth is only the beginning of giving life, maybe the smallest part of giving life, like a seed that still needs the sun and soil, needs so much to still blossom. I thought of how much Marjan had already given all of us and how much she'd keep giving.

Then Marjan shook her head, a sad smile etched on her face.

"I keep thinking grief feels like climbing a staircase while looking down," she said. "You won't forget where you've been, but you've got to keep rising. It all gets farther away, but it's all still there. And you've only got one way to go and you don't really want to go on rising, but you've got to. And that tightness in your chest doesn't go away, but you somehow go on breathing that thinner, higher air. It's like you grow a third lung. Like you've somehow gotten bigger when you thought you were only broken."

I climbed through the hatch onto the deck and saw Daniel and Pearl sitting across from each other near the starboard gunwale, bent over a piece of paper spread between them.

The sun brightened Pearl's hair to the color of a flame and her hair tossed in the wind like a flickering candle. Daniel traced something on the paper with his finger and Pearl leaned forward, her small hand following his.

I walked closer to them so I could hear them but pretended to inspect a crack in the gunwale. I heard Daniel say, "You use the sextant to measure the sun's distance from the horizon."

"This is boring," Pearl muttered.

"You'll have to learn to read maps and calculate distances," Daniel said.

"Why?"

"So you can go wherever you want."

Listening to them talk, I could see Pearl sailing away on her own, her little brown body barely a spot on the horizon, standing on the deck of some ship I'd never been on, moving toward a destination I couldn't imagine. She was as new as this world I'd never fully know.

Daniel saw me out of the corner of his eye, stood, and walked over to me.

"I thought it'd be good for her to practice," he said cautiously. "Hope that's okay."

"I want her to learn," I said stiffly. In the evenings I'd been continuing to teach Pearl to read with Abran's books. Her favorite was *The Jungle Book*.

Pearl remained bent over a map, twisting the sextant in semicircles. She wrote down a number on a pad of paper next to her knee. She leaned again over the map and made another measurement.

Daniel and I watched her. The sun glowed on her back, bronzing her skin. Her face was furrowed in a frown. The wind made the edge of the map curl and she kept smoothing it with an impatient hand. At times like this, when she was immersed in something, she seemed like someone I barely knew, and it made me happy in a wistful way.

It made me remember her birth and how she felt like a stranger even then. And how even before her birth, I had feared losing that little stranger. Not losing her was the one thing that kept me going, I kept telling myself. What Marjan had said sounded nice, and I wanted to believe it, but I feared it couldn't be true. That after too great a loss I'd simply be snuffed out. That being broken simply meant being broken.

Daniel stood so close I could smell him, that familiar scent of wood smoke and some dark flower that grew at the roots of trees. Like a forest in autumn. In the distance I heard the calls of seagulls.

"I should get back to fishing," I said, though my feet stayed planted on the deck. The seagull cawing grew louder and louder and I looked out over the water. A flock was diving into the water to the east of us and coming up with fish wrestling in their beaks. I gripped the gunwale. I'd trolled in that spot only a half hour before and had come up empty.

"You can rest for just a minute," Daniel said.

I still was having trouble reconciling what Daniel had done with who I felt he was. I had also always had trouble reconciling the different sides of Jacob, trying to understand how the man I married could be the man who hurt me even more than the floods could. I had spent hours stewing over it, combing through memories, looking for clues. I could read the devil into his every word and gesture, but some memories resisted this. They reminded me of a man I loved and who seemed to love me.

Back when Row was just a baby, I had awakened once to Jacob bringing me breakfast in bed. He had kissed my forehead and tucked my hair behind my ear before setting a tray on my lap full of eggs, strawberries, and toast.

"What's this for?" I asked.

"For you. You've been working hard. I know how lucky I am to be with you," he said.

Sunlight from the window turned his hair a brighter red, his fair skin almost porcelain. I placed my palm on his cheek and murmured thanks.

"I'd best get the coffee. Almost done," he said, standing up and leaving.

The scent of coffee wafted upstairs and I listened to his movements down in the kitchen. Warmth enveloped me and I stretched out in bed. Row would be waking soon, her catlike cry spreading through the house like clockwork in a half hour. Everything in its place. Like we were a still-life painting you could stand in front of and find pleasing.

Early on, Jacob had been obsessed with me, as if I were some creature he hadn't seen before. What was grouchiness he mistook for mystery, what was cynicism he mistook for intelligence. I married him because I thought he was so taken with me that he'd never leave me. That I'd never relive those moments on the front stoop waiting for my mother to come home.

How wrong I'd been. But had I been wrong about all of it? Should I dismiss the beautiful times I'd trusted him? How could

I reconcile that the man who brought me breakfast in bed was the same man who betrayed me?

Since Jacob was a carpenter like Grandfather, part of me thought he'd actually be like Grandfather. Stable, patient, a calm, steady presence. Someone I needed and could trust.

Pearl squealed. "Mom! It's my bird!"

Pearl danced in a circle and pointed overhead to a bird that coasted above us. It was smaller than the other seagulls and darker in coloring, and it did not cry out to the others. It circled our mainsail and then coasted along with us, keeping pace with the boat.

"It's the bird I caught!" Pearl said, running up to me and tugging my arm.

I squinted up at it. "I don't think so, honey."

"Of course it is," Pearl said impatiently. She spun around in a circle again, her arms spread wide, the bird flying above her. She twirled and twirled. Her hair spread out from her like wildfire.

Daniel smiled as he watched Pearl and said to me, "You know, I think it might be her bird."

Every good thing will return to you, my mother used to say. I had forgotten it until now, watching Pearl's shirt billow around her. Every surface of the ship felt impossibly delicate, wood windblown to the texture of driftwood, sails above us bleached to the softness of sheets hung on a clothesline. Even we felt delicate at that moment: three bodies on the deck of a ship, cold water for miles, our three hearts beating furiously like wings.

CHAPTER 41

IT GREW DARK during supper, shadows lengthening and then the window casting our reflection back at us as the light dimmed outside. Marjan hung the lantern from the ceiling and lit candles on the table. I hadn't thought about the long stretches of darkness we'd be encountering as we went farther north. How both the sea and the sky turned black so early, the final bit of light hanging on the horizon, like being inside a clam as it snapped shut.

We devoured the fish bone broth, barely speaking with one another. A bread basket sat empty in the middle of the table, each of us having been given a piece of bread the size of my palm. I suspected the yeast we'd traded for was almost gone. Daniel and I gave our bread to Pearl. I was sick of feeling her ribs poking through her skin when she lay next to me at night.

It reminded me of my own body when I'd breastfed her. How I was lucky my milk still came in despite the long days of hunger, but my flesh disappeared from my body, bones appearing where I'd forgotten they existed. My body put her first for a while, siphoning off nutrients to make milk, leaving me achy and starved. But after a few months, the tide shifted, and my milk began to dry up.

Grandfather traded fish for goat's milk at ports and we spoon-fed it to her from cups. She began to fatten up, finally getting as much as she needed. Grandfather and I fished around the clock and began trading for other foods for her: fruit, sourdough bread, cheeses. She surprised us both by growing into a chubby, happy baby, and I remember thinking for a while that this was possible; with Grandfather's help, I could actually raise her.

Marjan began stacking dishes. A small tower of crumbs built up in front of Pearl, and once she finished her bread, she scooped the crumbs into her fist and jammed them into her mouth. That evening, the crew and I discussed our plan for dealing with the guards at the colony. I showed them the map and suggested we anchor on the south side, where the mountain would be easiest to climb, so we could then descend into the valley below. I volunteered to go in first as bait. My plan was that the guards would take me captive and while they were busy subduing me, Abran, Daniel, and Wayne would attack them, taking them out. Thomas, Marjan, and Pearl would stay behind on *Sedna* and we'd signal with a flag once we'd killed the Lost Abbots. There was no telling what condition the community itself would be in by the time we arrived, but I hoped whoever was left would be grateful to be rid of their overseers. And hopefully they would partner with us to begin reinforcing the community against another attack. Because undoubtedly, the Lost Abbots would return for their collections.

After the meal Wayne surprised us by getting out his guitar and playing a few ballads and sea shanties. My heart warmed to him. I could tell he wanted to cheer us up.

Over his shoulder, I could see Abran leaning against the wall adjacent to the kitchen, smoking a pipe, his expression gloomy.

Wayne began playing a faster jig and Pearl got out of her chair and began yanking on Daniel's hand, trying to pull him up to dance with her. Finally he relented and stood by the side of the table, in front of where Wayne played. Wayne tapped his foot quickly with the beat and Jessa began clapping alongside. Daniel stood still and Pearl held on to his hand and spun and spun around him, a planet spinning and orbiting the sun. Daniel slowly rotated in the circle Pearl made around him, his hand holding hers as she spun, his face tender and enchanted as he watched her.

I sat and talked with Thomas. He had that quick, computational mind I'd seen in a few older people. They'd observe the world like they were collecting data and preparing questions in response. Pearl observed the world like she was listening to something very far away, like she had a third hand with which she reached out and touched something invisible.

Thomas told me about how he'd been an ecologist employed by the government before the Six Year Flood.

"I studied the salinity changes in the ocean," he explained wistfully. I could tell he was proud of the work he'd done and missed it. "My father couldn't have been more proud of me when I finished my Ph.D. I'd started out in philosophy, but then I wanted something more . . . concrete, more applicable. My father was a welder, and while I was still in school I'd work alongside him in his shop. Years later, after the government broke down and I migrated to Colorado, I returned to his work, not mine. People needed boats and new buildings high up in the mountains. Needed someone who could work metal. So that's what I did."

"The work you did," I said, "with salinity. These floods, are they just the beginning . . ."

"Of the end?" Thomas asked.

I nodded.

Thomas squinted like he was looking at something far away. "Could be. But you know what surprised me the most? The salinity didn't change as much as people thought. It fluctuated up and down in different oceans at different times, but ultimately it remained steady. Some of it was changes in ocean floor sediment from increased earthquakes. Some of it was increases in carbonic acid. Some of it I could never understand; I couldn't trace it. Maybe it was Gaia."

"Gaia?"

"There was this theory, over two hundred years ago, called the Gaia hypothesis. Essentially that all living matter on earth works together to create life, to make earth habitable. A regulation among matter to fight disorder. Life can't exist without fighting disorder."

"Do you believe that?" I asked.

Thomas shrugged. "It raises questions for me. Do all natural things but man conspire toward life, but man alone has a death drive? If life exists to fight disorder, will violence and disorder evolve right alongside us, the shadow that we need to keep breathing? If rage is a reaction to disorder, does that make rage the original life force?"

I stared at him. "What I want to know is if things will get worse. I want to keep fishing."

"You fish while you can," Thomas said gently.

Marjan set clay cups on the table and poured herbal tea in them. A bitter scent rose from the cups, and crushed dandelion leaves settled at the bottom. After a few more songs, Wayne handed the guitar over to Jessa and she thumbed through a few ballads quickly, in the corner, like she didn't really want to be heard.

Daniel had settled back at the table next to Abran, and as they talked, Abran's voice grew louder and louder, thundering over Jessa's quiet notes.

"It will be a 'he who does not work, neither shall he eat' sort of thing," Abran said. Abran leaned forward, hunched over his cup, elbows on the table, both hands around his cup in a possessive gesture.

"Even the children? The sick and elderly?" Daniel asked.

Pearl sat on the floor in front of Jessa, making her newest dead snake dance by twisting its body with the melody. Pearl had caught many snakes around the warm coasts of Wharton and a few more in Broken Tree, but she only had a few live ones left in her snake jar. After each meal Pearl warmed rocks on the fire Marjan used for cooking and set them at the bottom of the snake jar. I'd told her that we'd have to eat them all before we landed in the Valley because it would be too cold for them to survive there.

"Charlie likes the cold. I caught him up in Apple Falls," she had said. "Besides, I'll share my body heat with them until I make him a cozy home."

Thomas and I stopped talking to listen to Daniel and Abran. Abran rolled his eyes and moved his hand as if he were shooing a bug from the rim of his cup. "We don't have sick and elderly yet. Point is, everyone has a share and has to contribute a share. There won't be private property. It will be all communal."

My eyes narrowed on Abran. Rich of him, who stole the

ship's supplies to trade for alcohol, to say there'd be no private property. Nothing private for anyone but him.

Daniel's arm was draped around the back of his chair. He raised his eyebrows and took a slow sip of tea. "Really?"

Wayne slammed his cup down on the table. "And I guess there won't be any government or leadership, either?"

Abran glared at Wayne. "Of course there will be."

Thomas turned in his chair to face Abran. "Surely we'll do a vote of some sort? Come up with a system of laws?"

"I've already been working on a system of laws. But we'll sort things out. I have some ideas." Abran stood up to pour himself more tea and his hands twitched. Sweat beaded on his temples and he wiped at it with the back of his sleeve.

Marjan and I glanced at each other.

"I'd like to see those laws," Wayne said.

"I'm not finished with them." Abran filled his cup, set the teapot down, and remained standing, his fists resting on the table.

"You may be captain on this ship, but that doesn't mean you'll be some sort of king on land," Wayne said as he stood up.

The creak of the kerosene lamp rocking on its hook and the groan of the ropes straining against the wind filled the silence. I rubbed my thumb over a crack in my clay cup sharp enough to cut, but my thumb was so callused it didn't even scratch.

Abran tilted his chin up and the light caught in his bloodshot eyes, their surface dull and watery.

"You do what I say here, you'll do what I say there," Abran said, his voice low and even.

Wayne's knuckles whitened on the back of his chair.

"We'll vote on who leads," Wayne said.

"No," Abran said. "You'll answer to me or be banished from us."

Wayne tossed the chair behind him and lunged at Abran, knocking him into the wall. Abran flung a fist at Wayne, but Wayne rammed his head into Abran's chest, slamming his back into the wall. Abran punched Wayne's back and clawed at his neck.

Thomas and Daniel ran toward them. Thomas caught Wayne's shoulder and tried to pry him from Abran, but he caught one of Abran's punches and fell backward.

Daniel grabbed Wayne around his torso and wrenched him off Abran. Abran shoved Wayne once Daniel pried him loose, and Daniel and Wayne sprawled across the floor.

Abran charged toward Wayne. I stepped forward, caught Abran's arm, and plowed him backward toward the wall. Abran's right fist came at my face and I ducked. I grabbed his other arm, twisting it behind his back, and yanked his head back with a fistful of hair.

Wayne scrambled to his feet, his shoulders arched and his fists held out as though he would lunge again. Thomas stepped between Abran and Wayne, putting his hands out toward each of them.

"Everyone just calm down," Thomas said, looking between the two.

Marjan picked up the chair Wayne had thrown and Jessa leaned his guitar against the wall. The cabin had a deflated feeling to it, like something had been sucked out of the room. The air around us had shifted and we were all rearranged, on edge, looking at one another like strangers.

I let go of Abran and stepped away from him.

"We will vote for leadership in the Valley, Abran," Marjan told him softly. She clasped her hands in front of her, her chin tilted slightly down, looking at Abran with a stern expression.

Abran looked around at all of us and let out a sigh of exasperation.

"Whatever. You know, whatever." Abran raised his hands at us, palms out, in a gesture of both resignation and defiance.

"We need to pull together. Be more careful. We're low on almost all our resources," Marjan said.

"That's on her! She's our fisher and she's gotten nothing!" Abran shouted, pointing at me.

"Don't put all this on her," Thomas said. "I see her out on deck fishing before the sun is up till after it is down. And I see you slipping around the ship, doing God knows what. And when they had Behir, she was the one who first shouted to stop the ship."

"Little good that did," Abran said and spat on the floor. His face burned almost as red as his bloodshot eyes.

Marjan caught my eye and nodded once.

"Just give us a second," I said, pushing Abran in front of me out of the cabin.

It was so dark, despite the moon and stars, that my eyes took a few seconds to adjust. Abran twisted his arm from my grasp.

"You've got to pull yourself together," I said.

"I'm not letting you take all this from me." Abran swiped his hair behind his ears and pointed in my face.

"Abran, I'm not trying to take anything from you. You're in withdrawal, you're not thinking straight."

Abran stared at me and let out a low laugh. "Don't act like you care about us now. Not after what you did."

"Listen. We want the same thing. To get to the Valley alive."

The sound of the wind filling the sails, the fabric swelling and flapping, drew around us in the silence. Everything on deck shone with a gray-blue glow in the moonlight, as if we'd been dipped in the water and it clung to us. Abran turned his face from me, his profile sharp as cut stone.

He held out his palms, his fingers cupped as though holding something. "Everything is slipping through my fingers," he said.

The fear on his face gripped me. Beyond the withdrawal symptoms, beyond the attack from the Lily Black, this crossing terrified him more than I could understand. That night his brother was murdered haunted him like something he had not just witnessed but had done. Maybe taking responsibility was the only way to lessen the helplessness he had felt that night. That was how I dealt with terror, how I wrestled some semblance of control back into my life.

"If you blame yourself for the bad, credit yourself for the good, too," I told him. I reached out and touched his arm. He nodded. I left him on the deck alone and went back into the cabin to get Pearl. My hands shook when I touched her small shoulders. We still had so far to go.

CHAPTER 42

I PLACED MY hand on the small of my back, where a dull ache was turning to a deeper, throbbing pain. I gestured to Pearl to help me lift the halibut, a fish twice her size, with gills the length of her arm. We heaved the halibut a few feet from the down-rigger, where I could butcher it on deck without tripping over it to check the lines.

When I straightened I looked across the sea, watching the dawn turn the sky red in the east. Pearl sat at my feet, rubbing her thin arms.

"Red sky in the morning, sailor's warning."

I turned and saw Daniel standing beside our halibut, his eyes on the horizon line.

"Hm?" I asked.

"An old saying. Red sky means a storm system is moving to the east," he said.

I shrugged. *Sedna* had done better than I'd expected with the northern storms. Last week we'd run through a series of small storms that delayed our progress. One of the mainsails tore during a storm, causing us to lose even more time when we took it down to repair it. But with the exception of the torn sail we'd sustained little damage. Some ropes and a block needed to be replaced, but that was typical wear and tear.

Our biggest concern now wasn't how *Sedna* was handling the storms, but the timing of our progress. According to Daniel's original calculations we should have been a hundred miles farther northeast by this time. We didn't want to arrive at the Valley in winter, when currents in the north were strongest and mooring the ship along the rocky coastline would be more dangerous.

"Did you notice the birds flying low yesterday?" Daniel asked.

"Yeah," I muttered, squatting in front of the halibut, inserting my knife at its vent, and sliding it up its belly toward the base of the gills. I hadn't noticed the birds. I'd kept my eyes down on the sea all day searching for halibut and schools of cod.

"Air pressure is changing. No birds today. They've disappeared. And yesterday—the clouds in long rows, like fish scales. This storm could be much worse."

"So we'll board the windows if you think the winds will be bad," I said. The giant eye of the fish stared up at me, the black hole of its iris so large, I felt I could drop inside it.

Daniel stepped past me to the gunwale, arms crossed over his chest, squinting in the growing light.

"We may not be able to ride this one out," he said quietly.

I pulled the gills and entrails out. "Well, why don't we just redirect north for a while? We may miss it."

Daniel sighed and shook his head. "I've charted out both going straight north and straight east, and either way, with these currents, we'd be hitting crosswinds. And it wouldn't guarantee we'd miss it. Only thing that'd increase that chance is slowing down."

"We're not doing that," I said. I glared up at him, my hands stained red. I was dizzy from the stench of guts. Why couldn't he go make himself useful?

"It'd be our only chance to avoid the worst of this storm."

"We don't know yet how bad it will be," I said.

"We should slow down," Pearl said, standing up between us. "I hate storms."

"I know, honey," I said.

"No, you don't," she said defiantly. "I *hate* storms."

I wiped my hands on my pants and reached out to touch Pearl's shoulder, but she jerked it from my reach.

"Pearl, just because there's a storm doesn't mean we'll sink," I said.

"You never listen to me!" Pearl cried, stomping her foot. She spun on her heel and ran across the deck to the rigging, which she swiftly climbed, the handkerchief tucked in her pocket waving in the wind like a red feather.

Daniel watched Pearl and then turned to me. "Can you get Abran to put it up for a vote? To slow our course to avoid the storm?"

"We can't reach the Valley in the dead of winter. We don't have time to slow our course," I said. I turned back to the fish, sawing its head off.

"Myra, you're the only one who can convince him."

"I don't trust you," I spat out. I wiped my brow with my sleeve and squinted up at him.

A line formed between his eyebrows; a hurt expression tightened the corners of his mouth.

"I want us to get there in one piece," he said.

"Then you'd better work on that," I said, turning back to the fish.

Daniel disappeared into the cabin and it was quiet, only the sounds of water lapping the side of the boat and my knife cutting through scales and flesh. I stood up and dragged the box of salt toward the fish and began cutting off the dorsal fin.

Voices tumbled out of the cabin, getting louder and louder until I recognized who they belonged to. Daniel and Abran.

I wiped my hands on my pants again and hurried into the cabin. Daniel and Abran stood across the table from each other. Marjan stood near the curtain covering the kitchen, her hands clasped in front of her, her head down. Abran's face was already flushed and his hands were balled into fists. Daniel stood still, as immutable as stone.

"If we slow down, northern currents will be worse, plus there'll be more ice around the coasts once we reach the Valley. It could make landing impossible," Abran said.

"I get that, but *Sedna* may not survive this storm," Daniel said. "Slowing down and avoiding it is worth the risk of losing time."

"We should put it to a vote," Marjan said softly.

Abran sent her a hard look. "No. I'll make the decision."

"I can't navigate through—" Daniel started.

Abran slammed his hand on the table. "You'll navigate through whatever you need to."

Abran turned from the table and leaned against it, his chin resting on his fist, and saw me standing in the doorway.

"I suppose you want us to slow down, too?" Abran asked me.

I glanced at Daniel and then back at Abran. They both had let me down; I didn't trust either of them.

But Daniel knew what he was talking about, knew the weather and the currents. We could lose the mast and the mainsail if it was as bad as Daniel thought it could be.

But what would happen if we made it to the Valley so late in winter that we couldn't navigate the coastline? We were already low on supplies; we needed to be able to anchor and get to land. And each day that passed was a day closer to Row boarding a breeding ship. Each moon that rose, white as an iceberg drifting in a black sea, gave me an ominous feeling, a sinking in my gut.

I imagined Row in the Valley when the epidemic came. Imagined her eating breakfast in a small canteen, maybe a biscuit or a bowl of oatmeal. And then the sounds. People from the village running, limbs thrashing, heads turned behind them to keep an eye on whatever they were fleeing. Clamoring and screaming, sounds of footsteps on hard ground.

Would she first think it was water coming for them? Roaring up over the mountainside?

And then an arrow shot through a woman in front of her. People colliding with her as she tried to flee. The smell of blood clinging in the air, a bitter taste in her mouth. She might have ducked into a church that doubled as a saloon, a small brick house with a window facing the well.

Maybe she crouched beneath a window, breathing heavily, blood thrumming in her ears as she tried to slow her breath. When she looked through the window, maybe she saw two raiders drop a body in a well. A body with sores and blackened limbs.

Or maybe the whole time she was at a house tucked away in the mountain, missing all of it, only to come outside once the village had been half burnt to the ground, the stench of disease heavy in the air.

However it had been, it didn't matter now. What mattered was that I get there in time.

My lip itched and I swiped a fish scale from my face. My hand left behind the taste of blood. I avoided Marjan's and Daniel's eyes. "Let's board up the window here in the cabin. Do some storm prep, but don't take down the sails," I said.

Daniel let out a long exhale, and when I looked at him his disappointment hit me like a hard shove.

Abran nodded. "We'll keep northeast. Keep on track, full speed ahead." Abran strode from the cabin and Marjan disappeared behind the kitchen curtain.

I went to the shelves and pulled down a small bucket of nails, my hands buzzing with a nervous energy. When I grabbed a handful, rust left orange smears on my palms.

Daniel stopped next to me before leaving the cabin.

"This isn't the way to get back at me," he said softly.

"You overestimate how much you factor into my decisions," I muttered.

Daniel sighed and shook his head. "I'll drop the sea anchor if I need to. I don't care what he says. I'll go overboard before this ship sinks."

A hard wind shuddered the door to the cabin violently after he left, and I felt a lurch in my stomach. The makeshift hinges rattled against the wood and I jumped forward and slammed the door shut, but it still shook, vibrations that pulsed against my hands.

CHAPTER 43

By lunch the wind had grown stronger and howled around the cabin as we ate. Everyone was silent, keeping their eyes on their bowls. The sky darkened by midafternoon, the horizon disappearing. It had a flattening effect, like we were being pressed down by some hand above us. I kept reaching for Pearl—tucking her hair behind her ear, straightening her shirt, nervous gestures that belied my confidence. Pearl swatted my hands away. Even the air was different; it smelled sweet and pungent and carried a certain sharpness, like a line pulled taut.

Marjan began putting everything in the kitchen into cupboards and spare boxes and nailing them shut. Daniel avoided Abran, but Wayne asked Abran if we could run before the wind with no sails.

"No, we're not lying ahull yet. We're going through it," Abran said.

A chill spread through me. I knew Abran felt he had something to prove after Broken Tree, but I hadn't expected such recklessness.

Daniel reefed the mainsail, and when Abran saw him anger flashed in his eyes. Abran ran to Daniel and shoved him.

"I said to run full speed ahead!" I heard Abran shout to Daniel over the wind.

Daniel elbowed Abran out of his way and turned back to the mainsail.

"I will maroon you!" Abran roared at Daniel.

A wave rose and collided with *Sedna*. We rocked like a cradle bumped in the night. White spray blew across the deck, blinding cold.

I ran into the cabin and began tying all my fishing rods together with a rope. Pearl came in after me, tugging at my sleeve.

She whimpered. "Mom, we'll go down."

I wrapped the end of rope around the shelves and knotted it. "Wrap my hooks in this cloth and stuff it at the bottom of that basket," I said, handing her a rag.

Pearl stamped her foot. "You aren't listening to me!"

I gave her a handful of lures. "These, too."

Pearl obeyed, her lips pressed together in a tight line. "I hate you," she murmured, just barely audible above the wind.

I gritted my teeth and finished weaving a rope around the shelf and the handles of baskets and buckets. "Are you sure you don't hate storms more?"

"I don't want to be in the water." Her expression was pleading, her eyes wide. She leaned toward me as if she wanted to bolt into my arms.

I knotted the rope, dropped to my knees, and pulled her into my chest.

I spoke into her ear, the soft smell of her a comfort. "You won't. We aren't going to capsize. Or sink. Daniel knows how to navigate a storm."

I spoke with more conviction than I felt. I kissed the tips of my fingers and pressed them to her lips. A small smile crossed her lips.

Abran sprang into the cabin, slammed the door, and collapsed into a chair.

"Son of a bitch," he muttered, running a hand through his hair. He jiggled his knee and tapped his fingers on the table.

When he looked at me his eyes held a wild, off-kilter look of astonishment. "The water is cold," he said.

I took Pearl's hand and we scrambled out of the cabin, toward the hatch.

At the stern, Daniel locked the rudder, keeping the bow pointed into the waves. The sky was almost black, as if ink had been poured over us. The clouds lowered over us, pressing down on us. A tower of water built, rising and rising as it approached Sedna's bow, black and looming, a wall we'd have to go through. I grabbed the mainmast to steady Pearl and myself, thinking of my mother looking up at the water before it crashed around her.

Pearl clasped my hand so hard, pain shot up through my arm. My love for her burned brighter, a dazzling clarity, a part of me that couldn't be touched.

The cold hit first, like a pebble twitching in my bones. Then the deck got so slick that our feet slid as if we were on ice, my arm around the mast our only anchor as our bodies lurched sideways. A second wave hit and it tore us from the mast, sending us sprawling and sputtering across the deck.

The water foamed and rippled across the deck, and Sedna righted herself and swayed as though ready to fall. Daniel ran toward us. He grabbed me beneath my arm and hauled Pearl and me to the cabin with Pearl wrapped around my waist, her face buried in my neck.

The bow rose on a wave, sending us stumbling forward, and then dropped with a crash. The hull hit the water and a crack split the air, so loud that it cut through the roar of the wind and the thunder of the waves.

Daniel, Pearl, and I fell through the cabin door and stumbled to our knees.

Wayne shouted at Abran over the din, "There's a hole in a joint down in the hull. Water pouring in and we're getting battered. Thomas is down there now, trying to stem the flow—"

Abran didn't look at any of us; his eyes drifted around the floor. "It's too late," he muttered.

Daniel pulled himself to his feet. "Just get belowdeck and help with the leak!" Daniel yelled at him.

Jessa was holding her stomach and vomited into the water at our feet. Wayne grabbed her arm and pulled her toward the door.

"We need to get the sea anchor dropped," Daniel said to me, rummaging through the boxes on the shelves. "Why the hell are none of these marked?"

Marjan scurried over to us. She pulled the sea anchor from a wood crate. It was a bundle of torn sails stitched together at the end of a long rope, like a heavy, raggedy kite.

The ship tilted to the right and we all slid across the wet floor. I caught Pearl in my arms and she collided against me before we hit the wall. The tables and chairs drifted with us, wood on wood screeching above the roar outside.

Daniel pulled himself up first and staggered toward Marjan. He grabbed the sea anchor from her. "Get Pearl down in the hull!" he shouted at me.

I hacked up a mouthful of salt water and pounded Pearl's back to get her to do the same.

We couldn't just drop the sea anchor. We needed to drop the mainsail and heave to. And Daniel couldn't do all that alone.

"Marjan, please take Pearl down," I shouted to Marjan. I took Pearl's shoulders and tried to turn her toward Marjan, but she whipped around and grabbed me around the waist.

"No!" she wailed. "No! Come with me!"

"I have to help Daniel," I said, my chest going tight. "You won't be alone. I'll be right down, I promise."

Her little body shook against mine and I pried her loose.

"Please, don't leave me," she murmured, a sob catching in her throat.

"Marjan, please," I said.

Marjan lifted Pearl and carried her through the cabin door. I caught sight of Pearl's face in a flash of lightning, a burst of light in her stricken eyes, her hair fuzzy from the salt water and wind, like she'd been rubbed until she began to fray.

Daniel and I slipped and floundered toward the stern, the cold, dark roar making my mind buzz. The dull roar in my ears seemed unchanging; it seemed to come more from within than without. Water everywhere, uncontainable, a rush and force that crushed and covered. Panic rose in me, flashes of those early days when the floods and storms buried everything I knew. The cars flipped over, crashing against houses. The old tree pulled up from its roots as if a great hand had yanked it up. The birds tossed against fences or houses by the wind.

Daniel held on to the downrigger and my arm, keeping us from being tossed into the sea. My fingers were numb and stiff as I tried to work the sea anchor's rope around the twin bollards. A wave built before us; the crest began to take shape. I got the rope knotted and tossed the sea anchor over the gunwale. Daniel and I both ducked as the wave hit, water engulfing us.

The rope pulled taut, and we braced ourselves against the gunwale as the ship began to drag and turn, straightening so it faced the waves head-on. We could still go broadside and capsize, I thought, but I pushed the thought away and focused on Daniel already scrambling across the wet deck toward the mainmast.

Daniel and I worked at the block and tackle, but Wayne had reefed the sail so tight that we couldn't loosen it. I couldn't see the rope, the mast itself hazy as a dark shadow. My numb fingers slid over the rope again and again, not able to pull any slack and loosen the knot.

"Get belowdeck!" Daniel shouted at me, shoving me aside.

"We could lose the mast!" I shouted back, but my words were lost as another wave crashed. Daniel caught me around the waist with one arm, his other linked around the mast, and we both tossed to the right like rag dolls, our feet slipping on the deck, water swirling around our ankles.

When we regained our balance, I elbowed him out of the way, my fingers finding the rope again. The deck leveled, as if all the wind and waves had stilled momentarily, motion sucked from our small world. My heart sped and a hot rush unfurled in my veins. Before us, another wall built, taller than the others, a wall like the one that had folded around my mother.

Daniel lifted me and half carried, half dragged me toward the hatch, lifting it and pushing me down below. He jumped down after me and pulled the lock into place, the sound of the metal clink lost amid the howling wind and roaring waves.

CHAPTER 44

I HELD PEARL against me, cradling her head under my chin, her body curled up against mine. She was no longer shaking. She had gone still and listless. I tried speaking to her a few times, to murmur something of comfort to her, but she didn't respond. I felt that she had backed away into some hidden room within herself and shut even me out. My small sailor, afraid of the sea.

We all were in the quarters, perched on beds. Thomas and Wayne had stuffed the hole in the curved wall with rags and hammered wood slabs over it. The pressure from the water opened new channels between cracks in the wood, which splintered and moaned. Water spread across the floor slowly, rocking back and forth as *Sedna* moved. Splinters of wood floated on the water like small ships being cast aimlessly about before being tossed into the hall, out of sight.

Sedna rammed against troughs again and again. It felt like an echo reverberating in my head. Crashes above, again and again. We didn't have enough wood on board to build that many spars. I could smell the sweat on everyone, salty and sweet, laced with panic.

A small window at the top of the wall let in flashes of lightning. Everyone flared in front of me and disappeared, the illuminations making it feel like they weren't actually in the room with me. The sensation was familiar, the aching fear that I'd be buried in a watery grave, always reaching for air and never finding it.

I returned to thoughts of my mother. The basket of apples as it fell from her arm. Was her body now a home for fish and plants? Her rib cage a roof for sea anemone?

Terror shuddered through me. We'll never make it through this, I thought. This is how the water takes us. I saw myself in my ocean grave, underwater light bluing my skin, my hair floating like seaweed, coral sprouting from my bones. A new thing in a new world.

Please, I bartered with any god, any creature who had power. Please don't let us sink. I felt about for something to offer up in exchange. Our crossing flitted past my mind, my desire to reach Row.

No, I thought. Not that.

When I stopped searching for Row it was as if I'd accepted everything I'd come to half believe about myself. That Jacob was right to abandon me. That I couldn't really make a life out here. Ask me for something else, I bartered. Don't take my last child.

Pearl stroked one of her snakes in her lap. I ran my finger along it, its skin strangely soft. It recoiled from me. Lightning struck; it opened its eyes and so did Pearl. Then it all went black again.

EARLY-EVENING LIGHT CAST a dim glow in the quarters. Some of us had dozed, fallen asleep with our dread. The storm must not have lasted long if it wasn't night yet. I almost wished it was night so we wouldn't have to see the damage by daylight right away. I feared seeing it would knock the breath out of me.

The water was a foot high in the quarters. Only a trickle of water came in now, forcing its way past the boards hammered over the hole. Pearl was shaking from cold, and I wrapped her in a blanket.

We climbed out of the hull silently. We had survived, but there was no celebration or spirited gratitude, only a shaken core, the question that lingered unspoken: yes, we'd made it through the storm, but will we make it through the calm after the storm? Which I knew was worse. All those days after the floods were always more difficult than the floods themselves. The rebuilding was what shook you to your marrow.

Looking across *Sedna*'s deck, I thought of the small towns in Nebraska that'd been hit by tornadoes; the leveling, the sharp edges of broken things, the misplaced objects too large to lift: car leaning against a tree, house with no roof.

The deck was strewn with water and wreckage—cordage and bits of wood, nails and shredded sail. The door of the cabin was missing. So was the mainsail. But the mainmast itself was still standing, and I let out a relieved exhale. Ropes lay frayed in heaps about the deck. The top yard lay overboard, still tied to the mainmast. The foresail was torn and fluttering in the wind.

The downrigger lay toppled over, split at the base like a tree struck by lightning. I cursed myself for not thinking earlier of removing it. It would be the last thing to be repaired, if we even had any material leftover to repair it.

I resisted what I saw; wanted it not to be true. Couldn't the storm have been a dream and everything still be in its place?

Anguish clenched me in its fist and I struggled against it. There wasn't time to mourn. How could we stop and mourn when there was so much to do?

The water around us was unbroken, as though nothing had happened. The sky was gray and the water looked softer somehow, as though the world had been scoured and cleaned, and now was letting out a fresh breath.

Thomas was the first to speak. "I'll check the spars and spare wood," he said.

"We don't have time to rebuild tonight," Abran said.

"We at least need to get some of the rigging cleaned up. Reinforce the hole in the hull. Do an inventory of the cordage that can be salvaged," I said. I steeled myself inwardly; we needed to move forward.

"So we'll just drift tonight?" Marjan asked, the first time I heard fear creep into her voice.

"We still have the sea anchor," Daniel said. "It will slow us some so we don't drift too far off course. And we have the foresail." I could tell from his tone that he doubted how much he could navigate with it.

My chest tightened. "Wayne, can you check the rudder?" I asked.

He nodded and made his way through the wreckage toward the stern.

"Do we have enough material for a new mainsail?" Marjan asked.

"Not for one of the same size," Thomas said.

This seemed to break something in Pearl. She dropped my hand and stepped away from me.

"You disagreed with Daniel," she said, speaking to the floor.

"What, honey?" I asked, squatting down, trying to look into her eyes.

"You made us go through the storm. You didn't care. You never care about me. You only care about her. Get to the Valley. Get to the Valley," Pearl chanted, her tiny hands squeezed into fists at her sides. She raised her eyes to meet mine. "I HATE YOU!" she screamed in my face.

Stunned, I blinked and was silent. I remained frozen, squatting in front of Pearl. Everyone shifted, their feet stirring small ripples in the water. Shame coursed through me. I remembered the looks on their faces when they discovered I'd betrayed them to search for Row. Judgment and anger were like objects I'd received from them and tucked inside me.

"Pearl," I said, reaching to touch her shoulder, but she jerked it away. "Pearl, if it were you—"

"It's not." Pearl jutted her chin out, her eyes dark. She crossed her arms in front of her. "You love her more."

"I can't," I said softly, my heart breaking. I never could make the right choice, could I? What was I teaching her about herself?

Wayne yelled from the stern that the rudder was still there.

"We need to get the yard out of the water. It's turning the boat," Thomas said. Jessa went with him and Daniel muttered something to the others, asking them to see what was left in the cabin. A dead fish floated past us. I could tell they pitied me and wanted to give us space.

"I need to check our location," Daniel told me, his voice barely audible. He said it like an apology.

Pearl dropped her arms to her sides and lifted her face, her chin quivering. Her eyelashes fluttered.

"I can't love her more," I said. "You two have already taken all I have. There is no more, there's only everything. If it were you there, I'd make her go through this. But that's not how it happened." I brushed a tear from her cheek. "I'm sorry I let us go through the storm."

"You never listen to me," she said.

I heard Jacob's voice in hers. How many times had he said those same words to me? I dropped my eyes to the watery deck. I was weary of all of it; weary of the choices, the responsibilities. For a moment, I wanted to disappear into the deep and float into oblivion.

Pearl stepped closer to me and laced her fingers in mine.

Her touch startled me. "I'm sorry," I said and meant it. She swiped her tears away with the back of her hand.

"I need to go feed Charlie. He's grouchy," she said.

I nodded and let her go back to the hull. As I watched her drop through the hatch I thought of how wrong she was.

Resentment burned in me. I wanted to tell her that it wasn't that I loved Row more, but that I had other, darker things in me that turned my decisions. My rage and my fear. They got all mixed up with my love and I couldn't separate them. They were like the sky when it melts into the sea, how you can't tell where one begins and the other ends.

She'd never be able to understand the weight of it all. The impossible choices. We were living this life together, but we might as well have been in separate worlds for all we knew of each other. I hid from her as my mother hid from me. And what was

she hiding from me? What dark currents swirled in her, mixing
with her love, eddying out of chasms that I could not see?

A fish swam past my feet. A small gray fish with a cut on its
belly, leaving a red swirl of blood in its wake. I snatched it up
and it fought my hand, scales shuddering in sunlight.

CHAPTER 45

THAT NIGHT WE got the yard out of the water and organized the damaged materials into piles of what could and could not be salvaged. The following afternoon I settled on the deck and leaned against the gunwale to stitch the foresail back together. Marjan had given me a small crate of scrap fabric to sew into the holes and tears. I was considering how to best fish without the downrigger when Daniel came and sat next to me. I shifted my body away from him and kept stitching.

"Saw you got some cod this morning," he said.

Two cod, after four hours of work. We needed more if we weren't going to go on even tighter food rations.

"Thomas and Wayne almost have a new yard built," he said. "Doesn't look half bad, actually." When I didn't say anything he went on. "Jessa has been working on the mainsail. It will be smaller. Quite a bit smaller. But it should work."

"How late will we be?" I asked.

"Late enough to worry about stronger currents when we anchor."

I bit my lip and rethreaded the needle, then positioned the fabric over a tear and began stitching the edges.

"Are you worried they're following us?" I asked.

The wind pushed the sail into a clump around my knees and I swore. Daniel leaned forward and helped me smooth it on the deck. He moved around me in a tentative way, as if he pitied me after Pearl's outburst. Or maybe he sensed my shame at deciding to try and run through the storm. I felt that shame like a piece of plastic caught in my throat, like something I needed to cough up, but had no words for. I imagined it like some hard thing I swallowed that would sit in my stomach and outlast me. The way when you cut open a seagull you'll sometimes find bits of plastic in its gut, small hard things that rattled around inside of it, never dissolving.

"A little," Daniel said. He straightened a fold and pressed the sail flat. "When my mother was at the end, she always sang this song. 'If I had wings, like Noah's dove, I'd fly the river, to the one I love . . .'" Daniel sang, in a low, clear voice. "It was some old song her mother would sing. I thought for the longest time the song was about my father, her longing for him."

Daniel went quiet, and I thought he was finished telling his story, but then he started up again.

"Then I noticed she was looking at me intently when she'd sing it and one night she reached for my face." Daniel reached out and brushed my cheek with his knuckles. "She was losing her sight by that point and it was like she was looking for me. She said, 'Don't go yet, don't go yet.' I told her I wasn't going to leave her, but that didn't settle her. It wasn't until after she died that I realized she was trying to tell me not to give up. She could tell I'd gone cold inside. Cold and empty. I thought I was with her at the end, but in a way, I wasn't."

Seagulls called out in the distance, their voices a relief. It had to be clear water for miles. I knotted the thread, cut it with my teeth. Daniel watched me. I kept my eyes on the fabric, waiting for him to go on.

"That's what I liked about you," Daniel said so softly that I leaned toward him so I could hear. "You never went cold. Not even for a while."

I realized why he was making me uncomfortable. His kind words to me were like water given to a thirsty man. I'd gulp it down and ask for more if I didn't restrain myself. I had made it this far by living alone and asking for less of this world than I'd ever thought possible. A few necessities to survive, but not much else. I was proud of how starved I could be. But longing for more remained in me like a steady fire I hoped wouldn't give me away.

Both our heads were bent over the fabric, his hands holding the sail down against the wind, mine clutching the needle and spare fabric. I noticed a single strand of gray hair at his temple. He seemed too young for it. The wind lifted my hair and sent it in a dark flurry around my face, and I pushed it back. It gave me an odd quickening in my veins, to sit next to him, to see myself the way he saw me.

"So Abran was part of the Lily Black," Daniel said, looking at me for confirmation.

I pressed my lips together and gave a slight nod.

"It's just if they follow us, Jackson will tell his crew they're going for Abran and to take over the Valley. They want a stronghold in the north. That's how he'll clear it with his commander. But for him, it will be for me. He promised. He keeps his promises."

I squeezed my eyes shut and opened them again. I didn't want to think about the possibility of being followed. "Tell me about him," I said.

"He always protected me." Daniel shook his head and looked at me with so much pain in his face, my heart clenched. "One winter, we were ice-skating on a small river and I fell through. Jackson leapt into the icy water and pulled me out and then built a fire on the bank so we could warm up before walking two miles back home. He had me sit with my feet and hands to the flames while he kept getting brush to feed the fire. He lost three toes and I made it through just fine. It was . . . not even a choice for him. Just who he was."

I pulled the thread tight, the stitches puckering the fabric like a scar.

"We always were rivals. I was my mom's favorite. That didn't bother him too much, though, until that night he came home for us. He started talking all about the Lily Black and what they were doing to rebuild society. But our mom had heard rumors about Jackson instigating the use of biological warfare during the war. Took out half of Turkey. She told him he was no son of hers."

A muscle in Daniel's jaw twitched and he blinked quickly. I swallowed and looked down. I imagined them around a kitchen table, a mother disowning her son.

"So Jackson told her, 'You know what Daniel did to get your insulin? He beat people up and stole from them. Tracked them down and beat them until they gave him their insulin. But I guess that's okay because he's your favorite. I guess he can't do any wrong.' She just told Jackson to get out of her house. And the look on his face. He'd come back to save us and now he was being thrown out. The shock and disbelief. I don't think I've ever hurt as much as he did in that moment."

Daniel lifted his hands from the sail to rub his face, and the sail fluttered in the wind like a broken wing. I pushed it back down.

"So he took the boat and insulin I'd gotten for her and sailed away. I understand . . . but I can't forgive it. Especially with what he's doing now. I can't stand by."

"That day—in the church," I began. "You came so close. To what you wanted." I let the unspoken question linger in the air.

Daniel shook his head. "I guess it wasn't just me and him anymore," he said.

I remembered how bewildered and frightened Pearl was that day in the church. Gratitude toward him swept through me. I reached out and grasped his hand. The touch sent a jolt to my bones and I let go of his hand and returned to my crooked seams.

Daniel looked out across the deck to where Thomas and Wayne were carrying the new yard toward the mainmast.

"Myra, you still believe it's you against the world. You think you can plow straight through a storm if need be. I will find a way to get you there, but you've got to trust me," Daniel said.

I scowled at him with what I knew was a childish, petulant expression. The look you have when you're wrong and someone else is right and you're almost glad of it.

He shook his head at me. "I would do anything for you. And the way you're looking at me tells me you already know that."

His eyes wouldn't leave mine, so I nodded once, a curt dip of my chin. I felt myself starting to give way, the cracks in my walls growing to fissures. I looked down at his hands still on the sailcloth, the calluses at the edges of his palms, the long scar traveling up his index finger. I wanted to touch them again, but I

repositioned the fabric over the sailcloth, pricked my finger with
the needle, and brought it to my lips just to taste something.

WE WORKED ON the repairs from dawn until dusk for over a
week, but even once the repairs were done something still felt
broken. I wondered if it was the solitude; this was the longest
we'd ever gone without seeing another ship. It'd been a month
since we'd left Broken Tree.

Thomas helped me scrounge up some old plywood and metal
rods to reinforce the downrigger. Marjan and I nailed scrap
wood along its base and fastened the metal rods along the shaft
with wire.

"We need to just replace the shaft," I muttered, pressing on
the downrigger. It shifted from my push.

"We could throw a net over, see how much weight it will
hold," Marjan suggested. "See where the strain is the worst and
reinforce it more."

I attached a net to the downrigger and tossed it overboard.
We both sat on the deck, watching the downrigger lean to the
left. Marjan got a piece of wood; I pushed the downrigger upright and she nailed it in place.

We sat back down. The downrigger strained against the
weight but held. We were both quiet and I was thinking of the
dream I'd had last night, from which I woke, startled, to Pearl's
light snore. I'd dreamt everything in the sea had died as if a
poison had run through it. Or maybe it had gone too hot or too
cold and there was nowhere to migrate, just miles and miles of
blue poison. The water was suddenly all wrong and no creature

could change fast enough to keep up, so each fish shriveled and drifted to the seafloor, where hundreds of them piled, one on top of the other. Tiny mountains of mass graves under the waves.

"What if all the fish dry up?" I asked Marjan. "The water changes somehow, becomes inhospitable? I've hardly been able to catch anything lately."

Marjan's face remained placid, only faint lines on her forehead and on either side of her mouth. Her dark eyes were unfocused, like she was in another place. I suddenly wanted to know what she'd done and what she remembered. Not just what she'd done in her life, but what she'd done that she didn't want to.

"Then we won't fish," Marjan said after a minute of silence. Marjan was sitting cross-legged, hands in her lap.

Her calm unnerved me. "Easy for you to say," I muttered and winced as soon as I said it. "I'm sorry. I—"

"With no one depending on me?" Marjan asked. Her voice went cold, but then a faint smile appeared on her lips. She shook her head. "In a way it is easier. And harder."

I squeezed my eyes shut and leaned back, my hands behind me. I breathed deeply, trying to expand my chest, a heaviness suffocating me.

"I'm sorry. I just . . . sometimes I don't know what I'm doing. I'm trying to save her, but I won't be able to protect her," I said. "Not in this world."

"Not in any world." Marjan peered across the deck and up at Thomas in the rigging, nailing a small metal block against the new main yard. When she looked back at me she seemed softer and smaller. The sun was shining in her eyes and she squinted. "My mother used to always say there's wisdom in suffering. But if I have any wisdom, it hasn't come from what's happened to me, so much as from the suffering I've brought on myself."

"What do you mean?"

"My daughter . . . when she drowned. She wasn't ripped from my hands by a flash flood like I said." A sad smile crossed Marjan's face. "Sometimes I like to think that's how it happened."

The hesitant, halting way she spoke reminded me of my mother. The rhythm was not unlike the sea, pushing forward and then pulling back.

"Before the schools closed I was a teacher. Math and science. I'd heard stories of how teachers tend to treat their students like children and their children like students. You teach your kids and give to your students. I always thought, Oh, I don't do that. But I did. Especially with my only daughter. Always expected more of her, put more pressure on her. After we migrated during the Six Year Flood we stayed in Kansas or Oklahoma for a short while. Became friends with another family with two young sons. They fished and their sons worked by diving in the shallows for clams and other small creatures. They shared their food with us and we shared with them. My sons dove with their sons and my daughter didn't want to. Said she was scared to go under the water. But I told her, 'You need to face your fears. You need to contribute. This is what we have to do now.' And I told her to dive with the rest of them."

My heart began to beat faster. Marjan set her palms on the deck between us, spread her fingers wide, her knuckles knobby with age. I tried to focus on the wood deck visible between her fingers.

"A week later they were diving in an old house for fish and she got stuck. Couldn't find a way out. The other kids thought she'd already come up. There was this moment . . ." Marjan squinted, and I could tell she was returning to that place and time, perhaps remembering the water, the exact way the sunlight fell on its surface. "This moment that was just the beginning of denial, denial I still struggle with. People say denial is a stage, but it isn't. I always wrestle with acceptance. Want to believe she could actually be here, that things could have gone another way."

I squeezed my eyes shut and sweat broke out along my back. I tried to swallow, but my mouth had gone dry. No, I kept thinking. No. It shouldn't have happened that way, not to Marjan.

"I went down for her body because I sent her down there." Marjan's voice went soft. "She was so light in the water. Like a feather. Like she hadn't even been a little girl. Like I'd dreamed her."

Marjan turned her face to the side and the sunlight caught her black hair, casting a blue sheen across it.

"So when you sacrificed us all to get to Row, I thought: That's a terrible thing. And it is. But I also thought, she's busy breaking herself. The world will break you, but it's when you break yourself that you feel you really can't heal."

"It wasn't your fault," I said, shaking my head at her.

Marjan bit her lip. "Sometimes I believe that, too."

I could hear seagulls diving into the water, their wings furiously flapping as they pulled a fish up out of the water. The net's rope was so taut it vibrated against the gunwale. Something was stirring in me, a surge of pressure building in my veins, something that needed to get out. I couldn't look at her, so I leaned forward and looked down at my hands.

"When Row was born her shoulders were these tiny curves. Barely even there. Like her skeleton hadn't formed yet. Like she wasn't ready to be out in this world," I said, something catching in my throat. I rubbed the back of my neck. "How?" I asked, my voice hoarse. "How do you go on?"

Marjan was silent a moment, watching me. She bit her lip and squinted until her eyes were slits. "You do the hardest thing. The most impossible thing. Again and again."

I couldn't do what she'd done, I thought. I couldn't go on like she had. The downrigger moaned against the pressure and leaned toward the gunwale like it'd bolt off the ship. Neither of us moved to pull in the net. I blinked furiously so the tears wouldn't spill. I wanted to reach out and grasp her hand, but I stayed still. There were no maps for any of this. Only people who had gone before, leaving trail markers behind for the rest of us.

Marjan made me think of a line Grandfather kept repeating over and over in the days before he fell asleep and never woke up. *From the water we came and to the water we will return, our lungs always hungering for air, but our hearts beating like waves.* It had seemed sad at the time, foreboding, but now it seemed somehow comforting, something that spoke of vigor.

Marjan sighed. "Myra, you don't need fish in the sea, you don't need dry land, so much as you need hope. You're strangling yourself."

I looked up at her and she held my gaze, her dark eyes unrelenting. I was surprised by the despair I saw in her eyes. Marjan always seemed so steadfast, so resolute in the face of hard times, but there was a black gravity in her, too. Hope

would always hold despair in it, I realized, despair born of what
I'd seen and done. I'd carry those images and those acts in my
body and hope would sit right next to them, neither feeding nor
extinguishing them.

I remembered finding my father hanging. He was so cold,
his face mottled. Wanting more from life than it could give you
looked like weakness. You should accept what it gave you and
trudge on, I had thought. After we took him down, the rope left
a line at his throat. It looked like a flood line, as if the sea had
risen right up under his chin and he had grown tired of treading
water.

CHAPTER 46

I DIDN'T KNOW what rules we were following anymore. So I stayed up late one night, making lures by candlelight in the cabin. An ill-fitting new door had been constructed from plywood and it thudded rhythmically against the doorframe with each wave.

I tied dead insects onto hooks and wove bits of fabric and thread together to look like insects or worms. I was running out of thread, trying to think of where I could scavenge for more, when Daniel opened the door to the cabin.

"Don't tell Abran," I muttered.

Daniel glanced at the hooks laid out before me and shrugged. "Wasn't going to."

He sat next to me. In the candlelight he looked older and more remote, the angles on his face deeper. His high cheekbones gave way to his beard, which almost hid the new gauntness of his face. His silence and still presence made him seem like a man come from an ancient time, a time I didn't have access to.

"How far are we?" I asked.

"About six hundred miles southwest."

I inhaled sharply. Almost there. I had thought I would be excited, but I only felt an odd trepidation, something caught and bottled in my bones.

"What is it?" Daniel asked, touching my arm with the tips of his fingers.

I shook my head quickly as if to wake myself up. "Nothing."

The wings fell off the dead fly I was pinching between two fingers, trying to get it wedged on a hook. "Shit," I muttered. I took a deep breath. All evening I had been thinking about Jacob, wondering how he felt all those years after he left. Had he regretted it? Had he felt any guilt? Or had he died soon after he had left, with little time to feel anything at all? I wanted to speak to Daniel about it but didn't know where to begin. The longing I had felt as Daniel and I repaired the sail burned even brighter now, a flame that kept jumping and reaching.

"What you said," I started, and then paused. I gritted my teeth and pierced the fly's torso with the hook. "About wanting a reckoning. I . . . for so long, I tried to believe Jacob wanted to come back for me. I waited. And waited. When he didn't come back for me, I told myself something got in his way." I looked up at Daniel, my eyes burning. "Nothing got in his way."

I had a vision of myself, at the bottom of the sea, releasing sea creatures one by one from the dark seafloor. Claws, fangs, tentacles. Things I knew intimately. Rising toward the surface.

"You don't know that," Daniel said, scooting his chair closer to me, his eyes not leaving my face.

Saving Row was the only thing I could admit to wanting. Was there a part of me that wanted to see Jacob again? Did I want the chance to destroy him, as he destroyed me?

"If he were there . . ." I trailed off into silence.

"He's still their father," Daniel said. He watched me like he was reading my thoughts. "What parents do to each other . . . it matters."

I blinked down at the dead fly shaking in my hand. "Of course, think of the children," I muttered sarcastically.

"I'll be there with you, Myra," Daniel said, his voice low and soft.

"You don't always get to take care of everything," I snapped.

"I know. You never let me take care of you. Or Pearl."

"We don't need care."

"Yes, you do," Daniel said. His eyes didn't waver from mine, and I looked away.

A growing heaviness descended on me. What would happen in the Valley felt irrevocable, something in an ancient story that had already been written. I had the odd sensation of being watched by my future self, some future self who whispered in my ear, asking me to pay attention.

I knotted a piece of twine around the dead fly. I ran a hand down the back of my neck and it came away damp with sweat. I was flustered. I needed Daniel to leave. Letting him in was giving in to the wrong impulse, feeding longing that needed to be squelched.

"I appreciate how much you've helped me," I said, turning my body slightly away from his. "I should finish up." I cleared my throat and squinted down at the fly.

Daniel's chair scraped on the floor as he scooted it closer. He placed his thumb under my chin and turned my face toward his. "I don't care about helping you. I'm not your helper."

We stared into each other's eyes and I felt warmth in even the soles of my feet. An ache built in my stomach and beads of sweat gathered between my breasts. I remembered when I first pulled him onto my boat, his limbs long and heavy under the high noon sun, dark lashes fluttering as he regained consciousness, skin glistening from water and light. Even then, under my fear, I felt some calm certainty about him that I didn't understand.

Daniel cupped my face in his palms and dropped one hand to trail down my neck. He rubbed a fistful of my hair between his fingers, the strands' friction making the gentlest rasp.

"Don't you understand? I can't lose you," he whispered.

The tenderness in his voice made me feel like I was collapsing. I leaned into him and he kissed me, his mouth rough and hungry on mine, our tongues darting, breath mingling.

His beard was rough against my face and I grasped his neck, his muscles moving and pulsing beneath my palms. My heart beat quicker and quicker, matching pace with his.

Daniel lifted me onto the table. He slipped his fingers beneath my shirt and pulled it off. His hand on my skin sent a hot stirring between my legs and I arched into him. He was hard against my belly and I grasped the back of his head, his hair sliding through my fingers, his mouth trailing down my neck.

Edge of his teeth, rough hair on his arms. A smoky, salty scent along his hairline. His chest heavy and warm, the taste of his skin. I felt like I couldn't breathe enough. Like I was softening to liquid, dissolving.

His fingers slid between my legs, my hips rolling against him, my whole body opening. When he entered me I tilted my head back, hands around his neck, my neck as exposed as the belly of a fish, the room almost upside down. The light from the candle swirled in the darkness. He moved inside me and my head clouded and cleared, clouded and cleared, until I couldn't rise any higher and was held suspended, aloft.

The room returned slowly, like awakening after a deep sleep. Rough wood on my fingertips, the chill from outside finding its way in. It seemed so cold. The night so silent.

CHAPTER 47

AFTER A WEEK of sailing in clear waters and cold but steady wind, we hit a patch of fog so thick we couldn't see three feet ahead of us. The horizon and sun disappeared. Daniel kept pacing in the cabin and swearing.

"We could be coming up on icebergs anytime. The map says depending on the season, they could already be in these waters," Daniel told me when I stopped in the cabin for a new fishing pole.

I touched his shoulder and smoothed his hair back. "We'll be okay," I said with uncharacteristic optimism. He laid his hand over mine.

While being with Abran had been a break from myself, being with Daniel was a kind of coming home, a centering. Abran had been useful to me, but it wasn't just that. I had been immediately attracted to his charisma, his certainty, the easy way he moved about the ship, like he could have been born there. I wanted some of that ease. When I first came on *Sedna* I was on someone else's property for the first time and felt a new vulnerability. I needed Abran's touch to soothe that vulnerability.

Being with Abran was like one of those children's games where all the thrill is in the chase and never the catch. Where you like most the moment when your fingers are inches from their back and they pull away from you, able to dart from your reach. The pleasure of wanting and not having.

But Daniel gave me a deeper kind of desire: for possession, for a future, for a kind of living within each other. Perhaps I could feel a future with him because he was the first person since Grandfather that I felt safe with. Perhaps his love for Pearl made me feel that we were partners from the beginning, that we could work together for a dawn on another shore. My attraction to Daniel had grown slowly and steadily until it overtook me, moss spreading over a tree until the whole trunk was green and stayed that way until it fell to the forest floor. I could feel him even in my blood, as if he inhabited me just by looking at me. There had been no awkwardness between us after that night in the cabin. Instead what remained was a deeper understanding, like we'd spoken at length after a long silence.

I returned to fishing, filling the salt barrels with cod and halibut and some small gray fish that I'd never seen or heard of. We were nervous it could be toxic, so Wayne volunteered to try it.

"The king's taster," he joked, trying to lighten our mood, but no one laughed as we watched him chew and swallow.

He didn't show any signs of illness a day later, so Marjan cooked it with what was left of the potatoes and we all tried to savor our first full meal in days. We had gone on food rations the previous week and I could hear our stomachs rumbling in the night.

Normally I depended on reading the water to fish, but fog kept rolling over us. So I kept fishing like a blind person, tossing lines over the gunwale, hooking up the net to the downrigger, reeling it in more frequently since the downrigger couldn't take much weight. The rope holding the net was beginning to fray, but it was the only rope we had left. We had no more twine to repair it, so I hoped it would hold until we made it to the Valley.

Daniel had us reef the mainsail to slow our speed.

"I can't navigate through icebergs if I can't see them," he kept saying. I laid a hand on his shoulder and felt his muscles coiled and tense as newly twisted rope. He spent all day in the cabin calculating distances or standing at the bow, straining to see beyond the fog, searching for the sun.

One day, Marjan called out to me. She stood at the gunwale, near the bow of the ship, binoculars in hand. I left the downrigger and went to her.

"Look," Marjan said, handing me the binoculars and pointing straight ahead.

I peered through the binoculars but couldn't see anything past the fog.

"What?" I asked.

"I saw a ship," Marjan said. She twisted her hands together and then pointed straight ahead.

I looked again but didn't see anything and didn't want to. I had stopped worrying about the Lily Black. We'd been so isolated so long, only water and sky for miles and miles, that seeing another ship felt like a distant, unlikely possibility. Underneath the disbelief, fear thrummed and grew.

"Are you sure? Maybe you imagined it. This fog can make it look like things are out there, but it's just more fog," I said.

Marjan shook her head, biting her lower lip, her eyebrows furrowed. I reached out and rubbed her arm. There were dark bags beneath her eyes. She was taking our dwindling resources the hardest, straining to make meals out of the grain stuck in the weave of a burlap sack. We did still have a few inches of grain in barrels and a few canned goods left, but we couldn't afford to waste a single crumb. We didn't know how long it would take to land at the Valley or how long it would take us to find food once we landed.

I told Marjan not to worry. Once she left to make supper I climbed the rigging to speak with Daniel. He peered at the sky and made a small note in his notebook. I told him Marjan thought she saw another ship.

His face hardened and he stopped writing.

"Do you think it's them?" I asked. My hair blew in my face and I kept pushing it back.

When he didn't say anything, I quickly added, "It could be anyone."

"We could go farther north," Daniel said. "Anchor and dock from that side."

"The map says anchoring on the south side is best," I said. "It's a sheer cliff to the north and a longer journey into the Valley from east or west."

Beatrice's map showed that the Valley would only be accessible from the southern side of the island. The west and east would be a long journey on foot, over the mountains, and the north was a treacherous coastline and a maze of rocks and ice. There were a few steep cliffs on the southern side of the island, but in the southeast there was a small inlet where we could anchor the ship and take the canoe to shore. That part of the shore was a flatter coastline with only a few miles to cross before reaching the Valley.

"I'm just trying to think of alternatives," Daniel snapped.

He rubbed his face, his nose red from the cold. "Don't tell any-one else about the ship yet. This fog will clear soon and we'll make a plan." He squinted up into the sky. "I hope."

I climbed down from the rigging and returned to the down-rigger to pull up my net. I cranked the downrigger, throwing my weight behind each crank of the lever. The wood handle stung my raw skin, my fingers chilled to the bone. The rope moaned against the gunwale, and when the net surfaced the water I braced myself against the lever, the extra weight pushing against me.

I gritted my teeth and glanced at the rope. The fibers unrav-eled in its weak spot, the strands snapping and fraying. It split in a sharp pop and the net splashed back into the water.

Everything in me brightened in panic and I leapt forward to grab the rope, but it disappeared over the side.

I looked over the gunwale, the dark water rippling, too clouded to even cast my reflection back at me. I sank to my knees and pounded my fists on the deck and swore.

"Mom?"

I turned and saw Pearl behind me. She stepped forward and stroked my hair, pulling it into a bundle at the base of my head. Her small fingers were so cold, I cupped them in my hands and breathed on them.

"YES, I CAULKED the weak spot in the hull. Dammit," Jessa snapped at Wayne.

"The floor was wet in the quarters this morning," Wayne

said. His handlebar mustache stuck up on either side of his mouth, and he kept trying to flatten it with his palm.

"Well, stop harassing me. I'm dealing with it," Jessa grumbled.

Daniel stood at the cabin window, arms crossed, shoulders hunched up to his ears. He hadn't slept last night; he kept tossing and turning, waking me from my light doze. Before dawn, he was on deck, binoculars to his eyes, searching the horizon. The fog was just beginning to clear. The rest of the crew thought he was keeping an eye out for icebergs.

Marjan and I stacked the breakfast dishes and went over a plan to stretch the food. With no net for trawling and our dry goods almost used up, we'd have to depend on line fishing.

"Mom! Mom!" Pearl ran into the cabin and grabbed my hand, pulling me out the door.

We burst into the cold air and there it was. Greenland's mountains. And behind them, the Valley.

The mountains rose up out of the water, a startling green, their reflection in the sea below clear as a carved object. It felt like I could reach out and touch them. The wind whistled around *Sedna* and enveloped us as though it was lifting us up, giving me the heady sensation of flight.

Pearl clutched my hand and beamed up at me, and I dropped to my knees and hugged her.

"We're almost there," she whispered into my hair. She said it with excitement, but I felt a sudden foreboding. I had expected to feel only relief, but I also felt fear—fear of what I would find among those mountains.

The others followed us out of the cabin. Gasps, claps, cheers, whoops of joy. Wayne slapped Thomas on the back. Marjan exhaled, closed her eyes, and clasped her hands together. Abran put his hands on his hips, shook his head as he let out a relieved laugh, and hugged Jessa.

Even Daniel couldn't suppress a laugh. He turned and swept me up in his arms, lifting me to my toes. His grin split his face in two, wider than I'd ever seen it. I buried my face in his chest and breathed him in. Everyone's joy was contagious and I pushed aside my dread. I felt a stirring in my chest and the vision of the cottage by the sea resurfaced in me. But this time I saw Daniel in the cottage with Pearl and Row and me. Boots by the hearth, candles on a table. Wildflowers dried and drooping from a cracked cup.

We pulled apart and Daniel went into the cabin to get the binoculars so we could survey the coast better and look for the inlet.

I pulled my fur hood more tightly around my face. Not since winters in Nebraska had I seen my breath ghost before my eyes. It felt nostalgic. The air tasted like a cool glass of water. Like everything would be all right.

The fog lifted around us. Pulled back its tendrils and revealed icebergs ahead of us, surrounding the mountains. The green of land was so bright it had cut through the fog, but now we could see it more clearly, the folds of the mountains, the rocks along the coastline.

"Will we be able to navigate around the icebergs?" I asked Daniel when he returned.

Daniel scanned the water around us and nodded. His expression was placid again, his mood subdued.

"We're small enough that it should be fine. Just need to go slow. I'll ask Wayne to trim the mainsail again," he said. "We could be there in a day."

We glided past an iceberg. It looked so serene, a brilliant white. It made me think of the face of a woman with her features rubbed off, erased.

I turned from the north and looked south, to see the water we'd gone blindly through. Nothing but water, no icebergs, no rocky outcrops of mountaintops. We'd been lucky. To the south there was still some fog in the distance, clouding the horizon. I looked up, into the clear gray sky, and saw a bird.

It wasn't a seagull. Its head was too small, its legs too short. It was a land bird. I squinted. It was pale gray and it flew as if it were struggling against the wind; it couldn't ride the wind the way gulls did. Even if we hadn't seen the Valley, this was our sign. We were close to land. I was close to Row.

A dove. Like Noah's dove, I thought. A warm feeling spread in my chest and I smiled to myself. Hope. Like Marjan had talked about. What I needed.

A flock of seagulls flew from the southwest, appearing suddenly out of the fog like a ghost. They squawked to each other wildly, their voices so erratic and overlapped they sounded panicked, like they were screaming out to one another. As if they were fleeing something.

They passed the dove, their shadows darkening *Sedna* as they flew over us. I looked back at the dove, which seemed to be flying in a straight line. Like it was flying toward something. On a mission.

I blinked. It wasn't a dove; it was a pigeon. Like the pigeon I'd seen released at Ruenlock.

The fog pulled farther back and I could see the horizon line, a dark gray streak where the sky met the sea, like a blade. And to the south, directly behind the pigeon, a dark ship sat on the horizon.

CHAPTER 48

DANIEL HANDED ME the binoculars. It was a ship twice the size of ours that looked like an old warship, but made of plastic and tires and metal sheeting, rather than smooth wood. Its bow had a thick metal ram, which caught the sun and sparkled. A black flag with a white lily in the middle billowed in the wind and the hull bore the name *Lily Black*. Daniel's brother wasn't just a high-ranking captain in the Lily Black, he was the captain of the tribe's flagship.

The ship grew larger by the minute, coming full speed at us, its sails stretched full with wind. There were gasps behind us and then silence. I couldn't breathe, a cascade of terror rolling up my spine. Did we need to sail for the northern side of these mountains? It was more treacherous, but fleeing felt like our only option. We were smaller, so we could maneuver through the ice better than they could.

"They're at the horizon, so twelve miles or so," Daniel said.

When I turned, I saw that the crew was looking at me. Abran was as pale as the ice that surrounded us. He walked forward to the gunwale, placed his hands on it, and dropped his head between his shoulders.

The crew spoke over one another, panicked, speculating.

"Have they followed us all this way? They already got revenge for Ruenlock."

I glanced at Daniel, but neither of us said anything about his or Abran's connection with the Lily Black. I remembered what Daniel had said about the crew tracking down Abran and taking over the Valley colony, while Jackson hunted Daniel.

"Maybe they plan to take over the Lost Abbot colony at the Valley. I've heard they're trying to take over the north," Marjan said.

"And preexisting colonies are easier to take over than new communities," Thomas said.

"Which means we wouldn't be in this fix if we'd known the Valley was a colony in the first place," Wayne snarled at me.

"We're smaller than they are," I said, ignoring Wayne. "Let's slip between the icebergs, cut up north, and get to land. Hide in the Valley."

"The ice field is worse up north. What if we're trapped between them and ice?" Wayne asked.

I secretly hoped the Lily Black would get stuck in this ice field and we could still land on the south side of the mountains, where a small bay would protect us from the rocks and waves. But if the Lily Black made it through this ice, Wayne was right—the north wasn't a safe plan.

I turned back to the ship. It was a double hull, with at least six sails, and through the binoculars I could see cannon holes below the main deck. The ship looked like it could hold thirty men, maybe more, not counting the slaves belowdecks.

"We shouldn't have . . ." Abran was muttering. The resources hidden in the cave. The murder in the saloon at Broken Tree. Behir.

Regret also surged through me and I tried to tamp it down. I grew dizzy. I clenched and unclenched my fists to startle myself clear.

"Let's try to make it through the ice," I told Daniel.

He nodded and ran to the tiller.

I looked at Jessa, Thomas, and Wayne. "Armory."

They nodded and ran for the hatch, jumping down and letting it slam shut with a thud. We had handmade bombs, rifles, knives, bows and arrows. Weapons that would help mostly in close contact; nothing like the cannons that could rip us to shreds from a distance. Or the ram that could sink us.

"Seal the water," I told Marjan. She left for the cabin to pull good water from the cistern and seal it in plastic water bottles.

Pearl clutched my hand so tightly, it was losing feeling. I squatted in front of her.

"No," she said.

"Pearl—"

"NO!" she screamed in my face. "I don't want to be alone down there!"

I felt so queasy, I thought I'd vomit. She looked at me defiantly. Her face before me seemed frozen for a moment, as if she were a photograph, as if I knew this all would soon be a memory and I was resisting the slip of time. I registered her every surface with a clarity that stunned and frightened me. I didn't want her out of my sight.

You need to get moving, I told myself, trying to shut my thoughts down. You need to get her a pack in case we get separated. I ushered Pearl into the cabin with me and grabbed an empty knapsack. I rummaged through the shelves, filling the bag with a flint rod, a thin coil of rope, a wool blanket, a jack-knife, and a few of the water bottles Marjan was filling from the cistern. I raided the kitchen cupboards for food and found a small tin of salmagundi and a jar of hardtack biscuits.

Then I pulled Pearl toward the hatch. She clawed at my wrists and pried my hands from her shoulders.

"It won't be long," I lied. "I'll be coming down to check on you."

"What if the water starts coming in?"

I imagined a cannonball splitting *Sedna*'s hull, water pouring in, the mad roar and rush of a cold force that could bend metal. And Pearl in the middle of it all, her small form shaking.

My stomach clenched. I gritted my teeth and tried to steel myself. My nerves began to snap shut, like an oyster shutting out the sea.

"It won't. And if it does, I'll come get you," I said, climbing down the ladder with her.

"The water is cold here," Pearl said.

This stopped me. I had been busy thinking of cannonballs and bullets and fire, calculating distances for different attacks. But *Sedna* sinking would take all of us at once. The water would be so cold that we couldn't hang on to scrap wood and float to a rocky outcropping. Blood would freeze and rattle in our veins.

The hull stank of mold and mildew. Ever since we got the leak from the storm, it had been musty and damp in the hull. I led Pearl down the short hallway into the food storage room and tucked her between some near-empty barrels of grain.

Footsteps thundered above us. I needed to get back up to help. Pearl grabbed my arm.

"Stay with me," she murmured.

"I would if I could, honey," I said. I kissed her forehead and smoothed her hair back from her face.

"The water is too cold to swim in," she said, her chin trembling.

"I know. But you won't be in the water." *Sedna* shuddered, and for a wild moment I thought we were brushing against an iceberg, but then she moved clear and easy. Just a rough wave.

I tried to steady my breath. "I'll come back for you," I promised.

Pearl trembled, but she leaned back between the barrels, her face full of trust.

"Okay," she said.

BACK ON DECK, Thomas and Abran were at the mainmast, trimming the sails.

"What're they doing?!" I yelled at Daniel back at the tiller.

"We need to trim the sails, we're going too fast. I can't navigate through this ice," Daniel yelled back.

"If we slow down, they'll be close enough to fire the cannons," I said. I ran a hand through my hair and swore.

An iceberg lay up ahead and Daniel steered us to the right. Jessa and Wayne loaded rifles and checked bombs in the cabin. Marjan loaded the water into backpacks. I slung a rifle around my chest, stuck an extra knife in the sheath at my waist, and stepped out of the cabin.

The *Lily Black* was only a mile away, on the starboard side, charging toward us. The ship's sails were black, giving it the appearance of a dark beast bounding toward prey. Several men and women moved about on deck, carrying guns. Daniel's brother stood at the bow, his hair brushed back by the wind, so still he looked like a statue.

Two women carried a wooden ladder with curved ends. To climb aboard. Like using ladders to scale walls, only our walls were the gunwales. They intended to hook us and send men aboard.

My breath went short and shallow, my hands clammy. The pigeon, which flew almost as fast as the *Lily Black* sailed, was now almost over us. So pale it almost blended in with the sky. I looked beyond it, back at the ship. Smoke billowed from a makeshift chimney in its cabin.

"Marjan!" I called out. I wasn't worried about deck fires, which would be easy to extinguish. I was worried about the sails burning, the flames fanned by the wind, inching downward toward us like a candle burning.

Marjan emerged from the cabin and I pointed to the smoke and we both ran for the buckets tied to the stern. We dropped them over the side of *Sedna*, hauled them up by the rope tied to their handles. We dumped the salt water into the now drained cistern, the water foaming and eddying in small currents.

After I'd dumped my fourth bucket into the cistern, Abran caught my arm.

"Myra. If I don't—"

I shook my head and tried to pull away, but his hand tightened around my arm.

"Just try and fulfill my promise. To my brother. If it's you and not me," he said. His eyes were bloodshot, the skin under them so creased and puffy, he looked like he hadn't slept in weeks. His skin was ashen. I reached out and laid my palm on his cheek.

"We want the same thing," I said. A home. Somewhere with a future that we'd actually want to be in. I didn't understand how I hadn't known this all along. It didn't stop with rescuing Row. It stopped with making a life for all of us.

He nodded. He took my head in his hands and kissed the top of my forehead.

Behind him I caught sight of the canoe, fastened to the cabin's west wall. It only held four people, so we always took turns rowing to coasts. There would be no escaping on it. Even if it could hold all of us, the Lily Black would follow us in it.

A single shot rang out and I flinched. The pigeon dropped dead a few feet away, a splattering of blood seeping into the wood deck.

A piece of paper was rolled and tied to its ankle. I squatted before it and pulled the paper loose.

The crew huddled around me.

My heart rose to my throat when I saw the words. "You have one of ours. Hand him over," I read aloud. They meant Abran, I thought, but Jackson wouldn't stop until he had Daniel.

"I'll go," Daniel said. Daniel walked toward the canoe and began to unfasten the rope.

"Daniel, wait! It's not you," I called out to him.

An awful churning began in my chest. A chill spread in my veins.

Row was so close. I could see the Valley. After all this time, she was almost within reach. I had come too far on this journey to be sunk by cannons now. Pearl was in the hull. My mouth went dry and I tried to swallow. I imagined sending Abran out to them, paddling through the icy water to his death.

The image made me light-headed. My thoughts skidded and jumbled. There was a line that couldn't be crossed, and Jacob had taught me where it was. I remembered Jacob wanting me to abandon my mother and grandfather and to leave early with him before the water reached Nebraska.

I had that same reaction now—the tightening in my gut, the refusal in my chest. After losing my mother and grandfather, I was certain I'd never feel that way about anyone again. But that same irrational loyalty tugged at me. The same loose-limbed feeling of vulnerability. The same defensive resolve. We weren't handing over one of our own. I intended to rescue Row, and I still would. If I had to survive the Lily Black to get to her, I would.

The crew glanced at each other and I was careful not to look at Abran.

"So someone on this ship is a raider?" Wayne asked, his eyes narrowed in suspicion.

"Someone on this ship *was* a raider," I corrected him. "We aren't giving anyone up. There's no reason to believe they wouldn't still attack."

Daniel returned to working the canoe loose. "We don't have a chance making it with them on our tail. I'll go. This began with me; it will end with me."

The crew exchanged confused looks. "What does he mean?" Wayne barked.

"That isn't the point," I snapped at Daniel.

"This isn't just your choice," Wayne said to me. "Abran, what do you think—"

Abran ripped the handkerchief from his neck, exposing the scars.

"I was Lily Black," he said, pointing to his scars. Everyone turned to him in shock. His stoicism began to collapse, his face knotting in fear and pain.

"All this time . . ." Wayne said, a sharp edge to his voice.

Jessa crossed her arms and took a step back, eyes narrowed at Abran. Marjan showed no surprise, but Thomas ran a hand over his face. Everyone grew silent and distant.

We can't withdraw from each other, I thought. I had spent my whole life withdrawing from people. We needed to pull together. "We ignore it and continue on. They are too big to navigate this ice," I said with more certainty than I felt.

A sad, resigned look flattened the planes of Abran's face. He shook his head.

"We'll never escape them, Myra," he said softly.

"If he goes, they may let us go," Jessa said, her voice high and anxious.

Abran nodded and began to cross our circle toward the canoe. I wouldn't see him hanging from the bow of the Lily Black's ship. My vision tunneled.

"NO!!" I roared, shoving Abran so hard he fell to the deck.

I spun around toward the crew with my fists raised, and they shuffled backward. I saw myself through their expressions: the caution, the shock. The way a person looks at a dog with teeth bared and hackles raised. I must have looked like a woman possessed.

"We don't hand over one of our own," I said quietly.

The crew exchanged looks. Marjan nodded. "I'll get the flag," Marjan said.

Marjan came out of the cabin with the orange flag, the flag that meant a refused request. Now we weren't *Sedna*. We were defiance. Orange as the sky before dark.

For seconds after we raised the flag, there was silence. Then came a sound like air sucked in quickly. A strange tension filled the air, like a line strung between us and them, a fast vibration. And then only sound.

CHAPTER 49

I FELL TO the ground and the explosion rattled in my ears. Wood splintering, water pouring in, *Sedna* heaving. Marjan lay near me, her hands over her head. Thomas peered over the gunwale; screamed at Daniel to get to the tiller. We were hurtling toward an iceberg.

Smoke clouded the air. There was the thick metallic scent of ammunition. I stumbled forward to duck behind the gunwale. A lit arrow struck the deck next to my foot. I ripped the arrow out, stomped out the flame.

Wayne and Jessa fired rifles over the starboard gunwale. I ducked behind the gunwale with them and fired. The rocking of the ship made aim almost impossible, and I'd never been a good shot anyway. I was always better with an enemy in one hand and a knife in the other. Bullets splintered the gunwale. I looked over the gunwale and saw their cannonball had skimmed the front of *Sedna*, flattening the tip of the prow. Bits of wood littered the sea around us and the top of the bow yawned open with splintered planks.

Across the deck, Abran and Marjan tossed buckets of water against the cabin, where a small fire had spread. The *Lily Black* slowed as it maneuvered between two icebergs, but it was less than a half mile away.

Bullets were too small. We needed fire. If only I could hit

their mainsail. We needed to drown them in this ice water. I had to get to the cabin.

I slung the rifle across my chest and ran low to the ground toward the cabin. A smattering of bullets pocked the wood around me. I heard a scream from the bow of the ship, but the cabin blocked me from seeing who it belonged to.

I burst into the cabin and ran for the kitchen. I fumbled with the matches at the stove, lighting the kindling and fanning it until it caught flame.

I rummaged through the weapons laid out on the cabin table, found a bow and set of arrows. I tied a rag around the tip of my arrow. With shaking hands, I found the rubbing alcohol where Marjan kept it hidden in a secret cupboard. I poured it on the rag and held the rag against the flame until it flared.

The second cannonball hit when I emerged from the cabin. The impact roared through me and shook *Sedna*. I fell to the deck as the ship quaked under me, the burning arrow scorching my chest.

I pushed myself off my chest back onto my heels. The extinguished arrow lay on the deck and I cursed.

Pearl, I thought. Had the cannonball pierced the hull?

There was a dull roar, like water rushing. Voices clamoring. Disoriented, I pulled myself to my feet, ready to dart back into the cabin to relight the arrow.

The *Lily Black* plunged toward us, water spraying up on either side of its bow. Its ram was about to hit us broadside.

"Get out of the way!" Abran screamed from somewhere behind me. He grabbed my arm and flung me to the deck.

The *Lily Black* rammed into *Sedna*, the impact like an earth-
quake in my spine. People collapsed to the deck on both ships.
Our sails reversed, the wind knocked out of them. We leaned
together toward the right and I thought we'd flip over straight
into the sea, but the ships leveled. They threw grappling hooks
over, hooking our gunwale, straining to pull us closer. *Sedna*
couldn't pull away.

They'll board us soon, I thought numbly, my mind jumbled.

Thomas ran toward a grappling hook and cut the rope with
his machete. Another was tossed over.

I tucked the extinguished arrow in the quiver on my back and
slung the bow across my chest. I crawled to the hatch, pulled it
open, and dropped down. Breath lurched in my throat when I
plunged into the icy water.

"Mom!"

I squinted in the hull's shadowy light and saw the silhouette
of Pearl, shaking, ankle deep in water, standing in the hallway
between the storage room and quarters. Mold mixed with sea-
water and explosives made a sharp and bitter odor, like a soiled
hand over my mouth.

Pearl clutched a burlap sack that was rustling and bulging,
the bodies inside coiling and curling over one another. She had
gone into the quarters to get those damn snakes.

"It's cold," Pearl whispered.

I splashed through the water and lifted her. The roar of water
coming in the ship blocked out the noise from above, as if we
stood under a waterfall. I ran down the hallway to the hatch,
pushing her up the ladder ahead of me. I had to get her off this

ship. My mind hollowed except for this one thought. The canoe hung from the cabin; we needed to get to it quickly. Maybe she could make it to the Valley even if we couldn't.

Once above, I could barely see through the smoke. I looked up and saw that our mainsail had caught fire. Smoke billowed above us, blackening the sky. Marjan swung in the rigging, blood coating one arm, trying to dump a bucket of water on the sail.

Screams, thundering footsteps, rifle fire swirled around me. Explosions from bombs broke the chaos into intervals, like the chimes of a clock. Several men on the *Lily Black* held the hooked ladder upright, trying to get the angle right before letting it fall and hook over our gunwale.

Ahead of me, Jessa loaded her rifle. A gunshot rang out and she jerked once and crumpled to the deck, folding over herself like a rag doll.

I ran with Pearl around the port side of the cabin to where the canoe hung. All the feeling had gone from my fingers and I fumbled with the knots. Finally, I got them loose, and Pearl lifted one end of the canoe and I lifted the other.

We lowered the canoe over the side of *Sedna,* rope feeding through our hands until we couldn't feel the canoe's weight. I grabbed the rope ladder hung on the cabin wall, threaded it through the shackles on the gunwale, and dropped it over the side of the ship.

Pearl was wearing the warm boots I'd bought her, and I bent down and tightened the laces.

"When you get to land, if these have gotten wet, you build a fire with your flint and dry your feet before crossing the mountain, you understand?"

Pearl nodded.

"Hurry," I said, reaching for Pearl to help her over the gunwale.

Pearl jumped back and shook her head. "The water is cold," she said.

"You won't be in the water," I said. I could feel my resolve ebbing away, so I hardened my voice. "Get on the ladder."

Pearl's eyebrows knitted together, her chin quivering. "I don't want to go alone."

My heart sped like hoofbeats on my chest wall. Looking into her eyes split me in two, so I looked out over the sea, tried to imagine the route she'd row through the icebergs, toward land.

I wanted more than anything to go with her, to get off the sinking ship, to make for the Valley and find Row. You've told Pearl you wouldn't leave her, I thought. I felt a straining in my ligaments, a tightening in my joints. As though I would burst.

The night Pearl was born rose before me. The flashes of lightning, the high waves and rolling thunder. Pearl's screech, high as a nocturnal animal on the hunt. Her limbs flailing and then settling once I wrapped her tight in a blanket. A sleepy look crossing her face as if she had half returned to the place she had come from.

I'll fail you, I had thought, holding her in my arms.

Grandfather died a year after Pearl was born. His hands knotted as tree trunks, thin wisps of hair wet with sweat. He rambled on and on the evening he died, telling me, *The world is more than all this. You'll see that you're more than all this.* He had said it like it was a promise.

Grandfather's face had startled me before he passed. It was

so full of trust, a gentle easing into another place. Like Pearl's face after she was born, as she lay heavy lidded and drowsy, her body warm with that before world of where she'd been and where she'd return.

Maybe we all were born with trust and then lost it. Maybe we all had to find it again before we left.

I had brought the crew this far; I couldn't abandon them now. I wasn't alone and drifting anymore; that person was gone. Everything in me reached for Pearl, yet I also felt a resistance in my bones. A knowledge that some choices are places and some places are where you cannot live. I had to go where I could live. I had to finish what I started and to keep stretching toward a future I had no right to believe in.

"I can't leave the crew, honey," I said, my voice cracking. "Head for the Valley. I've shown you the map. Aim for the inlet, go over the mountainside down into the Valley."

Tears streamed down her cheeks. I didn't want it to be my last image of her, so I grabbed her chin and roughly wiped her tears away with my thumb.

"I'll be coming for you. I'll be right behind you," I whispered.

Pearl's eyes flickered with hope at this. "I know you will," she said softly. Her hope broke over me like a wave, threatening to drown me. Doubt spiraled inside me, like tiny fractures running through my every bone, cracks and fissures widening with each breath.

Our breath fogged before our faces and when I pulled her into a hug I smelled her familiar scent of brine and ginger, as steady and unchanging as her heartbeat. Her red handkerchief poked out of her pants pocket, so I tucked it down, thinking of that moment it had flown up from Grandfather's face into the wind before Pearl caught it.

"I can't come after you until I take care of this first," I whispered in her ear.

She nodded. I boosted her over the gunwale and she swung her leg over the edge, catching the ladder. Halfway down the ladder she looked up at me, her expression tender, the canoe floating beneath her, bumping the ship gently.

It felt like pulling my own heart out and sending it away. It won't be the last time you see her, I repeated to myself, over and over, unable to believe the words.

She settled into the canoe and took up the oars in her hands. She looked so small in the canoe, the water a blue expanse. Even the sky and ice burned a light blue. And she, a tiny thing unlike all that surrounded her, the blueness so whole it looked like the world could swallow her.

CHAPTER 50

I PULLED MY thoughts from Pearl to *Sedna*. If I was going to get back to Pearl, I had to focus.

The *Lily Black*'s ladder was already hooked to our ship. We had no boarding netting, so they'd swarm us quickly. We didn't have enough ammunition. We were too outnumbered to survive hand-to-hand combat. Panic built up in my chest, threatening to choke me.

My mind went fuzzy. I felt as though I was moving in a dark room stuffed full of gauze, not able to breathe, hands out, trying to make room for myself in my own mind. I looked down at the water. So blue. Unlike the water in Nebraska, always green or brown, full of dirt.

When I began to fish, Grandfather scolded me for fishing without intention, throwing lines in before I observed the water. Thinking that as long as hooks were in the water the fish would bite.

Watch the water. You must submit to it. Don't fight it, Grandfather would say as the boat rocked gently under a hot noonday sun.

I looked back and forth between their ship and ours. Our ship was past saving, I thought numbly. I coughed from the smoke as the mainsail burned down toward us. I had to accept that we'd already lost *Sedna*.

I thought of Pearl saying we'd sink. We'd be in the water. She was right, I thought grimly. *The water is cold,* she kept saying as though it were a secret she was confiding in me.

I looked across our deck and starred at the *Lily Black*. Wayne threw a bomb and it exploded in midair, flinging someone from their ship into the water.

The water. The icy water. If only we could get them in it, we could take their ship. Use the *Lily Black* to sail into the inlet and find Pearl.

I ran into the cabin where the bombs lay in boxes on the table.

Abran was in there, fumbling with a match in one hand and a bomb in his other.

"We need to toss these over. Help me," Abran said.

I grabbed the bomb and match from his hand and darted out of the cabin. I ducked as I ran, gunfire spraying around me. I placed the bomb at the base of the gunwale where the ladder was hooked.

Wayne fired his rifle from behind the gunwale, trying to pick the raiders off as they crawled along the ladder toward our ship. Two women and a man crawled along the ladder, machetes slung through their belts and rifles strapped to their backs. Wayne fired once, missed, and pulled the trigger again, but no bullet rang out.

I struck the match along the rough wood and lit the bomb. Lunging toward Wayne, I grabbed him by the arm and hauled him backward, away from the gunwale.

"What the hell are you doing?" Wayne yelled at me, trying to break free of my grasp.

I shoved him toward the cabin.

"Duck!" I screamed, pulling Wayne down with me to the deck and covering my head.

The bomb blew bits of wood over us, a cascade of sawdust and smoke. The ships rumbled, shifting in the sea. I scrambled to my feet and dashed over the debris.

The gunwale was gone where I'd placed the bomb. Their ladder was in pieces, littering our deck and the sea. The man who'd been on the ladder now thrashed about in the icy water.

Daniel climbed to his feet near the mainmast and took aim with his bow and arrow. I ran toward him and yelled at him to come help me.

In the cabin, I snatched our last strong rope from a bin, uncoiled it, and handed him one end, holding on to the other end myself.

"What're you doing?!" he yelled over the raucous noise.

"Wait," I commanded, a hand on his chest, holding him back. I peered out of the cabin.

As I expected, they were throwing over more grappling hooks. The hooks caught on the gunwale on either side of the hole I'd blown. I felt *Sedna* shift toward them. They were pulling us close enough that they could leap on board without the ladder.

"Crouch behind the gunwale," I said, pointing to the left of the hole. "I'll go to that side," I pointed to the right side. "When they jump on, we'll sweep them into the sea."

Daniel nodded and we ran to the opposite sides, crouching down behind the gunwale. The rope lay unfurled between us, lying in a wide arc on the deck. The smoke was so thick it was like a fog, making everyone indistinct.

When the first man leapt through the hole toward us, I looked at Daniel and nodded. We both stood and yanked the rope tight between us, shoving him backward into the water. He screamed before he disappeared beneath the waves.

We dropped down again, slackening the rope between us. Another jumped on and the rope sent him flailing backward into the water.

Marjan screamed above and I looked up. She was in the rigging with a rifle, picking the raiders off from her higher vantage point. An arrow protruded from her shoulder, her white blouse darkening with blood. She struggled to hold on to the rigging with one arm, her foot slipped, and she wavered in the tangled ropes before falling to the deck.

I closed my eyes and winced at the sound of her body hitting the deck. I kept them closed a few more seconds, arrows whirring above my head. Goddammit, I whispered. Goddammit.

I felt the rope jerk in my hands, Daniel already pulling it taut, and I stood just in time to catch a woman and fling her into the sea.

There was a pause. No movement. A chill coursed in my veins. They must have realized what we were doing. A storm of bullets peppered the gunwale and Daniel and I dove flat to our stomachs. Arrows flew over, striking the cabin, the deck, sailing on past our ship and into the sea beyond.

Two men jumped on at the same time, their machetes out to chop the rope, but we raised the rope and flung them back before they could catch it with their blades. We squatted again, panting for breath. Six, I thought to myself. How many were left?

Another jumped on and we stood, pulling the rope tight, but

the raider ducked, our rope pushing past him until it made a straight line, touching only air.

The raider swung his machete over his head, chopping our rope in two. He lunged at Daniel, machete raised, and an arrow stuck in his back.

Abran, taking cover behind the cabin, reloaded his bow.

I pulled my long knife from my belt and braced myself. Several raiders jumped on at once. One threw a hatchet toward me and I ducked. It splintered the gunwale behind me.

The man pulled a knife from his belt and lunged at me. I sidestepped him, grabbed his hair, yanked his head back, and slit his throat. He crumpled at my feet and I lurched to the side as another raider swung a machete at me.

A scream erupted from the cabin and I turned to see Abran, face blanched, his hands fumbling around a sword stuck in his gut. Jackson stood in front of him, hand on the hilt of the sword, and ripped it out of Abran.

Blood dribbled from Abran's mouth and he fell to his knees, his face blank, his muscles paralyzed.

"NO!!" I roared, stepping toward them, when I was jerked backward by my hair and tossed to the deck. A woman raised her machete over me and I rolled to the side right before her machete struck the floor where I'd been. An arrow pierced her chest and she stumbled and fell.

I looked back at where Abran lay. Daniel was near him now, crawling backward on the deck, away from Jackson. Daniel's hand left a bloody streak on the wood in his wake. Jackson stepped toward him.

I dashed toward them, leaping over fallen bodies. Jackson

raised his sword, his eyes on Daniel, only a few feet away from him. I tossed myself at him with all my weight. We tumbled across the deck. He clawed at me, catching my throat. The world narrowed as I gasped for breath.

I kicked him in the gut. His grip loosened and I rolled to the side, grabbing a fistful of his hair to arch his neck open for my blade.

Out of the corner of my eye I saw Daniel coming at us, knife in his good hand, when someone rammed into him. A frenzied screech. Blood across the deck, spraying across my vision.

Jackson caught my shirt and ripped me off of him. I rolled a few paces on the deck before finding my footing. He fumbled about the deck for a weapon, his hands rough and red, his movements wild and panicked.

I pulled my second knife from the sheath at my ankle and lurched forward with both knives. He blocked my first blow to his neck with his forearm. I slashed my second knife into his gut, pulled it out swiftly, and struck him across the neck.

He leaned back from me, hands at his throat, blood pouring over them. He tried to say something, but the words came out a gurgle.

Like the calm after a storm, it took me a moment to notice the sudden stillness. No more bullets or machetes or bombs. Only the wind, pulling *Sedna* into pieces. The creaking and moaning of a sinking ship. Small fires and smoke. Torn sails fluttering and cut ropes swaying. Broken glass and wood all about our feet, the whole ship a weapon, ready to cut you. Everything sharp except the bodies, all lying in a posture nothing like repose.

Daniel crawled to his feet, his attacker lying facedown. He slipped in the blood and caught himself on his palms.

Jackson saw Daniel out of the corner of his eye and shuddered. He slumped against the gunwale and seemed to will himself to leave this earth before his brother could reach him. Before he went still, his eyes clouded over with a great sadness that looked like emptiness, as if he were being sucked out of himself.

I couldn't get the taste of blood out of my mouth, bitter and metallic. I spit and wiped my face with the back of my arm, trying to keep the blood out of my eyes. I turned in a halting circle, my knife held out in front of me, moving like a compass without north.

Daniel crouched beside Jackson as he cradled his injured hand to his chest. A finger hung loose by a tendon. He laid a hand on Jackson's heart and then moved his hand up to his face to gently thumb his eyes closed.

A breathless, giddy relief began to build in me until I looked beyond our deck. The southwestern coast thrust toward us, waves pushing us onward, hurling us toward the rocks.

CHAPTER 51

SEDNA'S BOW WAS buried in water, the stern lifting upward in a tilt. Daniel and I clung to the gunwale as we scurried to the starboard side.

I kept my eyes on the *Lily Black*, waiting for more of them to emerge. Thomas clung to the mainmast and used the flagpole as a crutch. Both the *Lily Black* and *Sedna* were flying toward the rocks, but *Sedna* would sink before it crashed. We had a better chance of surviving shipwreck on the *Lily Black* than sinking on *Sedna*. We needed to gather everyone and move quickly.

"Thomas!" I called out, waving for him to follow us.

He limped toward us. Blood stained his pants on one leg.

"Where's Pearl?" Daniel asked me.

I stared at him in confusion and then realized that no one had seen me put her on the canoe. A numbness spread through me; I felt the sky would blot me out.

"I put her on the canoe," I said. My chin quivered and my knees buckled.

Daniel stepped forward and caught me from falling. "We're going to find her," he said.

I nodded in a daze, leaning against him. Daniel shook me hard.

"Myra, we're going to find her. Come on."

A slave came above deck on the *Lily Black*. We all froze, staring at each other. My grip tightened on my knife. He backed up until his back touched the gunwale and then turned and leapt into the icy water.

Daniel, Thomas, and I clambered around the side of the cabin. Marjan lay slumped against it. I dashed toward her and knelt. Her face was ashen and her eyelids fluttered when I lifted her chin. I touched the belt tied in a tourniquet around her upper arm.

Abran. He was trying to save her when Jackson attacked him.

Abran lay on his side near Marjan's feet. I reached out and ran my fingers through his hair. I should have been there to help him, I thought. A chill ran through me. It shouldn't have ended like this.

I remembered him laughing as we lay in bed, his boyish smirk and messy hair. How he'd roll over and read me his favorite passages from books, saying words I rarely heard anymore: *ebullient, resplendent, succulent*. I thought also of the haunted side of him, the shadow he carried. But more than that, I thought of the charming man who had enough vision and hope for a village, the eager heart so pure it was sure to break.

I'm not going to let you down, Abran, I told him silently, touching his hair again.

Wayne stumbled out of the cabin and almost tripped over Marjan and me. He carried the backpacks Marjan had packed full of water and food.

He dropped them at his feet and knelt beside Marjan. "I'll get her," he told me. Daniel and I strapped the packs on and I struggled to my feet under the weight.

"Marjan, we're getting on the other ship," said Wayne, his rough voice unusually soft. He lifted her up over his shoulder. *Sedna* lurched, her bow sinking deeper. Water was halfway to the mainmast. The grappling hooks from the *Lily Black* strained against *Sedna*.

Daniel cut the ropes of the grappling hooks from the gunwale.

"Myra!" Daniel called out to me. "Hurry!"

We all gathered at the hole I'd blown in the gunwale. One by one, we leapt and fell onto the *Lily Black*, Daniel and I catching Wayne when he landed so Marjan wouldn't fall. I turned, pulled out my knife, and sawed the last grappling hook's rope until it snapped.

The sea around *Sedna* gurgled, pulling her deeper into it. The foremast disappeared, entering the water at a slant.

I looked about the *Lily Black* for an anchor but saw only wreckage. An anchor could slow our landing, easing the inevitable crash. Or it could keep us like a ball on a string, to be tossed again and again. Better to be flung once and bear the violence.

White water surged toward us, crashing on board, foaming at our feet. *Sedna* drifted farther from us and crashed against a rocky outcrop. She splintered into flotsam.

As *Sedna* was sucked into darkness, the *Lily Black* surged closer to the rocky shore, the water against our back like the hand of God.

"To the mast!" I yelled above the waves. We stumbled to our feet, our fingers scraping the wet wood for balance.

We clung to the mainmast and each other, the ship breaking up around us with each small collision. A rumble of rocks beneath us tearing open the hull. The roar of the ship colliding with a rocky outcrop on the port side. Each crash deafening, sending a spray of icy water into our faces.

I swallowed the bile of panic rising in my throat. We barreled toward the coast. I gritted my teeth and thought of Pearl, her red hair a flare of color amid the gray sea and white ice, the front of the canoe breaking the water in small ripples. The *Lily Black* shook so hard my bones rattled, and I squeezed my eyes shut.

When I opened them I saw only the coast coming at us. Rocks, sand, surf, a bleak gray sky above. The bones of a whale on shore. I blinked. The skeleton was half the size of the *Lily Black*, a surreal object that looked out of place, mistaken. A shipwreck already before us, victim of the wind and waves.

In one final push we were lifted out of the sea and into the air, tossed like a child's toy.

I SAT UP, pain coursing through my body. I lifted Daniel's leg off my arm. He blinked and shook his head as if trying to shake water out of his ear. Blood left a trail down his temple and cheek, dripping off his chin. I reached out and wiped it with my thumb.

I struggled to stand, my left leg weak and throbbing under my weight.

"We need to get off," Daniel said, his voice groggy and distant. The wreckage could be pulled back into the sea with the tide.

Daniel lifted Marjan over his shoulder. Thomas leaned against Wayne and hobbled forward. The ship had the crushed and scattered look of something pummeled with a hammer. Broken wood, scrap metal, fallen sails strewn across the deck, tripping us up.

I squinted up ahead. The rocky shore was covered with moss

and lichen. To the right stood a steep cliff, with a sheer drop of fifty feet. To the left, the gentle slope of a mountain rose, streams and small clusters of aspens breaking its face. The whale skeleton rested at the foot of the cliffs, fully intact, as though it could acquire flesh and swim back into the sea.

Several seabirds picked around a few tide pools. The air hummed with their raucous calls.

We were lucky it was low tide. The sea foamed, only a foot deep under us, and the *Lily Black* shifted its weight, already settling into the coast. It was so cold I kept breathing on my fingers.

I helped Daniel over the broken gunwale and he jumped into the shallow water. He stumbled and fell to one knee, Marjan's head bobbing backward from the impact. I leapt down, the cold water piercing me like a blade.

"We need to get her warm," I told Daniel, running up the coast ahead of him to find driftwood. Marjan breathed in shallow bursts and struggled to keep her eyes open. I knew there might not be more we could do than keep her comfortable.

I stumbled to my knees in the wet sand and cursed. We were miles from the inlet where I'd told Pearl to go. Abran was gone. Pearl was gone. None of it was how it should be.

My head rang and I kept blinking, trying to settle my vision. Rocks loomed up and seemed to float in space, as if I were still on water. Noises blared in my ears, stirring panic in me. Even the sunlight seemed too bright somehow. Calm down, I told myself. Do the next thing.

I scooped up a few pieces of driftwood and Wayne followed me, searching the beach for kindling. I squinted against the wind whipping the sand up from the beach, fearing that we wouldn't be able to start a fire. I scraped lichen from rocks with the back of my knife and tucked it in my pockets.

I scanned the shoreline to the east and west. I couldn't see any sign of Pearl or the canoe. I tried to find hope in not seeing a canoe floating alone on the waves or broken up beside the rocky shore. But the pit in my stomach lurched and grew. I wanted to leave them and go look for Pearl.

You need to settle down and come up with a plan, I thought. Get your bearings. You're going to need help. I forced myself to look down at my feet for driftwood.

Daniel gently eased Marjan to the ground in a small hollow on the beach. He helped her recline against a large black rock. A fallen tree trunk protected one side from the wind and a thorny bush protected the other. Thomas carefully lowered himself down next to Marjan, stretching his injured leg out straight in front of him.

I dropped the packs and driftwood next to them, opening one pack and rummaging for matches. Daniel carefully peeled Marjan's shirt away from the wound on her shoulder. Her eyes were closed and she wasn't grimacing. She was already drifting away from us and the pain.

I knelt in front of Marjan and arranged the driftwood into a pyramid. I stuffed lichen and dried leaves into the cracks. The first three matches were too damp to light, but the fourth did, and I shrouded it with my palms, blowing on the lichen to spread the flame to wood.

Daniel ripped Marjan's shirt in two and wrapped it around her shoulder in a makeshift bandage. I began to take my jacket off to lay it on her, but Daniel said, "Don't. I'm already warm." He took his jacket off and tucked it around Marjan's upper body.

Liar, I thought. Fresh blood pulsed from above her hip and I reached forward and gently felt around her side. Blood colored my fingertips. She winced and jerked away from my touch. Her face had grown as pale as yellowed antique china. I felt the rough edge of a broken arrow protruding from just above her hip. I'd thought all the blood had come from her shoulder wound.

"There's an arrowhead lodged above her hip," I told Daniel in a whisper, hoping Marjan couldn't hear. "The rest of the arrow must have broken off when she fell from the rigging."

"No wonder she's lost so much blood," Daniel muttered, running a hand over his face. "Keep her comfortable. Wayne and I are going to check the ship for extra supplies before it's pulled apart by these waves."

Marjan turned her head toward me and tried to say something. Her throat worked against itself, trying to swallow. I brought a bottle of water to her lips and she took a sip.

"Pearl?" Marjan asked.

Pressure constricted my chest and I shook my head. "She . . . she's lost. She's not here."

Two seabirds took flight next to us, calling out to one another, their caws strident under the calm gray sky.

Marjan reached out and took my hand and squeezed it once. "You do the hardest thing," she whispered.

I nodded, pressing back against the wave of emotion building in me. I felt like I was *Sedna*'s flotsam, crashing into the rocks, breaking into many pieces that would all sink, never coalesce.

"Bury me at sea," Marjan said. "I'll be with the rest of them."

I thought of Marjan finding her daughter's body stuck in that house. Had she been caught up in the curtains in a living room? Stuck in a windowless bathroom? I thought of Marjan turning her daughter over underwater, the cloud of her hair swirling around them, and seeing her face.

I thought of the migrations. How once I passed a baby who nursed from her newly dead mother. What did it mean to enter an era without marked graves?

But I nodded and squeezed her hand.

Marjan's eyelids fluttered and her lips moved, forming ghost words I couldn't hear. It felt like she was reaching out one last time. I stroked the top of her hand with my thumb. She locked her dark eyes on mine, but I couldn't tell what they said. I searched her eyes for blame, but only found a vague searching, as though she wanted to know her own name.

With her other hand she clutched her necklace, her fingers moving over the four beads.

I heard footsteps behind me.

"We found blankets," Daniel said, his voice stopping short and silence rushing in. He dropped a pile of wool blankets next to me.

Marjan's eyes fluttered shut and the hand at her necklace fell to her lap. Her hand in mine went limp.

I leaned forward and brushed the hair from her face. Her skin felt surprisingly soft, after all these years. I tried to whisper a good-bye, but no words would come out. I couldn't speak because I didn't want to hear my own voice. I wanted to hear her melodious voice; I wanted her words.

A dark heaviness grew in me, spreading from my chest to my limbs. I leaned back on my heels and looked out to sea. A bird crouched at the edge of a tide pool. Something living wriggled in its mouth.

CHAPTER 52

DANIEL AND WAYNE pulled a door from the wreckage of the *Lily Black* and we laid Marjan's body on it. I found some small purple flowers growing amid grass farther back from the shore, picked a bouquet, and set it between her hands. I wet a piece of cloth in the surf and scrubbed the blood from her skin. She lay pale and damp and cold, like a flower blooming underwater.

Thomas laid two flat pebbles on her closed eyelids. I stayed by Marjan's side as the others prepared for her burial. When I closed my eyes I still saw her face. I felt deadened, like my spirit had left my body and roamed somewhere else.

A cape of rocks jutted into the sea and Wayne and Daniel carried her out onto it, Thomas and I trailing behind. I feared a wave would send her crashing back against the rocks once we put her in the sea, but the water had calmed as the tide began to slowly rise.

Daniel and Wayne climbed down through the rocks and eased the door onto the water. The sea pulled her away. We watched her drift away from us for a few moments and then a wave rose and swallowed her. We didn't see her come back up.

The sea became a still, smooth surface again. Seagulls cried overhead and several dove into the water, hunting where she had disappeared. The water taking her made me think of the man Pearl and I dropped into the sea before all of this had begun. The one who told me that Row was in the Valley. Back when it was just Pearl and me. Maybe this all had begun before even that. Maybe something in me was set, like an alarm, ready to go off. But I thought of this distantly, as if it had happened in another life, to another person.

We were quiet as we headed back to the fire. Wayne set more driftwood on top of the embers. Thomas wrapped himself in a blanket. I tried to ground myself in simple movements, willing my mind to become steady and clear again. I washed the cloth we'd used as a bandage for Marjan. I knelt next to Thomas and cleaned the cut on his leg, hoping the salt water would help prevent infection until we could scavenge for medical supplies.

Daniel piled everything he could find from the ship next to the fire. Cans of sardines, bags of flour. Jugs of clean water. A few jackets and a spare set of boots. More matches and a tiny tin of kerosene. Not as much as we'd hoped, but the hull was too battered and submerged to get into. The icy water would choke someone out before they could find anything. Daniel had only been able to search the cabin on deck.

I began to allow myself to scan the sea and land for Pearl. A prayer kept buzzing on my tongue, willing her to appear around a rock or bend.

I touched Daniel's arm. "It's time," I said.

He nodded. "When we get back we should break up wood from the ship."

I realized what he meant and looked at the few skinny aspens on the mountainside. Ever since we'd landed, my thoughts had been delayed and stuck; I'd noticed things a few moments after I looked at them. I made connections about what everything meant after it should have been obvious. We were stuck here,

I now saw. We couldn't build another ship from so little wood. If what was in the Valley wasn't what we needed . . . I didn't let myself finish the thought.

"I have to go find Pearl," I told Wayne and Thomas.

"Where is she?" Wayne asked, his brow furrowed.

"I put her in the canoe," I said.

Wayne scanned the sea and I knew he was doubting that she had survived.

"I told her to go to the Valley," I explained. I wanted them to say that they were certain she was there and perfectly fine.

"What about the epidemic?" Wayne asked. "Is it still active?"

I felt a clench of fear. I didn't know how long epidemics of the plague lasted in villages, but I'd heard fleas could carry the disease longer than humans or rodents.

"Possibly," I said. "But we need shelter, so we'll have to risk it." I squatted before the fire and stoked the flames with a stick. "We should get going before it gets any darker."

"Myra, just you and I will have to go," Daniel said gently.

"What?" I asked, glancing up at him. "We need help with the Lost Abbot guards. There are probably several of them still here."

"Shouldn't we stick together?" Wayne asked Daniel. "She got us into this."

I stood up and brushed sand from the front of my pants. "I didn't mean for all this to happen." I wasn't sure how much of the blame for our misfortune fell to me, but I felt all of it in my gut, a heaviness I couldn't shake. It lay like a dull weight, right under the thrumming panic in my throat when I thought of Pearl.

"This isn't all her fault," Daniel said.

I held my palm out to stop Daniel. I couldn't parse out what was and wasn't my fault, but I could take responsibility for setting us on this course. "It is. It is my fault."

Wayne stopped short and stared at me, surprised. Then he turned and looked out to sea and shook his head. "I knew. Knew there had to be some other reason you were so hell-bent on getting here. But I still wanted to take a chance on it. Thought it could be good." Wayne took a few steps forward; kicked a pebble into the sea foam. Wayne turned his eye on me like he was appraising me for the first time and finding something he didn't expect.

"Thomas can't travel with that leg," Daniel said. "He needs rest and warmth. And someone should stay on the coast to keep a lookout." Daniel and Wayne exchanged looks. A Lost Abbot ship could sail through those icebergs any day to stop and collect taxes.

Thomas stared out at the sea, his face pale, his arms shaking from fatigue or cold. "I'll be fine here alone. Besides, how will you two find Pearl and deal with the guards?"

"You're too injured to be left alone. And besides, if there's any trouble, you won't be able to make it over the mountain alone. Maybe we'll find Pearl without alerting the guards. Slip in, slip out," Daniel said.

Wayne shook his head. "Unlikely. No way they'd not recognize a new person."

"We don't have time to plan this all out," I said, grabbing my backpack. "We'll have to take it as it comes."

Wayne looked at me and then nodded. "Thomas and I will stay behind and keep salvaging from the ship," he said. "You two go on so we don't slow you down."

Daniel pulled the map of the Valley from one of the packs and unfolded it.

"We'll have to go over the mountain," Daniel said, his eyes on the cliffs to our right. "Those're too steep to scale." I looked up and saw a seagull dive from the cliff, over us, into the water. So that's where they'd been diving from as they hunted the coastline.

I grabbed the map from Daniel and pointed to it. "Shouldn't we go first to the inlet? See if Pearl is there?" A part of me didn't want to enter the Valley yet, afraid of what I'd find. Besides, what if she was at the inlet and we missed her entirely by going straight to the Valley? We were supposed to land at the inlet. This was never the plan. Behir, Jessa, Abran, Marjan, all dead. Pearl, missing. It wasn't supposed to be this way. My mind kept shuddering away from the facts, kept reaching for something else to be true. This can't be how it ends for us, I thought.

"It's at least twelve miles," Daniel said, pointing to the length of coastline that separated us from the inlet. "You told her to head for the Valley. If I know her, she's already there."

Already there. Alone, in the cold.

I gritted my teeth and nodded once. I turned toward the fire and squatted before the supplies, rolling up a jacket from the pile. "Well, help me. We'll need to take some of this with us," I said.

CHAPTER 53

DANIEL AND I climbed steadily for two hours before the dark set in. There were so few trees that it felt like we were the only things between the mountain and the black sky, which pressed down on us like a flat palm. The wind whipped our skin raw and took the breath from our mouths. I could smell moss and wet rock, but little else. Often when I was on land I smelled wood smoke, salted fish, the bustle of other bodies around a port. But here it felt like we were alone in the world, the only two people left.

On the map, the distance between the coast where we landed and the Valley was marked as six miles, so Daniel and I guessed we could make it in several hours. But the cold and rough terrain wore us down faster than we expected. I couldn't feel my face or hands or toes anymore. Daniel held a small lantern in front of us, but it would burn out before dawn. The stars were shrouded by clouds and the moon was a thin scythe, offering only the lightest veil of light.

"We have to stop for a bit," Daniel said.

I heard an animal scurry across a rock into shrubs several feet away. Startled, I stared into the dark after it, seeing only shadows.

"Let's keep on," I said, pulling the map out of my pocket, my hands shaking as I tried to hold it in the lantern light.

Daniel snatched the map from my hand. "We'll freeze. We're lighting a fire, here, now. There's a rock there. It will block the wind."

The wind pushed against my back and I braced myself against it, wavering like a sapling in a storm. Something hot rose in my throat and sweat broke out along my neck.

"Hey," Daniel said gently, touching my arm. "We're not going to reach her any faster until we pause and get our bearings."

Something in me was breaking against my will, my resolve slipping away. I nodded and collapsed behind a tall jagged rock. A cluster of small, prickly trees grew to the right of the rock, giving us some break from the wind. We got the fire started and huddled next to it, wool blankets pulled around us and over our heads. Daniel studied the map by the firelight, pulling out his compass and checking the position of the moon. I leaned close to the fire, letting it heat my face.

"We're on track. It should only be another hour. Take a few sips of water," he said, handing me the canteen.

I held it limply and thought of Pearl, alone in the cold. I tried to remember what she had been wearing when I put her on the canoe. A light blue sweater, a brown pair of trousers, and the boots Daniel had bought her. Her little red handkerchief sticking out of her back pocket. A wool stocking hat. No gloves that I could remember. I closed my eyes and winced, squeezing my hands into fists and opening them again in front of the fire, letting them drop so close I felt a burn.

"Myra," Daniel said sharply. He leaned forward, caught my wrists, and pulled my hands back. "Stop it."

I want to feel something, I thought. My eyes searched his.

"It's not going to change anything," he said, as though he read my thoughts.

"I need her more than she needs me," I said. The words came unbidden to my lips.

Daniel didn't say anything at first. He watched the fire and I wondered if he'd even heard me.

"That's not true," he finally said, his voice soft.

My hope that Pearl and Row and I could all be together again had been a vision that couldn't be true. Ungrounded, foolish hope. A bird without wings.

I couldn't wrap my head around it. The journey, the storm, the attack. How I'd deceived the crew in the beginning. How we came all this way for Row and now I'd lost Pearl. It felt just and cruel, some ancient order rising up and asserting itself, Sedna sending sea creatures up from the depths of the sea, determining the fates of men.

"What did you feel?" I asked. "When your brother . . ."

Grass shuddered in the wind and the trees shifted and echoed down the mountainside. Daniel picked a berry off a bush next to us, squeezed it between his thumb and finger until it burst.

"It didn't feel right. It felt . . . incomplete. Empty. I wanted to rectify what I'd lost." Daniel shook his head. "You can't always rectify something; you can only rebuild."

Daniel stoked the fire with a stick, ashes crumbling from driftwood and scattering on the wind.

"What if I can't find either of them?" I asked, my voice catching.

"That's not going to happen," Daniel said. He didn't move; his face was as still as a carved stone. The firelight cast shadows flickering across his face. An owl's hoot broke the silence and its yellow eyes glowed a few yards away in a tree.

"Jessa . . . Abran . . . Marjan . . ." I began.

"That's not on you."

I glared at him. He was acting like none of it mattered. If it wasn't my fault, how else could I make sense of it? Taking responsibility for all of it was the only way I could accept it as real. The only way I didn't feel as helpless and out of control.

"Of course it is," I snapped.

"What you did—deceiving them—yeah, that's on you. But not all the rest."

I shook my head. I'd lost Pearl because of what I'd done. It was punishment.

"There were times I didn't even want to be a mother," I whispered. I squeezed my eyes shut and felt a hollow ache in my bones. "I didn't want to be responsible for other lives. There were times I wished them away."

I had feared losing them, but there were moments that desire lurked right at the edge of that fear. Set loose from them, I could give up, I told myself. I could slip away into the water, no longer fighting, no longer pretending to be strong.

But now I had lost both of them and I still couldn't give up. The breath in my throat felt like a curse. It kept coming and coming, steaming before my face, mocking me. My own body betraying me.

"I can't go on," I told Daniel. I turned to him, my voice strained, my eyes burning. "I can't. I don't have anything left." My hands went to my chest, scratching at my coat, clawing for skin. "It's like my heart's been chipped and chipped away."

The way waves change the shape of a rock, beating it into something new.

I yanked at my coat, clawing it off me. I dug at my upper chest and neck, the cold air rushing in, the bright pain of nails on skin a relief.

Daniel grabbed my wrists.

"Myra. Stop. Myra!"

"I want to be done," I sobbed, falling into his chest, my body growing weak and heavy.

Daniel cradled my head against his chest, tucked my body against his.

"I don't have anything left. I have no heart," I murmured.

"Myra, you aren't hurting because you have no heart, you're hurting because you're carrying two other hearts in you. You'll always have them. You'll always have to carry them. They're your gift and your burden."

I shook my head against him, my hair a tangle in my face. I couldn't go on; I didn't feel I had it in me. I didn't even know what direction to take or how to move forward.

You do the hardest thing, Marjan had said.

You must become someone you haven't had to be yet. The thought came from somewhere in me I didn't know existed. I thought of flying fish, the ones that rose up out of the water into the sky, their fins flapping like wings.

I thought of my father and how despair must have had him in its clutches. Not only despair about what had happened, but despair about who he couldn't become.

A year before he hung himself he'd been in a fire at the factory where he worked. An electrical accident where light flared in his eyes and left him half blind. The world he lived in became one of shadows.

Unbidden, a memory I'd forgotten flashed before me. It was a spring day after the accident and I was sitting in the grass, hunting worms to use for bait. My mother sat on the front stoop and my father walked home from a day spent looking for new work. Every day he roamed the streets, knocking on doors of boarded-up shops, begging for a place on a farmer's crew.

On this day he stopped a few feet from my mother. "I couldn't see your face until I got here," he said softly.

Her mouth tightened and she glanced at me and took a deep breath. I knew even then she was trying not to cry. She stood and took him by the hand and led him inside.

During that year I also took him by the hand and led him around and told him what I saw. For me, it had been fun. A game. For him, it must have been like crawling back into the womb. Sounds and shapes muffled as he drew ever more inward into himself and what he could no longer do.

Wind howled across the rocks and clouds moved across the moon, darkness and then a glow of soft light. It felt like we sat on the edge of the world.

I was happy to be your eyes, I thought. We needed each other. If I was enough you would have stayed.

Something turned over in me, hackles rising in resistance. I hadn't come all this way for someone else to decide who I was and what I was worth. I hadn't come all this way to stay in one place. I might still be that child, but I was someone else, too. Like the sky becoming sea, the horizon shifting, ever rising.

I rested against Daniel, the fire slowly warming us. I let time pass. After a while, I placed my hands on the rock and pushed myself up. Clouds drifted east, a cast of starlight lightening the landscape. Clusters of small flowers grew between rocks. The dark descent into the Valley stretched in a long shadow.

CHAPTER 54

WE ENTERED THE Valley before dawn broke. A soft pink glow on the horizon gave us enough light to see as we came down the mountain. From a distance, the Valley looked like a village recently abandoned, smudged with fog. Buckets upturned in the streets, a feral cat prowling the rim of a well, doors left hanging open, clothing and household items dumped on lawns, smoke-less chimneys, a radiating silence.

As we got closer I smelled death. Pungent, heavy, a stench even the wind couldn't clear. I swallowed hard. No sign yet of the Lost Abbots' guards.

Funeral pyres lay scattered around the perimeter of the vil-lage. A base of stones, a jumble of charred wood, bones, and ash. From one pyre a thin tail of smoke climbed up the sky. A raven circled over a distant pyre, then dove to the ground, dis-appearing behind a shack.

Some shacks on the outskirts of town looked hastily built, with metal siding nailed to wood boards. Other buildings farther into the village were made of stone with thatched roofs. Some had been painted in bright colors—crimson, yellow, bright blue. Colors that looked too bright against the gray and green land-scape. Out of place. The prettiness mixed with the smell of death and became disorienting, an irritant.

We came down the mountain on a little path that had been dug out by footsteps between the rocks. The purple wildflowers

I'd placed in Marjan's hands grew at the foot of the mountain here as well. The village stretched about a mile to the east from where we stood.

"You go east on the south side, I'll go east on the north side. We'll meet at the other end," Daniel said.

The feral cat jumped off the well. My stomach turned over. The well was boarded over, but the stench of a rotting body still escaped.

"Okay," I said.

"Myra." Daniel reached out for my hand and squeezed it. "We're going to find her."

I nodded and squeezed his hand back. The sheen of resolve I saw in his face buoyed me. He really believed it.

We parted ways and I crossed to the south edge of town, heading east. The closest building to the well had graffiti painted on the metal siding in bright red block letters: BODY IN THE WELL.

I remembered the shopkeeper at Harjo when I'd first heard of the attack. How her voice felt like it was coming from far away. The sudden claustrophobia of all the shelves in the shop.

I scanned the village and crept behind a crumbling stone wall. The air felt woolen, too thick to breathe. A shadow moved past an open doorway in a nearby house. I crept to the doorway and paused on the threshold, peering into the dark house, my hand resting on my knife.

A creak in the floorboards split the silence. I stepped inside, my eyes adjusting to the dim room. Sunlight seeped through lace curtains. They must have been carried up from below when the water rose. Strange, the things people brought with them when they fled to higher ground.

The room was filled with an odd assortment of furniture—an old dining room table, a small settee, several kerosene lamps hanging from the ceiling. The house smelled of dirt and feces and urine and rotting food. Every surface was smudged with mud. I stepped into a bedroom, my knife out in front of me.

A thin woman, about my age, sat on the bed. She held her hands up in front of her; her eyes wide.

"Please," she mumbled in an accent I didn't recognize. "Please."

"I'm not going to hurt you," I said, lowering my knife. "Is anyone else here?"

She shook her head no but I still scanned the room and kept the knife in my hand.

"Have you seen a small girl?" I asked. I held my hand at chest level to indicate Pearl's height. "Reddish hair, light brown skin. Wearing a blue sweater." I realized it was absurd to give so many details. Any strange girl would be recognizable in a village wiped out from illness.

The woman shook her head no again, but it seemed she did so more from fear than giving a real answer. Her eyes clouded and I felt her retreating from me, as though she were stepping deeper into herself. She dropped her hands to her lap and sat perfectly still.

I backed away and left the house. The sun had dried up the fog and the air was beginning to warm. I continued on past abandoned houses, searching for any sign of Pearl. For a fleeting minute, I forgot that I had come all this way for Row.

Movement behind the window in another house. I gripped my knife tighter and waited for someone to appear in the doorway. No one did. Perhaps it'd been an animal. Or the person was hiding from me. Or stalking me.

I was almost halfway to the east side of the village. A few more houses lay ahead, and past all of these, at the very south-eastern edge of the village, a house stood all alone, about four acres from all the others. Behind this house a steep slope rose. I looked at the map. This slope led up to the cliff close to where we had shipwrecked on the beach.

I walked past the other houses, drawn to that final, separate house for some indiscernible reason, as though a magnet pulled me toward it. As I approached the house and the base of the slope I saw a bright red piece of fabric on the lawn. I looked again. It was Pearl's handkerchief. I bent and picked it up, rub-bing the fabric between my fingers.

I crept toward the house, listening. If the Lost Abbots had captured Pearl and were holding her inside, I needed to surprise them. But I couldn't hear anything over the seabirds calling out to each other from the cliff, where they watched the water and dove to their prey below.

Everything except the seabirds felt impossibly still. Even the wind didn't seem to touch this part of the Valley.

Like almost every house, this one's door was ajar. The house was built of smooth wood planks that had been sanded. The joints fit perfectly, having no cracks between the boards stuffed with mud, moss, and wood chips like the other houses.

"One day, I'll build us a house," Jacob had said years ago. This had been on a picnic along the Missouri River, after he'd ask me to marry him. It was the most romantic thing anyone had ever told me. He'd only made furniture for us at that point, but he dreamed of making us a house. I believed his dream and when I daydreamed about the house it looked almost like this one. Something small and simple, tucked into a quiet space.

Blood thudded in my ears. I crept toward the house, up the porch stairs. One of them creaked and I froze, listening. I thought I heard voices, but I couldn't tell if it was my imagination.

I stood on the threshold and peered inside. Homemade furniture—a side table and a rocker—sat against a wall. They were as recognizable as a person's smell. Furniture Jacob had made.

The voice I thought I'd heard before now grew louder. It was Pearl's voice.

I felt like I was underwater, clawing toward the top. The need for air building in me, my lungs pumping, nothing coming in.

I charged through the living room toward her voice. I burst into the kitchen. Pearl sat with her father at the kitchen table, holding a teacup.

CHAPTER 55

JACOB. I STARED at him, frozen, too shocked to swallow the gasp that came from my lips. My hand drifted to my chest as though to slow my heart. My spine gone rigid, my mind blank, I stood in my stung skin and couldn't take my eyes off him.

I shook myself. "Put it down," I told Pearl.

Startled, Pearl obeyed, carefully setting the teacup on the table. I ran to her and snatched her up in my arms, inhaling her in a quick gasp, while keeping my eyes on Jacob. I set Pearl down next to me, my hand on her shoulder, keeping her rooted slightly behind me. She still wore her burlap sack of snakes slung over her shoulder.

The kitchen was cramped and littered with dishes on a small cart and shelves. A child's drawings were pinned all over the wood walls. Sunlight came through a window over the table, which looked out onto the grassy slope. Looking through it, you couldn't see the sky, so it seemed like a wave of grass was about to envelop you. I ached for the movement of the sea, to not be bound to one room with one man, everything so stable and still.

Jacob hadn't changed except he was thinner and looked frailer. His hair was still auburn, his face unlined, his eyes brown and soft.

"Hi, Myra," Jacob said softly.

The way he said it made me feel weaker, like some defenses were falling without my permission. I struggled to buoy myself against him. His familiar form, the angle of his chin, the way he sat leaning forward over the table, his eyebrows raised slightly as if about to ask you a question about yourself.

Pearl looked at me and said, "He says he's my father. I told him my father is dead."

"Myra, is she . . ." Jacob couldn't finish. His cheekbones stood out; his face was gaunt. "She called me a family friend. You . . . must have a photo."

I remembered the photo I had of Row and Jacob, the one Grandfather and I would show at trading posts all those years ago. Pearl used to like to look at it.

"She said, 'You must be Mom's friend. Where's Row?' I took a closer look at her. I . . . couldn't breathe. Her standing here. I thought . . . she was a ghost, an apparition. I asked who her mother was and she said your name." Jacob looked at me and his eyes shone with tears.

"He fell down," Pearl said flatly.

Jacob laughed, a tear falling down his cheek and splashing on the table. "It's a miracle."

"You are nothing to her. You are nothing," I said.

Jacob's mouth flattened in a thin line and he gave a small nod to this. "We've never been kind to each other, have we?" he asked.

I didn't know what to say to this. His betrayal, his abandonment of Pearl and me, was sometimes all I could remember. It was easy to forget all the small moments of selfishness and apathy, the myriad ways we'd turned our backs on one another.

The times he left the house and spent days with people I'd never met instead of helping us prepare to leave. The times he raised concerns and I turned my back to him, pretended he wasn't speaking at all. I didn't want to remember those; it mixed everything up and made it hard to think straight.

I held my knife out in Jacob's direction. My hand trembled so badly that the blade shook. Anger pulsed through me, and the room seemed to narrow. Beneath my rage I felt the unfurling of vulnerability, the exposed shoot of longing edging toward light. I wanted to know everything and to have all my questions answered, but I also wanted to silence him.

"Where's Row?" I demanded.

A flicker of pain crossed his face and he glanced down. I felt dropped, suspended. I wanted to feel the impact on the other side. I needed to know. Maybe it was the only thing I came for.

"Where is she?" I asked again.

"The illness . . ." Jacob said. He didn't look different, but his voice was different. Softer. The voice of a broken man. He lifted his eyes to me and I closed mine. His voice hollowed me like a knife scraping guts from the belly of a fish. I stood, weightless, feeling emptiness vibrate in me.

"I'll show you," he said softly as he stood up.

We exited the house and he led us around toward the back. There was an ax wedged in a tree stump and a pile of firewood next to it. A few tools lay on the ground, below a window with a broken shutter.

The wind had picked up and came down the slope, making the grass wave. My hair blew in my face. The sky grew darker but the grass shone golden and bright.

We walked around a small garden and lean-to shed and I saw it. A pile of stones and a wood cross, halfway up the slope.

WHEN WE REACHED the grave, I fell to my knees in front of the stones and waited to feel the impact. Waited to be on the other side of grief. All these years I grieved that Row wasn't with me, but I couldn't grieve the loss of her life. Now I was on the other side, the side of knowing the full extent of my loss.

I waited and waited, but nothing came.

Pearl knelt beside me and took my hand in hers. When she touched me I collapsed inside, like glaciers running into the sea, a slow erasure. I turned to her, sank my head on her small shoulder, and sobbed. She stroked my hair.

I remembered Row's face, the way she'd wrinkle her nose when she smiled. Her teeth so tiny, I'd wonder when they'd grow to fit her. Her voice so high pitched it sounded like birdsong. I reached for more memories of her, wanting to go back in time.

I held Pearl and breathed her in again and again until it comforted me. When I finally leaned back on my heels I saw Jacob out of the corner of my eye, standing apart from us, his hands behind his back, his head down. This wasn't how I imagined it. Kneeling at Row's grave with Jacob standing nearby. I had imagined Row, Pearl, and me together, and Jacob gone, as if he'd never existed.

Gradually my numbness gave way to anger, that familiar burning fire. I glared at Jacob, but his face was free of expression as he looked back at me, the lines around his mouth forlorn, his eyes heavy with fatigue.

"When?" I asked.

Jacob bit his lip and looked down. "I made the grave four days ago. They wanted to take her with them—to work the ship. But she got ill."

If we'd gotten here just a little sooner, I could have held her. Felt her skin when it was warm, looked into her eyes. Heard her voice. How I could treasure even the curve of her eyelashes, the roughness of her elbows. Cup each in my mind and keep it, sustenance for every day to come. Just like when she was younger and I'd pinch each of her fingertips and together we'd watch the blood return. Both of us mesmerized by her body, her wanting words for every part and its sensation, and me content to witness life unfold before me. Never real enough anymore in my own body, but in hers, a glorious awakening for each of us. She, my second awakening, my second birth.

Jacob squatted and repositioned a stone on the grave. The grass rippled around him, his auburn hair bright against the gray sky. He shook his head and went on. "The epidemic wasn't over like we thought. They didn't let me . . . have her body. They burnt it with the others. I buried a few of her favorite things."

I stood up, shocked. Pearl stood up next to me and dusted off the front of her pants. She hated dirt. She wasn't used to it. Everything seemed to smell of dust and earth and the misshapen underground things that dug through soil.

"You weren't with her?" I asked.

"They took her from me months ago. They took all the girls around her age. They kept them in the holding cell," Jacob looked down the hill to small stone buildings near the middle of town. "They let me visit her there at first, but then they said she got sick and needed to be contained. I didn't even know she'd died until after they burnt her body. I tried to fight them when they took her and was beaten so badly I almost died. I tried, Myra, I tried," Jacob said, spreading his hands in a pleading gesture, creases forming between his eyebrows.

"If you tried you wouldn't still be here," I said. Row had no one to care for her in her last days. No one to hold her hand. A cold wind shook the grass. "Why are you still here?"

A flicker of hurt crossed his face.

"How do you know—" I started.

"No breeding ships docked here. I kept watch." Jacob jerked his head toward the cliffs, from which you could see the entire southern shoreline. "One morning smoke clouded the sky from a funeral pyre and the holding cell was almost empty. Row and another girl had died overnight. They had no reason to lie to me."

I imagined her lying on some dirty pallet in one of the buildings I'd passed. Perhaps a cinder-block one-room building or a stone cottage with too few windows. I imagined her thirsty for water, chills shuddering through her small body. Guards at the door, food delivered on a tray slid across the floor.

No, I thought. It can't have ended that way for her.

I wanted to reach for my knife, but I kept my hands free. Wiped them on my pants and tried to breathe past the red. I had known Jacob could be ruthless in his weakness, but I never imagined what shape it could take, how much it would affect me.

"They told me I'd make it worse for her if I kept fighting them on it," Jacob said. "Don't you see?" Jacob raised his arms and turned, gesturing to the valley below, the cliffs, the sea beyond. "We're all alone now. It's not like it was before."

I could have told him what I knew now: that you could choose to be alone like you could choose anything else. Nothing out in the world ever changed it being your choice. Hope would never come knocking on your door. You had to claw your way toward it, rip it out of the cracks of your loss where it poked out like some weed, and cling to it.

But I didn't tell him; I could barely speak past the rage crowding my throat. "You never believed in Pearl and me. In either of us," I said, my eyes narrowing and my body tensing like a rope pulled through a block. "So you left us to die."

The golden grass swayed in a gust coming over the cliff and down the hill. The smell of vegetation drying out in the winter cold rose off the ground and swirled past us. Soon this hill would be covered in snow.

Jacob squeezed his eyes shut. "There wasn't room."

"Wasn't room?" I asked, my voice almost inaudible.

Jacob dropped his head in his hands and then let his hands fall away. When he spoke, he spoke like he was reciting a story he had memorized a long time ago. "It was Davis's boat—I met him a few weeks before the dam broke. He and his family were planning to flee and he said there was only room for two more people. I asked him—I asked him if I could bring just one extra person, so I could bring both you and Row, but he said no; he threatened to not let us come at all. Especially once he found out you were pregnant . . ." Jacob's voice cracked and he looked at Pearl. She stared back at him, her face expressionless, her arms limp at her sides. A faint stirring came from her burlap sack. "And besides, I had asked you about it that day you were weeding the vegetable patch and you refused to come. I couldn't wait for your grandfather to finish the boat; I was going mad. Losing my nerve. I knew that dam was going to break."

Waves crashed against the rocks below, a steady thrashing, the lull between each collision filled with a low moan from the wind.

"You could have waited. You could have said something more," I said.

"You never listened to me, Myra!"

"You're trying to put this on me now? You planned to leave. You followed through with that plan and abandoned us, but it's my fault?"

"It's not your fault. It's just . . . you always were waiting on me to become your father."

I tensed at the mention of my father. Hair stood on the back of my neck and sweat lined my palms. The shriek of a small animal came from farther down the Valley; something was hunting it. Perhaps a hawk, talons in the prey's belly. I shook my head at Jacob, but I knew what he said was true.

Jacob hurried on. "You were always treating me like I was weak and couldn't be trusted. Always giving me that look you're giving me now."

"What look?" I asked.

"The look that says you're expecting me to disappoint you."

"You've always fulfilled that expectation."

Jacob closed his eyes and sighed. "The guilt almost killed me after I left you," he said. "I wanted to die. But I stayed, to take care of Row."

"You did a great job of it," I spat out. Self-loathing curled within me. How did I ever love him?

"I'm sorry, Myra. I'm sorry, but . . . I couldn't have done it any differently." He shrugged, spread his arms wide, and then dropped them at his sides. "There's not one right thing left in this world." Jacob's chin trembled and he blinked back tears. A bird flew low over us and landed on the cross atop Row's grave.

"You did what was easy. You've always done what's easiest for you," I said.

Jacob shut his eyes, and when he opened them I saw panic. He dropped his head in his hands, knuckling his eyes. He looked down the hill, over the Valley, as though searching for something. I suddenly had the odd feeling that he was waiting on someone to arrive.

The bird stamped its feet and clawed the wood cross, impatient. I glared at it. It bobbed its head at us like it was waiting to be given something, a treat for a job well done.

There was a metal clasp around its ankle. The world narrowed.

"You told them," I whispered, looking back at Jacob. He had sent a message to the Lost Abbot guards that strangers had landed in the Valley. To alert them to come for us.

CHAPTER 56

My knife was in my hand before I realized I had grabbed it. I lunged at him, and he stumbled backward and turned and ran up the hillside.

I ran after him. He looked over his shoulder at me, his legs pumping furiously, his hair shaken loose behind him. The fear in his eyes mirrored my own terror, the half knowledge of what I was doing fluttering through my mind. I caught up to him after a dozen strides and leapt at him, catching the tail of his shirt, both of us tumbling to the ground, rolling over rocks and dry grass. In a fleeting image I remembered wrestling on our bed back home in Nebraska over a letter he didn't want me to see, our limbs tangled, our faces close.

I rolled out from beneath him and struck him hard in the back with my elbow. I lodged my knee into his back, pushing all my weight into it. He choked for air and tried to claw at my leg but couldn't reach it.

I grabbed a fistful of his hair and yanked his head back and set my knife to the side of his throat. This was also what I had wanted, I discovered with a shudder of horror. I had wanted this almost as much as I'd wanted to see Row again. To reverse the past. To not be the powerless one.

"Don't," Jacob rasped.

My hand tightened around the knife and my body constricted.

His eyes were fixed on something down the hill, and I followed his gaze.

Pearl stood below us on the slope, to the side of her sister's grave. She took a few steps toward us, her chin tilted upward, the grass rippling around her ankles, her form the only moving thing against the gray sky.

I felt like I was hurtling toward shore again on a broken ship. Airborne. Several strands of Pearl's red hair lifted on the wind. The perfect curve of her chin. The voice in that small throat.

She didn't deserve any of this. To see her mother kill her father. How much had she already seen that she shouldn't have? A sob built in me and I let out a guttural wail, short and brief, a burst of darkness. Like expelling bloodlust, with only grief flooding back into the emptiness it left.

"Let me help," Jacob whispered. He tried to lift a hand from the ground, but it shook so badly, he dropped it again. "Let me deal with them so you can run."

"I don't trust a word you say," I growled. I rolled him over so I could see his face but kept my knife pointed at him.

"Myra, when she came to my house I didn't know . . ."

"Didn't know she was your daughter? But you'd send another child to them? Is that what you do? Summon them when people land on these shores?"

Jacob closed his eyes. "I'm proud of nothing I've done. When I realized who she was . . ." Jacob's voice broke and he bit his lip. He explained how he first saw her in the distance and sent the message to the guards. "They torture me if I don't keep watch. That's why they let me live out here. I keep watch from the hillside and from the cliffs for any approaching ships. When she came up to my house it was like seeing a ghost. She's haunted me for years." Jacob shook his head. "Just let me do this one thing. So you both can get away. Since Row passed, I've been needing to do something. I think this whole time I was waiting for you."

I looked into his eyes and saw that he meant it. Jacob had often hidden the truth from me, but he couldn't lie outright to my face. He lacked the courage and certainty to be convincing and false.

Instead of gratitude I felt a rush of power. I could deny him everything, just as he had done to me. I remembered back when I was on *Sedna*, how I wanted to find something between revenge and absolution, but I didn't want that now. I didn't want to give him anything. I wanted to take every choice from him and to cut him down.

"There is no redemption for you, Jacob," I said.

Jacob eyebrows pulled together. "I know," he murmured. "I can't save you. But you can save yourself. They'll be here any minute, Myra."

The seabirds on the cliff suddenly took to the air, their wings a frenzy, as if in answer to some inaudible call. White chests, black wings, a stripe of orange above their beaks. Beating the air, necks outstretched, eyes on something beyond.

You do the hardest thing.

Pearl was walking up the hill toward us. Small purple flowers fluttered amid the tall grass beside Jacob. I now noticed that they looked like the flowers he'd set on the tray that morning he made me breakfast in bed. I had forgotten them, the way they smelled like honeydew, the soft purple when a sunset disappears into darkness. I had forgotten also how we'd fought the night before, about what I couldn't remember. Some disagreement about rations or Row or how to deal with migrants passing through.

He had been trying to reconcile, I thought. Trying to help us move on from whatever we'd fought about. He hadn't been good at a lot of things, but he'd been good at that. At reaching out and trying to rebuild.

I needed to move on. Pearl and I both needed to. And cutting him down wouldn't help with that. Pearl stopped beside me, waiting to see what I'd do. I released Jacob and leaned back on my heels but watched him warily and kept my knife trained on him.

"This doesn't change what you've done," I said.

Jacob crawled backward from me. He pointed to a cluster of bushes and saplings about twenty feet down the hillside.

"Hide there. I'll tell them you already escaped in that direction," he said, pointing in the opposite direction of the bushes. Voices came from his house and he glanced down at it and swore. "They're already here. Shit. I can't take down three of them, but I'll try to buy you time. If they kill me, you need to run. Down into the Valley. Hide in empty houses. Now go."

I grabbed Pearl's hand and pulled her toward the bushes. We crawled through the saplings, tucking ourselves low to the ground, behind a bush heavy laden with berries.

Jacob started walking down the hillside toward them. All three of them had come. A bald woman led the pack and two men followed her, one scrawny with a limp, the other tall and barrel chested. We could see them between the berries and branches, but we couldn't hear them when they began to speak.

The woman swung a small ax in circles. Irritation knitted her brow. She said something to Jacob and jerked her head up the hillside to where I'd attacked him. She'd seen us, I knew, with a drop in my stomach. She'd likely been able to see us from the house when we were exposed on the hillside.

Jacob gestured, waving two flat hands back and forth, disagreeing with something she was saying. Her face remained impassive, her mouth set in a firm line. Nausea swept over me.

The large man shifted impatiently, wiping his knife on his shirttail.

The scrawny man swiped his knife at Jacob, but Jacob jumped back, pulling a knife from his belt. Jacob flung the knife at the scrawny man and it stuck in his chest. The man stumbled backward and fell to the grass.

His two companions stared in surprise at Jacob. Even I was surprised by his change. The Jacob I'd known was the kind of man who ran from a fight. For the first time he seemed like Pearl's father. He was standing the way Pearl sometimes did, feet apart, shoulders squared, as if he knew the world would never belong to him, but he'd stand straight regardless.

The woman swung the ax at him and he ducked and lunged at the larger man, arms around his chest, trying to wrestle him to the ground.

Pearl found my hand and squeezed it. When I looked into her eyes I saw what we both knew: that we'd watch him die here. Beyond that knowledge, her eyes were dark and unreadable, as though shutters had been pulled shut over windows. My breath went short and shallow and I tried to swallow, but my mouth felt stuffed with wool.

This isn't going to work, I realized. Jacob was right; he couldn't take them all down alone.

I couldn't think straight without the movement of the sea. The smell of the earth, the branches overhead, all pushed down on me, making me feel caught and helpless.

I remembered the way Jacob had looked at me as I walked down the aisle on our wedding day. Adoration on his face, anxiety in his hands as he squeezed them together.

I remembered how sometimes I could feel like I was in his skin, beset with uncertainty and burdens. I'd watch the way he stood in the light from the window and know the whole world felt different to him than it did to me.

I remembered how he wouldn't look at me when he loaded Row onto the boat. I still held all the same rage in me, still could not forgive him, could not even think it. But that didn't change how we'd all die if I didn't do something.

Jacob grappled with the larger man, trying to wrestle him down, but the man punched Jacob, who fell to the ground. He scrambled to his feet again as the woman swung her ax at his belly. I squeezed my eyes shut and when I opened them Jacob was on his knees, blood pouring from his stomach.

I felt gutted myself. I squeezed a fistful of grass and yanked it up, a burst of earth smelling fragrant and foreign. I bit my lip so hard I tasted blood. Hide in empty houses, he had said. But until when? Until they came looking for us. We were only a few dozen feet from them. They'd search these bushes first, the only shelter on this otherwise bare hillside. If we ran for the Valley now, they'd see us. I needed to end this now.

CHAPTER 57

"STAY HERE," I told Pearl.

"No," she said, beginning to stand.

I grabbed her shoulder and shoved her down. "Do as I say," I growled.

They turned in circles, searching the hillside for any sign of us. I crept between the trees and stepped out between the bushes into their view. They saw me and began to walk toward me, and I turned and walked up the hillside, away from Row's grave below, closer to the cliff's edge.

I stopped a few feet from the edge. The grass was so dry, some of it broke where I stepped, and it lifted away on the wind coming up off the sea. I smelled wood smoke from our camp below. The smoke made me think of what the Valley must have smelled like when the Lost Abbots first invaded, how everything goes dark and dirty when you're being cut down. The fire, the cannons, the bodies on the ground. Your life a cloud you can't see through.

I was shaking. I hunched my shoulders up to my ears, tucked my head forward, lowered my eyes. Made myself small.

"My daughter," I gasped once they were close enough to hear. "She fell." I looked over the edge of the cliff, as though peering at a body below.

The man had a cut across his forehead and he wiped his arm over it to clear the blood. The woman's face was creased and pale. Her ax swung loosely from one hand. She set her mouth in a firm line and her eyes flitted impatiently between me and the edge of the cliff.

I clutched my chest as though in grief and swayed closer to the edge of the cliff.

"Hey," the man said, stepping forward to grab me from the edge.

I twisted my wrist from his grasp, stepped behind him, and pushed him over the edge. I heard the woman gasp. He didn't fall as I expected, something I could see moving from one place to another. He simply disappeared and then reappeared on the ground below.

I took a few steps away from the edge, facing the woman. The air was a weapon that could only be used once, now that she knew my intentions. I pulled my long knife from its sheath. The woman raised her ax and held it with both hands as though ready to swing it like a baseball bat.

A shrieking startled me, the wild scream of some animal hunting in the dark. Down the hillside, Pearl ran toward us.

The woman swung her ax at me and I ducked and lunged at her, swiping my knife at her neck. I nicked her skin and her hand flew to her neck. Her eyes darkened and she lifted her ax to her shoulder again and stepped toward me.

Behind her, I could see Pearl getting closer and closer. The woman swung her ax at my belly and I jumped backward. It caught me just above my right hip and pain ripped through me; my bones went watery and I fell.

Pearl crested the hill and stood near us, her red hair billowing in the wind. Her hands were empty, one hand at her side and the other resting at the opening of her satchel.

I tried to scramble to my feet, to tackle the woman before she could reach Pearl, but my legs gave out beneath me and I collapsed to the ground.

Blood dripped from the blade of the ax. The woman lifted it higher again to swing it at Pearl. Sweat poured into my eyes and I gritted my teeth, flinging myself toward the woman. I drove my knife through her boot, sticking her to the ground. She screeched and yanked at her foot, trying to pull it up. She jerked her foot up, with the knife still stuck through it, and stumbled backward and fell.

"Pearl, run!" I screamed. I tried to pull myself up again, but my legs buckled beneath me in weakness. I pressed one hand against my wound and I leaned against my other hand, knuckles digging into the dirt.

Pearl glared at me in annoyance. She reached into her satchel and pulled her hand back out, a snake writhing in her hand. It was one I hadn't seen before, and in my clouded mind I wondered why Pearl was showing off her snakes.

Then the woman's eyes widened in horror and she propped herself up on her elbows and scrambled back, her heels kicking up small clouds of dirt. She made small screeches as Pearl stepped closer with the snake. Terror. They were vipers, I realized. Pearl had disobeyed me this whole time. Astonishment and relief seeped through me. Pearl threw the viper at the woman, arcing past me in a brown streak. It landed on her chest, and when she lifted a hand to hit it, the viper spit venom into her eyes.

The woman screamed, clawing her eyes as the snake slithered away into the grass. Pearl took another step closer and tossed another snake on her chest. It struck her neck rapidly three times, fell away, and disappeared into the grass.

The woman crawled backward, closer and closer to the cliff's edge, until a few rocks tumbled down the cliff, rattling as they hit rocks at the bottom.

"This one's Charlie, my favorite," Pearl said politely, as though introducing him. She held him behind his head and her other hand cupped his coiled body as though he were a teapot.

The woman's eyes were slits, swollen red skin rising around them. I remembered reading those pamphlets handed out at ports, the ones I made Pearl study to learn which snakes were poisonous. Viper venom burned like an iron brand. It hardened blood in your veins, your body twitching for oxygen, pain radiating up your spine.

My own sight was going out, the world flattening and becoming distant as my vision blurred. I pulled my hand from my side, where I had been clutching my wound. Bright red in the sunlight. I felt surprised, though I already knew my blood was outside of me now.

"It'll take a whole day before you go," Pearl told the woman. "But since you have more bites, it may not take so long."

I collapsed to the grass when I heard the woman's body hit the rocks below. The last thing I saw were birds overhead. Several seagulls rose up over the cliff's edge, flying over Pearl and me, flying past Row's grave, disappearing over the opposite horizon like ghosts.

CHAPTER 58

I WOKE IN Jacob's bed. Jacob's thick flannels and heavy trousers lay stacked on an open shelf beside the door. A small cluster of purple wildflowers leaned in a cup on the bedside table. Sunlight fell through the open doorway leading into the kitchen.

Daniel stepped into the room, the heels of his boots scraping against the wood floor. He stood slightly stooped, gazing at me through a lock of hair in his eyes. A white bandage was wrapped around his palm. Sunlight glinted in the glass of water he held. I inhaled sharply. Daniel and the glass of water: they made a beautiful shape I could hold on to for a while.

He held it to my lips and I drank, the liquid cleaning my senses, clearing out the brambles in my mind. He left and brought Pearl into the room. She stood before me for a minute before speaking. Her face had changed in the hours she had been apart from me. Her eyes had a heaviness I knew I couldn't reach.

"I wanted to meet her," she said softly.

"I wanted you to, too," I said. She has stood before too many graves, whether in water or earth, I thought. I swallowed the thickness in my throat.

Pearl crawled into bed with me and tucked her face into my neck. Her back shuddered and she let out a sob. I stroked her hair and murmured to her. Sometimes, it was easy to forget how small she actually was.

· · ·

IF I SAT up I could see into the kitchen and watch Daniel and
Pearl rummaging for food. There wasn't much left, but they
found a rotten tomato, a half-empty bag of flour, and two eggs
in an icebox. Daniel cracked an egg in a wood bowl and smelled
it, then cracked the second one. They must not have been ran-
cid, because he lit a fire on the stove and fried them up for us.
After he finished cooking the eggs, he mixed water with the
flour and made a lumpy kind of pancake in the skillet.

We ate in silence. Pearl licked her thumb and pressed it into
the crumbs to lift each one from the plate. I looked past Daniel
and Pearl at the table, to one of Row's drawings on the wall.
It was a charcoal picture of a whale. Perhaps a picture of the
whale that had washed ashore on the beach below us, because
the whale she drew was not in water, but caught on land.

I rested for a day, careful not to move and break open the cut
in my side, where Daniel had tightly wrapped an old bedsheet
around me. The next afternoon I told Daniel, "We should be
getting back to the others."

"Rest a few more hours." Daniel explained that he'd signaled
to them with a flag and written a note telling them we were safe.
He'd wrapped it around a rock and dropped it to them from
the cliff.

"They aren't going anywhere, and we left them with enough
food and water," Daniel said.

He pulled a chair next to the bed and sat, taking my hand
in his.

"Pearl and I are digging a grave for Jacob next to Row,"
Daniel said. "The ground is frozen, so it'll take us a few more
hours to break it up."

I nodded. Daniel watched me as if he wanted me to say something, but I didn't speak.

"I was thinking of my mother this morning," he said. "Something about the light here. In our last days together, she'd raise her fingers to touch sunlight and turn her hand over, like the light was running water, moving over her skin." Daniel shook his head and rubbed his thumb over the top of my hand. "You get used to loss like you get used to water. You can't even imagine what it'd feel like to not be with it, not have it all around you."

I thought of how during the flood, bodies would wash up on every new shore the water made. The sun taking skin and flesh, the bones polished with each wave.

Row is gone, I repeated over and over, trying to make myself believe it. I would need to learn how to mother myself in the wake of her loss. I would need to make room for both my loss and hope, to let both abide and change as they would.

A bruise bloomed on Daniel's chin. I touched it gingerly and he flinched. His eyes were so clear, they made me feel like I was falling. He reached out and brushed hair from my face. I leaned forward, pain radiating from my wound, and kissed him.

THAT AFTERNOON, I stood, testing my balance. I could see Daniel and Pearl through the small window. They carried apples in baskets. There must be an orchard somewhere near, I mused. They walked side by side. As they got closer, I could see tears on Daniel's face that he rubbed away with the back of his hand, keeping his chin up so she couldn't see. I knew he had thought we might never find Pearl again and had only been fronting confidence for me that night on the mountainside.

I rummaged through Jacob's dresser drawers for more warm clothing. A cold wind ripped down the hillside, making the small house shudder. I shoved wool trousers aside and picked out a heavy sweater stitched with thick yellow yarn. A drawing poked out from under the sweater.

It was another of Row's drawings, showing a river and sand-hill cranes. It looked just as it had that day all those years ago; her memory was also my memory. One crane was drawn in midflight, above the river, heading for the upper corner of the paper. At the bottom, in a child's near-illegible scrawl, was the word *mother*. I imagined her tucking herself into the memory on the same days I had, sheltering inside of it, a shared space for the both of us.

I went breathless and dizzy. I leaned against the wall and slid down, head resting on my knees; the picture dropped on the floor in front of me. I let myself weep, let the ground hold me up.

I felt like the earth during a flood, so much pouring upon me— not just the grief, but the longing, too, and I knew I had to sit and wait it out, all of it building and building, crushing me under its weight, my heart shifting in the depths, every part rearranged.

WHEN WE MADE it over the mountain, back to the camp on the beach, fog was just beginning to clear. Relief spread across

Wayne's and Thomas's faces when they saw us approaching. They leapt up and hurried toward us, taking the bags from our shoulders and hugging us.

Thomas and Wayne had pulled all the salvageable wood and rope from the *Lily Black* and laid it across the beach to dry. But I knew it wasn't for rebuilding a ship and sailing. There wasn't enough wood for that, but beyond that, we were weary of the sea. We belonged here now, if for no other reason than it was where we'd wrecked. Where we'd have to rebuild.

We made a fire behind the large black rock and huddled together. While we were gone, Thomas and Wayne had collected mussels in a pail. We cooked them over the fire, talking about the village while we ate.

Daniel and I described the epidemic, the empty houses, the poisoned well, the dead Lost Abbot guards. We talked about how the Lost Abbots would return soon. They'd likely moor in the inlet to the east and climb up the mountainside into the Valley to make their collections. And we'd need to be ready for them.

Daniel had seen a large garden and orchard on the northern side of the village, now untended and gone to seed. We could turn over the soil and prune the branches, encourage new growth. Move into some of the abandoned houses and fix them up with salvaged wood from the ship. We could make a ladder to drop down the cliff side so we'd have easier access to the shore for fishing. A ladder we could pull up during attacks.

On our way back through the village, we'd seen a few more people milling about their homes and through the streets. They moved like they were still frightened, but more daring with the guards gone. Curiosity shone on their faces as they watched us walk through the village.

As I walked I planned how I'd speak to them. I didn't have Abran's charisma, his ability to pull people together, but I'd have to try. We needed their help if we were going to build the safe haven Abran and his brother had dreamed of.

But questions flooded my mind. Would they join us? How safe would we be with strangers? What history and secrets did they keep that would be the unwitting foundation of our community?

I looked at each face around me in the firelight. Before all this, it had been just Pearl and me, alone in the world. And now, each face was like a buoy in the dark sea. Thomas with his spirit that seemed untouched by darkness. Wayne with his willingness to step into the fray. Daniel with his steadfast presence. And Pearl, with the wildness of an animal I'd never want to tame. I felt a maternal protectiveness toward each of them. I would lead them into whatever would come, would try to fulfill my promise to Abran. When the water buried the earth, it felt like it was erasing us. The whole world a grave. But we would rise with the horizon if it continued to rise; we'd mark the sky with our silhouette before disappearing over the edge of the earth.

I remembered the time I took Row fishing with Grandfather and we had a fish in the boat that was flapping its fins against the air.

"Fly, fly," Row had said.

We dropped him in the water and he swam away.

I had thought at the time that she'd said that because she wanted us to return him to the water; that she hadn't mastered the difference between *swim* and *fly*. But now I think she could have just been talking about flying, since she wanted everything to be a bird. I've also longed for that kind of rising. For everything to rise above earth, above certain death, to have some part of you that always rises and lets you hover above what you've lost.

There was a pull in me toward denial. Toward believing Row could be out there somewhere. But I knew that was the kind of hope that betrays. The kind of hope that's an illusion, that shackles you to your desire. I needed hope built on real possibilities. Hope that we could make it here; that I could care for these people. Jacob had no reason to lie to me, and the Lost Abbots had no reason to lie to Jacob. They could have put her on their breeding ship at any point they wanted; it was what they did all the time.

It was time to accept it all and find a way to go on. Row was gone; she had lived her life mostly without me. No more clawing for a different truth than that. She was mine and she also wasn't. She was wholly her own. And our memories bound us as tightly as our bodies before her birth. Her spirit would remain like a fire in my bones.

I saw now that I hadn't just sailed to rescue Row. I had sailed for some part of myself that hadn't been born yet, sailing toward her, as if she were some ghost from a future I needed to create.

I had waited so long to prove myself wrong. To prove that I have room in me for everything I've lost and will lose, that the room in my heart will grow with loss and not contract. And I hadn't just found it to be true; I'd made it true. I am not the shards of a broken glass, but the water let loose from it. The uncontainable thing that will not shatter and stay broken.

I noticed Pearl had left the fire, and I glanced around the shore for her. She danced in front of the whale skeleton, sand flying from her feet. Twirling and twirling. Her hair a flurry around her face. Her figure tiny against the skeleton and the gray sky and sea beyond, the horizon a line so faint it was hard to place.

A warmth came from within and I smiled. She must be dancing to some music in her head, I thought. But then I heard it. The seagulls above, on the cliff, no longer diving for fish. Their voices lifted on the wind, bright and singular as bells. It sounded like they were singing.

ACKNOWLEDGMENTS

To Victoria Sanders and Rachel Kahan, for their faith in this book and for helping make it better, and to Hilary Zaitz Michael, Bernadette Baker-Baughman, Jessica Spivey, Benee Knauer, and the HarperCollins team. I'm so lucky I get to work with you all.

To my writing group: Theodore Wheeler, Felicity White, Ryan Borchers, Amy O'Reilly, Bob Churchill, Drew Justice, and Ryan Norris; to Kate Sims for being a great book critic; and to my professors for always being so generous.

To Adam Sundberg, for providing a wealth of knowledge and perspective on environmental history. Any and all errors are my own.

To my family for always being so supportive of my work; to my father for building me an easel when I was a toddler; and to the one and only Fetty, for teaching me to read and write and for continuing to be my first reader to this day.

To Don, for keeping the light.

To my sons and to my husband, for everything.